Walls of Ancient Stone

K. L. Schaefer

CHAPTER 1

The drums beat louder and the music reverberated from the stone walls of the chamber. Daveeka kept on dancing, thrusting aside the cold chill of fear that made the fur rise along his back.

Blindfold covering his eyes, he moved in time to the quickening music, feeling with the sensitive, unfurred soles of his feet for the slight change in texture marking the edge of the small rectangle of rug on which he danced. Step off that rug in any direction, and he would land on a carpet of sharp barbarythorns, their tips coated with poison.

Daveeka's pointed ears swiveled, aiming for Teo, as he tried to pick up some sound from his partner's direction. If they had stayed together thus far, their movements precisely coordinated to form a pleasing pattern, Teo should be at the same end of his own rug, ready to pirouette.

Yes, he could hear a faint swish of fabric, almost drowned out by the heavy beat of the drums. *So far, so good.* They might well qualify for the priesthood this night, in the Kiari Spring Dance, if Elenath smiled on them. It was the only Dance done in pairs, and so it was especially difficult.

Briefly, he recalled joining the Kiari two summers ago. It had been ten years since he'd become an adult, and still his pouch was empty. As a result, he remained without status or worth, just one of the many childless males on the bottom rung of rillenu society. But in the Kiari, lack of a child was not important. A male could be valued for other things, such as courage and ability in the Dances.

The music thrummed slowly, with the beat of the drums marking the time to which his feet must move. With each repetition of the basic melody, the drums throbbed louder and faster.

Daveeka held the long skirt of his robe gathered in his hands, pulled up above his knees so his feet and legs would be clearly visible to the watchers. He moved in the intricate sequence of steps that he had practiced with Teo, sometimes following traditional patterns and sometimes using new routines they had worked out together. With his bare feet, he could feel the faint guide-patterns he'd woven into his rug, allowing him to keep track of his position.

His heel encountered the slight roughness of the warning border. He had almost gone too far, but he needed enough room for the next sequence. Skipping forward into a short jump, he landed with one knee bent before him, the other knee briefly grazing the soft nap of the rug.

Feeling the edge, the four long toes of his forward foot arched up and back as far as possible, avoiding the barbed thorns by the merest fraction. *Sloppy.*

Above the insistent beat of the music, he could hear indrawn breaths and soft exclamations from the crowd. It had apparently been closer than he'd realized, unless they were reacting to something one of the other dancers had done. There was no way he could know.

The huge room was packed, childless males having come to watch the Kiari ritual from most of the thirteen male Families that owed allegiance to the female Family Thennevar. Most of them were not members of the cult. They had not the courage to dance on the rugs, not even once, which was all that was required for initiation. Only true devotees of Elenath would risk their lives by dancing repeatedly in the rituals four times a year.

Of course, anyone who died in the Dance was thought to go directly to Elenath, to receive a place closer to Her than even an Honored Father could obtain, but it was only among the Kiari that this was believed, and there were varying opinions even within the cult about the exact nature of the afterlife.

If too many of us die in this Dance, it will weaken our cause in the eyes of all those outsiders who are watching, Daveeka reflected. Immediately, he felt guilty for harboring such mundane considerations during the sacred Dance. It was not fitting for someone who hoped to be admitted to the priesthood tonight. He should be trying to reach the Dancer's Ecstasy, to hear the Voice of Elenath in the music, even if only briefly.

Perking up his ears to mimic a confidence he did not feel, he moved along the full length of the rug, placing his feet rhythmically, toe then heel, as if he were trying to balance on an imaginary tightrope. Ten steps, and he was at the far end of the rug.

A stifled scream followed by a moan of dismay from the crowd. One of the other dancers must have made a misstep, come down on the thorns.

Teo! he thought in sudden fear. Then he calmed himself, realizing the scream had not come from close by.

He felt himself almost a part of the music now, caught up in the excitement of the melody. Confidence burned in his heart. He could do anything! He and Teo would survive this Dance and become priests. It would happen.

On a sudden impulse, he let go his skirt with one hand and traced an intricate floating gesture through the air, fingers evoking the flutter of snow in a light breeze. At the same time, he went into a rapid spin. Some of those watching would recognize it as Myerta's classic move.

He stopped the spin abruptly, and began revolving in the opposite direction, fighting the dizziness caused by the sudden reversal. He let his hand fall to his side, clenched into a fist. The audience might read that meaning also, if they could. Myerta had been executed on the High Wall only three quarns ago, at the urging of the Marloosh Fathers. His partner had been exiled to the Farms. Myerta had spoken out too loudly and too often against the Fathers.

Cold fear washed through Daveeka's mind, and he quenched his brief show of anger. Perhaps he should have accepted his station in life without complaint, rather than risking the Fathers' displeasure by rug-dancing. After all, childlessness was nothing more than the common fate of the vast majority of males.

Even if he had to spend the rest of his life cleaning and maintaining the barracks where the Thennevar guards lived, that was better than dying on the High Wall, or being exiled to the jaram Farms.

He'd heard the stories brought back by males who'd been drafted for the autumn harvest on the Farms. Having to work even by day in the fields to get the crop in quickly, despite the scorching sunlight; the constant battle to clear more land from the poisonous and dangerous forest; overseers who pushed the slaves mercilessly, in the slim hope of receiving an Invitation to a Birthing if the harvest was good enough.

Small wonder most of those drafted never returned. And to be sent there for the rest of one's life—

Thought of the Farms disrupted Daveeka's concentration. He almost lost his balance, stumbling sideways. Catching himself before he could step off the rug, he tried to turn the stumble into a swooping turn on half-bent knees.

He could ill afford such clumsiness. With a determined effort, he banished everything from his mind except the music. The pipes shrilled in the traditional flutter on this verse, warning that the Dance was drawing to its conclusion.

Briefly, he wondered how many other couples still survived, of the eleven that had started.

It was time for he and Teo to attempt their special move. If it failed—

Daveeka shivered, imagining the viciously barbed thorns tearing into the tender soles of his feet, the poison inexorably working its way through his body. He executed a short sideways glide, stopping in the middle of the long side of his rug that was nearest to Teo.

Again, he swiveled his ears, anxiously listening for the swirl of Teo's robe, his breathing, anything that might confirm his partner's position. Above the music, he caught a whisper of movement to his right. Teo was where he belonged, at the near edge of his own dancing-rug. He would be expecting Daveeka's signal.

Daveeka executed the stationary stomping step they had agreed upon, knowing Teo could hear him over the background noise. Taking hold of the skirt of his robe in only one hand, he stretched his right hand out toward his partner, careful not to let it seem like an obvious reaching motion. *Come on, Teo. Where are you?*

The sensitive bare skin of Daveeka's fingertips grazed Teo's unfurred palm. He signaled the timing with slight movements of his fingers. Second beat. Ready? Now!

They clasped hands and jumped, each aiming for the other's rug. If they missed, they'd come down with their full weight on the carpet of thorns separating them. Daveeka had seen this jump performed several times, by the higher Kiari initiates. Once, he'd seen it fail. If he and Teo could do it, they'd surely be judged worthy of becoming priests, despite the relatively short time since they'd become members.

Daveeka's feet encountered soft rug, not lacerating thorns. The warning margin was under his left heel. It had been a near thing!

He whispered a short prayer of thanks to Elenath. Without losing his grip on Teo's hand, he tried a few short steps, orienting himself on his partner's rug.

Whispers, choked exclamations, a hiss of indrawn breath from the watching crowd.

Wait, he thought with grim satisfaction. *You haven't seen the rest of it yet.*

The music was frantic now. One more repetition of the melody, maybe two, and the Dance would be at an end.

Teo's hand trembled in Daveeka's grip, but he gave the quick squeeze that meant he was all right.

Daveeka squeezed back. They hadn't much time to finish their maneuver. Teo's thumb pressed suddenly once against the back of Daveeka's hand, meaning "No. Leave it at this."

Daveeka wasn't willing to comply. He pressed his own thumb twice against his partner's hand, expressing disagreement, commitment to continue.

One beat. Two. Teo gave in. He repeated Daveeka's pattern. He would go on.

Daveeka went back to signaling timing, trying to pick up where he had left off. Ready? Go!

They leaped again.

Releasing his partner's hand, Daveeka stumbled slightly as he landed. His outside toe caught on a barbed thorn, flesh tearing as he jerked loose. He clenched his teeth against the sharp pain and cursed to himself. It was only one toe and he had pulled free immediately, so the poison wouldn't be sufficient to kill him, although his foot would doubtless be painfully sore by sunrise.

There were no cries of dismay, no scream of pain, so Teo must have made it safely onto his own rug also.

Daveeka let his feet move in the patterns they had practiced. Finish this measure without mishap, and it would be over. His foot hurt, but he set himself to ignore it.

Hoping to salvage something despite his misstep, he executed the intricate, cross-foot-and-kick routine they had originally planned, trying to place his bleeding foot in exactly the same spot after each step while acting as if he had not been hurt at all. Panting with exertion, he curled his injured toe as far back as possible, in an attempt to minimize the blood that would stain the stark white of the dancing-rug. Too much would proclaim his ineptitude, show him unworthy of being a priest.

Elenath, Mother of All, Dark Mother, be with me and strengthen me, he prayed.

Blood pounded in his ears as the music shrilled louder. There was nothing now in all the universe save the frantic melody and the patterned movements, with the sharp burning agony of his toe as counterpoint. His feet moved without conscious effort, faster, wilder.

Suddenly, he had the insane urge to break and run across the thorns, directly to Elenath. Other dancers had done that on rare occasion. No more back-breaking work, no more abuse by the Thennevar guards whose barracks he cleaned, no more frustration and pain. It would be so easy. The large dose of poison he would receive would act quickly.

His ears twitched and his feet fairly craved the embrace of the poisoned thorns. He would become a legend amongst the Kiari, one of the honored ones. Fear burned away in the tumult of melody. He could do it. He could—

Blinding white light flashed behind his covered eyes. Dazzled, he faltered briefly in his dance. A faint voice whispered in his mind, drowning out the tumult of the music.

No, my child. You are not yet summoned. When it is time for you to come to Me, you will know.

The music built to a frenzied climax, then crashed to a halt. Silence filled the room, echoing off the thick rock of the walls. Daveeka's ears rang with the aftereffects of the music, slowly fading.

Rationality seeped into his mind. Had he imagined that faint whisper? He held his position on the rug, waiting as he heard the scratch and rasp that meant the mats of thorn were being carefully drawn back and piled by a wall.

He continued to hold his long robe up above his knees, unmoving. Very soon, he felt the blindfold being removed from his eyes.

Blinking in the harsh white light filling the room from the poor-quality glowweeds suspended from walls and ceiling, he glanced at Teo. He wanted to say something to his partner, but his mouth was dry and he was panting for breath.

Teo's eyes shone with excitement, pupils fully dilated so his eyes appeared solid black against the light gray fur of his face. Had he also heard—?

The tips of Teo's ears drooped mournfully above his head when he looked down at Daveeka's rug and saw the bloodstains.

Daveeka made the quick Kiari gesture signifying he was all right, the injury was minor, by touching the tips of all three fingers to his thumb. Teo brightened.

"Dav?" he said, between gasps, his voice low-pitched and soft so as not to carry far in the buzz of conversation and speculation filling the room. "Did anything … strange … happen to you? I mean, I know we're not supposed to talk about it, but …"

Daveeka nodded, still out of breath.

Teo's eyes glistened darkly. "Do you think that was the Voice of Elenath?"

"I don't know. Maybe." Although he would have liked to ask his partner what he had heard, by Kiari custom such things were not to be discussed. He made the short, chopping dancer's gesture warning Teo to silence on the subject.

Teo nodded his understanding. Then he said timidly, "Dav, if we do become priests, please don't say anything that would …" His voice trailed off as he saw the annoyed backward slant of his partner's ears.

Daveeka looked around the rock-walled chamber. On five of the other rugs, dancers sat huddled over lacerated feet, trying to stifle sobs of pain. One was already in convulsions from the effects of the poison. They were immediately hustled off to the infirmary, but there was little hope for any participant so badly cut that he was not standing up at the close of the Dance.

Daveeka winced in sympathy. His own gashed toe was of little consequence, considering what had happened to those others. For the dancers, who kept the soles of their feet soft and sensitive, nothing quite compared to the agony of an injured foot. And when the poison began working—

Elenath had taken a heavy toll this time, accepting their sacrifice as was Her deadly way. Other than the Kiari, few rillenus recognized Her in Her aspect of Death-Bringer, preferring to see Her only as Mother of All. Daveeka had nothing but contempt for those simple fools, who were quick to run to Her for comfort but never acknowledged Her darker side. It was like expecting you could have the lovely moons without the harsh sun, or the gentle night without the cruel day that followed. Like the mortal females who were Her living avatars, Elenath dealt out both pleasure and pain as, in Her wisdom, She deemed proper.

A brief twitter of pipes signaled the end of the ritual.

A bright bunch of flowers was thrown from the audience to land on Daveeka's rug. More followed, also falling on Teo. Daveeka swept up the first bunch, waved it above his head, kissed it, and tossed it back to the crowd. Teo followed suit, making a single graceful movement of the traditional Kiari acknowledgement of praise.

Seeing the procession of priests start across the room, Daveeka sank down into a cross-legged position on his rug. He straightened his robe, refastening the hooks at the disgracefully collarless neck and smoothing his coarse gray fur where the fabric had disarranged it.

An elderly Kiari priest passed among the now-seated dancers, touching the tips of each one's ears and reciting a brief blessing before placing a vial containing eight small green glass beads in his hands. A younger priest followed behind, returning to each dancer his own special padded shoes.

When the old priest came to Teo and Daveeka, he looked at them impassively, no hint of expression in the angle of his ears.

Although Jeremael had taught them both the traditional parts of the Dances, he could not show favoritism to his pupils now. He opened both hands, one before each of the two seated candidates.

Daveeka's heart leapt to his throat. Resting on Jeremael's palm, a vial of blood-red beads sparkled next to the expected green ones. Gravely, he picked up the vials and kissed them, catching a glimpse of Teo doing the same. They had made it! They were accepted as priests.

Jeremael's assistant laid Daveeka's shoes on his rug. Seven zigzag lines of beads crossed the arch of each shoe, two each in yellow, brown, and blue, one in green; one line for each Dance he had performed.

Reverently, Daveeka placed the beads inside his shoes. Then he held out his hands, palm upwards, as Jeremael knelt before him. The palms were shamefully calloused and work-worn, not like the tender palms of the Fathers, who never stooped to manual labor, but he couldn't help that.

The old priest took Daveeka's offered hands, holding them steady as his assistant used a short, sharp knife to jab the fleshy part at the base of the thumb. Blood welled up in the cuts. His hands trembled with the pain, but Daveeka resisted pulling them away.

As the blood spread on his palms, the priest let go. Daveeka pressed his hands to the toes of his shoes, allowing the blood to soak into and stain the tanned beige kullup hide. He watched the ritual repeated for Teo. Now they would both be priests.

Teo's eyes locked with his. The watching crowd cheered and chanted, but Teo and Daveeka saw only each other, ears quivering with exultation.

The Kiari began a wild song, the drums taking up the beat, as Jeremael's assistant crushed jaram leaves and bound them to the cuts he had made, doing the same to Daveeka's gashed toe. The jaram would deaden the pain, at least temporarily.

As soon as this was done, the rest of the Kiari rushed forward, hoisting Teo and Daveeka into the air and carrying them around the room to the strains of a clamorous melody. Although a number of others had successfully completed the Dance, only he and Teo had distinguished themselves sufficiently to be accepted into the priesthood.

At the feast that followed, the two rillenus sat in the place of honor at the head table, flanked by the other surviving dancers. Pungent jareesh flowed in plentiful quantities, and they dared to drink, now that they didn't have to worry about the dreaming-drug impairing their performance. Some Kiari danced drunk, but Daveeka and Teo knew better. Jareesh might inhibit fear, but it also inhibited caution.

The food was good, the jareesh a more potent grade than was usually available to males. Teo's eyes reflected love and desire. As the last grains of sand fell through the blue timeglass, showing it was almost dawn, Daveeka was no longer thinking clearly.

Someone proposed a toast to the two newly made priests. They stood to acknowledge it. Teo glanced warningly at his partner and quickly mumbled a few shy phrases of thanks to the crowd. Then he tried to pull Daveeka back down onto the cushions.

Daveeka had other ideas. He raised his ceramic cup of jareesh, waiting for a semblance of quiet before he spoke.

"To our esteemed and generous Fathers," he said, angling his ears to emphasize the sarcasm in his voice, "who keep a firm hold on their power and authority by primarily recommending each other to the females for Invitations to Receive infants."

The room became abruptly silent.

"They have yet to learn that ability and worth are not solely determined by whether or not a male receives a child."

Urgent whispers spread throughout the room. Even some of the dancers shifted uneasily on their cushions.

"And especially to the Honored Father Fahlin," Daveeka continued recklessly. "If his proposal passes at the Conclave this winter, childless males will have less chance than ever before to obtain an Invitation."

Teo tugged on his partner's robe, but Daveeka ignored him. He lifted his cup higher, slopping deep red liquid over the sides as he did so.

"May She Who Rules turn Her Face from Fahlin, and confound all his plans!" Daveeka proclaimed. He sat down. Enthusiastic applause from several Kiari drowned out the initial stunned silence, but most of the crowd just stared, ears flattened back in fear.

"Are you crazy?" Teo whispered. "If Fahlin hears about this, he'll have you sent to the Farms."

"Don't care," Daveeka declared drunkenly. "S'true, isn't it? They keep all the babies for themselves."

Teo sighed but said nothing more.

After that, the banquet faded into a blur for Daveeka, the festivities lasting well beyond sunrise and into broad daylight. He and Teo stayed to the very end, knowing other Kiari would cover their work assignments for the following night, as was the custom.

At last they staggered back to the room they shared in the upper levels of the Marloosh lodging house, arms around each other.

When Daveeka awoke that evening, he found Teo already up. His head pounded with the ache of too much jareesh, his injured toe throbbed, and his eyes took a while to decide that they would focus.

He glanced at the timeglass. The yellow day glass was still running, but there wasn't much sand left to fall. Sunset soon.

He stretched luxuriously, reveling in the knowledge that no one would come to summon them to work, as usually happened once the sun went down.

"Teo? What are you doing up? We don't have to work tonight, remember?"

"I remember. I'm just straightening things up a bit, since I woke up early anyway."

Daveeka stretched luxuriously, watching the other rillenu as he bustled around the room they shared. Teo was naked, having apparently not yet taken the time to put on his robe. The regular pattern of symmetrical darker stripes showed up clearly in his pale gray fur. Daveeka crossed his arms behind his head and just lay there admiring his partner's markings. They were much nicer than his own random splotches of varying shades of gray, which had none of the symmetry that was so admired by the females. Unlike Daveeka, Teo's lower belly had the slight sag of a once-opened pouch, along with a more prominent swelling beneath his fur along the upper edge of that pouch. As always, Daveeka had to stifle a twinge of envy. His partner had worn the short robe, had known what it was like to carry a son, even though he was several years younger.

Yes, he told himself, *but that son died before leaving his pouch, and he'll surely never be Invited again. Females think a male whose infant dies before it's taken is unlucky. Besides, you know the grief Teo carries in his heart over that child. How dare you envy that?*

Before he could feel too guilty, Daveeka reminded himself that it was only normal for rillenu males to envy each other. They all did it. It was part of male nature to be envious, just as it was part of female nature to be intelligent and wise enough to rule over all the Families. The females were the ones who had been created in the image of Elenath, sharing in Her Divine Wisdom. Males were only males, after all

He caught Teo's eye, then turned the blanket down, patting the mattress invitingly with one hand while simultaneously displaying his own unclothed body and fixing his partner with an exaggerated leer.

Teo gave a short laugh, coming back to the bed. His hand slid familiarly over his partner's body, resting lightly on his abdomen, over the tightly closed opening of his pouch. Daveeka stiffened, but didn't pull away. He trusted Teo. There was nothing to fear from his touch, even there.

Daveeka slid an arm around his partner, but Teo smiled and pulled away. "Let me take a look at your toe first."

He unwrapped the bandage carefully and discarded the wilted jaram leaves.

Daveeka winced as Teo cleaned the inflamed cut in his toe, applying fresh jaram leaves and a new bandage.

"It should be getting busy in the Marloosh lodging house soon," Daveeka said, in an effort to divert his mind from the pain that had been reawakened in his toe. "The full moon that begins Ninth Nanth is only a few nights away."

Teo giggled as he took a jar of the thick ointment the Kiari used to keep the soles of their feet soft and sensitive. He scooped some out and began massaging it into his partner's feet. "Yeah. Usually when the weather turns warmer, so do the females."

It was a well-known fact that the females summoned more Fathers to the mating rooms during the Spring nanths than at any other time of year. Daveeka wondered, as he had many times before, what it would be like to mate a female. Only Fathers did that, and, during Harvest, a few specially chosen slaves, who were put to death afterwards as part of the Harvest Ritual. Most childless males would never be granted access to a female. But that long silky fur would feel so incredibly wonderful beneath his fingers! Such a thing must surely be ecstasy beyond measure!

Enough! he chided himself. *My own handsome partner should be sufficient for me. I have no reason to lust after some forbidden female.*

"If I were a Father," he said, trying to pull his mind and his desire into a different direction, "I could do something to ensure that more childless males Received children."

"Dav, you say that all the time. If you were a Father, you'd find you couldn't change things at all. It isn't that easy. Besides, our life isn't so bad, is it? We could be on the jaram Farms."

"Yeah, yeah. You hate working in the kitchen, Teo. Admit it."

Teo shrugged. "Oh, it's not so bad this time of year. I'm always warm, and there's a lot of interesting things to taste."

"Taste, sure. But the best food gets served to the guests and the Marloosh Fathers."

Teo put away the ointment and reclined on the mattress, seeming in a better humor now. "Dav, be reasonable. That's how it's always been. Fathers are Fathers, after all." His dark eyes sparkled mischievously against the fine gray fur on his face. "Want me to snitch some fresh cranels for you?"

"You wouldn't dare."

Teo giggled again. "Sure I would. But it'll cost you."

"How much?"

He snuggled his body against Daveeka's, taking one hand and guiding it down toward his belly.

"Idiot," Daveeka breathed into his partner's ear. "Do you think you have to bribe me into doing that? I can barely keep my hands off of you as it is. Your fur is so fluffy and soft, I could spend the rest of my life just petting you."

Suiting his actions to his words, Daveeka pulled Teo tighter up against him and began stroking his partner's back, sometimes going with the lay of the fur and other times going backwards, digging his fingertips through the ruffled hairs and just lightly touching the skin beneath.

Teo's body arched with pleasure, squirming happily as he wrapped an arm over Daveeka and returned the favor.

Daveeka's fur was more glossy and sleek, lying much flatter down against his body than normal. Although this was much less favored by most males than fluffy fur that had more body to it, Teo never seemed to mind. His caresses were fully as ardent as Daveeka's as they tangled themselves around each other, both trying to reach every part of his partner's body. Legs entwined, the unfurred soles of feet ran frantically up and down against leg fur, while hands groped for new places to explore as their mutual excitement rose.

Teo buried his face in Daveeka's shoulder, using just the very tip of his tongue to tease the tingling skin beneath the fur. They rolled over each other, freeing the arms that had been pinned under them so that different fingers could reach for more contact in new places.

Daveeka's sore toe kept him from being too active with that foot, but he made up for it as best he could. They were in no real hurry, as the longer the build up lasted, the better it would feel when they finally gave up their fluid to each other. It took time for the pressure to grow, for that exquisitely sensitive place just inside and under the base of his penile sheath to fill until it was ready to overflow and provide the wonderful pleasure of release.

They broke apart for a moment, lying next to each other with only fingers gently stroking the other's body. Daveeka ran a finger over the raised edge of Teo's pouch. Teo gasped and stiffened, then allowed himself to relax. That was their signal that Teo would welcome being opened. If he wasn't ready or didn't want it, he would have shaken his head instead of relaxing.

One finger slowly pushed its way between the outer layer of skin and the inner lining of the pouch, covered with a layer of short downy fur. Slowly, Daveeka reached further inside, his entire body thrilling at the exquisite feel of that fur beneath his fingertips. As he moved lower, he kept his hand flat in order not to stretch Teo's pouch, since that would be somewhat uncomfortable for him. Finally, he reached the small soft teat, where a baby had once drawn his nourishment for three nanths, before it died. He took it between two fingers, kneading it very gently.

Teo moaned with delight, as his penis began to stiffen and extend from his sheath.

Daveeka was just beginning to respond himself when a noise in the corridor outside the room caught his attention. Teo also froze, listening. Two pairs of pointed ears swiveled toward the faint sounds. Someone was coming.

The footsteps stopped at their door. Daveeka removed his hand swiftly and they rolled away from each other, pulling the coverlet over themselves.

"Enter," Daveeka called, trying to squelch the frustrated annoyance in his voice.

Arvale pushed the curtain aside, casting a scornful glance at the two of them still lolling about on their mattress this close to sunset.

"Daveeka sardhan Marloosh-Sharemmi," he said formally, "you are commanded into the presence of the Honored Father Fahlin."

His message delivered, the young rillenu reverted to his usual snotty self, concluding archly, "Although I can't for the life of me imagine why Fahlin would want to see you."

Teo clutched his partner's arm. "Now you've done it. I warned you about saying anything against—"

Daveeka gestured impatiently for him to be quiet. "Thank you, Arvale. I shall attend the Honored Father immediately."

It hurt to have to be courteous to this arrogant youngster, but Arvale wore the short robe of a male carrying a child in his pouch. The Honored Father Syron had made sure Arvale's name was included on the list of males recommended for Invitations. As a potential Father, Arvale no longer had to work in the guard barracks. He was already training to be a clerk in the Office of Room Assignments for the Marloosh lodging house. If all went well, he stood an excellent chance of being Invited to Receive additional children. It would be foolish to antagonize a potential Father unnecessarily.

Daveeka sat up slowly, making sure the edge of the coverlet hid his arousal.

"How are the repairs in the East Wing coming along?" the younger rillenu inquired superciliously, leaning against the side of the doorway.

"Fine. No problems." Daveeka reached for his long robe on the chair near the bed. He pulled it over his head, groping for the sleeves.

"Well, some of the guards have been complaining about drafts."

Dav gave a short snort of laughter as he stood up and simultaneously tugged the robe down over his lower body. "The East Wing butts up against the outlying walls of the Palace of Family Thennevar, so any draft is the product of their own imaginations. There's no breeze strong enough to find its way through those walls."

He forbore to point out that Arvale should have known that. The stone walls surrounding the Palace were extremely old, but they were solid and impenetrable.

He slid his feet into his dancer's shoes, admiring the blood-stained toes that now marked him as a priest. The thick layer of spongy carpetmoss lining the shoes was beginning to get worn.

He'd have to replace it soon, if he wanted his feet to be properly protected. He drew the laces tight around his ankles.

Arvale frowned at the shoes. "Haven't you tired of that Kiari nonsense yet? I thought you knew better, but I suppose one can't expect wisdom from someone with an empty pouch."

The youngster's smug pride was beginning to rub Daveeka's fur the wrong way. Arvale wasn't a Father yet. He didn't have the right to be so overbearing.

Before Daveeka could reply, Teo said softly, "Not every son lives to leave the pouch, Arvale. Not every male who Receives becomes a Father."

"Maybe not." Arvale gave a short laugh. "But I've got a better chance at it than either of you two."

Seeing the hurt in Teo's eyes, Daveeka took Arvale's arm and propelled him through the doorway, saying, "Come on, let's go before the Honored Father gets angry."

Daveeka followed behind the young rillenu without further comment as he headed for the wide stone steps that led down to the Fathers' luxurious rooms, well underground and far from the cruel light of the sun. Daveeka did his best not to limp.

Once they were in the lower corridors, garlands of fresh glowweeds draped from hooks along each side of the corridors lit the way with a pale rose light, much more comfortable to the eyes than the harsh whitish light of the fading glowweeds in the upper parts of the male quarters.

Family Marloosh had the finest, reddest glowweeds to be found outside the female Houses. But that wasn't too surprising. Even though Marloosh was a small Family consisting of barely one hundred males, they were responsible not only for the guards' and servants' barracks but also for providing accommodations for all males from the outlying Families when they came to the female Palace for business, mating, or Receiving. The service they provided within the lodging house was exemplary, but that was only to be expected of males who lived and worked so close to a female Family. Some of the females' style was bound to rub off on them, or so most of the visiting Fathers said.

The two rillenus threaded their way through the maze of tunnels and corridors until they reached the Honored Father's chambers.

Arvale opened the fancy embroidered curtain barely a hands width, not daring to step inside until Fahlin acknowledged him with a nod of the head.

"Honored Father, I have brought you this male, as you have requested," he said, with nothing but devout humility in his voice.

"Very good, Arvale. Admit him, and then you may go about your business."

"As you wish, Honored Father."

Arvale held the curtain aside. Eyes downcast, Daveeka entered the room. The Honored Father Fahlin reclined on a pile of cushions, writing on a sheet of parchment on the low desk before him.

Daveeka bowed, remaining in that position until Fahlin should deign to notice his presence.

It took a while. In the meantime, Daveeka occupied himself with worrying. If Fahlin had found out about that little speech he'd made at the Dance yesternight—

"You may be seated," Fahlin said at last.

Daveeka sank to the floor, crossing his legs as he did so. Several decorated cushions lay scattered around the room, but those were for the use of Fathers. Other males sat on the hard stone, and were grateful not to be left standing.

"How may I serve my Family, Honored Father?" he asked humbly.

The elderly rillenu leaned against the padded back of his own cushion as he fixed Daveeka with a hard stare, his dark eyes glittering no less than the fine gems embroidered into the elaborate collar, almost a short cape, that encircled his neck.

By its designs and width, the collar proclaimed him as the Honored Father of one daughter and seven sons, the highest-ranking individual in Family Marloosh. A few other Fathers had as many as ten sons, but no daughters. Only Syron could compete with Fahlin for leadership of the Family, and he had a daughter, but only three sons. Not only that, but Fahlin had one of the coveted crystal Shapes hanging from a silver clasp in the middle of his collar, which bestowed upon him even more prestige. A Shape was very difficult for a male to obtain.

"I doubt very much whether one such as you can serve the Family in any way," Fahlin replied dryly. His sharp eyes rested on Daveeka's red-stained shoes. The older male's ears angled slightly backwards. "Especially since you've become involved with that Kiari trash and taken to dancing on rugs."

"But I do it very well, honored one," Daveeka replied, careful to boast only obliquely of his having achieved the priesthood. It could be possible that Fahlin knew what the bloodstains meant, but he couldn't tell for sure.

"Hmph. Perhaps if you applied yourself more to your proper work, you might do that well also."

"Repairing and cleaning rooms is not very interesting. Possibly if I had a more challenging assignment, I might—"

"If your pouch weren't still empty, perhaps you would have a better assignment. In the meantime, I'd advise you to keep better control of your tongue. Is that clear?"

"Yes." Daveeka looked at the floor. Fahlin had heard about what he'd said, then. He'd be lucky if all he got was a flogging.

"Good. If it happens again, there will be a suitable punishment. This time, I'll let you off with a warning."

Such mercy was not Fahlin's usual mode of operation. Daveeka gathered his feet under him, hoping he could leave before the Honored Father changed his mind.

Fahlin gestured for him to remain seated. He began shuffling through a stack of rolled parchments on a low stand next to his elbow.

Uh-oh, what else is wrong?

Finding what he wanted, the old rillenu unrolled a sheet of parchment and laid it across his knees. "Since we have been unsuccessful in dissuading the Mistress Annilee from her choice, I am obligated to deliver this to you. I'll read it."

"I can read it myself."

Fahlin's lips set in a disapproving line. "You shouldn't be wasting time on such a thing. You'll be taught to read, should you ever become a Father. Next, I suppose you'll try to tell me you can read femalespeech also." Despite the scorn in his voice, he shoved the parchment across to Daveeka, probably hoping that he would not be able to read it after all.

With a trembling hand, Daveeka picked it up. The insignia of the female Family Thennevar, beautifully drawn, occupied the entire top third of the page. It was followed by a formal request that the male known as Daveeka sardhan Marloosh-Sharemmi be brought to the Thennevar Palace at the proper time to attend the upcoming Birthing of the Mistress Annilee. He was offered Ninth Position in the Receiving.

Daveeka swallowed hard. This was an Invitation. To him. And it was from Mistress Annilee, the only daughter of the Exalted Mother Marlieth. There must be some mistake. When and if Annilee became a Mother, she'd be next in line to head Family Thennevar.

Daveeka laid the parchment carefully in his lap, staring at it in disbelief. Something odd occurred to him. A female's pregnancy was always confirmed and announced on the first night of the nanth prior to the nanth of the expected birthing, and her Invitations went out immediately after that. The full moon signaling the start of Ninth Nanth was only a few nights hence. Females never waited this long to Invite someone, unless something happened to the original male chosen.

Maybe she had had to make a last-minute decision and had chosen him on impulse because of the Kiari ritual? There were always rumors that such a thing had happened, but they usually turned out to be unfounded. Could it be—?

Fahlin cut short Daveeka's reverie. "It might be best if you declined the Invitation."

Daveeka cringed as if he'd been hit. "Why?" he choked out.

"Ninth Position, as even you must know," Fahlin explained unctuously, "does not guarantee an infant. Most females bear no more than eight at a time, if that. The last Position is there only in case there might be one more than is usual. Seventh or Eighth would give you a better chance. If you show yourself to be cooperative in this matter, I might be able to arrange a better offer for you in the future."

There was more to it than that; there had to be. He'd never heard of anyone being urged to turn down an Invitation. And besides, while a childless male was permitted by law to take Seventh, it rarely happened. Even Eighth normally went to a lesser Father.

"You're afraid people will think I got Invited because of yesternight's rug-dancing, aren't you?"

Fahlin's eyes narrowed and his ears slanted backwards. "Some foolish males might make that ridiculous assumption, yes."

"Are you so sure it's ridiculous?"

The old rillenu snorted. "Of course it is. How would the females have heard about your silly ritual so soon? It's coincidence, nothing more."

Fahlin might well be right, but Daveeka didn't feel it. Gossip traveled surprisingly fast sometimes. And there were rumors that some females sent males to the Dances to observe and report what had gone on, ostensibly to take pleasure from hearing about the deaths that always occurred.

"Consider," the Honored Father continued smoothly. "If you're right and the ritual actually made the difference, you should be getting more Invitations in the future. This is Mistress Annilee's first pregnancy. It will be unusual if she can bring even six babies to birth, much less nine. And there is little chance that one of them would be a female, in case that's what you were hoping for."

That possibility hadn't even crossed his mind until Fahlin brought it up. He dismissed it instantly. Female infants were very rare and almost always went to those in First or Second Position.

"Such was not my expectation, honored one. But I wish to accept this Invitation. The Birthing will be quite soon. If I am unsuccessful, I can always accept other Invitations later."

"Hmph," Fahlin grunted again. "I suppose I shouldn't have expected any more cooperation or respect from one of the Kiari. But if you go against me in this, you'll be very sorry."

Daveeka cringed at the chill in Fahlin's voice, but he didn't give in to the Honored Father's obvious desire that he refuse the Invitation. It might well be the only one he'd ever get, despite Fahlin's offer. Mistress Annilee was probably unaware of the inappropriateness of her current choice.

Or was she deliberately defying her own Family by Inviting a dancer?

Seeing Daveeka's hesitation, Fahlin extended his hand in an imperious gesture. "Give it to me. I will return the Invitation to Family Thennevar along with the proper apologies."

Daveeka shivered slightly. He distrusted Fahlin's motives. The old rillenu was too anxious, too insistent. He probably wanted the chance to get this Invitation for some favored male, perhaps one of his many young lovers, as Syron had probably done for Arvale.

Still unwilling to give up, Daveeka shook his head.

"Perhaps," Fahlin went on, "it is time you were considered for a different job. Something in the Office of Room Assignments maybe, since you would appear to be able to read. Would you like that?" His hand remained out, all four fingers now curling slightly with impatience.

Daveeka's ears pricked up. Yes, he would like that very much. To be one of the scribes who handled the rooming records, prepared accounts, or even assigned visitors to the different rooms, keeping track of whose status entitled them to which degree of luxury. It was a job he'd always wanted, but it was an assignment seldom given to childless males. He'd give anything to be able to quit working in the guards' barracks. Not only was the work backbreaking and boring, but one or another of the powerful males would inevitably make fun of him and rough him up if he dared to answer back. It was a common practice among the guards, but most unpleasant.

Fahlin was offering him a chance at a much better assignment. All he had to do was decline this Invitation. And yet, there was something not quite right about Fahlin's offer. The Honored Father was afraid, despite his show of confidence.

If someone like Daveeka, Kiari, over-aged, outspoken about his resentment toward the Fathers, and without reasonable hope of advancement, could Receive a child as a result of his prowess at rug-dancing, what could that mean to the other Kiari? Could the male Families afford to let someone bypass the approved routes to Fatherhood so easily?

You're trying to buy me off. Well, it won't work.

"I choose to accept the Invitation," Daveeka stated quietly, rolling the sheet of parchment and placing it in his pocket in the traditional gesture of acceptance. He hardly dared raise his eyes to Fahlin's face.

"Very well." The old rillenu's voice was as cold as the bare rock walls in winter, his ears flattening straight backwards with anger. "But be very sure that you do not disgrace Family Marloosh by your behavior, should you be fortunate enough to actually Receive a child." He leaned forward from his cushions as Daveeka hastily rose to his feet. "Mark my words, dancer. If you behave poorly, you'll wish you had been content with your present lot. There are many males on the Farms who got there by being too rash to take the advice of their betters."

"I understand. I won't disgrace Marloosh," he promised, forced into bravado by Fahlin's scorn. *And more than that,* he thought. *I won't disgrace the Kiari.*

"I doubt that." A cold gleam came into the old male's eyes. "However, I find myself curious to observe the behavior of one so sure of himself. I'm certain you wouldn't turn down the offer of the Head of your Family to be one of your attendants at the Birthing, would you?"

Fahlin, one of my attendants?! Elenath forbid!

Fahlin's eyes bored into him, but Daveeka refused to quail before that hostile gaze. "I would be greatly honored by your presence," he said with a bow. But he couldn't resist adding, "Perhaps I'll Receive a child, and have something more to do with my life than dance on rugs."

Fahlin's ears flattened back once again. "Watch your tongue, worthless one. You dance very close to the edge of your rug right now."

Daveeka stifled a start of surprise. The Kiari expression sounded strange on Fahlin's lips. Strange and ominously threatening.

"I'll see you when you're summoned," the older male said, waving Daveeka away. "And we'll find out if you have any smart remarks to offer when it comes time to enter the birthing chamber."

Daveeka retreated quickly from Fahlin's chambers, hurrying up the stairs and towards his own part of the extensive building complex. In the light of the glowweeds, he took the parchment from his pocket and unrolled it once again, staring in disbelief at the graceful script. For this precarious opportunity, he had incurred Fahlin's wrath. He almost turned back, ready to repent his insolence and return the document to the Honored Father.

And yet, Mistress Annilee had requested him, against all odds and, probably, against all advice. He couldn't turn it down.

He would be a symbol of success to the Kiari. And when he was a Father, he'd find some way to get Invitations for more of the others, instead of just using his influence to further his own interests. He could make a real difference. He could—

He could be in a lot of trouble. Daveeka recalled the look on Fahlin's face, the way his ears had flattened as he sent him away. After this, the Honored Father would be out to get him.

Daveeka shivered, then continued on his way to his room. His injured toe, forgotten until now, began throbbing mercilessly as he climbed the stairs and hurried through the hallways back to his quarters.

He had no sooner stepped inside the door curtain than Teo asked anxiously, "What did Fahlin want? Is everything all right?"

Daveeka took the Invitation from his pocket and laid it on the mattress in front of his partner without saying a word.

Teo's indrawn breath whistled through his teeth. "Annilee dhan Thennevar-Marlieth!? Beloved, this is quite an honor! Do you think it's because of the Spring Dance?"

Daveeka's ears perked up. "What else?"

"But someone like Mistress Annilee! I could understand a less important female Inviting a male who wasn't on the official lists, but I can't imagine the Exalted Mother Marlieth letting her daughter get away with this."

"It's only Ninth Position."

"Yes, but even so ..." Teo shook his head, at a loss for words.

Daveeka smoothed the short fur on Teo's cheek tenderly. "Will you be one of my attendants at the Receiving?"

"I'd love to. But wouldn't you prefer someone with more experience, since this is your first time?"

Daveeka's mouth twisted into a wry smile. "Oh, I have someone with lots of experience." Teo just looked a question at him, so he went on, "The Honored Father Fahlin."

Teo's eyes went wide. "Fahlin?!"

"It was his idea, not mine, believe me."

"But why would he—"

"I think that the Honored Father would very much like to see me squirm." He took Teo's hand, giving it an affectionate squeeze. "Don't worry, I have no intention of giving him that satisfaction."

"That's ... easy to say, Dav," Teo murmured, his eyes breaking away to look at the floor. He had been drugged nearly unconscious at his own Receiving, having to be held down by his attendants. It wasn't at all unusual the first time a male had his pouch opened, but Teo was quite ashamed of it, nonetheless.

Daveeka reached out to stroke the fur of his partner's arm in a pattern of reassurance. "I'm sorry. I didn't mean that to embarrass you."

"I know. May the Mother of All grant that you do better than I did." He looked up. "I mean it, Dav."

"I might be lucky enough to Receive a child. We might soon have a son to raise."

"Yes. Yes, I hope so." But behind Teo's brave words, Daveeka knew there hung the unspoken question: And if you should become a Father, what of us?

Daveeka answered the question by raising Teo's hand to his lips and kissing his palm.

"Don't worry, Beloved, I'll never desert you. Never!"

<h1 style="text-align:center">CHAPTER 2</h1>

Shortly before sunset three nights later, Daveeka sat soaking in the bathing room in a deep tub carved from the rock floor, enjoying the hot water, when Teo rushed through the curtained doorway.

"Teo, come join me …" Daveeka began, then stopped when he saw the look on his partner's face.

Teo unfolded the red robe that hung draped over one arm, holding it up carefully. The soft, shiny fabric was embroidered with the Marloosh Family emblem, a deep purple chonendron blossom, lovely, tempting, and devastatingly poisonous. The robe was made to open up the entire length of the front, female-style, rather than to be pulled over the head as male robes would be.

"They said I should give this to you," Teo said uncertainly, a mixture of admiration and unwilling envy in his shaking voice.

Daveeka stared. "I'm summoned to the Birthing?"

Teo nodded. Hanging the rich garment carefully on a hook, he took up a towel and a brush. "Come on out and dry off. I'll brush your fur. We're expected at the Thennevar main gate at moonrise."

Daveeka hurried out of the tub, dripping water all over the floor and cursing his poor timing.

As soon as he was dry and his fur had been brushed and fluffed, Teo applied a fresh bandage to his swollen toe. Then he picked up the robe, holding it open for him. Daveeka took the fine fabric between his fingers, not quite able to believe it was real. It felt as soft and light as a moonbeam.

"Put it on. We haven't much time."

He slid his arms into the sleeves, almost afraid of tearing something. Then he took a few steps, watching the way the fabric flowed around him and enjoying the feeling as he moved. It was almost like having nothing on at all, but not quite. Oh, how wonderful it would be to wear a robe like this when he was dancing!

They hurried back to their room so Teo could change into his best robe and Daveeka could grab a warm cloak. He tucked his Invitation into a pocket, resisting the urge to unroll it and read it just one more time.

Fahlin stood waiting for them in the lobby of the Marloosh lodging house, regally dressed as befitted his high rank. He said nothing to the two younger males except, "Hurry up. You're late."

Teo and Daveeka followed Fahlin out the door, shading their eyes against the still-bright twilight as they rounded the corner of the lodging house and trotted along beside the high stone walls of the female Family's huge compound.

The evening air smelled of wetness and damp earth, with mist rising above the lower-lying areas of the flat plain spread out around them. The buildings of the town clustered close to the hill on which the Thennevar Palace was built, thinning out as the distance increased. To the north, herds of kullups grazed peacefully within the fenced pastures belonging to the male Family Dziedzic. To the south and west lay Family Suvinn's fields, awaiting the coming of warmer weather for the spring planting. But the source of Thennevar's true wealth lay far beyond the western horizon, where the jaram Farms clung to the edge of the forest, producing the high-quality jareesh that made Thennevar one of the richest Families in this area.

Long shadows stretched across the landscape as the sky dimmed into full darkness. It promised to be a beautiful night, albeit somewhat cool.

But Daveeka had no eyes for the familiar scenery. Ahead, by the Thennevar main gate, he could see a group of people standing in clumps of three or four, the other Invited males and their attendants.

Most of the other rillenus faced east along the thick moss-covered stones of the High Wall, where the sky already showed a piece of the huge red-orange orb called Elnanth, the moon sacred to the Mother of All. The two unnamed smaller moons, ugly white and only half full, hung high among the stars, but no one paid too much attention to them. They were only Her male consorts, and thus of little account.

Daveeka shivered as his gaze involuntarily jumped from the rising moon to the execution area next to the main gate in the Wall, but much higher up, roughly four times the height of the average rillenu. A section of the thick stone had been hollowed out in order to provide a place for the execution of males convicted of serious crimes in full view of the public.

The decomposing remains of Myerta's body still hung chained by wrists and ankles to the stone. It would not be taken down for another nanth or until the next execution. It was barely a nanth since Daveeka had watched Myerta die, standing in the crowd of Kiari in front of the High Wall. The memory of the doomed dancer's screams as he was slowly eviscerated still echoed in Daveeka's head, setting the fur along the back of his neck on edge. He looked away, no longer able to bear the grisly sight of the hanging body.

As he drew closer to the waiting males, Daveeka cautiously inspected the others who had red robes trailing from beneath their capes. These would be his fellow candidates for the Receiving. None of them looked familiar, so they must be from other Families.

A surge of irrational antipathy towards the other candidates welled up in his mind, but he thrust it aside Rillenus were civilized; males no longer fought to the death for access to a female about to give birth.

Nevertheless, each candidate stood a bit apart, leaving his attendants to form a symbolic barrier between himself and the others.

As Daveeka approached the group, some of them turned to look him over. Above the quiet undertone of whispered conversations, he thought he caught the word "Kiari" repeated scornfully several times, along with a few worse epithets. Someone even jerked a thumb towards the execution platform, as if to indicate that that was the proper end for all rug dancers.

Daveeka's party had barely arrived when the heavy gate swung open. Several adolescent females appeared, gesturing for the males to follow them inside but not deigning to speak to them.

They were the first females he had ever seen this close, so Daveeka stared at them as inconspicuously as he could. Long silky fur, so deep gray that it was almost black. Short rounded ears. Delicate features, framed in a fluffy ruff of lighter fur.

Absolutely exquisite! His hands ached to caress them and feel that silken fur slide through his fingers, but he knew he must not. Touching a female unbidden was a serious crime.

Teo reached for Daveeka's hand, twining his fingers with his partner's and calling him back to reality with a sharp squeeze. Following the other males, they filed through the opening in the thick rock wall and crossed a broad courtyard.

At the other side of the courtyard, the little procession passed through an arched doorway into a massive building. Once inside, the males shed their cloaks, regarding each other with thinly veiled curiosity.

Except for Daveeka, all of the red-robed males wore the embroidered collars that showed them to be Fathers. Although only one was the elaborate collar of an Honored Father, the other collars all had many bands of decoration, each band done in a special pattern depending on the number of the son it represented. Even the lowest-ranking Father had five sons to his credit.

Daveeka's eyes went wide. He hadn't realized the rank of the company he was keeping. He could never hope to compete with these experienced Fathers for the right to Receive a child.

No. He didn't have to compete. He had already been Invited. The idea that he'd have to fight for a child was a leftover instinct, nothing more.

The other candidates were taking their Invitations from their pockets, handing them to the young attendants. Daveeka did the same, catching the displeased angle of Fahlin's ears out of the corner of one eye as he gave the parchment into the dark-furred female hand.

"There's nothing to be afraid of," Fahlin declared superciliously, as if he were instructing a terrified youngster. He spoke just loudly enough to be heard by the other males. "The acolytes will take you to the Temple, until it's almost time. We'll be waiting for you outside the Birthing chamber."

Several of the other Fathers snickered knowingly. So the dancer was an ignorant coward, eh? They'd expected as much.

"I know what happens," Daveeka replied, annoyance edging his voice with sharpness. It hadn't even begun, and Fahlin was harassing him already. Well, he'd show them! "And I'm not the least bit afraid," he added, lifting his chin and glaring at the older rillenu.

Fahlin had no time to respond. One of the young females gestured imperiously, and the red-robed candidates left their companions behind, following her through a doorway and down a winding corridor.

Last in line, Daveeka was able to inspect his surroundings without being noticed. Scarlet red glowweeds festooned the hallway, casting soft shadows on the walls as the small party proceeded along the hall and down a long flight of stairs. The walls and low ceiling were painted with intricate geometric designs in muted tones, and faintly luminous carpetmoss covered the floors. Even through his padded shoes, he could feel the softness of the thick moss.

Rounding a wide curve and paying more attention to the decorated walls than to where he was going, Daveeka narrowly missed stepping on the heels of the person in front of him when the other male halted abruptly at the entrance to the Temple. He looked up, and caught his breath.

The huge main lobby of the Marloosh lodging house would have been dwarfed by the size of the room in which Daveeka now found himself. The ceilings arched away into darkness, illuminated only where thick woven ropes of glowweed hung suspended in graceful loops. All the walls were covered with heavy embroidered fabrics, muffling sound. At oddly-spaced intervals around the Temple floor, carved stones in various shapes sat atop low pedestals, surrounded by cushions. There were so many that he would have had trouble counting them, even had he been allowed enough time to do so.

In the very center of the vast room, dominating everything else by its sheer size, brooded the ancient statue of Elenath. She was seated cross-legged, Her hands reaching down to hold either side of a raised platform. At the back of the platform hung a heavy veil, obscuring Daveeka's view of something that appeared to be suspended above a firepot, since he could see flames flickering behind a metal grillwork.

Daveeka stared around the huge Temple. He had heard of its size and the incredible statue, but seeing it in person was entirely different.

The young female beckoned them onward. Daveeka trailed behind the other males, strangely unwilling to approach closer to the statue.

A number of the scattered cushions held females of varying ages, some seated cross-legged, others kneeling or reclining. Some of them seemed to be contemplating the strange stone sculptures, while others faced the statue of Elenath. Several rose to their feet and left when they noticed the party of males approaching. He stared for just a moment too long at a female with a young girlchild in her arms, earning himself a fierce scowl and flattened ears from the Mother.

The young acolyte escorted them to cushions directly in front of the overwhelming statue. She went to the steps leading up to the platform, where a series of crystals hung suspended from a frame, dangling on fine metal chains. Taking the lowermost crystal between two fingers, she struck the others in a swift pattern, producing an eerie melody of crisp, chiming notes.

As the sounds died away, she climbed the stairs, performed an involved bow, and reached briefly behind one side of the veil. Holding a small glass cup in one hand, she went back down the steps and then went to each male in turn, dipping the fingers of one hand into the bowl, then sprinkling him with strangely scented water. Very hot water, Daveeka noticed with surprise, as a drop hit one of his ears.

Ritual completed, the female sank down onto a cushion beside them. Covering her face with both hands, she began reciting a rapid chant, swaying slightly from side to side as she did so.

Although Daveeka could easily hear her voice, he couldn't make out many of the words. Of course, she would be chanting in the ancient formal version of femalespeech, which was even harder for a male to understand than everyday femalespeech.

Daveeka stared up at the statue, knowing he was supposed to be praying for the Deity's assistance, petitioning Her for success at the Receiving. If it were Her will, he might soon have a child, which would mean he had been designated as one worthy to wield power over his fellows. Since the females were the earthly representatives of Elenath, it was not unreasonable that Her choices should be manifested through them.

But even among the ones Invited, not all would Receive. Infants were born dead at times, or as Fahlin had reminded him, there might well be less than nine babies in a Birthing. Still, if he found favor in Elenath's eyes, if he were among the chosen ones She honored with Her blessing …

He should be praying, but all he could do was gaze at the statue. From where he sat, his view was partially blocked by the veiled whatever-it-was on the platform She held in Her hands, but he could see Her face and upper body. She had rather large and pointy ears, for a female. And Her sculptured fur, though longer than a male's, didn't look quite as long as he'd have expected.

But Her face. Her eyes seemed to look into his very soul, as they glittered in the reflected flame from the back of the firepot. Shadows shifted around the top of Her head, mingling with the shadows cast by the glowweeds hanging from the ceiling. It was impossible to make out clearly the angle of Her ears. One moment She appeared pleased, the next angry.

The echo of that faint whisper he had heard during the Dance crossed his mind. He shivered, still not absolutely certain he hadn't imagined it.

Entranced, Daveeka never knew how much time actually passed while they sat in the Temple. He had just begun to wonder what was behind the veil when an elderly female came softly to their attendant and whispered in her ear. She rose to her feet.

As the young female led them from the Temple, Daveeka realized with a guilty pang that he had entirely forgotten to pray for a child. Well, it was too late now. Elenath would either look upon him with favor this night, or reject him. Either way, he would never forget this probably once-in-a-lifetime visit to the Temple. What was behind the curtain? And what was the meaning of the odd stone sculptures, and—and—

Such knowledge was not for the likes of him, he reminded himself sternly. Males hadn't the intelligence to comprehend such things, nor the refinement of spirit to appreciate them.

Just the same, he was curious.

As Daveeka walked into the soothing red dimness of the Birthing chamber, he dragged his thoughts back to more mundane realities. He mustn't get his hopes up too high. His chances of actually Receiving an infant were not that good, especially since he'd probably just insulted Elenath by not praying properly.

His eyes adjusted to the dim red light as he followed Teo and Fahlin around the semi-circle of padded couches, going to the last one at the far side of the room. Ninth Position.

Mistress Annilee would already be in her place, behind the curtains that blocked the center of the semi-circle from view. Daveeka wished he could see her and at least find out what she looked like. If only he could ask her whether she'd chosen him because of his rug-dancing, or for an entirely unrelated reason.

He strained his ears for a sound from behind those heavy curtains, but he could make out nothing other than the nervous whispers and soft comments of the rest of the males now taking the Positions they had been assigned.

Daveeka wondered briefly whether Annilee was as scared as he was. Or were females by their very nature beyond fear?

He sat down on the edge of his couch, took a deep breath, and exhaled slowly. His status in Marloosh was low enough already. He did not need to have it further lowered by dissolving into a terrified and hysterical coward at this point. It was entirely understandable, of course, since it wasn't easy for a male to face the prospect of having his pouch opened for the very first time.

Almost as if he'd read Daveeka's thoughts, Teo leaned close, whispering faintly into his ear, "If you don't behave well, the rumor will get around quickly." He nodded towards the other males in the room.

Daveeka was suddenly very conscious of a number of curious eyes looking his way. "I know."

"It could also ruin your chance at another Invitation." Teo lowered his voice further. Even so, it shook sadly as he concluded, "Females don't like cowardly males."

Daveeka touched his partner's hand, resolve flooding anew through his mind and washing away his nervousness. "I can do it, Beloved. Don't worry."

"Watch out for Fahlin. He'll certainly try to rattle you," Teo warned.

Daveeka reclined on the couch, his head and shoulders raised by the padded back. He deliberately tried to relax as Teo unfastened his robe and opened it to either side, draping it over the edges of the couch and leaving him essentially naked, although his arms were still in the sleeves. Although he wasn't used to having his furred penile sheath exposed like this, he reminded himself that this was necessary in order to provide access to his pouch, should there be an infant for him. None of the other candidates acted even the least bit embarrassed, so he decided there was no need to be ashamed of his obvious maleness under these circumstances.

Teo and Fahlin sat down beside him, one on either side. Teo placed a hand gently on Daveeka's exposed belly, over the taut, fur-covered flesh that formed the outer skin of his pouch. Daveeka winced slightly, but did not pull away, only slitting his eyes open far enough to see his partner's face.

Ever since he'd received the Invitation, Teo had been coaching him, trying to get him accustomed to being touched in this way, teaching him to relax instead of tensing against the irrational fear that made him want to push the other male's hand away. But there had been such a short time to prepare. It would have been better if they had had most of the nanth, rather than just three nights.

Daveeka tried to convince his tense abdominal muscles to relax. *Picture yourself dissolving, melting into the ground*, Teo had told him repeatedly during their practice sessions. Daveeka melted, feeling the dead weight of Teo's hand on his belly and accepting its presence. If he couldn't stand his partner's touch on the outside of his pouch, he'd never be able to calmly accept the presence of the hoped-for infant actually inside his pouch, against the unfurred and extremely sensitive inner flesh.

He'd heard stories about Receivings, and how terrified first-time Fathers sometimes had to be held down by their attendants and even, as a last resort because violent struggling could harm the infant, drugged into total unconsciousness, when the time came for the tiny newborn to crawl into its Father's pouch. All Teo had been able to tell him about his own experience was that he couldn't really remember all that had happened, since he'd been drugged at the time. Perhaps that was just as well.

Teo's hand moved slightly, fingers kneading muscles that insisted on tensing despite Daveeka's efforts.

Fahlin touched his shoulder and Daveeka opened his eyes to see him holding out an ornate ceramic cup filled with pale red jareesh. Wordlessly, Daveeka shook his head in refusal. He wouldn't give Fahlin the satisfaction of knowing he was scared.

"Take it, Dav," Teo said softly. "To be brave doesn't necessarily imply that one must be foolhardy as well. It's not very strong and it's no more than has been offered, and probably accepted, by any of the other males here."

Daveeka relented and sipped at the sweet liquid. He could tell from the taste and the color that the jareesh had been very much diluted. They'd undoubtedly save the stronger potions for later. Nevertheless, he took care to do nothing more than sip.

From behind the curtain came a short gasp and a stifled moan, accompanied by the sound of murmuring voices. Daveeka's ears swiveled and he almost sat up, but he couldn't catch the words. He wasn't likely to understand anyway, since the females would be using femalespeech.

Although he wished he could see what was happening on the other side of that shielding curtain, he also knew it wasn't any of his business. His business was to be prepared to Receive a child, nothing more.

Daveeka glanced around the room, trying to see how the other candidates were reacting. The draped walls of the Birthing chamber swallowed sound, but the hushed conversations between the other males and their attendants formed an unintelligible background murmur. They all appeared calm enough, but then, they had each carried numerous infants already.

Daveeka lay quietly, yielding himself up to the feeling of Teo's fingers on his stomach. Teo probed gently but insistently, sometimes touching the opening of his partner's pouch.

Annilee's occasional gasps became panting sobs, but Daveeka only half noticed that now. He drifted, slightly light-headed but fully conscious. For the first time, he let himself consider the possibility that he might really be successful.

He would wear the short robe of a potential Father and be treated with respect and consideration. And if the child lived to leave his pouch, he would have a son. He'd be entitled to the decorated collar of a Father, although it would be nowhere near as wide as the ones the other Fathers wore, since it would only indicate a single son. And his belly would no longer be shamefully taut and flat, but would have a respectable sag, mute testimony that his pouch had held a child. He would have a responsible and interesting job in the Marloosh lodging house. Life would be full of challenge, instead of boredom.

And maybe, just maybe, he might be able to use his influence to help some of the other Kiari Receive children also.

So lost was he in this pleasant daydream that it took a loud moan from Annilee to recall Daveeka to reality. He started awake, only to feel Fahlin's hand on his shoulder, pressing him down.

Daveeka did his best to ignore the interruption and concentrate only on how very much he wanted a son. He distracted himself by wondering if there might be a female amongst the babies.

Perhaps once in ten Birthings a female was born, but seldom at a first Birthing such as this. Still, statistics were only statistics. It was always possible.

Not that it would make any real difference to Daveeka, though. Females were almost always among the first to be born at any particular Birthing, which was strange, since they were so frail and tiny. All too often, they didn't even survive the birth. Amongst the male babies, the bigger and more vigorous ones tended to be born first.

But when a female infant did survive, and when the fortunate male who Received it was able to successfully carry the child until the females took it from his pouch, that person would gain the highest status possible for a rillenu male, that of Honored Father, ranking just under the females themselves. If the daughter later died in infancy, as so many did, this would have no effect on the Honored Father's status.

Daveeka had the irrational feeling that he wouldn't be this nervous at all, if only he were near Annilee, able to stroke her dark fur and feel her hands caress him gently. It seemed as if that would somehow banish the tension gathering in his gut.

It wasn't that it hurt so much to have your pouch opened, even for the first time. It's just that it was an instinctively terrifying sensation, seeming to threaten severe internal injury, even though in actual fact it was not harmful in and of itself. At least that's what he'd been told, so in the rational part of his mind he knew he had nothing to fear.

And yet he saw nightmare images of someone reaching into him, tearing him apart, pulling his insides out as he screamed in agony.

A muffled commotion and sounds of movement came from behind the curtain. Curious, Daveeka opened his eyes.

A tall, stately female in a light-colored robe bustled out from between the heavy folds of the drape, hurrying over to the male who had First Position.

"That's the Exalted Mother Marlieth," Teo whispered in awe. "Mistress Annilee's Mother."

Daveeka stared, drinking in the sight of the powerful female, the ultimate ruler of Thennevar and the thirteen male Families who owed allegiance to it. No jeweled collar or other distinctive clothing marked her out as the Exalted Mother, nor did anything proclaim the number of her daughters. Females had no need to advertise their rank, as it was assumed to be known.

Light glittered off a long gold chain of large crystal beads that hung suspended from an enameled clip at the neck of her robe as she hurried across the room, but that was the only decoration she wore.

She leaned over the couch, blocking Daveeka's view of the Honored Father in First Position.

"The baby's not a female," Teo whispered. "If it were, the Exalted Mother would have announced it by now."

Her back was to Daveeka and he couldn't see what was happening. No matter; he knew. She would lay the first of Annilee's babies on the belly of the male in First Position, then wait to see if it had sufficient vitality to crawl into his pouch on its own.

Just thinking about it made Daveeka's stomach do flip-flops. He felt suddenly dizzy and short of breath. His ears flattened.

Fahlin gave a small snort of disgust. "Not so brave after all, eh, dancer?"

"All right, Dav, all right," Teo soothed. "Lie back and close your eyes. You shouldn't be watching that anyway. Soon enough when it's your turn. Easy now."

Knowing his partner was right, Daveeka listened to the darkness behind his closed eyelids and pictured himself floating in a pool of warm water, slowly dissolving the fear that lay like a hard lump in his belly.

Annilee's soft panting cries continued to disturb the expectant silence, and every so often Daveeka heard footsteps and the rustling of fabric. All must be going well. "She's birthed seven healthy babies so far," Teo whispered. "No daughters, but no one really expected there would be." Daveeka felt his partner's breath tickling the stiff hairs inside his ears and knew he must be leaning over him.

"I wish I could see Annilee."

Fahlin's voice came roughly to his ears, harsh with displeasure. "No male may watch a Birthing. It awakens dangerous feelings. Surely, even one such as you should know that."

Teo spoke rapidly, almost interrupting Fahlin in his eagerness. "Here's the eighth infant now! If there's one more …”

Daveeka tried to see, but the bodies of the various attendants blocked his view of the Father in Eighth Position.

Teo buried his face in his hands, whispering a prayer Daveeka could not hear.

There was only silence behind the curtain, but the other males, successful and ecstatic, conversed excitedly amongst themselves. Although no one had Received a daughter, eight healthy sons were more than could reasonably be expected from a first Birthing.

For a time, nothing further happened.

"There," Fahlin stated positively, "I told you that you wouldn't be successful."

Daveeka's ears drooped mournfully. He had gotten himself into trouble for nothing.

Then the Exalted Mother Marlieth came out from behind the curtain, flanked by several other females. She leaned over him, and he saw that she carried an incredibly tiny infant in her cupped hands.

"No! I don't believe it!" Fahlin's voice cracked into an undignified gasp.

The infant was barely the length of a finger, much too small. At first glance, Daveeka feared it wasn't even alive and was just being shown to him in order that he might confirm its lack of life. Then the tiny chest moved a fraction as the infant took a precarious breath. It was alive, but it wasn't very strong. Perhaps it wouldn't survive at all. It seemed strangely unformed and incomplete.

Then it hit him. This one was a female! Last-born, pathetically undersized, barely alive, but distinctly a female.

Instead of the total hairlessness of a newborn male, it was covered with fine dark fuzz. This was impossible. The odds against it were …

The Exalted Mother hesitated for a moment, her exquisite ears half-flattened against her head as she stared at Daveeka's face. "Hear: thiss ve daughter."

She spoke slowly and distinctly in a simple version of femalespeech, in the hopes that he would understand despite the strange accents of the sibilant female dialect. At Marlieth's announcement, the room became very quiet.

As Annilee's Mother, Marlieth should have sounded pleased at the birth of a female. She did not. With an annoyed shake of her head, she dumped the too-small infant onto Daveeka's belly, just above the opening of his pouch.

Daveeka felt the tiny scrap of life struggle briefly, making weak crawling motions. Then it lay still.

He wanted desperately to touch it, but Teo and Fahlin held his wrists pinned to the couch.

No! Don't give up! I don't want you to die, he thought frantically at the limp little creature.

The infant had to reach the warmth and safety of his pouch quickly. If it could not, it was surely doomed.

Daveeka heard a rustle of movement. He looked up to see another female coming towards him, wrapped in a light cloak. Her long fur was mussed and disheveled.

Marlieth said something in the female dialect, fast and unintelligible, but an angry exclamation judging by the intonation. The approaching female answered in a gasping whisper as she sank down on the opposite edge of the couch.

Daveeka swallowed the lump of fear in his throat, half his mind on the infant lying motionless on his belly. "Mistress Annilee?" he asked softly, wonder etched in his voice.

Her dark eyes turned to him in surprise. Then she said very slowly, "You ve Daveecha, na?"

He nodded eagerly, overcome with an intense yearning to feel her fingers touching him, wiping away his anxiety with a soothing caress.

"Ve danser, na? Chiari?" Her voice turned cold, her eyes narrowed in suspicious appraisal.

He hardly dared to nod. She had known he was a dancer, then. But why did she seem to disapprove?

Marlieth spoke again to her daughter in rapid femalespeech. Although it was mostly a garble to Daveeka's ears, he almost thought he caught a phrase about something being better dead.

"Na!" Annilee extended a hand toward her tiny child, but Marlieth grabbed her wrist.

Her actions injected sense into her words. The Exalted Mother would rather see the infant die than be carried by the likes of him. No! They couldn't do that!

But wait—didn't Annilee's opposition imply there was an alternative?

"Please," he begged, "don't let her die."

Both females inhaled sharply. Their small ears swiveled toward Daveeka.

"Understhanding uss ve you?" Marlieth asked sternly.

Daveeka stared at them blankly and shook his head. He certainly couldn't claim to know femalespeech that well. It had been only a lucky guess.

Annilee hissed out a few sentences, pointing angrily to Daveeka and demanding something of her Mother. It sounded as if it were something she had every right to expect.

With obvious reluctance, Marlieth agreed.

Fahlin tried to say something in halting femalespeech, but Annilee cut him off with a gesture. Then she turned back to Daveeka. "Hear: a female it ve permitted to assist, while yet life iss. But you must ask thiss. Courage have you sso to dho?"

Daveeka didn't hesitate long enough to allow himself to consider what her statement implied. His heart was too torn by the sight of the motionless little thing lying against the short fur of his belly.

"Yes," he said hoarsely, hoping he had correctly understood her words. "Yes. Save her, if you can."

Hearing the sharp intake of Fahlin's breath, Daveeka knew he'd let himself in for something unpleasant.

Annilee glared at her Mother in triumph. Barely able to contain her fury, Marlieth sat down next to him on the couch.

Daveeka shrank back, fearful of accidentally touching an Exalted Mother without permission. Males had been put to death for less.

Teo, recovering from his initial shock, held the drugged cup quickly to Daveeka's lips. Daveeka swallowed what was left without hesitation, as Marlieth gently stroked the tiny infant with the tip of a finger. It reacted with nothing but a feeble squirm, but it was still alive.

The Exalted Mother nodded at the two females who attended her, and they moved to either side of Daveeka's couch, taking hold of his wrists and shoulders and pinning his arms away from his body. Teo and Fahlin moved down to hold his legs.

Marlieth's free hand went to the opening of Daveeka's pouch. Amazed that one such as she would even deign to touch him, Daveeka almost forgot to be afraid. She inserted the tip of one finger under the lip of skin forming a slit across his belly. Although he couldn't stop himself from attempting to pull away, he turned the instinctive movement into more of a twitch than a struggle, not wanting the females to think he was a coward.

With a sharp glance, Marlieth slid the intruding finger first to one side of the slit and then the other.

Daveeka forced himself to notice that it really didn't hurt; it just felt strange, almost as if someone were actually poking inside his body, not just under a section of skin and muscle that was external to his abdominal wall.

With a quick and certain movement, she slid her hand all the way into his pouch, bridging her fingers slightly to separate the inner surfaces and form an open space.

Daveeka was winning his battle with the dark tide of terror caused by this abrupt intrusion when Fahlin brushed roughly against his foot, jarring his half-healed toe. The unexpected pain lancing up his leg was enough to shatter his concentration and calm.

Suddenly overwhelmed by instinctive panic, Daveeka struggled wildly. He fought against his captors, unable to free himself from the many hands that held him down. Marlieth meant to tear him apart, pull his insides out! He had to stop her—

No. That's silly. Fahlin did that deliberately. Be calm. Stop fighting.

Daveeka gave the Honored Father a black look, even as he squelched the irrational fear that had momentarily claimed him.

The Exalted Mother was only trying to help the infant. He must believe that. It still felt as if she intended to tear him open, but he worked at convincing himself she would not, in fact, do so.

But why did the Mother have such a strange expression on her face, her eyes squinted, her lips pressed together in an expression of pleasure? Her small rounded ears stood upright. He'd have sworn Marlieth was enjoying his terror.

No, he must be imagining things.

Daveeka was still busy reacting to the presence of the Exalted Mother's hand within him, when Annilee reached over and carefully prodded the infant toward the opening. Had it been male, it would have been left to die if it couldn't make it into his pouch, and there would be no one holding that pouch open to ease the way. Apparently, the rules were different for females.

Intent on willing the infant to survive, Daveeka lay still. He let himself sink back against the couch, Marlieth's hand still forcing him open.

From the corner of his eye, Daveeka saw Teo staring down at his belly with a look of horror on his face. The pupils of Teo's eyes dilated suddenly and he slid to the floor in a dead faint.

The infant began to crawl weakly, urged on by another push from Annilee. Marlieth's hand was deep inside him, near the bottom of his pouch. The pressure of her arched fingers against the sensitive membranes was beginning to hurt, but it was bearable. It was more of a stretching feeling than true pain. By the time his child was ready to leave the pouch, he would have been stretched much further than this.

Keeping that thought firmly in mind, Daveeka fought against the tendency of the muscles in the outer wall of his pouch to contract.

"Goodh. Very goodh," Annilee murmured, her head bent to watch her daughter's progress.

Daveeka shuddered as the small creature dragged itself forward. If Marlieth hadn't been holding him open, it would never have had the strength to push its way inside.

He couldn't see it now, but he could feel its underdeveloped arms and stubby legs moving against the tender bare skin of the inner surface of his pouch. Nothing had ever touched him there before. If he had already been opened and had carried a child, he wouldn't be so sensitive. He would even have developed the fine downy fur that normally lined the inside of the pouch, if it had once been opened. Now, however, having never been exposed to the air, the skin inside was soft and moist.

Annilee absently caressed his head with her free hand, between his laid-back ears. Much of the tension seemed to flow out of Daveeka's body at her touch. He willed his ears to stand up, wanting to show that he trusted her and wasn't afraid.

The infant had reached the deeper recesses of his pouch. He felt it brush against his teat, then it took the tip into its mouth. If it had enough strength, it would suck the teat back into its throat, remaining thus attached for eight nanths. The baby's sucking and the pressure of its body against the lower pouch would cause lactation to begin.

Daveeka hardly dared hope the infant might live. It seemed all right now, safe and secure where it belonged. Maybe ...

Slowly, Marlieth released the tension. As she withdrew her hand, he allowed himself a sigh of relief. His pouch sagged open slightly now, and the infant made a distinct, if rather small, bulge low on his abdomen, not far above the base of his penile sheath.

He had done it. If the infant survived, he would be a Father!

Languidly, he closed his eyes, dreaming of what it would be like. He and Teo would have a child to raise—

But wait, this was a daughter, not a son.

Daveeka had no time to follow that thought through to its conclusion.

Teo had revived by now. The tips of his ears drooping sadly forward toward his face with shame, he put an arm under his partner's shoulders and helped him sit up. The females retreated behind the curtain.

The infant shifted slightly and Daveeka turned his attention back to his daughter. He had Received a baby, and it was alive. That was all that mattered right now.

Teo touched his shoulder tentatively. "Dav, want to watch the presentations?"

There was a sadness in his voice that didn't match Daveeka's feelings at all. He wanted to ask Teo about it, but this was hardly the time.

After the drama of his Receiving a female infant, the presentation ceremonies seemed somewhat pale. Mother Marlieth went in turn to each of the males on the couches, giving them a beautifully woven short tunic as a gift of honor and appreciation. Each male shrugged out of the red robe he had worn for the Receiving, pulling the new garment over his head and arranging his decorated collar carefully around his neck. Then he was free to leave with his attendants.

As Marlieth moved from one to another, formally dismissing them, Daveeka realized why Teo looked so unhappy. They wouldn't be going home to Marloosh together. He was now dhamereth, a male carrying a female infant. As such, he would remain in the female Palace until his daughter was old enough to be taken from his pouch. For the next eight nanths, this would be good-bye.

Daveeka clutched his partner's hand. "Teo, I don't want—"

"Silence!" Fahlin commanded.

Marlieth approached them now. She held a short black tunic picked out with shiny embroidery of the moons in all their many phases, the two small male moons silvery and pale, while ruddy

Elnanth sparkled and shone in all her glory. The Exalted Mother held the robe out to Daveeka.

Almost, he hesitated to take it. Teo pulled the red robe down off his shoulders, leaving it lying over the couch, while Fahlin reached for the tunic, saying to Mother Marlieth as he did so, "Family Marloosh extends thanks for this honor."

Somehow, he managed not to sound honored at all.

The Honored Father gathered the cloth into folds and held it up so Daveeka could slip it over his head. The old male's face was a study in controlled hatred, his ears held unnaturally stiff and unmoving.

Teo arranged the robe as neatly as he could. "Stand up, Dav," he whispered. "You've got to go with them now."

"Teo—"

"It'll be all right, don't worry," Teo reassured him, helping him to his feet.

As the highest-ranking male of Daveeka's Family, Fahlin came to stand next to him, displacing Teo. He took Daveeka's hand in both of his, turning to Mistress Annilee.

"Family Marloosh gives this male into the care of Family Thennevar, according to custom and the Law of Elenath."

Fahlin placed Daveeka's hands into both of Annilee's.

"Family Thennevar acceptss, until ssuch time as my daughter dies or iss taken from hiss pouch," Annilee responded gravely, making a partially successful effort to suppress the sibilance of the female accent in order that it might be more intelligible to the males.

The expression on Fahlin's face as he looked hard at Daveeka told him clearly that he hoped the infant died first. But all Fahlin said aloud was, "Be sure you do nothing to disgrace your Family,"—his lip curled with scorn as he spat out the final word—"dancer."

"I'll be waiting for you to return as an Honored Father," Teo whispered, trying to sound cheerful despite his drooping ears. He turned to follow Fahlin from the room. As the heavy curtain at the door swung down behind Teo's back, Daveeka had to stifle the urge to run after him.

Annilee picked up a brimming cup of jareesh, offering it to him. When he shook his head and continued to look over to where Teo had disappeared, she sipped from the cup herself and held it out to him once again. This time he had to drink, or insult her. He touched the jeweled cup to his lips, intending to fake drinking. Then he changed his mind, taking several mouthfuls of the thick liquid.

It was strong, very sweet and sticky.

Annilee took the decorated cup again, raising it to her lips. With a disapproving frown, her Mother knocked it from her hands, splattering dark liquid down the front of her cloak. The ceramic cup rolled across the thick moss on the floor and smashed noisily against the stone wall.

Annilee pouted, then shrugged off the incident. She let herself be led away by her attendants.

Marlieth gestured to several of her female attendants. One of them took Daveeka's arm and propelled him toward the door, following the Exalted Mother. Shaky and already feeling the effects of the potent jareesh, he let himself be taken up several levels without paying much attention to where they were going.

When they reached a room and a soft mattress, Daveeka collapsed. Marlieth herself draped a light blanket over him. He tried to thank her, but she cut him off.

"Dhaughter na sshould you have Received, danssser. You pleasse me na."

With the swish and swirl of rich fabrics, she turned abruptly and left the room, leaving Daveeka to drift off to sleep wondering uneasily what an Exalted Mother might do to a male who pleased her not.

CHAPTER 3

When Daveeka drifted groggily back to consciousness, he had no idea how long he had slept. He reached across the mattress, muttering sleepily, "Teo?"

He encountered nothing but empty space where his partner's body should have been. As he opened his eyes and glanced around the unfamiliar room, memory of the Receiving came crashing in. He carried an infant, after all these years. And not just any infant, but a daughter!

Anxiously, he wondered if his daughter was still alive. Female infants were notoriously fragile, and this one had been so small and weak. He couldn't seem to feel it moving, but perhaps an infant that young didn't move around much. He concentrated on feeling any signs of life in his pouch. Over and above the stiff soreness of stretched muscles, he thought he could feel something unusual. Probably the infant's mouth holding onto his teat.

The light pressure of her tiny body felt vaguely pleasurable against the sensitive skin inside his pouch. Very gently, he touched the slight bulge under the fur of his belly. The strange sensation changed, almost hurting but not quite. Maybe he'd disturbed the baby enough to make her suck, and he just wasn't accustomed to that.

No matter, his daughter was definitely alive. That's all he really cared about for now.

He threw an arm over his eyes and tried to ignore his stomach's insistent demand for food, dreaming of how marvelous life would be for him. For the next eight nanths, he would live in the Thennevar Palace. At the end of that time, when they took his daughter … Well, he really didn't want to think about that. But after it was over, he'd be an Honored Father, with only Fahlin and Syron outranking him in his Family. And Syron was old, and in poor health.

Daveeka smiled to himself. If the Honored Father Syron were more discriminating in the number and quality of the lovers he chose, perhaps he would be in better health. As it was, Daveeka might soon find himself second in command to Fahlin, and even Fahlin was getting on in years.

Imagine what he could do then! He'd have the power and influence to begin changing things, at last. He could see that more childless males were on the lists for Invitations, instead of just other Fathers. He could make the Kiari more acceptable, and perhaps even stop the periodic persecutions entirely. Maybe he could get an Invitation for Teo, despite his having lost a previous son.

Of course, he'd probably never see his daughter again, once she was taken. If she survived leaving his pouch, he might possibly encounter her as an adult. But that was the price all Honored Fathers had to pay. If he had gotten a male infant, he could have kept him until he reached maturity at ten years of age, when he would have been sent to another Family in the annual exchange of sons.

He himself would also have been able to return to Marloosh, and Teo.

Daveeka got up before he could begin exploring that line of thought any further. It was strange to see his legs below the hem of his fancy new short tunic, but that would allow air to circulate freely to his pouch. His daughter would need that.

He explored his new living quarters. The room was large, hung extravagantly with nice pink glowweeds. Plump cushions were scattered around on the carpetmoss, and shelves filled one entire wall, stacked with clean new tunics just like the one he was wearing, plus several capes in varying lengths, in case he was chilly, and some nice silky leg covers to cover his legs without getting in the way of his pouch. There were also heavier tunics and leg covers on the lower shelves, plus a variety of shoes.

He flicked his ears with amusement at all the footwear. He wouldn't need any of them, as he intended to wear his dancer's shoes during the entire time he was here.

The tunics and other clothing were a different story. He fingered the soft fabrics with admiration. *All this, for him?*

His ears stood up straight with joy. *Who else would they be for?*

The room was warm, not drafty and cold like his chamber in the Marloosh childless males' quarters. Exploring, he found that the ventilation slits, instead of opening to the outside, led into tunnels in the solid rock of the wall. Warm air drifted through the opening, smelling of freshness and damp. Wonderful! Even Fahlin didn't live in such luxury.

But he was still ravenously hungry, and he thought he smelled fresh-baked bread. Cocking his ears toward the doorway, he could make out a faint rustle of movement. He decided to put on a fresh tunic and a pair of leg covers, since he had so many garments at his disposal. Then he pulled back the heavy drape in the doorway.

Instead of a bare corridor, Daveeka found himself in a beautifully furnished common room. A handsome young servant boy knelt by the low dining table, unloading a tray of food. The boy bowed. "Blessed be the one who carries a female," he said formally. "Welcome, Dhamereth." He bowed again, forehead to the ground.

"Uh … thanks." Daveeka glanced hungrily at the food on the table. A pot of kullup milk steamed gently over a small flame, next to a bowl heaped with fruit and a loaf of bread. He sat down, reaching for a cup to scoop up some milk.

The servant boy grabbed hastily for the cup, saying, "Let me. It's my job to serve you."

Somewhat uncomfortable with this, Daveeka sat back and allowed the boy to hand him a brimming cup of kullup milk. It was thick and creamy, not the watered-down, almost tasteless fluid he remembered being fed as a youngster.

Licking his lips with appreciation, he helped himself to a ripe cranel from the fruit bowl, just as the boy tried to pick up the bowl and offer it to him. The back of the youngster's hand knocked against the cup, and the spilled milk ran across the table. The boy mopped hastily at the mess, cringing and apologizing profusely for his clumsiness.

Daveeka stifled a laugh and bit into his cranel. The tart juice ran down his chin, and he recalled Teo's offer to steal some cranels from the Marloosh kitchen for him. Now, they were his for the taking. *Wouldn't Teo be surprised?*

If he knew. A small twinge of loneliness clutched at Daveeka's heart at the thought of his absent partner.

Waving away the young servant's attempt to help, Daveeka refilled his cup, peeking over the rim as he drank. The boy was attractive, with unusually small ears for a male and symmetrically dappled fur, but that wasn't surprising. Thennevar usually took the best-looking boys in each year's exchange of sons to be trained as servants, just as the stronger and larger boys would be assigned to the guards.

The youngster was obviously terrified, his ears flattened tightly back against his head. He looked to be about twelve years old, so he was probably still in his probationary period. No wonder he was afraid. Any youngsters who failed their training were sent to the Farms.

The boy was still apologizing.

"Am I your first assignment?" Daveeka asked, cutting off the apology.

"Yes, Dher Daveeka." The boy bowed his head and cringed, looking as if he expected a flogging.

"Relax. I'm not angry. What's your name?"

"Zillah." His voice held a quaver, and he didn't raise his eyes.

"I'm Daveeka."

"Yes, I know. Mistress Chezoar told me about yesternight's Receiving when she gave me this assignment," Zillah replied, his voice now filled with awe. "You must really have found favor in Elenath's eyes, to Receive a daughter in Ninth Position. That never happens."

"Um," Daveeka replied noncommittally. The silence lengthened. "Tell me, what do I do while I'm here? Do I have work assignments?"

"Oh, no!" Zillah exclaimed, unsuccessfully stifling a giggle. Then he looked at Daveeka fearfully. Seeing no anger in the angle of the older male's ears, he went on, "You really don't know?"

Daveeka shook his head.

"You can mostly do whatever you please. Most dhamereth spend as much time as they can mating as many females as will have them." At Daveeka's surprised look, the boy continued with an air of mature understanding, "You'll find a good number of females wanting to mate. They think any male already carrying a daughter will sire a higher proportion of female infants, so almost anyone will be glad to have you."

"What good does that do? I'll still be carrying my daughter when it comes time for their Birthings, so I won't get any Invitations."

"Of course not. But there's always a chance that they'll remember you later on. And then there will be Invitations."

This seemed a bit overdone to Daveeka. After all, Honored Fathers were always at the top of the recommended lists. They received plenty of Invitations. Still, wouldn't it be marvelous to have a chance to actually mate with a female? There were always plenty of fantastic stories about such a thing circulating in the quarters of the childless males. Maybe now he'd find out for himself how much of that was truth.

He glanced at Zillah, whose eyes shone with bright enthusiasm. It must surely not be fitting to discuss such a topic with a mere servant, but the youngster didn't appear ill at ease.

"Eight nanths of doing nothing doesn't sound particularly exciting. I'd rather use the time learning about the females. Tell me, are we allowed into the Temple?"

"Yes, as long as we don't disturb anyone. We can even watch their ceremonies, if we sit back by the walls. I do it sometimes, when I have a chance."

"Good." Daveeka took another cranel. "Can I look around the Palace, or do I have to stay in my quarters?"

Zillah waved one arm expansively, almost knocking the loaf of bread from the table. "Sorry," he mumbled, returning the bread to its place. "You're allowed to go everywhere, except through the doorways that have curtains marked with the Thennevar symbol. Only females can go there."

As Daveeka rose to his feet, Zillah leapt up ahead of him and bustled into his sleeping room. He came out with clothing in his arms. "You'll want to wear heavy leg covers and this fur cape. Our living quarters are kept warmer than the rest of the Palace. The females think it's stifling in here, and I suppose if my fur were as long as theirs, I would agree. Let me help you dress, then I'll show you around."

"That's hardly necessary." But Zillah insisted it was his duty, so eventually Daveeka gave in.

Before that night had ended, Daveeka was reasonably well acquainted with the Thennevar Palace. When he looked through the library, seeing shelf after shelf of scrolls and considering the knowledge they must contain, his biggest problem was keeping his mouth from hanging open in awe.

With Zillah following humbly behind, Daveeka strolled past rows of closely packed scrolls, some so thick he would have been hard put to get his arms around them, others small and dainty. Hesitantly, he picked up one of the smaller ones, untying its binder and unrolling it. Since Zillah said nothing and no one rushed over to chide him, he assumed males must be permitted to read the scrolls.

Much good it would do him, though. The ornate letters crawled across the parchment like malevolent worms, refusing to yield any clear sense to his eyes. Most of the letters seemed almost familiar; fancier than the corresponding ones in the malespeech alphabet, but not entirely different. Or were they even the same letters? He could be wrong.

Then and there, Daveeka resolved to learn as much femalespeech as he could. Such knowledge might be turned to his advantage, since very few Honored Fathers were fluent in femalespeech, and even fewer could read it. If he could become good at it, the Mothers might request him to handle their dealings with Marloosh. Besides, there were all those scrolls he wanted to read, so much he could learn. Suddenly, the eight nanths he'd be at Thennevar seemed like far too short a time.

Several nights later, while Daveeka sat in the common room puzzling over a scroll, Zillah came up behind him and peeked over his shoulder.

"Learning to readh ve you, Dher Daveecha?" he asked softly in femalespeech.

Daveeka jerked his head around to stare into Zillah's face. "Yesh, learning ve Ish," he answered hesitantly. The words felt strange on his tongue.

Zillah smothered a giggle. "Only females refer to themselves as 'Ish'. Males say 'I'. Just like 'hyou' and 'you'. And you've got to get the accent right on the verbs, so you can distinguish between male and female intonations. Get it mixed up and you'll find yourself in trouble. Females don't appreciate being addressed in male terms."

Daveeka's ears drooped slightly in embarrassment. How could he have failed to notice that?

"Learning ve I," he repeated slowly, careful to use the proper form of the pronoun.

"Better," Zillah replied. "But there needs to be a drawn-out falling inflection on the verb. Like this."

Zillah demonstrated, and Daveeka copied him until he got the hang of it.

The boy glanced down at the scroll in front of Daveeka. "Trying to learn just by reading the scrolls isn't easy. They're written by females, for females, so almost everything uses female forms. After awhile, you start to think that way, too." He spoke as if he knew what he was talking about.

"Zillah, how well do you know femalespeech?" Daveeka asked.

The servant boy shifted uneasily. "Well, servants are taught a little of it, but mostly only what we need to know in order to serve the females. The rest I just pick up on my own." He looked up at the older male in sudden fear. "I couldn't help it, Dher Daveeka. I hear it all the time and I …"

Daveeka understood. "But you're not supposed to be learning to read it, and you have been. Right?"

Zillah hung his head. "Are … are you going to report me to the Mothers?"

"No, of course not." The boy stopped trembling. "I'll make you a deal. I won't report you, if you'll help me learn, also. We can study together. How's that?"

"I won't get in trouble?"

"If anyone asks, I ordered you to do it. All right?"

"Oh, yes, Dher Daveeka! I'd love that."

Zillah was as good as his word. Each night, they studied femalespeech until the letters ran together and blurred before Daveeka's tired eyes. Many of the everyday words weren't spelled too differently from the corresponding ones in malespeech. Once he got used to the elaborate lettering, reading some of the simpler scrolls wasn't all that hard.

He grinned. Just like reading malespeech, any reasonably intelligent male could learn this. Except that most males never got the chance.

He went to the sundown ceremonies in the Temple every night, both for the chance it afforded him to practice understanding femalespeech and because he liked watching the eerie drama of the gathered females clustered at the base of Elenath's statue, reciting Her praises and petitioning Her favor.

Entire sentences began making sense to him. Soon he was singing the ritual chants under his breath, along with the females.

During the elaborate full moon ceremony that marked the beginning of Tenth Nanth, he understood much of what was going on when Mother Magdael and Mistress Havall were announced to be pregnant and special prayers were recited over them, asking that they might bear daughters. Invitations would soon be going out to the fortunate males chosen by the two pregnant females.

Mother Magdael was not young, but she was exceptionally beautiful, even for a female. Her fur was long, fluffy, and extremely dark; her ears very small and rounded. Watching her stand proudly before the statue of Elenath for the blessing, Daveeka stifled a small pang of regret that Zillah's prediction that he would be summoned often to the mating rooms had thus far not come true. Perhaps it was his Kiari status that deterred the females from mating him. Perhaps as they became used to seeing him around the Palace, they would become less reluctant.

As the ceremony concluded and Daveeka left the Temple, he was still musing wistfully over this possibility, unable to dismiss Mother Magdael from his thoughts.

"Daveecha," came a voice from behind him. He spun around to find himself face to face with the object of his musings.

Dropping to one knee before Magdael, he asked humbly, "How may I serve hyou, revered Mother?"

She studied him for a moment, seeming slightly uncertain despite her regal bearing. Then she made up her mind. "With me you come."

Daveeka rose to his feet. Eyes cast down, he followed Magdael from the Temple and along the hallway. When she pulled aside a curtain marked with the deep purple chonendron blossom that Daveeka recognized as the Thennevar symbol, his heart leapt into his throat. He was being admitted into the forbidden female section of the Palace.

Could this be the way to the mating rooms? He could think of no other reason she would be interested in him.

He followed meekly behind the Mother as she turned down a side corridor that became a curving stairway. The stairway ended in a dimly lit chamber, the focus of a cluster of doorways, all standing open with curtains drawn back. Magdael gestured toward one of the doors, so Daveeka went inside.

Deep red glowweeds illumined the small chamber with a comfortably dim light. He stared at the rich wall hangings as Magdael pulled the curtain closed behind them. She waved him over to the wide couch that almost filled the room. A small statue of Elenath sat in a decorated niche in the wall above the couch.

Definitely nervous now, Daveeka wondered what would happen next.

"You often in Temple ve. Undersstanding femalespeech?" she asked in her accented version of malespeech. Daveeka had noticed that it seemed easier for most females to suppress the sibilance of femalespeech when talking to a male than it was to change the word order and intonations used.

"Y … yesh. Sssome," he replied hesitantly.

Magdael nodded. "Goodh." She swept a hand around the room. "For you thiss firsst time ve, yesh?" the Mother asked, speaking slowly and distinctly.

"Yesh."

"Clothing off, on bed lie."

Obediently, he pulled his short tunic over his head and stripped off his leg covers and shoes. Then he lay down naked on the mattress, anticipating what was to come next. He was actually going to be mated by a female, and a most beautiful one at that!

Magdael sat next to him, fully dressed but allowing her long skirt to hike up almost to one knee as she crossed her legs. Her eyes roamed slowly over his body.

He found it hard not to reach for her. His fingertips longed to caress her thick fur; his arms yearned to hold her body against his. But he dared do nothing until he was told, for fear that he might do something wrong and anger her.

"Pouch sstill ve tight and daughter ssmall," she concluded. "Ssheath ve already sstanding."

Still he didn't move, frozen beneath her appraising glance.

Magdael took hold of his penile sheath, caressing him expertly.

His fingers curled in frustration.

"You wissh me more to touch, na?" Her voice seemed merely amused.

"Yesh! Pleasse!" he gasped. His hands were fists, his toes pulled down underneath his feet. His entire body seemed to ache for the slightest touch of her hands.

"Na ve it allowed you to touch me. Na ve it required me to touch you, except for thisss." She tightened her grip on his sheath. Already his moist and naked penis had begun to emerge from the tip. "When ve ready Ish mount you."

Judging from the tone of her voice, Magdael was greatly enjoying his apparent dismay as he realized fully what she had said. "No," he protested, then corrected himself. "Na! Hyou mussst – "

"Na ve 'musst' for femaless, foolisssh male. Sstay quiet and ssstill, or you ve punissshed," she hissed.

Defeated by her anger, Daveeka held his tongue. By now, he was burning with lust, his nerve endings craving sensual stimulation along with the sexual arousal.

All too soon, his penis was fully extended from its furred sheath, signaling his readiness. He realized he was close to releasing his fluid, even though he hadn't had nearly enough time to build up very much of it. Not to touch and be touched in return at such a time was almost painfully unsatisfying.

Magdael continued milking him dispassionately, as if she felt nothing and cared less.

He bit his lip to stifle a groan. It would all be over far too soon for him to reach that high peak of ecstasy that always came so easily when he held Teo in his arms.

With no further ado, Magdael let go of his sheath, hiked up her skirts and squatted over him, taking less than half of the full length of his extended organ into her body. Daveeka didn't dare to move, although he desperately wanted to push himself in all the way.

For long frustrating moments, the female remained still, crouching well above his groin, safely clear of the daughter nearby in the lowest part of his pouch. Then she moved, just a little, up and down, up and down, squeezing him tightly on the upstroke, but never taking him in any deeper than he already was on the down stroke.

Daveeka panted with the sheer effort of keeping still, while all his instincts cried out to touch, and feel, and bury himself fully into that delicious warm and grasping place.

"You now releasse fluid," Magdael said, a strangely lascivious grin on her lovely face, as if she truly desired to be filled by him.

"Na," he gasped. "Na ve ready. Need more."

Her grin spread wider, as her eyes narrowed dangerously. Again, she wrapped her hand around his sheath, but this time she slowly slid her fingertips downwards and began probing around the base.

Daveeka's eyes widened as he realized what she was going to do. "Na! Mistress, pleassse!"

She ignored him, pressing hard down and against the sac that held his fluid and the gland that lay beneath it.

He choked on a cry of pain, willing himself to release, but he wasn't ready, his sac not yet full enough.

She dug in harder, finally managing to force the hard contractions that would empty him into her.

This time he screamed, with the combined pain and pleasure of being forced to release his fluid in this way.

Magdael closed her eyes and tightened herself around him, then pulled up hard several times, as if she meant to suck him dry with her grasping opening. Then she let go and got off the couch, straightening the skirts of her long robe and smiling in evident satisfaction at a job well done.

"Glad ve you that Ish with gentleness took your fluid. Sshortly ve your sservant here to escort you to room." With that, she strode out through the curtain.

Daveeka just lay there, waiting for the spasms to stop and trying to breathe. No decent male would ever do what she had done. It was unnatural and disgusting.

As promised, Zillah appeared promptly.

"Come on, Dher Daveeka. Let's get you dressed and out of here," he said, attempting to be cheerful. "Sit up now, and I'll help you with your shoes and leg covers."

Daveeka did his best to comply, but he was still rather dazed by the entire experience. Once he had his clothes on, Zillah knelt in front of him, guiding his toes into his shoes. That done, the youngster stood up.

Daveeka couldn't help himself. He leaned forward and wrapped his arms around the other rillenu's waist, pulling him close and resting his head against the boy's narrow chest, at last finding some small relief from his frustrated desire to touch and be touched simply by having someone else pressed against his trembling body.

Zillah didn't appear to be surprised. He leaned forward, gently stroking Daveeka's back. Even through the clothing, it was marvelously calming.

"Are they … " Daveeka said, then choked on a sob. "Are they always like that?"

"Yes. Mother Magdael may be a little worse than most of the others, at least according to the gossip in the servants' quarters. But not by much."

"I don't understand why she even bothered with me, since she's already pregnant."

"Probably just curious about the new male. Don't worry. If Magdael liked you, she'll summon you again, after her Birthing."

"I'm not sure if I want her to do that or not," Daveeka admitted.

"You'll get used to it, just as the other Fathers do. Come on, now. We're in the part of the Palace where males are forbidden to enter on their own. I'm only here because I was summoned to attend you, and I know the way we have to go to return. We'll be in trouble if we don't get moving. No more talking until we're back where we belong."

With Zillah's guidance, they threaded their way through the maze of corridors in silence.

Daveeka didn't have time to reflect on his experience until they got to his room. Feeling somehow dirty in more than a physical sense, he asked Zillah to take him to the bathing rooms.

Soaking in the hot pool restored his spirits somewhat, even though it was much shallower than the pools to which he was accustomed. The water barely covered his legs when he sat cross-legged, but this was to prevent his accidentally allowing too much water into his pouch. His daughter could drown if that were to happen.

Zillah sat next to him, rubbing soapy water into the fur on his back. "You expected something better at the mating, didn't you?" the boy asked softly.

Daveeka tensed, but Zillah went on diligently scrubbing his fur, as if it were merely a casual question.

"Well, I … uh … didn't much enjoy it," he admitted carefully.

"Most dhamereth don't, especially the first time."

Daveeka turned around far enough to catch Zillah's eye. "If you knew that, why didn't you tell me?"

"It is forbidden to discuss such things with any male who has not yet been mated," he said stiffly, clearly quoting a rule. "That's why the Fathers never talk about it, except between themselves. The females don't want the childless males to find out that mating isn't really all that desirable. Since you now know, I am required to inform you that you are also bound by that rule, just as I am."

Daveeka thought about that, while Zillah finished soaping his back.

"Lie back in the water now, Dher Daveeka, so I can wash the front of your body."

"I can do that myself," Daveeka protested.

"Of course. But wouldn't you like to have me do it, considering what just happened?"

"Um … yes. It does feel wonderful when you touch me," he admitted. "I feel almost normal again."

Zillah's hands were gentle as he lightly soaped and rinsed the older rillenu's arms and chest, carefully keeping any water from running into his pouch. Then he worked his way up Daveeka's legs, massaging the muscles as he did so.

Daveeka lay still, feeling the tension draining from his body under Zillah's skilful ministrations. His touch alone was enough to relieve some of the sensual frustration that had been built up by the mating.

"Dher Daveeka, would you like me to do the rest, or let you do it?"

Daveeka had to think for a moment. Would he be comfortable with someone else's hands near his pouch? "You, please," he finally requested with a thin smile. "I have to get used to having my pouch touched by others, so I may as well start now."

"I've been trained very well. You can trust me not to harm your daughter."

Zillah covered the lip of the pouch with a small folded towel, then rapidly washed the entire area. His fingers skimmed carefully over the bulge of the infant, not pressing any harder than he had to. Daveeka drew in a sharp breath, but that was all. The young servant's washing of his penile sheath and between his legs was done in the same careful but matter-of-fact manner.

By the time Zillah was finished, Daveeka felt much better. "You're very good at this," he said dreamily.

"I'd better be, or I'd be in big trouble. Sometimes the females even allow me to caress them and give them pleasure. Of course, they never actually mate me."

"So they do like to be touched?"

"Oh, yes. But mostly only by other females." Zillah's ears perked up as he went on. "I may be pretty clumsy otherwise, but I'm one of the very few young servants who are summoned to their quarters every now and then."

"You mean they actually let you touch them?"

"Oh, yes. And usually more than just that, depending on which female requests my services." A subtle pride came into his voice as he continued, "I've even been used as a model when girls come of age and are taught how males are to be prepared and forced to release their fluid." He grimaced. "Sometimes that isn't much fun. However, since the girls have to get used to males as servants at an early age, I'm also learning to care for their infant daughters, since I have a very gentle touch and manner. They're afraid of the strange touch at first, but I know just how to pet them and hold them to make them happy."

Daveeka tried to decide if he was more surprised at hearing that or more envious of Zillah.

"I could tell you how to please the females, if you wish," the youngster offered. "Not like I do, of course, but things that are permitted in the mating room. There are ways you can move when they mount you that will please them. And they're usually flattered if you pretend to enjoy their touch on your sheath, even if you really don't. That sort of extra skill catches their attention, making it more likely you'll be summoned again."

Daveeka sat up abruptly. "I'd appreciate that, Zillah."

The youngster looked down at the soapy water, his hands now modestly clasped in his lap. "I've also been trained to please males, Dher Daveeka. It's part of my duty as your attendant."

Daveeka considered that. Eight nanths was a long time, and Zillah was certainly attractive and likeable. And yet …

"I appreciate the offer, but there's someone waiting for me."

Zillah nodded. "I understand. But I'll be here, if you change your mind."

"You can teach me that stuff about the females, though," Daveeka said grimly. "That might come in handy."

When Mistress Havall summoned him to the mating room several nights later, he knew what would happen, so he was able to gain some distance from what was being done to him. Even though he was afraid to try anything yet, he kept Zillah's suggestions in mind, making note of exactly when and how he might be able to implement them in future matings.

After a few more bouts in the mating rooms, Daveeka decided that he was, indeed, beginning to get used to it. It helped that he now expected nothing more than a disagreeable experience, followed by a bout of sensory frustration. He still hadn't gotten up the courage to try anything, but each time he promised himself that he would do it soon.

Meanwhile, his interest shifted to his studies.

He read children's scrolls from the library, then moved on to more adult things. In addition to attending the Temple ceremonies, he spent long periods of time walking the roof gardens or strolling around the permitted corridors, often near a group of females and always listening with his acute ears. Since males could hear better than females due to their larger ears, it didn't appear patently obvious that he was eavesdropping. He had to make an effort not to swivel his ears too much in their direction though, or he might have been noticed. Female ears were far smaller and less maneuverable. Although they could quite adequately use their delicate ears as an expression of emotions, the females couldn't use them to pick up sound to the extent that the males could.

Sometimes he sat unobtrusively in the rear of the Hall of Judgement, watching Marlieth and her Council of senior Mothers hand down decisions on problems and disputes brought before them by the thirteen male Families under Thennevar's jurisdiction. The Honored Fathers and ordinary Fathers of the individual Families handled most routine matters, with only the really important decisions being referred to the females.

But Daveeka's favorite remained the Temple ceremony. The regular nightly ritual was the only time he heard singing in the Thennevar Palace. Until the music had disappeared from his life, he hadn't realized just how much he would miss it.

Although most of the chants were relatively sedate, some seemed to cry out for a dance step to accompany them. And females never danced. Oh, they swayed a little from side to side while they prayed perhaps, but their feet remained stolidly in one place.

Later, in his room, Daveeka would hum what he could recall of the melodies, closing his eyes and pretending he had a dancing rug beneath his feet. He had insisted on wearing his Kiari shoes even in the female Palace, even though most people wore only light slippers, since all the floors were carpeted. He had to keep his feet soft and sensitive, if he hoped to continue dancing.

Each night he danced by himself, since it was the only way he could practice. He came up with the idea of drawing imaginary dancing-rugs on the carpet moss of the common room with chalk powder.

Although his daughter was still so small that her insignificant weight didn't hamper his movement in the slightest, he thought about the time to come when she would be older. Maybe, if he faithfully practiced his dancing, some traces of memory might be established in her mind. Perhaps when she was a child she might recall a bit of melody or a feel of movement.

Stopping abruptly in the middle of a turn, Daveeka smiled. *Yes. Let her remember me like that. It's the only memory I can give her. She'll never see me, since they'll take her before her eyes open.*

His own eyes closed, he whirled around again, happily immersed in thoughts of his child. And danced right into an obstruction that shouldn't be there.

Stumbling, Daveeka opened his eyes. Zillah had come into the room without being noticed.

"Sorry," the boy mumbled. "I should have asked permission to enter first." He looked up at Daveeka. "You're summoned to see the Mothers."

Panic stabbed through Daveeka's heart. "What's wrong?"

"Nothing. It's time for Annilee to examine her daughter, that's all. I thought you knew. She'll do that regularly from now on."

Daveeka winced at the thought of having someone's hand in his pouch. He hadn't been aware that was part of carrying a daughter. His hands closed protectively over the slight bulge of his belly.

Seeing the dismayed angle of the older rillenu's ears, Zillah added quickly, "Don't worry, you'll get used to it. It won't be done very often until your daughter's a couple more nanths older. Gets the baby accustomed to feeling her Mother's touch, so she won't be as likely to go into shock later."

Daveeka just stood there.

"Come on. I'll show you where you go. You don't have to be afraid."

Hesitantly, Zillah put an arm around Daveeka's waist and led him out into the hall.

"I'm not afraid," Daveeka protested.

Zillah just nodded.

But when he entered the examining room alone, Daveeka was afraid. There were seven females in the room, which included most of the senior Mothers in Family Thennevar, plus a few Mistresses. He could recognize most of them by now.

Annilee gestured impatiently for him to lie down on the couch, so he hurried over. Mistress Chezoar offered him a sip of jareesh, but he just shook his head and pushed it away. He preferred to know what was going on.

When Marlieth pulled his short tunic up to his chest and began instructing Annilee on how to open his pouch to examine the infant, he found that he could follow the overall gist of the conversation, even though it was in rapid femalespeech. Good. Concentrating on that might keep his mind off what they were actually doing.

Sitting on the couch with her back half-turned to his face, Annilee reached carefully into his pouch with one hand. It hurt as her fingers stretched him open, but he lay quietly despite the unconscious fears stirred to the surface of his mind. He told himself that he'd learn to get used to it. They wouldn't do anything to harm him or the infant.

He had to believe that, or he wouldn't be able to endure having Annilee's fingers so close to his vulnerable daughter. It would be horribly simple to pluck the tiny scrap of life away from him, despite the swollen end of his teat that filled the infant's throat and held it firmly anchored. Flesh rips, if subjected to sufficient force. It wouldn't take much to …

No. Daveeka pushed that thought away, clinging to the idea that Annilee desired the survival of this infant as much as he himself did. If nothing else, it would make possible her rise in status from Mistress, the term for any daughterless female, to Mother. And put her in line to inherit her own Mother's power and position some day.

Besides, hadn't he just heard Marlieth specifically instruct Annilee not to touch the infant this time, since it was still so small and fragile? All she was to do was check to see if the infant had begun excreting the hard fecal pellets that would have to be removed from his pouch by hand. The baby's urine would be reabsorbed by the pouch membranes, requiring only an occasional cleaning later on, as the baby became larger. Mistress Annilee was only practicing now, getting him accustomed to having her hand in his pouch so it wouldn't bother him in succeeding nanths, when she'd do it more often.

He tried not to let his eyes wander down to her hands. Instead, he concentrated on watching the soft red light glisten off the string of large transparent crystal beads each female wore on a golden chain hanging straight down from a clasp on her collar.

Each set of beads was made up of a different series of Shapes. Zillah had explained that each Shape had a particular meaning, ranging from the very simple to the very complex, depending on the configuration of the crystal. Although anyone could go to Elenath at any time in order to obtain a Shape, it wasn't all that easy to do, plus one might not get the Shape one hoped for. Once obtained, the wearer had to live up to whatever principle the Shape embodied. And that could be very easy or exceedingly difficult, depending on what that principle was. The crystal at the end of the chain was the newest one, and carried the most obligation.

The stone sculptures he had noticed in the Temple were representations of some of the more complex Shapes, placed there for the purpose of meditation on each particular concept.

Against the intricate patterns of the Mothers' embroidered robes, the beads sparkled and glittered. Yes, they were truly fitting decorations for females, their crystalline hardness forming a lovely contrast to the fine fabrics and long, dark fur. It would be an exquisite contrast to explore with his fingers, but he dared not touch a female uninvited. That was a good way for a male to lose his hand, if not his life.

"You see, Annilee? He has learned to behave very well, just as I said he would."

Suddenly, Daveeka realized his mind had translated Mother Marlieth's words without any hesitation at all.

"But why did I have to be the one to Invite him?" Annilee complained, her fingers still gently stroking the inner wall of his pouch. "Someone else could have done it."

"No one else was pregnant just then, daughter. And he was becoming an embarrassment to Family Marloosh."

"Fahlin should have been able to deal with him."

Marlieth gave a contemptuous snort at mention of the Honored Father. "Perhaps if you would think, instead of allowing the jareesh to think for you, you would see the logic of what was done."

"We'd have been better off if we'd simply disposed of the entire Kiari cult, the same way we disposed of Myerta."

Marlieth gestured impatiently at Annilee, silencing her. "Executing Myerta in public like that was a mistake. It solved nothing and only drew more attention to his teachings. Besides, the Kiari serve our purposes well, daughter. Never forget that. The cult diverts the energy of the worst of the potential troublemakers away from any effective action against the Fathers. And since it's generally the most devout believers who dance on the rugs, the high losses incurred conveniently eliminate the undesirables before they can do anything worse."

Daveeka fought to conceal his shock at hearing their callous view of the Kiari.

"Oh, I know all that," Annilee replied. "But the most this piece of childless trash should have Received was a son. Now, a stupid rug-dancer carries my firstborn daughter."

"You were the one who insisted the infant be helped into his pouch, Annilee," Mistress Chezoar pointed out gently. "It could have been left to die."

Annilee's ears slanted back as she glared at the older female. The bottom Shape on Chezoar's string was the square- bottomed, elongated pyramid that Zillah had said signified Truth in All Circumstances. She was obligated to speak the truth as she saw it.

"What, and lose my chance to become a Mother?" Annilee replied to Chezoar with a disdainful snort. "Do you think I want to remain a Mistress until I'm as old as you are?"

"No matter," Marlieth interjected. "Should this male become an Honored Father, he'll do our bidding without any trouble." She extended an elegant hand and lightly scratched the base of one of Daveeka's ears. "See how obedient he has become? No more foolish talk of getting Invitations for childless males, or anything like that. No, he seeks to please us now, even coming to our ceremonies to petition Elenath for the welfare of his infant. Most dhamereth wouldn't bother to do that. I think it's rather cute." She favored Daveeka with an approving look that had no connection whatsoever to the scornful words which followed. "Thus, my foolish daughter, it is possible to turn an enemy into a pawn."

The females had bought him off by giving him an Invitation, just as Fahlin had tried to buy him off with his offer of a better job. Could it be possible?

But females were the epitome of wisdom and virtue, made in the image of Elenath. Surely, they wouldn't resort to such underhanded tactics. Males might do such things, but not females, not Mothers.

Daveeka closed his eyes, feeling an almost physical dizziness as the pillars underlying his perception of the world trembled and threatened to collapse. No, it simply couldn't be true. He must have misunderstood.

"Gently, Annilee, gently. You're hurting him," Chezoar cautioned, noticing the angle of Daveeka's ears.

"So what? He's only a male."

Marlieth dismissed their interchange with a contemptuous gesture. "When Fahlin brings up his proposal in Conclave this winter, this one will gladly offer his support. Just think what that will do to the few other Fathers who would have dared oppose the proposal. Why, it will pass easily, without this former Kiari rug-dancer around stirring up trouble."

Did she truly believe he'd betray his friends like that? Fahlin wanted the male Families to adopt an official policy that would place further restrictions on the childless males' already slim chances at Receiving babies by cutting down the number of Positions they were permitted to accept. Once such a proposal had been ratified by the Conclave of the thirteen Families, it could be presented to Thennevar as the expressed desire of the male Families and could then be adopted as law by the females, if so desired.

Daveeka failed to stifle a gasp of dismay.

A dozen pairs of sharp bright eyes turned to him and he realized he'd just given away his understanding of femalespeech.

Marlieth's gaze raked slowly over Daveeka's body, making him feel exposed and naked as he never had before. He wanted to pull his robe down to cover his pouch and his genitals, but he didn't dare. "Hearing uss ve you?" she asked softly.

Terrified, Daveeka hardly knew how to respond. Would they think he had been deliberately eavesdropping on them if he admitted how much he knew? And yet, his very fear must have given him away already, his flattened ears revealing his understanding.

"Answwer," Marlieth demanded slowly and distinctly, "if you can."

"Ssmall understanding," he said, with much hesitation, while conspicuously botching the words and missing some of the sibilants in the hope of showing only a limited knowledge of femalespeech. "Study for ve learn."

"Goodh male," Marlieth said, tracing a pattern of encouragement in the fur of his thigh. "Ssstudy much. Learn much. Usseful ve."

Daveeka perked up his ears, but he was sorely puzzled at her attitude. He had expected anger.

The Exalted Mother turned her attention to the others, speaking rapidly in femalespeech and obviously not expecting him to follow her meaning. "Thisss one ve sssmart, for worthlesss male. Ve as Ish said. At Conclave ussseful ve."

Although he couldn't dare say it aloud, Daveeka had no intention of doing as Marlieth expected. He would certainly oppose Fahlin's proposal, once he became an Honored Father.

A twinge of guilt stirred his heart. What Marlieth had said before was true, to an extent. He had indeed done nothing since he'd come to the Thennevar Palace, except study and enjoy his unaccustomed leisure. He'd have to change that.

Annilee finished her examination of her daughter and rose from the couch. Her hand flicked Daveeka a negligent gesture of dismissal. As he pulled down his tunic and got to his feet, he recalled that Mother Magdael had had her pregnancy confirmed just four nights ago at the full moon ceremony. She would be sending out her Invitations soon, if she hadn't done so already. That gave him an idea.

So the Exalted Mother thought he had given up all his concern for childless males, did she? Well, he was going to show her that wasn't true.

"Zillah, is there any rule that would forbid me from approaching a pregnant female and asking her to consider certain males for her Invitations?" Daveeka asked casually as they completed their lesson in femalespeech later that night.

"Not that I know of. But it wouldn't do you any good. Why should they listen to you?"

"Why should they take the advice of the Fathers and choose names from their recommended lists? Yet they do."

"That's different. They've always done that. After all, how could the females possibly know enough about males to know which ones deserve to be Invited?"

"Well, I'd only be doing the same thing, providing them with information."

"Dher Daveeka, you're not even a Father yet. I don't think they'd take too kindly to your advice, at this point." His eyes flickered down to Daveeka's Kiari shoes. "You intend to ask them to Invite childless males, don't you?"

Daveeka nodded.

Two nights later, he stood at the entrance to the Temple, watching for Mistress Havall to leave after the evening ceremony. Last night, Mother Magdael had refused to listen to his request, curtly informing him she would choose males from the official lists submitted by the Fathers, as usual. But Mistress Havall was a youngster, pregnant for the first time. It was possible that she would be more sympathetic.

She walked regally across the Temple floor, in the company of two other young Mistresses. As she reached the archway, Daveeka moved into her path and genuflected, bowing his head and extending both hands towards her, palms upward. It was the formal gesture for a male begging the attention of a female.

"With Ish wissh you to sspeak?" Havall asked uncertainly, as one of her companions giggled.

Thus addressed, Daveeka was allowed to drop his hands to his sides and look up. Taking a small scroll from his pocket, he held it out towards her. "Mistress, here ve namess of five maless. That hyou look upon them with favor, I humbly beg."

The young female opened the parchment and scanned what he had written. Daveeka held his breath. It was unlikely that she would deign to tell him anything, but if she accepted his list it would indicate she would at least consider it.

Her delicate ears twitched slightly in puzzlement. "Thesse na Fatherss ve."

"Mistress, for lowesst three Possitionss permissible ve to Invite childless maless. Thesse maless—"

She cut him off with a wave of one hand. Her eyes narrowed as she studied him suspiciously. Daveeka thought she was about to toss away his list of names, but instead she tucked it into a pocket, then turned and hastened away down the corridor with her friends at her heels, leaving Daveeka still down on one knee, hope flaring in his heart.

But when Havall's Invitations went out, none of them went to childless males.

"Well, perhaps it's too much to expect success on the first try," he told Zillah several nights later as he sat eating the midnight meal. "I'll just wait and see which females confirm new pregnancies at the beginning of Eleventh Nanth and try my luck with them. There will be plenty of chances. After all, I'll be here for six more nanths. I've got lots of time left."

They were interrupted by the arrival of a servant at the doorway. He handed Daveeka a folded piece of parchment and then rapidly scurried away.

Daveeka gave Zillah a puzzled glance, then unfolded the message. Torn scraps of parchment fluttered to the table, some of them landing on the floor and others in his lap. Daveeka gathered them anxiously together—and recognized with a shock that they were bits and pieces of the list of names that he had presented to Mistress Havall.

Fearful of what this might mean, he continued to unfold the paper and read what was printed on it. All it said was, "You will stop this, now."

Wordlessly, Daveeka showed the message to Zillah. The boy sucked in a surprised breath.

"That's Mother Marlieth's handwriting," he whispered. Then he looked fearfully at the older male. "Guess you won't be writing any more petitions, huh?"

Daveeka crushed the paper in his hand. "I'll try again next nanth."

Zillah shook his head, but said nothing.

CHAPTER 4

During the rest of Tenth Nanth, Daveeka devoted himself to his studies, being careful to avoid Marlieth's attention. When three females were declared pregnant at the full moon ceremonies, he once again drew up lists of names of childless males. He had made so much progress in learning femalespeech that he was able to write the lists entirely in that alphabet, adding flowery phrases of petition and praise in the hopes of further impressing the pregnant females.

He had a chance to deliver only one of his carefully prepared missives before he was summoned into the presence of the Exalted Mother.

Annilee sat next to Marlicth on a heap of cushions. She held Daveeka's petition in one hand, waving it at him as he entered the room.

"Warned were you to sstop, yet thiss you gave to Misstress Ssarreth. Why ve you disobedient?" Annilee's voice was silky-soft, like her fur. Daveeka found it hard to resist. All his instincts made him want to obey the Mother of his daughter.

"Pleasse, Misstress. Only have I mosst resspectfully requessted that ..."

Annilee fixed him with a cold stare. "Hoped it wass that you would forget thiss foolisshness. Ssuch nonssensse na fitting for dhamereth ve."

"Revered Misstress, only I sseek—"

Marlieth cut him off with an impatient gesture. "Trouble you make, danser. Dissatisfaction you causse. Thiss na permitted ve."

Annilee tried again, her voice a warm purr. "Your cooperation we want, Daveecha. Much honor ve yourss, if with Fahlin you sstand at Conclave and hiss propossal ssupport. Many Invitationss you earn, for sself and friendss."

"If," Marlieth put in, "wisse you ve, and find friendss among Fatherss, na childless trassh."

Daveeka squirmed. "Fahlin'ss propossal ve wrong, Exalted Mother. Would prohibit childless maless from all Possitionss but Ninth. Now, only ve they permitted up to Sseventh. Further resstrictionss na needed."

"While childless oness perssist in refussing acceptance of their fate, insstead of having faith in femaless to choosse thosse who desserving ve, resstrictionss necessary!"

Daveeka said nothing.

"A partner ve yourss, na?" Marlieth glanced down at a paper on the table before her. "Teo?" When he nodded, she went on, "Perhapss that male ssoon found worthy of Invitation ve. You then pleassed?"

"Yesh, Exalted Mother. But ..."

"But?"

"Na will I ssupport Fahlin'ss propossal. Ve wrong."

"Hear: Ish sspeak the Will of Elenath. You will dho as ssay Ish."

Daveeka swallowed nervously. Could he possibly refuse to follow the orders of an Exalted Mother when she was speaking for the Deity Herself? Maybe he could explain, make them understand.

"Only wissh I to do right," he replied, voice barely above a whisper. "Childless maless desserve chance—"

Marlieth's ears flattened against her head as she rose to her feet, dark eyes flashing. She grabbed the collarless neck of Daveeka's robe with both hands, pulling him forward onto his toes. "You ssay me na, you ssssuffer," she hissed. "For thiss, punisshed ve, dansser."

Daveeka quailed before her fury, but he refused to give in so easily. "Ssuch propossal musst I opposse," he stated, surprising even himself. "Ability to causse pain na ssame as to ve right. Truth ve truth. Na changed by ssuffering."

A cruel smile spread across Marlieth's face. "Na? Perhapss remainss truth, but ssurely changed can ve itss perception."

Before Daveeka had a chance to realize what was happening, the Exalted Mother had summoned four guards into the room. She gestured curtly to a bench against the far wall.

Four pairs of hands seized Daveeka and pinned him down on the bench. Four pairs of eyes stared stalwartly at the walls, fearful of meeting the gaze of either of the females.

"Hiss disgusting sshoess remove," Marlieth ordered her daughter. Annilee unlaced them and slid them off, dropping them to the floor as if the beaded and bloodstained shoes had soiled her hands.

Marlieth went to a cabinet in a corner of the room and returned carrying a short stick.

Although he'd never seen one before, Daveeka knew immediately what it was. The hurat tree grew in the deep forests. Its bark was covered with short, needle-sharp thorns. While they weren't barbed or as long as barbarythorns, the body of each thorn widened quickly and could inflict a nasty puncture wound.

Daveeka stared at the hurat stick. Marlieth held it by a polished wooden handle, tapping it lightly against the side of the couch. A tremor ran through one of the guards. Daveeka could feel it where the male's hand gripped his leg.

Marlieth held out the stick to Annilee, her eyes never moving from Daveeka's face. "Hyou dho."

Annilee accepted the hurat wand, but her ears slanted backwards and her hand seemed none too steady. "My dhaughter—" she began.

"Will na damage dhaughter to punissh male who carriess."

"Daveecha na Father ve,"Annilee persisted. "Understandss doess he na—"

Marlieth dismissed her objection with an impatient gesture. "Undersstandss too well. Now will undersstand more." She nodded to Annilee.

Daveeka found his voice as the young female drew back the hurat wand, obviously aiming for the unprotected soles of his feet. He tried to pull away, but the guards held him fast. "No! Please !"

His words turned into a choked scream as the thorns tore into his flesh. Pain ran up his legs from his pierced feet, sensitive nerves shrieking protest.

When he opened his eyes, the hurat wand was directly in front of his face, thorns darkened with his blood. Annilee still held it in her hand, but Marlieth's fingers were clamped around her wrist, forcing her to hold the stick before him.

"Ssay me sstill na, dansser?" Marlieth asked, her voice like the rustle of silk along a knife blade. She let go of her daughter's hand.

Tears of agony ran from Daveeka's eyes. The room smeared and ran as he blinked. He had only been hit once, but the mere thought of a repetition of that blow was enough to make him tremble. Any rillenu's feet were sensitive, but as a dancer, his were even more so than average.

"Ansswer," she hissed.

He wasn't fast enough. At a gesture from Marlieth, Annilee hit him again.

"Sspeak, dansser," she demanded. "Or dansse again will you na."

He tried to force a humble retraction to his lips, knowing he could not win this game. But he couldn't betray his beliefs. It just wouldn't be right.

Annilee hit him twice, in rapid succession. Suddenly, the truth seemed much less convincing. All he really knew was the agony in his lacerated feet.

When his scream had died into silence, Daveeka whispered brokenly, "As you ssay, Exalted Mother. The Will of Elenath will I dho in the matter of the Honored Father'ss propossal."

Would Marlieth accept that, not noticing he hadn't exactly promised to obey her but only to obey Elenath? Granted, it was a fine point, since the Will of Elenath was normally made manifest through the Exalted Mother and the females. He lay there trembling, expecting to feel the hurat thorns slash into him once more.

But Marlieth was apparently satisfied. She caressed his thigh. "Goodh. Very goodh," she said softly. Then her hand clamped around his leg just above the knee, fingers digging into nerves. Compared to the searing pain in his feet, it was nothing, but she had made her point. "Na you forget, dansser. Na you forget."

The Exalted Mother turned away from him and strode from the room, gesturing for Annilee to follow her. The guards carried him to his quarters without a word.

Daveeka awoke from a drugged sleep to burning agony. He whimpered and tried to draw his knees up to his chest.

"No, Dher Daveeka. Lie still." Zillah's voice, his hand stroking the base of Daveeka's right ear in a deft imitation of a female's reassuring caress. "I heard about what happened." Zillah shook his head. "That was a dumb thing to do." But his voice held admiration, not scorn. "Whatever possessed you to defy the Exalted Mother?"

Obviously not expecting an answer, Zillah picked up a bowl of jareesh and held it to the other rillenu's lips. Daveeka pushed it away. The boy might think he had been quite brave to defy Marlieth, but Daveeka himself knew how easily he had been forced to back down. He wasn't exactly proud of it.

"You'd better have some," Zillah persisted. "You've been unconscious for quite a while. It's about time for me to change your bandages."

Judging by the amount of sand in the yellow timeglass that was currently running, it was the middle of the day.

"I've been out long enough already," Daveeka replied. He tried to collect his thoughts and push aside the grogginess he felt. The jareesh he'd been given earlier hadn't entirely worn off yet. His feet would hurt a lot more if it had.

Zillah shrugged and set the cup aside. He began unwrapping the cloth strips from one foot, removing the dressing as gently as he could.

Daveeka did his best not to pull away, but he couldn't help wincing as Zillah wiped the oozing punctures and then smeared them with a stinging ointment.

"Wounds made by hurat thorns can get infected easily," Zillah said, as he crushed several dark green jaram leaves between his fingers and pressed them against the wounds.

The pain subsided a bit as the juice soaked into Daveeka's flesh, deadening sensation.

"This foot already doesn't look so good," Zillah continued, as he applied a fresh dressing, binding it with a length of bandage. His fingers were skillful and gentle, but it still hurt. The young servant went to work on his other foot.

"Feel like eating something now?" Zillah inquired, as he cleared away the discarded bandages. When Daveeka nodded, he propped him up on a couple of pillows and brought over a bowl of steaming meat broth.

Daveeka swallowed several spoonfuls in silence, contemplating his throbbing feet. When those wounds healed, they would form nasty scars. He'd never be able to dance in the Kiari rituals again, since he wouldn't be able to feel the guide patterns in his rug. His eartips drooped despondently.

Zillah tried to distract him. "Mistress Chezoar says Mistress Annilee told her you acted just as stubborn as a female constrained by her Shape," he chattered.

The boy's words pulled a memory to the forefront of Daveeka's mind: Mistress Chezoar, at the first examination of his daughter, daring to speak up because her Shape of Truth in All Circumstances obligated her to do so.

"Zillah, if a female wears a Shape, can she be punished for living by its meaning?"

"No. If Elenath grants you a particular Shape, She approves your pursuit of what it signifies."

"Well, how about a male? Would the same thing apply to me?"

"I don't know. Very few males wear Shapes. Only a couple of Fathers. Why?"

"Oh, just thinking. Maybe I could go to Elenath for a Shape?"

Zillah's ears angled backward in discomfort. "From what I've heard, a Shape isn't an easy thing to get. Nor is it always an easy thing to wear. You're better off just doing as the Mothers tell you."

"Zillah, how do I get one?"

"I don't know. It's a very rare thing, even for females."

"You could find out."

The boy hesitated. "There may be a scroll explaining it in the library. We'll look for it when your feet have healed. Okay?"

"Now."

Zillah sighed. "No, not yet." He waved away Daveeka's protest. "What's your hurry? You can't even walk to the library just now." He aimed another spoonful of broth at Daveeka's mouth. "Have some more soup."

"Get me the scroll."

The boy squirmed uncomfortably, spilling some of the broth on the floor. He bent to mop it up. "You've got something in mind. I can tell."

Daveeka propped himself up on his elbows, wincing as the change in position pulled at the bandages on his feet. He took hold of the youngster's arm, forcing him to meet his eyes. "Get me the scroll, Zillah. That's an order."

"Okay, Dher Daveeka. But don't say I didn't warn you."

Before the night was over, the youngster reluctantly brought him a scroll describing the ceremony for obtaining a Shape, along with the Scroll of Meanings, which defined all 51 Shapes.

For all four quarns of that nanth, Daveeka was bedridden with a stubborn infection in his left foot. One of the deeper punctures under the arch refused to heal properly, forming a painful abscess that eventually had to be lanced.

Once each quarn he was carried by servants to his pouch examinations and cleanings by the Mothers. Next nanth, it would be twice a quarn, every three nights. He wasn't looking forward to that.

During these sessions, Daveeka prudently kept his mouth shut while Annilee examined the infant and cleaned his pouch. Several times, she even stroked his neck and the base of his ears, complimenting him on how well he was behaving. He thought he caught a hint of something that sounded like affection in the young Mistress' voice.

Meanwhile, he could do little but lie on his mattress, eat, read, talk to Zillah, and try to ignore the pain as much as possible. Mercifully, no female requested his appearance in the mating rooms during that time.

When the full moon of Twelfth Nanth rose, Daveeka was able to walk a bit. His feet were still wrapped in thick protective padding, but the punctures had mostly healed, replaced by tender scar tissue. He couldn't go as far as the Temple yet, but since he dared present no further petitions to pregnant females, it was of little consequence that he didn't learn immediately if anyone had been declared pregnant that nanth.

His daughter made a satisfying bulge in his pouch now, not heavy enough to inconvenience him, but enough to make him very aware of her presence. It was nice to feel her small body securely snuggled in the bottom of his pouch. His fingers ached to caress her, but that was forbidden. She'd stand a better chance at survival if she were accustomed to Annilee's touch, not his.

By halfway through the nanth, Daveeka could get around better. He gathered his courage and told Zillah he would go before Elenath for a Shape that very night.

Zillah glanced uneasily over his shoulder at the entrance to the common room. "I wish you'd reconsider, Dher Daveeka. If anything goes wrong …"

"Nothing will go wrong."

"You can barely walk."

"I'll manage. You told me that the dark of the moon was a good time to go to Elenath, didn't you?"

"That's what the females say."

"Well, then, don't worry. Want to come and watch?"

Zillah's eyes grew wide and his ears flattened. But he nodded his head.

It was almost morning. The Temple appeared deserted. Leaning heavily on Zillah's shoulder, Daveeka was able to keep some of the weight off his left foot as he limped across the cavernous chamber. The boy was right; he really shouldn't be walking this far just yet. His foot ached badly, despite the fresh jaram leaves that had been bandaged against it.

As they had discussed before starting out, they stopped before one of the stone sculptures set in a far corner of the Temple, a many-faceted Shape vaguely resembling a teardrop. Daveeka studied it closely, memorizing the angles and planes. This was clearer than the diagram in the Scroll of Meanings. As they walked around it, he checked its appearance from all sides. Then they continued on.

Mother of All, grant me the courage to go through with this! he prayed fervently, as they stopped at the steps before Elenath's statue. What if he were transgressing? What if She Who Rules did not smile on him today? Her Law was for females to have dominion over males. Would She reject his quest, and confirm Marlieth's judgement that he was in the wrong?

Daveeka gave Zillah a brief squeeze with the arm that was around the boy's shoulder, then released him. "Pray for my success," he whispered. Zillah bit his lip, but nodded.

From here on, Daveeka was on his own.

He went to the far side of the steps, where a number of crystal slivers hung suspended at varying heights on slender gold chains. He had often noticed the chimes during the rituals, when an acolyte's hand would set them tinkling.

Taking the bottom-most sliver carefully between two fingers, he drew a deep breath. Almost, he feared being destroyed by the Deity's wrath.

Nothing happened.

He studied the hanging crystals. Using the piece he held in his hand, Daveeka struck each in turn in a complicated pattern.

He sank to his knees, covering his face with his hands.

Shortly there came the gentle rustle of a robe, then the hiss of a breath, indrawn with surprise or anger. He dared not peek between his fingers at the acolyte who answered his summons. He simply knelt and waited for her challenge, all his mind on being ready to understand and respond.

"Before Elenath wisssh you to go?" She sang the ritual question in a complex chant. Daveeka would have to sing his answers using the proper melodies, or she could forbid him access.

He hesitated a moment, hoping his voice wouldn't break at the wrong time. The tune was better adapted to a female's voice range. "I wisssh ssso to dho."

"What sssseek you?" she sang.

There were several ritual answers to choose from. Some of them applied only to a Challenge, when a female demanded an answer from the Deity and took whatever Shape she was given as that answer. Daveeka intended no such daring. He sought a specific Shape, so he settled on one of the simpler responses.

"Whether Elenath upon me sssmiless, and my sssseeking approvesss."

The acolyte touched him lightly on the top of his head, the signal that he might uncover his eyes. "Go you," she sang in the final tune, gesturing toward the statue that towered over them both. "To your sssseeking, ve Ish witnesss."

Daveeka rose painfully to his feet and mounted the few wide steps leading to the platform suspended between Elenath's Hands. He held his breath as he climbed the stairs, very conscious of the nearness of the huge statue. He dared not raise his eyes to glance at it.

He stopped before the veil that hung down to almost waist height across the entire back of the platform. A shallow ceramic dish sat on a stand at one side of the curtain, its dark surface reflecting the flicker of the flames. Taking a deep breath, he reviewed what he had read.

Behind the curtain would be a large pot, filled almost to the brim with crystal Shapes. If he could reach in, locate the proper one, bring it out, and place it in the cooling dish, the Shape would then be his.

That had sounded almost too easy. The catch was that the pot was deep enough to plunge a hand in almost as far as the elbow, but it was kept heated by the firepot behind the grillwork. The deeper you reached, the hotter the crystals would be. Simple Shapes would be near the top. The complex designs were more deeply buried and harder to get at, complexity increasing with depth.

Daveeka swallowed the lump of nervousness in his throat and stepped up to the curtain. He thrust his shaking hand through the heavy veil. The calluses on his hands had begun to fade during the last several nanths of leisure, leaving them far more sensitive than ever before in his life. That wouldn't make things any easier. But a female's hand was soft and tender also, and that didn't stop them from getting Shapes.

Heat wrapped itself around his fingers, rising from the pot he knew must lie just beneath his outstretched hand. He reached down gingerly.

Even at the very top, those crystals weren't merely warm; they were hot. Hot enough to hurt if he kept his hand against them for long.

He closed his eyes and licked dry lips. Forcing his hand down again, Daveeka ran his fingertips rapidly over the exposed Shapes on the top. If he ignored the heat, he could feel the angles, identify particular Shapes by touch. Here was a pyramid with three faces, signifying Proper and Respectful Stability. Here, the flat rectangle of Unselfish Devotion. There, the cube of Beginner on the Path to Knowledge. The pointy crescent Shapes of Obedience to the Will of Elenath were particularly numerous. Any of those on the top would be easy to take.

He lifted his hand briefly, letting the burning in his fingertips subside. Unless he pulled his hand back outside the veil, he had all the time he wanted to consider what he was going to do. Squeezing his eyes more tightly closed and clenching his teeth, Daveeka plunged his hand boldly beneath the surface of the hot crystals. With his full concentration focussed on the angles and planes, he tried to ignore the scorching pain. His fingers sifted frantically through the beads, searching. Even the skin on the back of his hand began to hurt, as the heat soaked through his short fur. He couldn't make out the shapes, couldn't keep his mind off the searing pain in his fingers.

This was a ritual of the females. How dare he, a mere male, attempt such a thing? He couldn't do it. He hadn't the courage.

His breath came in rasping sobs as he pulled his hand once more free of the pot. Through slitted eyes, he stole a glance at the acolyte standing by the side of the veil. The expression on her face was bland and unreadable.

Maybe he should just grab something near the surface and be done with it? Simply getting a Shape was a great accomplishment, for a male. No one need know he hadn't gotten the one he had sought after.

His gaze traveled upward, to the statue brooding in the semi-darkness above him.

No one? What was he here for, except to determine if Elenath frowned or smiled upon his ideas? It needed his courage to persevere, but it would be by the Will of Elenath that the proper crystal would find its way into his fingers. That was what the females believed. No complex Shape was freely given by the Deity: it must be wrested from Her Hands, if it were to be received at all.

He gritted his teeth, closed his eyes, and reached once again down into the heat, forcing his hand quickly in past his wrist and almost to his elbow.

Sharp angles, flat surfaces, complicated Shapes he could not even visualize, much less name.

It had to be here. All 51 Shapes were in the pot at all times, although there might be only one of some of them and many of others. All you had to do was find the one you wanted. If Elenath did not approve your quest, it would not appear before your courage ran out.

Daveeka refused to consider that possibility. Keeping the desired image firmly in his mind, he continued sorting through the hot crystals. His hand throbbed in agony, making it harder to feel the Shapes now.

"Give up, danssser. Thisss na ve for malesss."

The grating whisper might have been in his own mind, but was not. He opened his eyes to see Marlieth standing next to him, her ears flattened back. She must have been summoned to the Temple.

Sudden anger flared through his mind at Marlieth's attempt at interference. He pushed his hand deeper. The pain in his fingers spun brighter and he bit his lip between his teeth, tasting blood.

A finely-cut crystal rested between thumb and first finger. Facets formed the proper angles, tapered to a sharp end. That was it. It had to be. And if not, he had at least not grabbed a simple Shape from the top.

Daveeka clutched the crystal tightly, fingers barely responding to his will. Elenath had put it into his hand. He mustn't lose it now!

With a strangled whimper, he pulled his clenched fist out of the pot and out from behind the curtain, dropping his chosen Shape carefully into the cooling dish. It clinked against the shining gloss of the ceramic bowl. He hardly dared look to find out if he had gotten the Shape he'd intended.

Marlieth's breath hissed through her teeth as she prodded the hot crystal with an elegant finger. Her head swiveled to regard Daveeka.

"Presssumptuousss male! The meaning of thisss Ssshape know you?"

"Yesh, Exalted Mother," he whispered, cradling his throbbing hand to his breast.

Against the dark finish of the cooling dish, the teardrop Shape signifying Respectful Disagreement with Established Authority winked and glittered in the flickering light of the firepot.

CHAPTER 5

Daveeka looked down yet again at his Shape, now hanging at the end of a short chain attached to his collar by the ornate clasp with its a design of a deep purple chonendron blossom, a lovely, tempting, and devastatingly poisonous flower. Somehow, it now seemed a very fitting symbol for Thennevar.

Even now, three nights later, he could hardly believe it was real. Elenath had shown Her approval of what he sought to accomplish. Well, at least She approved of his disagreement with those in authority. Was that the same thing? He couldn't be entirely sure, but it could be.

His hand was still somewhat swollen and tender from the burn he'd gotten, but it didn't hurt as badly as it had before. Of course, a generous dose of jareesh had helped a lot during that first night, but he had been able to decrease it after that. Tonight the pain was almost gone. It had been well worth it. Even the females showed him some respect when they saw the crystal at his breast. Against the black of the short robe he wore, it sparkled and glittered in the light of the glowweeds. Already he had acquired the habit of putting his hand around it and running his fingertips over his Shape, especially when he was thinking about something.

Now that everyone could see that he had found favor in Elenath's eyes, perhaps one of the pregnant females might actually pay some attention to his petitions on behalf of childless males. He began the laborious process of composing and lettering new scrolls to be used for that purpose.

Ironically enough, only one female was announced to be pregnant at the ceremony beginning Thirteenth Nanth, and that one was the Exalted Mother Marlieth.

From his place behind the gathered females in the Temple, Daveeka breathed a sigh of relief. It was useless to petition Marlieth to give Invitations to childless males, so he wouldn't have to test whether or not his Shape would protect him from punishment just yet.

Again, he reached to caress the crystal Shape. As the surfaces slid against his sensitive fingertips, he realized he was being a coward. Instead of avoiding it, he should petition Marlieth this nanth. In fact, he was obligated to do so, like it or not. If he didn't, he disgraced the Shape he wore. No female would take him seriously if he refused to live up to the destiny Elenath had bestowed upon him.

All right, he thought, *so be it. I demanded the right to disagree and I got it. Now I'll use it, whether Marlieth approves or not.* But his sore foot gave a warning twinge as he remembered the hurat thorns.

Gathering his courage, Daveeka approached the Exalted Mother as she left the Temple, kneeling before her and presenting one of the scrolls he had so carefully penned. Marlieth took the rolled parchment from his hand and tore it to bits without even opening it.

"Yours ve now right to asssk, dansssser," she hissed, "but none here ve who dare accept sssuch nonsssenssse." She raised her arms above her head, palms cupped upwards in supplication to the Deity. "Elenath, hear me! Mother of All, ssso ve my wordsss, ssso ve the world!" Her eyes swept over the nearby Mothers and her voice hardened. "On thossse who Invite Kiari trasssh, call Ish down the cursssse of bearing only male infantsss!"

She stalked away, leaving bitterness in Daveeka's heart. That curse would be known to every female in the Palace by morning. Few would dare defy the Exalted Mother now. Well, at least he knew there would be no punishment. That only added to his determination to keep trying.

Later that nanth, Zillah brought word to Daveeka when Marlieth's Invitations went out. First Position went to Fahlin, with the Honored Father Strucally from Family Scheld and the Honored Father Tekoa from Connemara getting Second and Third. All the rest of the Positions went to ordinary Fathers.

Daveeka's heart sank even lower when he heard the news. Strucally and Tekoa were two of Fahlin's cronies and allies. What was worse, this would give Fahlin an outside chance to Receive a daughter at Marlieth's Birthing. Even if he only got another son, it would still reinforce his status in Family Marloosh, but if he Received a second daughter, that would place him amongst the top-ranking Honored Fathers under Thennevar jurisdiction, greatly increasing his power and influence. There were only two other males in such a position, one from Family Ferlathan and one from Dziedzic.

Had the Exalted Mother Invited Fahlin for precisely this reason? Even giving him another son would enhance his ability to thwart Daveeka, once he became an Honored Father. Surely Marlieth would have other motives for her choice besides simply blocking him, but all this could well have been taken into consideration.

Much to Daveeka's surprise, the first female to take him to the mating rooms since his punishment was Mistress Chezoar. As he followed her obediently through the corridors, he studied her closely. All he could see of her fur was the back of her head, but he could make out a few telltale streaks of gray mixed in with the black. In a few more years, she would no longer be able to bear children. With no daughters this late in her life, she was very likely never going to become a Mother, since the younger females had a much greater chance of bearing daughters. If she hadn't done so by now, she would probably remain nothing but a Mistress for the rest of her life, the lowest possible status for a female.

She must be pretty desperate by now, Daveeka reflected. *Desperate enough to mate even me, despite my disfavor in the eyes of the Exalted Mother. Or maybe she mates every Honored Father, or potential Honored Father, that she can, hoping for a miracle.*

For the first time in his life, Daveeka found himself pitying a female. He shook his head in amazement.

Once they were inside one of the mating rooms, he dutifully undressed and arranged himself on the couch in the required position. All he really wanted to do was get this over with as quickly as possible. He sighed and told himself to relax, expecting to feel Chezoar's hand around his sheath.

Somewhat to his surprise, she directed her attention first to the niche where the small statue of Elenath stood looking down at the couch. Holding her hands palm up at waist level in the classic attitude for prayer, she stood there for some time, eyes closed and lips barely moving.

Hmm. She's a real pious one, isn't she?

Her Shape caught his eye, reflecting the soft light from the glowweed that outlined the niche. *Truth in All Circumstances. I wonder if she had sought that particular one, or gotten it entirely by chance. It must be almost as difficult to live up to as mine.*

Finishing her devotions, she sat down on the couch next to Daveeka. After so many disappointing experiences with the females, he wasn't even aroused.

Her fingers took hold of his limp sheath. He sighed again, resigning himself to yet another bout of sensual deprivation.

Her touch was gentler than he expected, her fingers only lightly encircling him, slowly, almost pleasurably. *Very strange. Maybe she's just bored with the entire process and in no great hurry this time.*

Regardless of the reason, he found himself reacting to what was very much like the sort of caress another male might use to arouse a partner. As his penis filled and stiffened inside its sheath, she increased the pressure of her fingers to match it.

His own fingers ached as he curled them into fists. His desire mounted, but was not fulfilled by other stimulation. This was almost worse than what the other females did, since the frustration lasted longer and grew stronger with each passing moment. If he could only …

Without thinking, he reached out with one hand and rested it on her thigh, which was still safely covered by the fabric of her robe. She sucked in a sudden breath, as if startled.

Horrified by the enormity of what he had done, Daveeka started to pull back his hand. But the Mistress did nothing, nor did she say anything to protest his action. She just sat there, stiff and unmoving. Even the hand on his sheath paused in mid-stroke.

Then she exhaled and her hand began moving again. She was surely aware of his own hand still lying on her leg, but still she did nothing, as if it wasn't there.

Encouraged, Daveeka dared to move his thumb very lightly back and forth against her leg. He wasn't touching anything but her clothing, yet he could feel the warmth of her body through the fabric. Just the thought that he had his hand on a female was enough to make the tip of his penis appear, already dark brown and moist.

Beneath the base of his sheath, he could feel that wonderful pressure begin to build.

Chezoar noticed and began stroking faster. He wanted to tell her to slow down, it was too soon, but he had already dared too much. She could have his hand chopped off simply for touching her. All he could do was look at her longingly, wishing she would understand.

Their eyes met and held. Her ears turned slightly inward, possibly indicating uncertainty. Still staring directly into her soft and liquid eyes, he shook his head just the slightest bit. Incredibly, she stilled her hand on his sheath.

The relief on his face combined with the slight relaxation in the angle of his ears signaled his feelings all too clearly.

Then a miracle truly did happen. Her hand moved, hovering for an instant above his leg, then settling tentatively on top of his thigh.

Daveeka's entire body arched, his head thrown back and a groan escaping from his lips. *This can't be real. I must be hallucinating. Females don't do this.*

But Mistress Chezoar did. Seeing his reaction, she drew her hand smoothly along the fur on his thigh almost as far as his knee.

His penis extended further as the pressure beneath it increased. When Daveeka closed his eyes and panted for breath, she stroked his other thigh.

His penis was now fully extended and he felt the pulsing contractions begin deep inside, but he wanted more, much more. He wasn't quite full, but he was close, his body quivering and shaking, desperately needing more of her touch.

But that was not to be. Noticing his condition, Chezoar mounted him immediately, taking him in deeper than any of the other females had ever done. She reached down to force his release, but before she could touch his groin, he jerked his hips up hard, burying his extended penis inside her body until the tip of his sheath touched her entrance. He couldn't stop himself even if he'd wanted to. He released his fluid deep inside her in a series of ecstatic spasms.

Only when he had finished did he realize what he had done. Pulling abruptly away from Chezoar, he began stammering out a frantic apology for penetrating her like that, terrified that such an affront would be enough to have his penis cut off.

When he noticed that the Mistress appeared just as shocked as he was, his pleas died away. She wasn't even listening to him. She crouched over him as if frozen in place. Carefully, he slid out from beneath her and sat up.

Her eyes were round and staring, her ears flattened down tightly against her head.

"Mistress? Mistress Chezoar? Did I hurt you? Are you … all right?"

Still, she didn't move. Was she paralyzed with anger? Or fear? Or just sheer astonishment? No matter what, this couldn't be good. Should he call for help? Should he run? He was in big trouble now. Could he do anything to make it better?

His eyes caught on the statue in the niche. The tiny face seemed to stare at him solemnly and calmly.

Touch her, came a whisper in his mind.

No, that was crazy! What if it just made things worse?

Then again, how much worse could it possibly get?

Rising to his knees and leaning forward, he placed a hand on the side of her face, drawing it along in the direction of her fur, then out and around through the luxurious long fur on her head back to her neck. Waves of delight ran through him as the silky strands of her fur slid through and around his fingers.

Chezoar blinked a few times. He repeated the same thing on the other side. Her eyes focussed slowly. Her ears perked up.

Daveeka was trying to decide if he should touch her again when she relaxed down to a cross-legged sitting position on the couch.

"Mistress?" he inquired hopefully.

"I am all right," she said slowly. "Just … surprised."

Instantly he bowed his head before her. "Please forgive this unworthy male for disturbing you so. I did not mean to presume … "

Her hand touched his head lightly. "You need not fear, Dher Daveeka. You have not offended me."

He breathed a sigh of relief.

"Sit up. I would ask you a question."

"Yes, Mistress?"

"Between males is there such … touching?"

"Oh yes. Very much. Did you not know?"

"What males do between each other has always been considered below the notice of females."

Daveeka was not sure what he should say about that, so he just kept silent. Chezoar considered this for a moment. "This must be our secret. Tell no one else."

"This I swear before Elenath, Mistress. I will tell no one."

"This I swear also." She glanced at the statue, and Daveeka followed her eyes. "This will be between the three of us only."

"Yes, Mistress." He looked meaningfully at the Shape she wore. "But are you not constrained to speak truth in all circumstances?"

"I am." Her lips quirked into a slight smile and one of her ears flicked. "But that does not mean I always have to volunteer the truth if I am not asked for it."

"Ah! I understand, Mistress."

She stood up. "I must go. Your servant will be summoned immediately."

"As you say, Mistress Chezoar. Thank you for your gracious mercy. I will remember it always."

She nodded solemnly as she turned away.

As he waited for Zillah, Daveeka had plenty of time to reflect on his experience. Not only that but he was newly overwhelmed with terror at how narrowly he had escaped what could have been a horrible fate. If it had been someone other than Chezoar …

His mind sheared away from considering the possibilities.

However, he couldn't banish the memory of the feeling of her hand on his leg, the long luxuriously fine fur between his fingers, the way it had felt to have his penis fully inside her as he released his fluid. Unlike the other times, it had been a good lot of fluid also.

By the time Zillah got there, Daveeka was trembling with a combination of fear and desire, which was ironically not too unlike his usual condition after a mating.

Zillah took one look at him and then said with evident sympathy, "She really worked you over, didn't she?"

Daveeka just nodded.

Once they were safely back in Daveeka's room, he took off his clothes and collapsed onto his bed.

"Dher Daveeka, don't you want your usual bath?" the servant boy asked with concern.

"No. I want something else."

"What is it?"

He turned toward Zillah, exposing his stiffened sheath and the tip of his swollen penis. "I want you," he said hoarsely.

"You're sure?"

"Yes."

Zillah cheerfully shrugged out of his robe and snuggled into the older rillenu's arms.

By the time Daveeka had gotten his fill of touching and being touched, they were both more than ready to give each other their fluid with gleeful abandon.

After that, the two of them often spent time together on the bed, especially after Daveeka had been mated. At first, he felt a twinge of guilt over what he was doing, but there really was no promise between partners that they wouldn't sometimes take pleasure with other males. He sincerely hoped that Teo would be doing the same thing during the time they had to spend apart.

Despite Daveeka's worry that Chezoar might have second thoughts and break her oath, nothing happened over the next few nights. As the nights turned to quarns, he began to relax, deciding she would indeed keep silent.

Now and then, he would see her at a ceremony or pass her in a corridor. She didn't allow so much as a flicker of her ears in recognition, and he did the same to her. He had just concluded that it was truly not going to be a problem when she took him to the mating rooms again, then continued to do so every few quarns, usually in an inconspicuous manner so as not to draw attention to them.

With considerable hesitation on both sides, they slowly explored more intimate touching and stroking. Not only was it not a problem, it was pure delight!

By the time Fourteenth Nanth rolled around, Daveeka felt pretty good about things. He could walk without much pain, his daughter was doing fine, and he enjoyed Mistress Chezoar's matings, even if not the matings with other females. But then, he had Zillah to console him afterwards.

He decided it was time to return to his long-neglected dancing practice. Drawing chalk marks on the floor of his room to represent his dancing rug, he closed his eyes. Humming one of the familiar tunes, he started out confidently enough.

Much to his dismay, he found himself making careless mistakes. At the climax of the routine, he turned full around, did a complex kick step, then flung himself into a spin, leaping sideways a carefully calculated distance. Then he opened his eyes and cursed.

Missed. He had landed just beyond the edge of his simulated rug. If this had been a true contest, he'd have been standing on barbarythorns, not the yielding carpetmoss on the floor.

Disgusted, he flopped down on his favorite embroidered cushion, panting and out of breath. When his left foot began to ache, he started wondering whether he should just give it up, since his scarred feet might never allow him to be really good at it again. Nevertheless, he had so enjoyed his dancing that he couldn't quite bring himself to quit. The melodies he hummed were too much a part of him, and besides, they carried poignant memories of Teo.

The doorway curtain shivered slightly. Daveeka heard the faint shuffle of feet. "Zillah, is that you?" he called.

"Yes, Dher Daveeka." The boy came diffidently into the room. "I was just watching you dance."

"How did you know what I was doing?"

"I … peeked around the curtain."

Daveeka laughed. "Spying on me, eh?"

Zillah's ears drooped. "You aren't angry, are you?"

Daveeka shook his head.

"It looks like fun," the boy said hesitantly. "Could you, maybe, teach me how to do it?"

"You really want to?"

"Yes."

"All right." Daveeka got to his feet. Taking Zillah's hand, he led the youngster over to the chalk-marked outlines of the dancing rug, then drew another close to it. "See that? That's your rug. Stand on it, just like this. Right. Now, watch me and do as I do."

Much to Daveeka's surprise, Zillah had a natural talent for dancing. His usual clumsiness disappeared entirely whenever he had music to guide him. Before three quarns had gone by, the boy had learned most of the basic steps and was working on the more difficult movements.

Daveeka enjoyed having a student. Perhaps he, himself, would never again be good enough to participate in the ritual Dances, but that didn't mean he couldn't hand on his expertise to others. He could also tell Zillah about the Kiari beliefs while he was at it, if the youngster showed an interest in that.

Five nights into the following nanth, Daveeka sat glumly at the table. Despite Zillah's urgings that he eat, his appetite had disappeared long ago, when news of the Exalted Mother's imminent Birthing had been brought shortly after moonrise. The Invited males from other Families would have been staying at the Marloosh lodging house for over a quarn by now, waiting to be summoned.

Thought of the Marloosh house brought back memories of the past, when he had dwelt outside the walls of the Thennevar Palace. Had it really been almost six nanths ago? It seemed much longer than that, as if it had happened in another lifetime and to someone else. The heavy stones of the High Wall loomed in his mind's eye, seeming almost to lock him away from his other life, and from Teo.

Was Teo still living in their old room? Ah, if he could only hold him again, if he could sleep with his partner's body safely cradled in his arms! There was such an emptiness where Teo should be. But it would be filled again, someday.

Maybe it wouldn't be entirely proper for an Honored Father to have a childless male as a partner, but Daveeka wouldn't let that stop him. Teo would be his again, in a little over two more nanths.

Two nanths. They would take his daughter then.

He shuddered, remembering what it had been like for Teo when his son had died after five nanths. He had been called into the Palace for the usual inquiry and examination after the death of an infant, but he had been released. Not many males who lost a son were that fortunate. Most were never heard from again, once they were summoned to the Palace. No one knew what happened to them, but it was assumed that they had been found guilty of negligence in respect to the infant's death and punished or perhaps sent away in disgrace to become a slave at the Farms.

Teo had reacted to his loss with deep depression. He had recovered only when his body eventually adjusted to the absence of the child in his pouch. Losing a baby suddenly was always traumatic, both physically and mentally.

It would be worse for him, he knew. He would have carried his daughter for a full eight nanths before she was taken. Daveeka tried to tell himself that was the price he'd have to pay to become an Honored Father. So what if it would hurt? The reward would be worth it. Other males had gone through it. He could, too.

His thoughts returned abruptly to the present. What was happening at the Birthing? With Fahlin in First Position, the best Daveeka could hope for was that the Honored Father would only end up with a son.

He considered going to the library to get a scroll to read, or going to the Temple to meditate.

No. Any male who had Received a daughter would be brought immediately to this common room, and thence into one of the private rooms facing onto it. He'd find out sooner by staying right where he was.

He stared at the sand running steadily through the blue timeglass. Half hypnotized by watching the falling sand grains, Daveeka jerked abruptly alert as footsteps shuffled along the hallway outside the door. Obvious curiosity would be unseemly, so he remained seated, watching the curtain across the entrance.

One arm around the shoulder of a Thennevar servant, Fahlin staggered into the room. Although he'd clearly taken a bit too much jareesh at the Receiving, his eyes sparkled with frenetic satisfaction as he glared at the other rillenu.

The tips of Daveeka's ears drooped. Fahlin carried a daughter, then. There would be no other reason for his presence here.

Mistress Annilee followed the Honored Father into the room. Pointing to the sleeping room furthest from Daveeka's, she ordered the servant to take him in there.

Daveeka thought he detected a hint of chilliness in the Mistress' voice. Recalling the contempt he'd once heard her express for Fahlin, he concluded she was far from pleased at the outcome of this Receiving. Or was he merely imagining things?

Annilee saw Fahlin settled in the empty room, then withdrew, leaving the servant to attend the Honored Father. Daveeka stared at the closed curtain across the entrance to Fahlin's room and cursed under his breath.

Although Daveeka tried his best, it was impossible to avoid Fahlin forever. Two nights later, he returned from the library to find the Honored Father halfway through his midnight meal. Daveeka considered ignoring the other male and going directly to his own room, but that would accomplish little. Instead, he settled onto a cushion by the table and allowed Zillah to serve him a cup of kullup milk.

At first, they did nothing more than exchange furtive glances, each sizing up the other in his own way. When Daveeka caught a glimpse of the Shape worn by the Honored Father, he was pleased to realize that it was nothing more than a simple pyramid, which he now knew to be quite insignificant, symbolizing Proper and Respectful Stability. Fahlin hadn't even needed to reach beyond the surface layer to get that one.

Daveeka forced himself not to smirk as he reached casually for his own complex Shape, taking it in one hand and rubbing it between his fingers as the Females often did with theirs. Fahlin couldn't help but notice it was much more complex than his own. The slight puzzlement in his expression allowed Daveeka to guess that the other rillenu didn't even realize the meaning of the glittering Teardrop.

Quickly recovering his composure, Fahlin regarded Daveeka, his ears at a satisfied slant. "So, dancer, I hope you've profited by your time amongst the females. Possibly you've had a chance to … uh … revise some of your opinions a bit?"

"I have revised a number of my opinions, Honored Father, but I'm not sure you would approve of my revisions."

Fahlin sighed elaborately. "I was hoping you'd have learned something by now."

The old male was being altogether too courteous. "What is it you'd like me to have learned?" Daveeka inquired cautiously.

Fahlin lounged back against the cushions. When he spoke, his voice was deceptively mild. "Perhaps just that it doesn't pay to buck the females."

"What makes you think I'd come to that conclusion?"

"Oh, nothing much. Just a stray bit of gossip I heard from the females regarding a certain foolish male who got a taste of the hurat wand."

Daveeka's ears flattened and he turned away.

"Oh, yes, I know all about that," Fahlin went on. "And I see that you're still wearing those hideous bloody shoes. Tell me, Daveeka, how well could you dance now? Could you still feel the patterns on your dancing-rug? Or would the scars on your feet prevent it?"

Inwardly, Daveeka flinched, but he forced himself to look Fahlin in the eye. "I have qualified as a priest, so I will not need to dance on rugs unless I wish to. Besides, I'll be an Honored Father soon enough."

Fahlin laughed. "An Honored Father dances in a more dangerous contest than any you have ever known. Are you prepared to learn the steps in that dance, or will you persist in being a fool?"

"What are you talking about?"

Fahlin casually adjusted the cushion behind him. "The Conclave this winter, of course. And my proposal. As you've already pointed out, it's possible you'll be an Honored Father by then. I'll still be confined to the Thennevar House and will be unable to attend, but you could be my representative, make the proposal in my stead."

"Syron is Second in Marloosh. Would not he be the proper one to do that?"

Fahlin shrugged. "Syron's old and sick. The Fathers of the other Families don't take him seriously anyway." He fixed the younger rillenu with an intense glance, ears set forward in the attitude of interested friendship. "I'd rather it be you. It would have much more impact."

Daveeka was too surprised to reply. *Did Fahlin truly believe I'd be willing to do such a thing?*

"Think about it." Fahlin picked up his cup of hot milk and sipped, regarding Daveeka appraisingly. "You could be Head of Family Marloosh, eventually. I won't live forever, you know."

Daveeka made a show of considering this in silence for a few minutes, fingering his Shape. He had promised to obey the Will of Elenath in the matter of the proposal. But what was Her Will? She had favored his quest for this Shape, hadn't She? Maybe …

"As a matter of fact, I'd be very happy to present a proposal to the Conclave." Daveeka paused, enjoying the pleased look on Fahlin's face and knowing it would soon fade. "Unfortunately, I don't think you'll like the proposal I have in mind. Perhaps we should restrict Honored Fathers to Seventh, Eighth, and Ninth Positions, and ordinary Fathers to Fourth, Fifth, and Sixth. Then we could reserve First, Second, and Third exclusively for childless males. That would be far more equitable."

"You can't be serious!"

"No?"

"That would undermine your own chances at more children. What could you possibly hope to gain by such a thing?"

"If each Father didn't have the opportunity to carry so many babies in his life, there would be almost enough for every male to have his own child."

"That's insane. Have you any idea of the number of Fathers we'd have then? Who would do all the work, if everyone were a Father?"

"I guess we'd have to change things a bit then, wouldn't we?" Daveeka suggested smugly.

"Change things a bit?!" Fahlin roared. "I offer you a chance at power and status, and you prattle on about changing things!"

Daveeka just sat there.

Fahlin slid suddenly from fury to icy reserve. "Very well, if that's how you want it. I should have known better than to think you would listen to reason, but I had to at least try." He rose to his feet and strode across to his own chamber, turning back briefly as he reached the archway. "I feel sorry for you, dancer. You just stepped off your rug." Fahlin jerked the curtain aside and left the common room.

"The Kiari like your proposal, Dher Daveeka," Zillah announced cheerfully three nights later when they stopped to rest during a dancing lesson.

"What proposal?"

The youngster looked perplexed. "What you said the other night to Dher Fahlin." When Daveeka just stared at him, Zillah continued, "I overheard your conversation with him. I think it's a terrific idea!"

Uh-oh!

"I only said that to annoy Fahlin," Daveeka protested.

"You mean you weren't serious?" The disappointment reflected clearly in Zillah's eyes and his drooping ears.

"Well … I … uh … Of course, it would be a good thing, but the Conclave and the females would never approve of it. You realize that, don't you?"

"Oh, yes. But just bringing up the idea would be a good start."

Daveeka realized unhappily that Zillah was right. "Such a thing would be far too dangerous to seriously consider." And then he remembered what the young rillenu had said earlier. "Zillah, how did the Kiari find out about this?"

The boy looked even more shamefaced, if such a thing were possible. "Well, servants talk, and word gets around," he mumbled. "You know."

"You mean you told people what I said?"

Zillah averted his eyes and nodded.

"And it got back to the Kiari so quickly?"

He nodded again, not daring to look up. "I … I've told some of my friends about the dancing I'm doing, and a little about the Kiari. And … and one of the other servants has a … uh … good friend who's a guard and the friend has often spoken favorably about the Kiari. So maybe …"

"So maybe there are sympathizers even here inside the Palace? And there are ways to get in touch with the Kiari?" Daveeka prompted him.

Zillah finally met Daveeka's eyes, his ears still drooping. "Yes, Dher Daveeka. But it's a bit risky."

"I'll guess it may be more than just a bit risky."

Daveeka considered the situation for a time, while Zillah squirmed uncomfortably. But Daveeka was the one who was the most uncomfortable of the two, despite his relative composure. He had a much clearer idea than his servant of what could happen if he truly dared to introduce such a proposal. Yes, it would be a good start, but it could just as easily spell the end of any power or influence he himself might gain once he was an Honored Father. Would it be worth the price, just to make a point? Or would it just stand in the way of any potential progress he might be able to make in the future?

"You shouldn't have said anything just yet," he finally replied calmly. "A proposal like that wouldn't stand a chance. No one would vote for it."

"Well, maybe you could think of something less drastic. Something the Fathers would vote for, if there were reasons for them to do so."

"You have a point there, my young friend. I'll have to think about it."

"You're not angry?" the youngster asked, visibly relieved.

"No, not really." Daveeka inclined his head in the direction of Fahlin's room. "But I know someone who's going to be furious over this. You'd better keep quiet about leaking the news. And watch your step around Fahlin. Understand?"

"Yes, Dher Daveeka. I understand."

For the next couple of nights, Daveeka kept expecting Fahlin to bring up the subject of the proposal again, but the Honored Father never mentioned it. Life went on.

Then one night, when Zillah had just finished drying and brushing Daveeka's fur and was helping him into a fresh tunic, Fahlin entered the bathing room. The servant boy hastily gathered the wet towels into his arms and started out of the chamber behind Daveeka.

"You, boy," Fahlin commanded, "stay here and attend me."

"I am Dher Daveeka's servant, Honored Father. But I'll go and summon your servant, if you wish."

Fahlin grabbed the youngster's arm. "No. You stay."

"Please, Dher Fahlin, I can't—"

Fahlin pulled him roughly towards the bathing pool, causing him to drop the load of towels. "I don't care. I want you," the old rillenu hissed. "Help me get out of my clothes."

Zillah was still struggling to get loose. Fahlin tightened his grip on his arm, jerking him forward. The boy stepped on a patch of wet rock, lost his balance, and stumbled hard against the Honored Father. They both tumbled into one of the deeper bathing pools, with Zillah landing on top of Fahlin and knocking him under the water. Daveeka raced over and pulled Zillah out of the pool.

Spluttering and cursing, Fahlin regained his footing. With one hand clutched protectively over the opening of his pouch, he had succeeded in preventing water from getting into it. His embroidered collar hung askew, sodden and dripping, and his brocade tunic was obviously ruined. Still standing in the shallow water, his ears flattened as he glared up at Zillah and Daveeka.

"Clumsy idiot! What are you trying to do, drown my daughter?" he roared.

"No, Honored Father! I didn't mean to … I fell … please!"

"Fahlin, it was an accident," Daveeka said, reaching out a hand to help the older male out of the pool.

"Accident, indeed! I say he hoped to drown my daughter. And you didn't help any by pulling him out first, instead of me. Perhaps this 'accident' was planned by the two of you."

"No! I swear—" Zillah cowered away from Fahlin, but the Honored Father fetched him a blow that sent the boy sprawling to the floor before Daveeka could calm him down. Zillah picked himself up and went running out of the room, as Daveeka helped Fahlin out of his wet clothes, doing his best to pacify him and make light of the entire incident.

The following night, a strange servant came to the room with the usual tray of delicacies for the first meal of the evening.

Daveeka picked up a slender pink chared stalk and took a bite, licking his lips appreciatively.

"Where's Zillah?" he asked the servant boy, just as Fahlin stepped through the curtain from his sleeping chamber.

"That clumsy little fool won't be serving you anymore," the Honored Father said smoothly. "He's being sent to the Farms."

"What? Just for accidentally knocking you into the water?"

Fahlin dismissed Daveeka's objection with a negligent gesture of one hand as he sat down to eat. "He should have been dismissed long ago."

"You can't do this."

"I already have. Your little friend is sitting in the dungeon right now. He'll be sent to the Farms next nanth with the rest of the condemned criminals, when the procession goes to the harvest."

"Fahlin—"

"What's the matter, Dher Daveeka?" the Honored Father said mockingly. "One would almost think you cared about that clumsy oaf of a boy. I thought you had a partner already. Teo, wasn't it? What happened to him?"

"Nothing. I mean, I still love Teo. But Zillah—"

"An impudent twit, nothing more. He wasn't even very pretty. Now, look at this young fellow here." Fahlin took hold of the new servant's ear, forcing his head back. "He's much more attractive, don't you think?"

When Daveeka didn't answer, Fahlin narrowed his eyes. "Besides, I suspect your sweet little servant boy had the habit of eavesdropping. You wouldn't want someone like that hanging around, would you?" His free hand reached under and up beneath the new servant's tunic, rubbing obscenely over the boy's unopened pouch. "This one is yours, of course. But if you don't want him, we can trade."

The boy looked to Daveeka, his ears flattened in sheer terror of what Fahlin was doing.

"Umm," the old rillenu went on, giving Daveeka a significant look, "His pouch hasn't even been opened yet. I do so love to be the first one to do that."

"You wouldn't," Daveeka protested, shocked to even hear such a thing mentioned.

"No? Why not? These are only servants. They're here for us to use, in whatever way we wish. It will be quite delicious to see the fear in his eyes as my hand slides deep into his pouch and stretches it hard, while my fingers pinch his delicate little teat. They try so hard to keep from screaming, but they never succeed."

With an oath, Daveeka threw his chared stalk onto the table, grabbed the boy away from Fahlin, and dragged him into his sleeping chamber. Fahlin's laughter followed behind them.

Daveeka fought to calm himself and cast his fury aside. True, he had heard rumors about opening another male's pouch for the first time, but he didn't know it was actually being done, especially without the other male's consent.

I've got to ask Zillah about – no, I can't. He's in the dungeon.

He glanced at his new servant, who was now crouched in the far corner of the room, huddled over and clearly expecting his new master to do as the Honored Father had suggested.

"Please, Dher Daveeka …" the terrified boy began, with a look that almost broke his heart.

He went over and knelt before the youngster.

"It's all right, boy. I'm not like him. I don't do that." He reached out and touched the younger rillenu's head, gently scratching behind the base of one flattened ear, offering comfort and reassurance. "Now, tell me your name."

"S ... Sinda," he stammered.

"Sinda. Good. Now stand up and don't be afraid. As long as you're not his servant, he can't touch you. If he so much as tries, you tell me. All right?"

The youngster nodded and rose to his feet. "Yes, Dher Daveeka. Thank you. I ... I'm ashámed that I reacted that way. Zillah told me you were a good master –"

"You know Zillah?"

"He is ... was ... a good friend of mine. Now he's going to—"

"Not if I can help it, Sinda. There has to be something I can do, some way to reverse the judgement against him."

But there wasn't. It turned out that Marlieth had signed the exile order herself, at Fahlin's request. She wasn't about to rescind it just because Daveeka requested it of her.

When he broke the news to Sinda, the boy broke down and cried.

"Don't give up hope yet," Daveeka comforted him. "After I become an Honored Father, I should be able to use my influence to have Zillah pardoned and brought home. If he can last just two nanths on the Farms, we may still be able to rescue him. And he probably won't get sent there right away. They'll wait and take him along with the other prisoners for the Harvest Festival. We'll get him back. You'll see."

From then on, Daveeka refused to speak to Fahlin, rising and leaving the common room whenever the other male came in.

At first, Fahlin seemed surprised that Daveeka would be so upset over a mere servant boy. Then his mood changed abruptly. Each time Daveeka saw him, he looked extremely pleased with himself. He was up to something, but Daveeka couldn't figure out what it was.

Then one night he returned from the library to find Fahlin sprawled on the cushions in the common room, waiting for him. He tried to ignore the Honored Father, striding instead towards his chamber, but Fahlin said softly, "You'd better think some more about my proposal to the Conclave this winter, if you ever want to see Teo alive again."

Daveeka froze. "What are you talking about?"

Fahlin pulled a rolled sheet of paper from one pocket and held it out to the younger rillenu.

Daveeka took it. It was a list of males to be drafted for temporary work on the Farms during the upcoming Autumn harvest. Every childless male lived in terror of finding himself on that list. At best, it meant three nanths of back-breaking work in the fields and distilleries. At worst, it could mean death. The jaram fields were dangerous.

Teo's name appeared near the end.

Daveeka caught his breath in a harsh gasp. *No! Not Teo! They couldn't!*

He gritted his teeth. Fahlin could. The Honored Fathers of each Family had the final say of who was drafted for the harvest. But Fahlin had forgotten one thing. "As soon as I'm confirmed as an Honored Father, I'll be able to get him and Zillah back."

"Might be too late by then, my young friend. A fairly high percentage of the draftees don't return after the harvest," Fahlin pointed out. "It wouldn't be hard to arrange for both of them to meet an untimely death, if you get my meaning."

Daveeka crumpled the paper in his fist.

"Of course, I could see that Teo's taken off the list," Fahlin said smoothly. "Maybe even your clumsy servant also, if you'd like to be a bit more cooperative about certain matters."

"I won't present your proposal, Fahlin, if that's what you're driving at."

"Think about it. The harvest doesn't begin until next nanth. You have time to change your mind." Fahlin rose to his feet, heading toward the door to the corridor. One hand on the curtain, he stopped and turned around. "And you had better change your mind, if you want to see your precious partner again."

Daveeka stared straight at the other male, saying coldly, "If you do anything to harm Teo, I'll kill you. By the Sacred Name of Elenath, I swear it!"

"Be careful who you threaten, youngster. You are not yet an Honored Father. Much can happen before your daughter is taken."

As soon as Fahlin had left the room, Daveeka slumped forward onto the table, his head resting on his arms. It had been bad enough when Zillah had been taken from him. But now Teo was in danger also!

He closed his eyes and wondered what to do. He couldn't abandon Zillah. He couldn't let Teo go to the Farms. He couldn't bear to be responsible for his partner's sufferings.

But he couldn't do as Fahlin wanted, either. He'd only been half serious about the proposal he'd mentioned, but if he turned around and supported Fahlin's proposal, it would break the back of any resistance that might be organized against it.

He delayed for several nights, putting Fahlin off by saying he was still thinking it over. There were a couple more quarns before the harvest. He'd come up with some way to get Teo out of it. If worst came to worst, he could keep stalling right through the harvest itself. That would at least prevent Fahlin from carrying out his threat to arrange a convenient "accident" even if it wouldn't keep Teo from being sent to the Farms. Teo was young and strong. He would survive. Zillah might be spared from the dangerous assignments, due to his youth. Daveeka would surely be able to get them both back once he was confirmed as an Honored Father. His daughter would be taken sometime during Second Nanth. That wasn't so long. They could make it.

Couldn't they?

Daveeka racked his brain for some better alternative. There must be something he could do to foil Fahlin.

But nights turned to quarns and he came up with no brilliant ideas. Fourteenth Nanth wore on, bringing cooler weather and the approach of the new year. First Nanth and harvest loomed closer with each sunset.

"Daveecha!"

He was already on his feet, having heard and recognized the pattern of Annilee's footsteps approaching the common room. She jerked the curtain aside, striding into the chamber. Her rounded ears lay flat against her head. Something was clearly wrong.

"Yesh, Mistress?"

"Ish musst to the Harvesst Fesstival go. You come with."

Two females were chosen by the Exalted Mother to attend the Festival each year. They would conduct the necessary ceremonies and mate with a number of males from the Farms.

"Misstress, our daughter ve now six nanthss old. Ssuch a long journey could be—"

"Aware ve Ish of thiss." Her voice rasped with anger, but not directed at him. "Alsso aware ve my Mother and Fahlin that thiss riskss my infant. My choice ve thiss na. Ish ve commanded sso to dho. In two nightss, we leave. Prepare."

She stalked away, leaving Daveeka stunned at this unexpected turn of events. A journey to the Farms would be difficult, in his condition. He should be resting, eating well and preparing himself to face the taking of his daughter.

Instead, he'd be at the Farms for the entire time of the harvest, expected to appear at the ceremonies with Annilee. They'd barely get back before it would come time for his daughter to be taken. Since Annilee was the one who had to open his pouch each day to clean and caress the baby, there was no chance he'd be allowed to remain safely behind in the Thennevar Palace. His sessions with her would have to take place under less than ideal conditions, leaving open the possibility of infection and sickness. Female infants were well known to be especially vulnerable to such things.

If anything happened to the child he carried before it was taken, he'd revert back to the status of childless male and would pose no further threat to the Fathers' hierarchy, nor would he be able to help Teo or Zillah.

Fahlin strolled from his room, ears at a cheerful angle. He had to have overheard what Annilee said. "Sure you wouldn't like to change your mind about things, Dav? Marlieth might be persuaded to appoint someone other than Annilee, if she had a reason to."

"You arranged this, didn't you?" Daveeka demanded.

"You give me far too much credit. How could a mere male arrange the assignment of females to the harvest?" Fahlin leaned against the wall, ears perked smugly. "Of course, I may have mentioned to the Exalted Mother what a shame it would be if Annilee went, and your daughter died as a result."

Daveeka's fingers longed to be around Fahlin's neck, squeezing, feeling the other rillenu strangle and die. But he could not. Any attempt on the life of a male carrying a daughter would lead to a sentence of death. In his case, that would be delayed until after his daughter was taken, but it would still mean throwing his life away for nothing.

"Fahlin, why don't you go mate with a kullup?" he said softly.

Striding past the other male and out of the room, Daveeka sought refuge in the Temple. He sank down onto a cushion before the statue of Elenath, praying for strength and courage.

Not for the first time, it didn't feel as if anyone was listening.

One hand reached down to his Shape, to caress the smooth surfaces in what had become an almost automatic gesture. He couldn't promise to support Fahlin's proposal. His opinion on that subject was well known. The Mother of All had even ratified his right to express that opinion. The Shape he wore obligated him to oppose Fahlin.

But if he did ...

As he stared down at the sparkling crystal, Daveeka began to understand why the Shape signifying Disagreement with Established Authority, however Respectful, resembled a teardrop.

CHAPTER 6

Daveeka followed obediently behind Mistress Annilee, with Sinda close beside him and her entourage of male servants in their wake. The courtyard of the Thennevar Palace bustled with activity, as those going to the harvest prepared to depart. Mother Magdael had been chosen as the other female to go. She looked as little pleased about it as Annilee did as she boarded the closed carriage in which the females would travel on the long journey to the Farms.

Harnessed to the heavy carriage, the eight spaldeens tossed their heads and stomped their cloven hooves, sending dust swirling through the clear night air.

Daveeka bowed his respect as Annilee was handed into the carriage, then he and Sinda went to take their places in the small buggy drawn up behind the ornate carriage. Servants scurried to crowd into open wagons, perching on top of the empty barrels. When the expedition returned, those barrels would be replaced by full barrels containing the first shipment of jareesh prepared from the previous year's harvest, now properly aged and ready for consumption or trade.

Marlieth had already pronounced her blessing on the departing females at the sundown ceremony earlier on, so there was no time to waste. The sun was well below the horizon and the almost full red-orange circle of Elnanth was mounting rapidly into the sky as the wide front gate of the Palace swung open.

From his seat in the buggy, Daveeka strained to see the crowd of assembled males drawn up in ranks outside the gate. They stood in silent resignation, heads bowed as the carriage bearing Annilee and Magdael moved past. These would be the unlucky ones drafted for temporary work during the vital harvest season, plus the boys culled from this year's exchange as mental or physical defectives, plus a number of condemned criminals. Only the first group would be returning to their Families once the crop was in and the distilling begun. If they survived.

Teo was somewhere in that mob, and so was Zillah. Daveeka tried to catch a glimpse of them, hoping to give them some small measure of encouragement with a wave of his hand. But the driver of the buggy flicked his whip over the head of his spaldeen and it moved off at a lively pace. The new slaves were all dressed in identical gray robes to denote their status, which made it hard to tell one from another. Daveeka passed by too quickly to recognize anyone, and the supply wagons pulled in behind, blocking them from view.

As the procession passed the entrance to the Marloosh lodging house, Daveeka realized with a start that someone was shouting his name. Then it was taken up as a ragged chant. A small group of Kiari stood together at the corner, waving to him. Several of them tossed flowers. A heavy pink calimand blossom landed in the buggy.

Daveeka swept it up in one hand. He stood, waved the flower over his head, kissed it, then tossed it back to his supporters, even as thcy wcrc lcft behind in the crowd. A few of them cheered again, recognizing the traditional rug-dancer's acknowledgement of a tribute from his audience.

He resumed his seat, feeling just a bit less alone. Somewhere on the dusty road behind him, Teo trudged with the other males. Perhaps he had heard. Perhaps his friends would cheer for Teo, too, and toss him a flower, if they dared.

As the expedition pulled away from the cluster of buildings surrounding the Thennevar Palace and moved into the open countryside, the drivers reined in their spaldeens to a slower pace. The females' carriage mustn't be jostled unnecessarily. A lone rider could have made the journey in half the time it would take for this crowded, straggling procession to do so.

Once outside the town, they were joined by a number of open flatbed wagons. The conscripted males swarmed on board, jostling each other in an effort to find enough space to sit down. The younger boys squeezed in amongst them, ears quivering with anxiety.

Daveeka craned his neck around the side of the buggy, trying to see what went on. In his pouch, his daughter shifted position, kicking him sharply. He relaxed back against the padded seat, hoping she would soon get used to the jostling and settle down.

Elnanth was long past zenith before a brief halt was called. Daveeka touched Sinda's shoulder and whispered softly, "Come on. Let's see if we can catch sight of Teo or Zillah." They dismounted from the buggy and tried to stroll back toward the end of the wagon train as if they were only stretching their legs. Guards dressed in Thennevar livery patrolled the dispirited party of slaves-to-be, watching that no one slipped away.

As Daveeka drew near, one of the guards approached him respectfully. "Please, dhamereth. Return to your place now. It is not seemly for you to be here." He was tall enough and strong enough to have bodily removed Daveeka had he wished, but he dared not manhandle one who carried a daughter without either extreme necessity or explicit orders from a female.

"I understand," Daveeka replied. He must be careful, must not cause trouble by singling out Teo in any way. "I'm going now. You need not be concerned."

He and Sinda walked back toward his buggy, disappointed at not having caught sight of his partner. Suddenly, Sinda touched Daveeka's arm and nodded slightly to the side.

"A cup of water, honored dhamereth? A sip of jareesh?" Zillah stood not far away from them, shifting nervously from one foot to the other as if he had never been in the company of such an illustrious male before. Daveeka almost caught him up in a hug before he realized the boy was carefully pretending not to know him. Zillah must have volunteered for the job of waterboy, hoping for a chance to speak to him.

"Water for me and my servant," Daveeka ordered harshly. "And make it fast."

With a show of humble eagerness, Zillah scooped liquid from the bucket beside him, offering the cup to Daveeka as he murmured, "I located your partner. Teo sends his love."

Daveeka took the cup. "I'll get you both off the Farms, Zillah. Once I'm an Honored Father—"

"Shh," Sinda warned, his eyes darting sideways.

Daveeka saw the driver of his buggy striding back from the bushes, where he had gone to relieve himself. He took a sip from the dipper and handed it to Sinda.

Zillah averted his head humbly as the driver approached.

"Let's have some of that jareesh, boy," the other male said cheerfully. "My throat's dry as dust."

Zillah clutched at the flask he carried strung over one shoulder. "I'm not supposed to … I mean, only females or—"

"Just pretend he's a female," Daveeka barked harshly, exchanging a wink with the driver.

They both laughed as Zillah hesitantly held out the flask. The driver took a long swallow, then tossed the flask back to the boy, grimacing fiercely. "Now get out of here. And keep your mouth shut, or I'll feed you to the outlaw males. They eat nice little servant boys like you."

"Yes, sir! I'm leaving," Zillah spluttered, grabbing his water bucket and running off as fast as he could.

"Outlaw males?" Daveeka queried. "What outlaw males?"

The driver spat on the ground. "Never heard the stories about them? Folks who live near the Farms claim they really exist, deep in the forests. But then, anybody who lives too close to the Farms isn't too bright, if you ask me. Come on, let's get back to the buggy. We'll be starting up again soon."

Daveeka stepped up into his place. "Any chance the stories are true?"

"Nah. Lot of nonsense. Chew on enough jaram seeds and you'd see outlaw males behind every bush too. Likely someone caught sight of some runaway slaves trying to escape into the forest and spun the whole tale from that. Not that runaways would last very long in the forest, anyway."

Like every other male, Daveeka had heard tales of the brooding woods at the boundaries of the jaram fields, the carnivorous poisonous plants that occasionally came crawling out. Rumor had it that when work parties went to clear new sections of the forest, barely half of the slaves sent out would come back alive.

The Farms were at the far edge of civilization, where the forests still held sway. Each year, the trees were cut back further, but it was an endless battle. However, jaram grew best on newly cleared land, in close proximity to those deadly woods. No one had ever been able to figure out why.

Forests were no place to go. Daveeka glanced out over the flat, safe plain surrounding him, taking comfort from the lack of tall trees.

After two long nights of travel and an uncomfortable day spent at the less than luxurious halfway house, the forests were more than a chilling rumor. Slowly, they became reality, beginning as a dark smudge on the horizon by the end of the first night, then growing the following night into a brooding boundary just beyond the jaram fields.

Yellow light flickered brightly from a building up ahead as the expedition drew nearer to the Farms. "What's that?" Daveeka inquired of his driver.

"The distillery. The vats are heated tonight, in order to cleanse them of any traces of last year's harvest. Nextnight, they'll be set boiling, full of the first jaram berries to be brought in this year."

There was no opportunity for further questions as the procession of Fathers from Family Scheld came out to greet the arriving females with all the pomp and ceremony they could muster.

Although Family Scheld was responsible for operating the Farms, none of their members actually worked in the fields. The Fathers, of course, ran the entire operation, but the childless males provided the workforce of overseers, guards, clerks, and skilled craftsmen. Scheld was both loathed and respected amongst the other male Families: loathed because of their association with the Farms, but respected because the jaram crop and the resulting jareesh provided the major part of the income of Family Thennevar, so the females looked on Scheld with favor.

Daveeka soon found himself ensconced in luxurious quarters not far from Annilee and Magdael in the elaborate building that was kept and maintained solely for the use of females and their entourage. Sinda bustled around, busily filling a bathing tub with scented hot water so he could wash the dust of travel out of his fur before going to sleep for the day.

Peeking through the closed shutters on his window, Daveeka watched the tail end of the consignment of males shuffle dispiritedly into the stockade that enclosed the slave compound. Even before the sun set again, they would be driven out to work in the fields, along with the rest of the slaves.

Daveeka awoke early the following evening, hearing the commotion as the first night of the dreaded harvest began. The sun was still in the sky when he was awakened, but by the time he was summoned to see Annilee for the now-nightly examination of his daughter, it was full dark.

"Sshe ve well and fine, Daveecha," the young Mistress said, stroking the base of his ears gently with one hand even while the other moved inside his pouch. He was used to that now. It hardly disturbed him at all. The baby squirmed with pleasure at Annilee's caresses. He could feel it wriggling and had to fight down the longing to touch it himself.

When she had finished, she sat back and pulled his short robe down. "Now come with. Fieldss musst ssanctified ve. Mating hutss ve prepared and thiss night'ss ssacrificess waiting." Her ears flicked with distaste, but she would do her duty and mate each night not only with him, but also with the two chosen slaves, who would be offered to the demons of the woods at the next sunrise. "Magdael ve already there."

As Daveeka rose obediently to his feet, Annilee touched his arm lightly. "Wait sshe musst, sssince you carry my daughter, ve Ish first."

Obediently, he followed Annilee outside and down the dirt road leading to the fields. Just beyond the high wooden walls of the slave compound, deep green jaram plants grew waist-high, bathed in Elnanth's orange light as the nearly full moon rose slowly in the early evening sky. The prickly leaves of the plants rustled noisily as a breeze passed over the fields.

The hard-packed dirt road continued through the fields in the direction of the threatening forest at the far edge, but Annilee turned off on a side path before they had gotten far from the cleared area of the Scheld buildings. The path had been recently widened, with the cut stumps of jaram still visible at either side. It led in an upward spiral around a small hillock, on top of which stood a circular stone hut.

Daveeka glanced over one shoulder as he climbed. Another similar hump of ground rose behind him, on the opposite side of the dirt road. Off in the direction of the looming forests, he could see groups of slaves working in the jaram, picking berries and loading them into wagons. Once the berries had been taken, the thorny stalks of the plants would be cut down and stacked, then methodically stripped of their leaves, which were used as medicines. After the stalks had dried, they would be added to the fuel for the distilling process, since the stalks burned with a fierce heat.

A stray thorn from a poorly trimmed plant caught in Annilee's skirt as she walked. Daveeka hurried forward to free her, careful not to snag his own clothing as he did so.

The jaram in this part of the field would be harvested last, since the females would be expected to live and mate amongst the ripe plants for as long as the harvesting lasted, drawing down blessings from Elenath on each night.

A group of males waited unobtrusively alongside the hut on top of the hillock, dressed in the colors of Family Scheld. All but two were Fathers, and several of them wore the wide collars of Honored Fathers. The other two wore only the coarse gray tunic of a slave. Those two would die horribly at the next sunrise and they knew it.

They all went down on their knees and bowed their heads to the ground as Annilee passed by, as was the custom when any female was in the fields.

Daveeka followed Annilee into the hut without a glance in their direction. He knew neither Teo nor Zillah was in any danger of being sacrificed, since it was always the worn-out slaves who were used, rather than the new arrivals.

He released the tied-back curtain across the entry. Deep rose light from the glowweeds shone on the sumptuous interior of the ceremonial hut, belying its outward simplicity.

He lay down on the soft mattress, hoping he was up to the task of being mated by two females in rapid succession. He was to be the first male who would symbolically enact the part of the passive fields of jaram, awaiting and accepting the beneficence of the Deity in mounting them and thus bringing forth the promise of new life. If one of the females became pregnant, it would be considered a sign of Elenath's special favor. If they both conceived, this year's jareesh was certain to be of excellent quality.

Annilee performed her role rather perfunctorily, perhaps thinking of the other males yet to come. Magdael was more enthusiastic in her attentions, forcing every last bit of fluid from his unwilling body. By the time Daveeka left her hut, he was frustrated and exhausted. From the top of the hill, he could see groups of slaves laboring busily under the watchful eyes of the Scheld overseers.

Daveeka left the relative peace of the undisturbed fields around the two sacred huts, following the dirt road back through where the slaves were working. Dodging an oncoming wagon that lumbered slowly forward on creaking wheels, he found himself face to face with one of the Fathers of Family Scheld.

The other male's eyes widened and his ears flicked attentively forward as he recognized Daveeka. "How may I serve you, dhamereth?" he inquired with a bow of the appropriate depth for a male who had only two sons greeting one who carried a female.

Daveeka had more than half expected a challenge. He drew himself up carefully, fixing his ears at an arrogant slope. "I wish to inspect the harvest," he said haughtily.

The Father bowed again. "Of course. Come with me and I'll show you around."

The slaves worked in silent misery, with the only noise being the commands and harsh curses of their overseers. The more alert and healthy ones, which included most of the newcomers, had been set to gathering berries, dumping them into long sacks suspended by straps from their shoulders. Since the red jaram berries grew in tight clumps against the stems beneath the prickly leaves and amongst short thorns, they were difficult to harvest without injuring one's fingers.

The overseers walked among the groups of slaves, exhorting them to work faster, even as the slaves strove to protect their bleeding fingers by picking as cautiously as possible.

"Haste is necessary," the Scheld Father confided matter-of-factly to Daveeka, "since the berries will be at their optimum ripeness only until the third quarn of the nanth. Of course, we'll continue to harvest them after that, but they'll rapidly become over-ripe, yielding only poor quality jareesh."

Daveeka nodded as if he understood and thoroughly approved of the system. Not far ahead of them, a young slave stepped on the edge of his robe and stumbled sideways. As he turned, Daveeka recognized him as Zillah.

Although the youngster caught himself before he could fall, one arm flailed into a tangle of jaram bushes. Zillah let out a scream as the thorns caught in cloth and skin at his wrist. He stood sobbing and trembling, afraid to move lest he should entangle himself even further, as one of the overseers headed his way.

"Clumsy oaf! Get back to work."

"My hand—"

"Well, pull it loose."

"No, please—"

But the overseer had already grasped his upper arm and wrenched him free from the thorns, raking them in deep gashes across the boy's hand as he did so. Zillah stood staring in shock at the blood dripping from his fingers.

"Now get back to work. You have a quota to fill, unless you want to be staked out to watch the sun for a day."

"I … can't," the boy gasped slowly, his ears drooping limply forward. It was clear he was about to faint from the pain.

The overseer glowered, his threat of staking out hanging in the air between them. Nearby slaves cowered away amongst the jaram, making themselves as nearly invisible as possible.

The overseer took Zillah by the back of his robe and shook him roughly. "Lazy scum," he said, beginning to drag the unfortunate youngster towards an approaching wagon, "I'll see that you're—"

But as the guard turned, he found Daveeka blocking his path. "You'll see that this boy is sent back to the compound to have his wounds dressed," Daveeka suggested quietly. "Or you'll answer to me for depriving Elenath of the work of this slave for however long he is incapacitated. I want him treated and back out in the fields by nextnight."

The overseer stared belligerently for a brief moment. Then his eyes fell from Daveeka's face to the collarless neck of his short finely-embroidered black robe, the crystal Shape, and the obvious bulge of his full pouch. He opened and closed his mouth several times in surprise before agreeing, "Yes, dhamereth. It shall be as you have said."

Daveeka stood off to one side as the overseer detailed two of the watching slaves to take Zillah back to the compound. The Scheld Father looked on with narrowed eyes and angled ears. "You shouldn't have done that," he said in an undertone. "It undermines the rightful authority of the overseers."

Daveeka's fingers played with the Shape at his breast. "I am commanded by the Mother of All to resist authority, if it is being misused."

He had deliberately stretched the truth a little, but as he turned and strode back toward the road to the main buildings, the Scheld Father trotted dutifully along at his side. "These males are but slaves, Dher Daveeka. It can be dangerous to show mercy to such trash," he said, ears tipped at the proper angle to express extreme respect. "It impairs their ability to meet the quotas."

Daveeka ignored him.

On the following night, dressed in his most elaborate tunic, Daveeka stood stiffly behind Annilee and Magdael on a raised platform inside the distillery. The heat rising from the boiling vats beat against him in waves, but he did his best to ignore it. The two females looked even less comfortable, their long fur making the heat harder to endure. It was a good thing that the ceremony would be over quickly.

The chief overseer of the Farm approached across the floor below, a huge wicker basket of scarlet jaram berries on his shoulder. He halted before the platform, hoisting the basket up at arm's length. Muscles bulged in his arms and shoulders as he strained to hold it steady.

Mother Magdael took a handful, lifted it, and inspected it with elaborate care. Then she nodded. Raising the first handful of this year's harvest above her head, she recited a brief prayer to Elenath. Then she stepped forward and cast the berries into the boiling water. Mistress Annilee did the same.

Crowded into the stone building, the Farm slaves stood watching in humble obedience. More gathered outside, silent, exhausted, rubbing burning eyes with lacerated fingers after working in the fields until long after sunrise. Their dark goggles provided only a limited amount of protection from the merciless light of day.

Daveeka searched the sea of faces, hoping to spot Teo. A dust-covered figure against the far wall raised one hand to his ear, as if to scratch an itch. Daveeka stared. That might be him.

Annilee hissed a soft command, recalling Daveeka to his duty. On behalf of the daughter in his pouch, he was expected to cast a handful of jaram berries into the vats also.

He approached the edge of the platform, bending clumsily to the basket. A hushed buzz went through the crowd.

Rumor of who he was had doubtless reached all the slaves by now. Seldom would they have had the opportunity to see a dhamereth in person. They would surely have heard of his origins as a Kiari rug-dancer and perhaps even be aware of his unorthodox opinions. Some of them would know what he had done in the fields just the past night, when he had helped Zillah.

As soon as he had tossed his berries into the vat, Annilee stepped up behind him, one hand caressing the back of his neck and his ears in a public display of approval.

A collective sigh swept the crowd. Daveeka wondered how many of them harbored the hope of standing in his place. After all, some of the slaves were only here for the duration of the harvest, while others served relatively short sentences. Not all would remain on the Farms for the rest of their lives. And if such an unlikely person as Daveeka, formerly an overage and childless male, could rise to such heights, might they not at least hope to do the same?

Hope they might, Daveeka reflected bitterly, but the odds were overwhelmingly against them. His apparent success would serve to feed the wistful flames of that hopeless hope, but it would keep them struggling dutifully into the fields night after night, while Magdael and Annilee conducted periodic tours of inspection when they weren't otherwise engaged in mating, each slave harboring the pitiful possibility that he might be noticed and make enough of an impression on one of the females to be sent an Invitation.

And then might one night stand where Daveeka did now, wearing the short robe of a potential Father.

Daveeka had to force his ears not to flatten as he thought of the way he was being used.

Time dragged by slowly, with each night's work taking its toll of slaves. One night, on the pretext of inspecting the facilities, Daveeka toured the infirmary, making sure that Zillah or Teo weren't there. The number of blind and badly injured slaves was horrifying. He stopped here and there, saying an encouraging word whenever he could.

Much to his surprise, he found his ex-servant sitting by the pallet of an unconscious slave, moistening the other male's fur with water to try to counter the effects of sunstroke. Zillah worked awkwardly, one hand still bandaged and in a sling.

"So, is your hand doing well?" Daveeka asked, casually squatting alongside him.

Zillah nodded, keeping his eyes downcast. "It is. I've been assigned to the infirmary until it heals. If I do well, I may be kept on here, instead of being sent back to the fields."

Daveeka nodded while pretending to examine the unconscious male lying in front of him.

"How is Sinda?" Zillah asked.

"Not as skilled as you are, but managing."

Zillah dared a glance, letting his ears perk up as if he'd just received a word of praise from the dhamereth, as indeed he had.

"Dher Daveeka, I must tell you something." Zillah kept his voice low, barely audible above the cries and groans of the other patients.

"Go ahead."

"Fahlin came to see me the night before I left the Thennevar Palace. He told me he'd get me away from the Farms if I'd kill Teo."

Daveeka nodded again, not allowing his ears to flatten with the sudden burst of anger he felt. Instead, he pointed to the slave's leg, as if instructing the servant to spread some water there also.

Zillah dipped his sponge into the water bucket, then ran it slowly over his patient's legs. "I won't do it, Dher Daveeka," he went on. "But I told Fahlin I would, so he wouldn't hire someone else. That should keep Teo safe for a while. I also warned him about it."

Daveeka wanted to give the boy a hug for his bravery and loyalty, but of course he couldn't. "I'll get you out of here, Zillah, if I possibly can. I swear it."

"I know you will, Dher Daveeka." He wrung out his sponge, keeping his eyes on his patient. "I can take a message to Teo, if you want me to. We've managed to get into the same barracks, but we're being careful not to let anyone see that we even know each other, much less that we're friends."

Daveeka thought quickly. He was spending too much time with one patient. People would start wondering why. "Tell Teo to meet me at the southeast edge of the second to last field to the north, during the Festival at the end of the harvest, if he can do it without endangering himself."

Zillah peeked up from the corner of one eye. "I'll tell him.
You can count on me."

Daveeka stood, murmuring carefully, "I know I can."

Knowing that Fahlin had already taken steps to have Teo
murdered did nothing for Daveeka's peace of mind. He could barely
sleep that entire day from worrying.

At sunset, he went as usual to the sacred hut to mate with
Annilee, but he found himself unable to respond, despite her
extensive ministrations. Aware of his obvious unhappiness and
anxiety, Annilee pressed him for the reason. He dared not tell her
all that was bothering him, but he told her of his partner's presence
on the Farms.

"Thiss male you show to me," she commanded.

Daveeka quailed. "Misstress, pleasse. Hyou not harm him?"

"Na, na." Her fingers reached to stroke his ears. "Only Ish
requesst he ve from fieldwork taken, eassier tassk given. Will
pleasse you, yesh?"

"Yesh, Misstress. Much," he said, trying to subdue the
quaver in his voice.

"Goodh. What ve hiss sskills?"

"Marloossh kitchen worker, Misstress. Very good he ve."

Annilee nodded. "Then usseful ve he in sslave kitchen.
Eassy to arrange." She gave him an indulgent look. "Now, ve again
happy, na? Father happy, dhaughter healthy, sssay we."

Daveeka hastened to assure her of his joy, although in reality
it was far more than just his partner's plight that weighed upon his
mind. Once assured of Teo's relative safety, he felt all the worse at
witnessing the suffering of the rest of the slaves, especially as the
harvest drew to a close and the death toll rose steadily.

The slaves were exhausted after two quarns of relentless
labor, bleary-eyed and careless. And the most dangerous stages
came last, as the work parties moved to the far edges of the fields
and approached the forest.

It was only then that they began encountering one of the
more aggressive species of infiltrating vines. While the body of the
plant remained safely in the shelter of the woods, it sent out long,
slender tendrils, which were expert at twining around jaram stalks
and concealing their poisoned ends amongst the berries. When an
incautious rillenu attempted to pluck the berries, he soon found

himself paralyzed by the poison but still fully conscious, while the implanted end of the vine slowly drained the fluid from his body.

Most victims were noticed immediately and rescued, but the poison was so strong that many of them died within a few nights anyway. One unfortunate was only discovered later on, when the stripped jaram stalks were being harvested. Daveeka happened to be nearby at the time and caught a glimpse of the hideously desiccated corpse. It was to haunt his dreams for days to come.

The two slaves who had found the body were staked out the following day face upward in the blazing sun for refusing to go into the fields again when ordered. By evening, they were half mad with pain from their ruined eyes. They were driven out to the harvest regardless, to work, blind. Both fell victim to the vines before the night was out.

No one else followed their example.

By the end of First Nanth, the long misery was almost over. All the jaram berries were packed in sacks in the storehouses, waiting their turn in the distillery. Most of the jaram leaves were spread out to dry and would be further processed into medicinal powders and potions, but some were carefully packed into large glass containers to be kept fresh and potent for pain relief.

A huge pile of thorny stalks lay drying, soon to be fed to the furnaces. More lay bundled in the fields.

The fires in the distillery burned night and day. The jaram seeds, skimmed from the tops of the boiling vats, were hand-sorted, most of them being set aside to be crushed in the mill and ground into a sweet, intoxicating paste. The larger and better ones were packed in bags as luxury items for sale to distant female Families, along with most of the top-quality jareesh, which had now been aged for a year and was ready for consumption.

With the harvest in and the distilling almost finished, it was time for the Festival. On the night of the full moon beginning Second Nanth, the gates of the slave compound stood open and unguarded. Barrels of poor quality jareesh made from last year's crop were brought out and set all around the slave compound, where the slaves were welcome to drink their fill. From the Honored Fathers all the way down to the most wretched slave, everyone had to be allowed to drink as much as he could. It was a ritual requirement.

Guards and overseers kept an unobtrusive eye on the drunken carryings-on, careful to have only a scant cup of diluted liquid themselves. The two females remained secluded in their sacred huts, but no males would be mated that night. None would even dare to approach, since the hills and huts were still taboo. On the following night, the females would move back into the lodging house, preparing themselves for the return to the Thennevar Palace.

Daveeka waited until the celebration was well under way before leaving his room. Everywhere he looked, gray-robed slaves sprawled in unconscious disarray. The only two he saw still on their feet were slipping cautiously off behind a wall, hand in hand and obviously intent on each other. There would doubtless be many others who had done the same thing, seizing this rare chance for privacy and a little free time to give each other their fluid.

With luck Teo would be waiting for him at the designated place. His heart beat faster at the thought of finally being with his partner. It had been so long.

He hiked across the empty fields, careful to avoid stepping on the sharp remnants of jaram stalks protruding from the soil here and there. He had told Teo to be at the southeastern edge of the second to last field to the north. That was far enough from the forest to be beyond the range of the dangerous runner vines, yet also away from the slave compound, which was next to the southern fields. No one would notice them there.

Yet, as he approached, he saw no sign of the other rillenu. Cut jaram stalks stood in tall bundles scattered irregularly around the field. Elnanth was still high in the sky, casting a comfortable light over the pastoral scene. Birds chirped here and there, gleaning the stripped fields for seeds and berries. A rhythmic churring of insects came distantly from the dark forest, just audible to Daveeka's sharp ears.

He shivered. That was one sound he had no desire to hear from closer up.

But where was Teo? Had Zillah failed to get the message to him?

"Psst, Dav! Over here."

Daveeka turned. Teo stood alongside one of the bundles of stalks, his gray slave's robe bright in the moonlight. His ears angled sideways in hesitation.

But there was no hesitation for Daveeka. He ran to his partner, clutching him joyfully in his arms, babbling his name.

"Easy, Dav," Teo gasped, laughing and hugging him at the same time. "You'll crush your daughter, if you don't stop holding me so tightly."

"I don't care, I don't care. Oh, Teo—"

"Come around here. I pulled some bundles of stalks together, and brought a blanket from the compound."

Needing no further urging, Daveeka crawled through the small opening into the sheltered cubbyhole of privacy Teo had constructed. Once inside, they fell again into each other's arms, urgently at first, then more slowly and languorously later on. In between bouts, they shared the small flask of good jareesh Daveeka had brought along. By the last time they gave their fluid to each other, they were quite as drunk as everyone else.

As Elnanth's lower edge was approaching the western horizon, they had fallen into an exhausted sleep, still clutching each other tightly.

"Uh-oh. Dav, wake up! We've got a problem."

Daveeka pried his eyelids open, then immediately shut them again. Bright sunlight slanted through the stalks that surrounded them, searing his eyes with its intensity. He blinked, then squinted his eyes open a fraction. "It's late."

"Yeah. Too late for me to get back inside the slave compound. The gate'll be locked by now."

"I could take you, make them let you in."

"Not a good idea. I've seen what happens to a slave if anyone shows him obvious favoritism. The other slaves resent it, and the overseers come up with reasons to abuse him. I wouldn't want to lose my job in the kitchen, just because people are jealous of our relationship."

"I don't think that would happen." Daveeka cut himself off before he could let slip to Teo that his privilege had been Annilee's doing. He wasn't sure how the other rillenu would feel about that.

"I don't even want to take a chance."

"We can't stay here," Daveeka pointed out, waving at the patch of bright sky directly above them. "Just our luck that it isn't even cloudy or overcast."

"What if we pulled all the bundles in so the tops touched, covered ourselves with the blanket, and kept our eyes closed and covered?"

"Teo—"

"No one would dare question where you were during the day, would they? And I don't think my absence would be noticed, as long as I show up in the kitchen by sunset." He laughed nervously. "Everyone's probably drunk, after Festival. I'll bet a lot of people won't be waking up where they belong."

"You're right. Besides, it would give us more time together, wouldn't it?"

"I was hoping you'd say that."

By midday, it was uncomfortably bright and hot inside the leaning bundles of stalks, but it was bearable. Sunlight poked through the cracks and chinks, but the two rillenus had torn strips from the blanket and wrapped several thicknesses of it around their vulnerable eyes. Every so often, one of them would peek out, squinting cautiously through a narrow opening between the fabric and shading his eyes with both hands, checking that no one was nearby.

Daveeka peeked through watering eyes at the glaring landscape, glancing over the fields and sun-shimmered buildings in the distance. Annilee's hut wasn't far away, atop its low rise. The forest shone with an intense green, uncomfortable but strangely beautiful in its own way. He found himself wishing for eyes adapted to this fierce light.

Then a band of figures appeared briefly near the base of the hill, rising abruptly from the ground and running in a half-stoop towards the entrance to Annilee's hut. They were gone from sight almost as soon as he saw them, leaving Daveeka wondering if he had seen them at all. He almost forgot to replace the bandage over his smarting eyes until Teo pulled him away from the low crawlspace leading into their hideout.

"Teo, something strange—"

"What?"

"Males. Running into Annilee's hut."

"Impossible! Who'd be out in the middle of an empty field in broad daylight, much less around the sacred hut? No male would dare such a thing."

"I saw it."

"It's the light. Your eyes are playing tricks on you."

Daveeka ran the image through his mind again, trying to fetch back the details. Five, maybe six, figures in long robes. Probably wearing protective goggles, certainly with the long peak of a sunvisor protruding from their foreheads. Slaves sent to glean the last scraps of jaram? But they had gone into the hut. No slave would do that.

"I saw it. I'm sure. I've got to go find out what's happening."

"Dav, that's dangerous. The sun's too bright. And the area around the huts is forbidden."

"I can go there. Annilee won't mind, if it's me." He wasn't as sure of this as he tried to sound. "Besides, I'll just look in, see that she's all right. I'll bet I don't even wake her up. The Mistress likes her jareesh. She'll be sound asleep, no doubt."

"I'm coming with you."

"No."

"Just to the hill. I'll stay out of the forbidden area, don't worry. We can take turns watching where we're going, so you don't damage your eyes with too much sun."

Seeing the logic in what Teo suggested, Daveeka let himself be persuaded. They crossed the empty field, first one then the other leading the way as they peeked briefly from under the bandages wrapped around their eyes. Teo stopped at the base of the hill.

"Take care," he whispered, squeezing Daveeka's hand. "I'll be right here, waiting."

His eyes teared uncontrollably, but Daveeka started up the hill. He was probably making a fool of himself over a mirage, but he couldn't shake a sense of menace at the memory of those hasty, stooping figures. Half blind, he moved as silently as he could up to the hut, then carefully drew aside the curtain and stepped into the semi-darkness, lifting his blindfold.

He'd just check to see that Annilee was sleeping undisturbed, make certain he'd been imagining the intruders, then he'd return with Teo to their hideaway, hoping his insane insistence on investigating hadn't damaged their eyes.

Still dazzled by the outside light, it took a moment for his pupils to adjust to the relative darkness. An arm snaked around his throat and he was pulled roughly backwards. Hands grasped his arms before he could begin to struggle. When he opened his mouth to scream, a rag was stuffed between his teeth, cutting short his cry.

Daveeka tried desperately to see his attackers. He could just about make out six males, several of them carrying knives. They wore the pale gray clothing of Farm slaves, with sunvisors pulled low on their foreheads and dark goggles pushed up above their eyes.

He would have demanded an explanation, but the gag in his mouth prevented it. He strained to see past them, to the mattress at the other end of the room where Annilee should be.

One of the tattered band strode over in front of him. The male wasn't tall, but he had the heavy body and muscular build characteristic of those chosen most often by females as guards. A jagged scar ran across his face.

The scarred male placed a hand on Daveeka's belly, tracing the outline of the baby within his pouch, as Daveeka stiffened and tried to pull away. "We're taking this one with us," he ordered brusquely.

"Bruefen, what do we want with him?" one of the others objected. "We've got the female already."

"Brainless oaf! Can't you tell he's carrying a female infant? There's no other reason for a male with a full pouch to be here on the Farms, dressed in fancy clothes and looking so well-groomed and sassy. He's no Scheld Father. Not in that get-up." Bruefen gestured with his knife and the arm slid away from Daveeka's throat. "I'm right, aren't I?"

Unable to speak, Daveeka just nodded.

Bruefen glanced around the inside of the hut. "Tie him and roll him up in that other rug, just like we did with the female."

"We're not prepared for two of them," one of the others objected.

"What's the matter, you can't carry one scrawny male and a female at the same time? Get moving!"

Unable to get his mind to fully grasp what was going on, Daveeka struggled against his captor. Where did they intend to take him? And where was Annilee?

Bruefen pressed the point of his knife against the side of Daveeka's distended pouch. "Make any fuss, and your daughter dies first. Understand?"

Daveeka nodded and went still while his wrists and ankles were bound together, and the rag in his mouth was secured tightly in place.

As two of the kidnappers cleared things off of one of the rugs, Daveeka caught sight of another rug rolled up into a bulky cylinder and tied at both ends. It appeared to be moving slightly. Annilee? In there? Blessed Elenath, who would do such a thing to a female?! It was unthinkable!

They had just laid him down on the other rug and begun to roll it up around him when Teo burst in through the doorway, ripping down the curtain and flooding the room with bright sunlight as he did so. Taking advantage of the momentary confusion, he threw himself on Daveeka's captors.

Bruefen grabbed Teo. His knife flashed and fell, once, twice, stabbing into the smaller male's chest.

Daveeka screamed his partner's name, but nothing more than an inarticulate noise got past the rag in his mouth. Bound hand and foot, Daveeka could do nothing but watch in horror.

The scarred male cut short his attack. Dropping his knife and grabbing Teo by the collar, he knocked his injured opponent's head against the stone doorstep. Teo went limp, blood beginning to soak through the front of his robe.

Breathing hard, Bruefen rose to his feet. He gave Daveeka a close look. "This one a friend of yours?"

Daveeka nodded frantically.

"Thought so. I could have killed him, but I didn't. He's still got a chance to live. Keep that in mind later on." He swept his eyes around the hut. "Okay. Tie our surprise guest up so he can't call for help when he comes around." He nudged Daveeka with a foot. "Then wrap up our second package here and let's move out. The sooner we're in the forest, the better."

CHAPTER 7

The last thing Daveeka saw as the rug closed over him was Teo, with blood seeping down from his forehead and soaking into the short fur of his face.

After that, it was all darkness and movement, as he was dragged over the rough soil while the kidnappers ran across the empty jaram fields. Trying to protect his daughter, he hunched his body over her as best he could, also shielding her with his bound hands, which had been tied in front of him. He could only assume Annilee was getting the same treatment he was.

When he was dropped to the ground, he could just make out Bruefen's voice ordering the others around. "We'll have to put them both in the one hammock, but it should hold. It'll just be harder to carry. I'll take one side, myself. You two take the other. Sheyden, Ailvar, trade off with them. Harizi, you scout ahead. We've got to make it to the river. If anyone spotted us, they'll be right on our trail. Ready? Let's go!"

Although it was now more comfortable lying in the hammock, it was getting harder for Daveeka to breathe. Through the double thickness of the rugs, he could feel Annilee next to him, squirming and struggling. She seemed to be trying to move toward the far end of the hammock, but was that where her feet would be, or her head? Bending his head as far back as he could, he strained to see if there might be an opening. Yes, there was a small patch of light. The kidnappers must have left the ends of the rugs loosely tied on purpose, since they appeared to want their captives alive.

If he could get closer to the opening, there would be more air. With luck, the same was true for Annilee and she was working toward the same goal.

With much effort and care not to put any pressure on his pouch, he was able to worm his way towards the light, at least far enough to breathe easier. He even managed to create a little space in front of his body, so that air would reach his pouch, once he pulled up his tunic and could hold it open as far as he could.

By then, Annilee had moved further in the opposite direction, so it was likely she had reached her goal also.

Daveeka was almost glad that he couldn't see where they were going, if they were headed deeper into the woods. He tried to push that out of his mind, letting himself dwell only on worry about his daughter and his partner, as he was jogged endlessly to and fro. He couldn't handle thinking any further ahead than that.

Eventually, he was lowered to the ground, then released from the suffocating folds of fabric. He caught only the barest glimpse of his surroundings, but the sight of the thick canopy of fearsome trees looming above him and the painful light of day, even filtered through those trees, left him almost grateful when a heavy blindfold was tied over his eyes.

His first concern was for his daughter. His wrists were still tied, but he fumbled beneath his tunic for the opening of his pouch, then lifted the outer part so far open that it hurt, in order that she would get more air. What if it were too late, and she had stopped breathing?! *Mother of All, let her be all right!*

He felt movement, and renewed sucking. *That's right, my little one. Be strong and live!*

Once he had determined that his infant was well, he turned his mind to other things. Listening intently, he could hear Annilee screaming fierce curses at her captors. She must also have been freed from the rug.

Her curses stopped abruptly as Bruefen ordered, "Gag her."

He then bent down over Daveeka, since his voice seemed to come from close by. "Now, dhamereth," he said, with a sarcastic sneer in his tone, "you going to keep quiet, or do I have to gag you too?"

Swallowing to try to ease his dry throat, Daveeka replied, "I'll be quiet."

"Good. At least you've got more sense than the female." He directed his voice to include Annilee. "We're going to be traveling in canoes from here on. Both of you keep in mind that it can be very dangerous if we capsize, especially for someone tied hand and foot. If either one of you gives us the least bit of trouble, I'll make sure you regret it. Got that?"

"Yes," Daveeka said promptly. Annilee just made a muffled sound.

With no further ado, he was lifted into a canoe and placed on the smooth bark of the canoe's bottom as it was paddled out into the river. Since he had heard voices talking about two canoes, he assumed Annilee was in the other one.

He let his pouch close, but kept his tunic pulled up. If he fell into the river, his daughter could drown if his pouch filled with water, so it was better left in its normal position.

From the bits of conversations he overheard and the effort it seemed to be taking, Daveeka guessed that they were going upstream, rather than with the current.

His thoughts wandered idly back to the Thennevar Temple. The huge statue, the feeling of holiness and awe, the night he got his Shape. *My Shape! Is it still there or have I lost it?* He lifted his bound hands to his chest, searching frantically. Yes, there it was, still clipped to his tunic, but it felt loose. He fumbled for the clasp. It had almost lost its grip on the fabric. He secured it carefully.

Already exhausted from being awake most of the previous day with Teo, plus the toll taken by the discomfort and fear of his capture, it wasn't surprising that the monotonous rocking of the canoe lulled him into a light doze.

All of a sudden, the going got more difficult. Amid frantic curses and shouting, the canoes fought their way through a stretch of rapids. At one particularly bad point, Daveeka's canoe knocked against something hard, shuddering and tipping almost to the point of capsizing. Water poured over one side, thoroughly soaking him.

Much to his relief, the canoe righted itself quickly.

Not long after that, the kidnappers reached their destination. By that time, Daveeka was a sodden and miserable mess, shivering with cold and apprehension. He felt the bottom of the canoe grind against the riverbank as it was drawn ashore, then his feet were untied and he was helped onto solid ground, where Bruefen removed the blindfold, saying only, "Show me that you can behave yourself and I'll free your hands later on."

The sun was well below the horizon, and Elnanth's orange light slanted down between the leaves of the trees. Daveeka stared dazedly at his kidnappers as they dragged the canoes far up onto the riverbank, replacing the clumps of bushes that camouflaged their landfall. Still tied, Annilee lay quietly now, water running in gleaming rivulets from her drenched clothing.

Daveeka managed a few tottering steps toward his Mistress before his arm was caught in a rough grip.

"Don't touch the female," Bruefen said. "We'll take care of her ourselves, don't you worry about that. Right, boys?"

The indecent comments and leers that followed the scarred male's remark did nothing to assure Daveeka of Annilee's well-being. He convinced himself they were merely idle boasts. Surely, no male would dare do what some of the comments had implied. Forcing a female to mate was … Well, it was simply unthinkable.

The outlaws hoisted them both once more into the hammock they had used earlier, then carried them down a narrow trail. After threading their way through a dense, tangled thicket of thorny vegetation, they came at last to a space cleared of underbrush, but shaded and overshadowed by tall hurat trees.

Daveeka shuddered as he passed the wide tree trunks. They were covered with thorns fully as long as his fingers. Far above, the smaller branches scraped noisily together as a light evening breeze ruffled the leaves. He still remembered the pain those thorns had inflicted on his feet, at Annilee's hands.

Small circular huts constructed of stone and mortar were interspersed throughout the clearing, most of them overgrown with vines or other vegetation and almost blending into the surrounding forest. Here and there, adult males went about their business, while a couple of young boys played games in the center of the clearing.

Daveeka expected a crowd to gather around the returning kidnappers, but instead everyone seemed to be giving Bruefen and his party a wide berth, all eyes shifting respectfully to the ground as they passed.

Annilee was taken into one of the huts. Daveeka tried to follow her, but Bruefen pulled him away. "Plenty of time for the female later, my friend. Right now, there's someone you need to meet."

He led Daveeka to one of the larger huts, opened a somewhat rickety wooden door, and gestured for him to enter. The inside was lit up with a harsh bluish light from several clumps of gauzy illovex bushes stuck to the walls. The poor light matched the rest of the primitive accoutrements in the rough cabin.

Against the far wall, a seated male glanced up expectantly from behind a table. His eyes widened and his ears pricked up alertly as he caught sight of Daveeka.

"So, Bruefen, how did you make out? What have you brought us?" he asked.

"Your plan worked perfectly, Clarlaw. We got a female, just as you said we would. And we got this male carrying an infant, as an extra bonus. He walked in on us just as we were leaving, so I took him along." Bruefen pulled a small leather bag from his pocket. "We also stole some excellent jaram seeds from the female's hut. I kept the biggest ones aside for you, but we have three bags in all."

Clarlaw rose to his feet, grimacing as if changing position was painful to him. He took the bulging bag, hefting it with apparent satisfaction before placing it on the table. He was extremely handsome, his ears small and his fur long and fine-textured, for a male.

He looked Daveeka over, taking in the fancy, if now somewhat bedraggled, tunic and the obvious swell of an infant in his pouch. When his eye fell on the crystal Shape at Daveeka's breast, one ear swiveled into an angle of ironic inquiry. "Ve dhamereth, na?" he asked in poorly accented femalespeech.

Daveeka drew himself up with an attempt at dignity. "Truth ve, that I ve dhamereth. Ssuch treatment as have I received from thiss male—" he glared at Bruefen "—ve unlawful."

Clarlaw laughed. "Excellent! He even speaks their language," he remarked to Bruefen, who appeared not the least bit discomfited by Daveeka's haughty words. Then Clarlaw turned once again to Daveeka. "When was your daughter to be taken? Soon, no?"

"Second Nanth. Why?"

Clarlaw nodded but ignored his question. "Bruefen, you did marvelously well. One adult female, and one new daughter. I couldn't have hoped for more."

The scarred male beamed under his leader's praise, but said nothing.

"I'll see that you're well rewarded for this," Clarlaw went on. "But right now, let's make our guest comfortable. He's dripping wet, and probably hungry and thirsty as well. Surely we can find a fresh tunic for him, and he'll need heavy leggings if he's to live here in the forest." Daveeka tried to say he had no intention of living here in the forest, but Clarlaw cut him off with a gesture. "Also, something to eat and drink, eh?"

With a short nod of understanding, Bruefen left the hut.

Clarlaw waved a hand at the mattress along one wall of the hut. "There's a blanket over there, if you'd like to take off that wet tunic and wrap up." He sat down once again on his cushions, emptied the leather bag on the table, and began sorting carefully through the shiny blood-red jaram seeds.

Meanwhile, Daveeka did as the other male suggested, pulling off his sodden tunic and shaking as much of the moisture as he could from his fur. The blanket was woven of coarse timmen fibers. It was uncomfortably scratchy against his tender fingers, but it provided some welcome warmth. He held his Shape unobtrusively in one hand.

Clearing his throat to get Clarlaw's attention, Daveeka asked, "You're the leader here?"

"That's right."

"I sort of expected it to be Bruefen."

"Bruefen's the one with the muscle. I'm the one with the brains." Clarlaw pushed thc last seed into its pile and looked over at Daveeka. His eyes stopped abruptly at the other rillenu's Kiari shoes. One small ear cocked forward in inquiry. "You have a name, dancer?"

"Daveeka. Daveeka sardhan Marloosh-Sharemmi."

"So, Daveeka, suppose you tell me about yourself."

Despite all that had happened, Daveeka found himself taking a liking to the other male. By the time Bruefen returned, he had given Clarlaw a brief summary of how it had come about that he had Received a daughter.

Bruefen carried a tray heaped with dark bread and fruit in one hand. With the other arm, he juggled a pile of clothing and a young child. At Clarlaw's nod, he set down the tray and dumped the pile of well-worn but serviceable clothing onto the mattress, inviting Daveeka to take his choice, then made himself comfortable also, setting his son down next to him.

As Daveeka sorted gingerly through the clothes, the baby began to whimper. Bruefen reclined on one side and lifted the front of his tunic, holding his pouch open so his son could crawl inside to nurse. The baby was too big to fit its entire body into the pouch, but it could still get its head and shoulders inside. An infant of that size would soon be old enough to be weaned.

It wasn't until Daveeka had shrugged into a faded green tunic and attached the clasp holding his Shape at his neck, pulled on leg covers, and begun to eat a chunk of bread that he realized the cozy little scene of a Father nursing his son wasn't exactly as it appeared. The baby was very dark, with fine and fluffy fur. And its ears had seemed awfully short.

"That's a female!" Daveeka exclaimed, almost choking on a mouthful of bread.

Bruefen nodded, while he and Clarlaw exchanged a glance. "Of course. Why shouldn't it be?" the renegade leader asked.

"Males don't keep their daughters …” Daveeka stopped, staring from one to another in puzzlement. The baby, disturbed by the commotion, withdrew her head from her Father's pouch and stared at Daveeka with wide dark eyes. "Her eyes are open.”

"Most babies' eyes are open when they're fourteen nanths old," Bruefen pointed out, as if this were the most natural thing in the world.

"Yes, but … You mean, you let …?"

"What would you like us to do? Give the baby to a female?" Clarlaw asked with a short laugh. "That's hardly possible, considering that the only adult female we have is the one Bruefen just brought us. Right now, that one has more to worry about than stealing our babies."

"If Mistress Annilee is the only female you have, where did you get the baby?"

"You ask a lot of questions, for a new arrival," Bruefen growled, his ears flattening. "Perhaps you shouldn't be so curious."

"No, that's all right. Let him ask. We want his cooperation, not his resentment." Clarlaw turned to Daveeka. "The little one is Bruefen's daughter, Varri. Her mother died shortly after the birthing, almost a year ago. She was quite old when we captured her, so many of her infants weren't vigorous enough to survive. We were extremely lucky to get a female infant."

"Yeah," Bruefen put in. "She couldn't stand knowing she had borne a daughter for us. Before that, she had only given us sons."

Clarlaw silenced him with a glance, ears slanting slightly. "We're hoping the new female will give us many children," he said smoothly. "She is perhaps the mother of your daughter?"

Daveeka nodded.

"I thought as much."

Daveeka looked at Varri, who had snuggled against Bruefen's chest and lay watching the others. "Will I be allowed to keep my daughter?"

"Sure. Why not? It's much better for the baby that way. At least, that's what we think. Look at Varri. Have you ever seen such a strong female infant at that age?"

Daveeka couldn't answer, since he'd never even seen a female of that age.

"We don't have many infants, but of the ones who survive their first two quarns in the pouch, very few die after that," Bruefen added. Although he seemed proud of having a daughter, he wasn't holding her and stroking her, as would be natural under the circumstances. Daveeka had seen males snuggle their pet scha'adis with more apparent affection than Bruefen showed for his child.

But that didn't matter. What was important was that Daveeka no longer had to face the taking of his own infant. A great weight lifted from his shoulders with that realization. "I think I'm going to like it here," he said cheerfully, helping himself to more bread.

After they had eaten, Clarlaw invited Daveeka to live in his hut with him for the time being. "Perhaps you'd like to rest?" he added. "You must be exhausted. I'll have another mattress brought in. Not very luxurious quarters for our honored guest, but the best we can do."

Daveeka acquiesced gratefully. He'd gotten precious little sleep the day before, between being with Teo in the fields and then being carried away by the kidnappers.

Teo. Cold fingers closed around his heart at the thought of his partner. *Did he still live?* It was possible, if he had been discovered in time and his wounds had been properly tended.

But Daveeka couldn't think about that now. He had to deal with the present situation, not waste his energy in vain worries.

"I'll cover the illovex so it'll be nice and dark," Clarlaw offered, "and you can take a nap. Bruefen and I have things to do outside."

Daveeka flopped down wearily as the other male draped a piece of dark fabric over the blue-glowing fuzzy bush clinging to one of the walls, plunging the hut into restful darkness.

Clarlaw waved Bruefen out the door, then hesitated, as if he wanted to leave but had something he had to say first. "Don't you think you'd better clean out your pouch before you go to sleep?"

"Huh?"

"Your pouch. You know ..." Clarlaw's voice in the darkness held an edge of vague embarrassment.

"I'm not allowed to touch my daughter. Mistress Annilee always ... " Then he stopped. "Where is she?"

"The female? Oh, she's perfectly safe. Don't worry about her. Do you really mean you've never cleaned your pouch or laid a finger on your own daughter, just because the females told you not to?"

Daveeka admitted he hadn't, feeling almost ashamed of his obedience.

"Well, you'd better learn to do it yourself. There won't be any females keeping tabs on you here." Clarlaw left the hut, pulling the door closed behind him.

Lying there in the dark, Daveeka thought about Clarlaw's words. He'd love to caress his daughter, but did he dare?

Why not? Annilee would never know the difference. And his pouch did need cleaning.

He slid one hand hesitantly under his borrowed tunic and into his pouch. He wouldn't hurt the baby. After all, if he carried a son, he would be doing this all the time.

His fingers groped blindly for the child's body. It felt strange to have his own hand touching the inside of his pouch. A peculiar double awareness of sensation, both from the interior surfaces and from his fingertips. Not bad. Nice, in fact. No wonder Teo enjoyed it so much.

One finger encountered the soft fuzz of the baby's body. He stroked gently. The infant squirmed with alarmed restlessness, not accustomed to his touch. Her mouth clamped reflexively on the teat deep in her throat. Not wanting to further frighten her, Daveeka kept his fingers well away from her head and face.

The little body felt so warm and appealing, fitting so nicely against the palm of his hand. He had to remind himself that too much handling wasn't good for an infant. Just a little longer, that's all. Then he'd clean out the pellets and leave her in peace.

She settled down, some of the tension already going out of the small curled-up body. It wouldn't take long for her to become used to his touch, if he did it regularly.

Giving her a final caress, Daveeka carefully removed the fecal pellets from the bottom of his pouch. It wasn't long before he fell into an exhausted sleep.

By the time he woke up, it was already night again. His fancy tunic hung beside the bed, now clean and dry, even if somewhat the worse for wear. It also had a long piece of what appeared to be heavy fabric sewn all the way around its lower edge.

Clarlaw sat on a pillow at the table, eating the first meal of the night. He watched Daveeka as he got up and examined the addition to his tunic.

"You'll need that, Dav, even if you keep to our clearing. Most of the dangerous plants in this area are low to the ground, so your legs need to be well protected. You'd also be better off wearing the leg covers we gave you, instead of those flimsy things you had on when you arrived, for the same reason."

"Won't that long skirt make it harder for my daughter to get air?"

The older male shrugged. "Doesn't seem to matter much to our infants. Out here, the biggest threat they face is dying along with their fathers, if they're stung by something poisonous."

"I'll take your advice," Daveeka replied, reaching for the heavy leg covers.

Once he was dressed, he sat down with Clarlaw and helped himself to some food.

"Dav, may I ask you a question?"

His mouth full, Daveeka nodded.

"I know that's a complex Shape, but I don't know the meaning."

"Respectful Disagreement with Established Authority."

Clarlaw's ears turned tightly forward with surprise, but all he said was "Uhmm. Never heard of that one before. Doesn't seem like the sort of thing one would expect in a ritual invented by females.”

Daveeka had never thought of it that way. “There are some other Shapes that are rather unusual also. The entire ceremony was created so long ago that no one knows who invented it.”

“Hmph. Not likely that any males were involved, no matter when it happened.”

During the next several nights, the outlaw leader acted as Daveeka's host, showing him around the settlement and introducing him to some of the other males. He pointed out the foraging parties setting out into the woods each night, but cautioned Daveeka against leaving the clearing himself until he had learned woodcraft.

"Very easy to die out there, if you don't know what you're doing. Besides, it isn't worth risking your daughter's life. Let the others do the foraging."

Daveeka was more than happy to leave the forest to those who wanted to enter it. He wandered around the little village. It seemed peaceful enough. There appeared to be a good number of adult males, all busily engaged in various tasks ranging from preparing food to weaving the coarse timmen cloth that made up the bulk of the clothing. Although he saw no males with full pouches or very young infants, there were some boys of varying ages. The older ones worked with the adults, while the younger ones and the toddlers played nearby. Surprisingly, Bruefen was among them, holding onto Varri as she tried to take her first steps.

Clarlaw headed over toward his second in command. “She’s doing very well, isn’t she?” he remarked to Daveeka.

“I never expected him to be there, playing with the children.”

“Why not? Someone has to be watching over the little ones to be sure of their safety.”

They stood there watching for a short time.

"Where did all of your people come from?" Daveeka asked at last.

"Our adults are runaway slaves from the Farms. But the boys have been born here, courtesy of our last female. We took her along with us when we first fled from the Farms.” His ears perked up at the thought. “Those were the good times, weren’t they, Bruefen? We thought we’d started an uprising, but it turned out that very few males followed our example. They were too afraid of the forest to make a break for freedom."

"Cowards," Bruefen declared contemptuously. "They deserve to be slaves."

"No one deserves to be a slave," Clarlaw replied.

Bruefen gave a disgusted snort, but didn't argue with his leader.

Any slave who could make it this deep into the forest surely had to know a lot about survival, considering the vast profusion of carnivorous and poisonous plants, not to mention the venomous animals, in the woods. Daveeka admitted to himself that fleeing into that terrifying wilderness wasn't something he himself would have dared to try, Farm or no Farm. By Bruefen's standards, that made him a coward.

"So you started all this?" Daveeka asked Clarlaw, waving his hand around at the settlement.

"We did. Me, Bruefen, Smarro, and Kobali, who died early on. It's been almost twelve years that we've been here."

"And the females leave you alone?"

Bruefen shrugged. "They got tired of losing every bunch of slaves they sent out to get us. We didn't even have to fight. The forest took care of that for us. Anyone who showed a particular talent for surviving and got as far as our village was invited to join us or die. Most of them were very happy to join us."

"Just as we hope you will be," Clarlaw added. "Once you see what we're like."

He led Daveeka over to the far perimeter of the clearing, where a new hut was under construction. They watched from a safe distance, but Clarlaw cautioned him to stay well away from the edge of the forest. Wearing heavily padded clothing, a work party hacked cautiously at a large bush, keeping a wary eye on the bush itself, the ground, and the overhanging trees even as they sawed off the branches.

"The most dangerous thing you can do to the forest is try to cut it down. Any sort of destruction seems to draw predators, both plants and animals," the renegade leader pointed out. "You can't be too careful, when you're actually clearing out underbrush. We learned that lesson the hard way."

Daveeka nodded. That would explain why the mortality rate on the Farms was so high, while the outlaws seemed able to survive fairly well even this deep in the forest. On the Farms, they were constantly trying to clear new land, in order to increase the jaram crop.

"If ever you have reason to be in the woods," Clarlaw went on, "be sure you do the least damage possible and move without disturbing anything. Once you learn how to do it, it isn't all that dangerous, but it's essential to realize you can't just go stomping around all over the place."

One of the work party yelled a sharp warning even as his machete sliced quickly through a slithering tendril of vine almost hidden in the dust and dead leaves on the ground. Everyone jumped back, and Clarlaw pulled Daveeka several paces backward as well.

The workers stared in terror at the slender vine, its severed end still twitching feebly. Leaving Varri behind, Bruefen rushed over immediately. "Well, what is it? Why are you all just standing around?" he demanded.

One of them pointed to the vine. The attached end writhed around uncertainly at ground level, as if seeking the rest of itself.

"Oh, is that all?" Wrapping the folds of his long tunic around his hands, he grabbed the vine, braced himself, and gave a hard tug. Surprisingly strong for its size, the vine held for a moment, stretching and quivering. It led off into the thick underbrush beyond the clearing.

Then something came loose. Bruefen staggered backwards with the sudden release of tension, but kept his footing. He reeled in a twitching mass of what looked like tangled root, ignoring the way everyone else moved rapidly away. As soon as it was all well clear of the bushes, he growled to the worker holding the machete, "Well, don't just stare at it. Kill the thing."

Gathering his courage, the wielder of the machete approached close enough to chop the predatory plant to bits. The pieces were gathered together very carefully and then tossed into a small cookfire nearby.

The excitement over, Bruefen scooped up his daughter and came back to Daveeka and Clarlaw. "That's one less jinko vine to poison us, eh?" he remarked, evidently quite pleased with himself. "What's the matter, Daveeka? Your ears look a little limp. Did it scare you?"

"I'm not used to them, that's all." Daveeka turned to Clarlaw, trying to ignore Bruefen's bluff amusement. He decided to change the subject. "So where is Mistress Annilee?"

"Oh, is that her name? So far, she's refused to even tell us that much. All she does is curse and try to fight us off."

"Don't pay any attention to Bruefen, Dav. In time, she'll come around. After all, it's not like she has any other choice." Clarlaw pointed to a hut near the middle of the clearing. "She's over there."

"May I see her?"

The two outlaw males exchanged a glance. Clarlaw nodded. They headed toward the hut.

"I'll let you look through the peephole, but that's it. Keep in mind that she's been refusing to accept anything but drinking water from us, so her condition isn't entirely our fault."

"That's not going to last much longer," the other male growled.

"Bruefen," Clarlaw said sternly.

"Yeah, yeah. I know."

Clarlaw slid open the small hole in the door, then gestured Daveeka forward.

Annilee sat hunched over at the far end of the hut. Her robe was badly soiled, her long fur tangled and knotted wherever it was visible. Her wrists were tied, but there was a substantial length of rope left between them, so she could still use her hands. A small clump of illovex provided some illumination, but it wasn't much.

When she saw that the peephole was open, her ears flattened and her eyes flashed fury. She spat in the direction of the doorway, then deliberately turned her back on them.

A few more nights passed and Daveeka was beginning to adjust to life in the outlaw camp. However, he noticed that he was never left entirely alone. No matter what he did, either Clarlaw or Bruefen seemed always to be nearby. Possibly the renegades didn't quite trust him as yet, but time would doubtless solve that problem. No need to complain.

One quarn into First Nanth, on the night of the first quarter of Elnanth, Clarlaw drew Daveeka down alongside him on a pile of cushions, asking casually, "So, are you glad that Bruefen brought you here?"

"I think so. I'm certainly grateful that my daughter won't be taken."

Clarlaw took a cup from the table and held it out to him. It was filled with small jaram seeds. Daveeka had never had the opportunity to chew the seeds. The large ones were highly esteemed, but even small ones like this were more potent than low-quality jareesh. He took one and nibbled on it experimentally.

"I figured you'd see things our way. There might well be a respected position for you here, considering you're a Kiari priest and all. There are those who might want to learn the dances, if you'd be willing to teach."

"I'd be happy to."

Clarlaw crushed a seed between his teeth. "You seem an intelligent sort. Yes, there could definitely be a place for you. You wouldn't have to pick timmen, or weave it, or do any of the dangerous jobs, like foraging."

"Clarlaw, there's one thing I'd like to know. How is Mistress Annilee doing?"

"Why do you ask?"

"Well, she's the Mother of the baby in my pouch, after all. And she didn't look too good when I last saw her, so I'm worried."

The other rillenu shrugged. "It's no big secret. She's fine, but she's still being held in isolation, due to her extremely uncooperative behavior, which you yourself have witnessed."

"I want to see her again." Daveeka knew he was being stubborn, but something didn't ring entirely true in what Clarlaw said. The other male lifted the cup of seeds once again, so Daveeka spat out the husk of the first one and took another.

"About Mistress Annilee … " he persisted. But already his stomach blazed with the warmth of the pure jaram essence and it took a distinct effort to keep his mind on the female's whereabouts.

"I've already told you, she's fine." Clarlaw waved one hand in an airy gesture, dismissing the subject.

"I want to see her." Emboldened by the cheerful haze that spread through his brain, Daveeka helped himself to yet another jaram seed. This time someone was going to take him seriously, or he'd know the reason why.

Clarlaw leaned back against the cushions, still chewing his first seed. "The female is otherwise occupied just now, Dav. It would not be wise—"

"Well, she can just stop whatever she's doing and take time to talk to me," he retorted, satisfied that he was finally getting a chance to assert himself.

Clarlaw's ears tipped into an angle of gentle amusement. "That isn't possible. Maybe later on tonight."

"Now," Daveeka insisted, rising unsteadily to his feet.

Clarlaw gave an elaborate sigh. "Very well." He rose also, picking up the cup and offering Daveeka another seed.

In some part of his mind, Daveeka knew full well that he'd had more than enough already, but he stuck a fresh seed in his mouth anyway.

Clarlaw took his arm, unobtrusively steadying him on his feet as he guided him out the door and over to the hut. This time, a guard sat in front of the door.

Surprised, the guard leapt to his feet. Clarlaw gestured and the male lifted the bar from across the door, pushing it open for them. Daveeka strode inside, letting go of Clarlaw's arm.

The scene that greeted his eyes as he walked in caused him to stop dead in his tracks. His mouth sagged open in horrified astonishment.

Stark naked, Annilee was on her knees, buttocks raised and face pressed to the floor. Smarro crouched by her head, gripping her ears tightly, while Bruefen knelt behind her, holding her hips and thrusting his groin roughly against Annilee's rump.

Daveeka's mind couldn't quite grasp what his eyes saw. Had the scarred male really forced his entire penile sheath into her, not just the extended part of his penis, which was all the females would ever willingly accept?

Annilee was struggling to pull away, but Smarro twisted her tender ears and ground her face into the dirt floor, smothering her cries of pain.

"Not quite so high and mighty now, is she, Dav?" Clarlaw asked softly. "Want to be next?"

Daveeka shook his head. Mate a female against her will? And so brutally? Never! Why, it was an unthinkable abomination!

But it couldn't be unthinkable, since Bruefen was doing it. He shrank back against the wall of the hut, thoughts coming dull and sodden through the haze brought on by the jaram seeds. As Bruefen finished and pulled free, Daveeka could see Annilee's genitals shamefully exposed. She was bleeding, the flesh around her opening torn raggedly.

"What's the matter? Never seen a female before?" Bruefen said mockingly, as Daveeka stared in shock.

Then Smarro and Bruefen traded places.

"Stop it," Daveeka gasped.

"Stop?" Clarlaw laughed. "What for? How do you expect her to get pregnant? Besides, it's good for morale. Being permitted to spend a little time in here with the female makes an excellent reward."

All of a sudden, Annilee squirmed out of Bruefen's grip. She twisted around, one hand reaching for her attacker's eyes. Her left ear oozed blood from a jagged tear.

Bruefen was too fast for her. He fetched the young female a resounding blow across the face, before he once again took hold of her ears and pinned her down. The two males laughed. Smarro resumed what he had been doing.

"Of course," Clarlaw remarked with apparent unconcern, "this new one is going to have to learn to be more cooperative. A few more sessions like this should take some of the fight out of her." He glanced at Daveeka. "Sure you don't want to give it a try?"

"No! No, I couldn't."

Bruefen tapped Smarro on the shoulder, jerking his head toward Daveeka. Smarro nodded, gave a few more energetic thrusts, then disengaged from Annilee and gestured magnanimously for Daveeka to take his place. "Sure you could. Come on. She's all ready for you. We'll hold her still, don't worry."

Daveeka shook his head. "I couldn't," he said again.

"What's the matter? Can't get it out? Maybe you belong down on your knees, just like the female?" Smarro jeered. He sidled over next to Daveeka, sliding his hand up under Daveeka's tunic. "Maybe I should just help you a little, eh?"

Breaking out of his shocked paralysis, Daveeka pushed the other male away. The shameful truth was that he was aroused.

Bruefen seemed quite amused. "Come on, dhamereth. How often have the females taken you to the mating room, whether you wanted it or not?"

"They didn't force me or beat me."

"No? What do you think would have happened had you refused?"

"Annilee never hurt …" he started to protest. The memory of Annilee wielding the hurat wand, lacerating his feet because he had dared defy Marlieth, flashed into his mind.

Something flared deep red inside Daveeka then, ripping through his civilized constraints and filling him with a burning hatred. Annilee was getting only what she deserved, what all females deserved. They did nothing but callously use the males they mated, leaving them frustrated and unsatisfied.

Yes. He would have her, here, like this. It would serve her right. Let a female see how it feels, for a change. Why not?

Pushing away from the wall, he walked stiffly across the room. Somewhat self-conscious due to the bulge of the baby in his pouch, he raised the skirt of his tunic only far enough to allow him access to Annilee as he knelt clumsily between her legs. Under other circumstances, he would have been disgusted with the sticky mess of blood and fluid oozing from her torn opening, but now it only spurred him on. He would teach her a lesson, let her know how it felt to be used and then tossed aside like trash.

Thrusting his hips forward, he drove himself into her mercilessly, as far as he could, hoping to cause more pain. Oh, yes, let it hurt!

"Lift her head," he commanded harshly. "I want her to know who's doing this."

Bruefen complied, jerking Annilee's face up from the ground and turning her to look at Daveeka.

Her eyes went wide as she recognized him. Blood from her mangled ear seeped between Bruefen's fingers and soaked into the short fur of her face. Her breath rasped between her teeth as she sucked in air. Her face contorted with disgust and once again, she spat at him.

She missed, but this show of resistance only led Daveeka to drive himself even harder against her, his hands grasping the long fur at her sides and yanking at it cruelly. "Honored Misstresss," he hissed in mocking femalespeech, "where now ve hyour privilege and hyour power?"

Annilee stopped struggling then. For a long moment, she only stared at him. Her eyes fluttered closed and she drew a deep breath. When she opened them again, Daveeka couldn't tell if he saw triumph or defeat reflected in their dark depths.

"Ability to causse pain na ssame as to ve right, Daveecha," she said in a strangled whisper as she threw his own words back at him. "Na sso?"

CHAPTER 8

Annilee laughed, a harsh and broken sound in the sudden silence.

Daveeka's lust died with that laugh. He broke free and ran from the hut, followed by the sound of Bruefen's mocking shouts.

How could he have done such a thing? He had proven himself capable of the same cruelty the females had shown to him, the same viciousness he had so self-righteously condemned in Mother Marlieth. How could he have found it enjoyable to inflict pain on someone else?

And yet, it had been enjoyable. Revenge was not without pleasure. It had felt good, in a way that hadn't been merely sexual. The truth was that he wanted to humiliate Annilee, break her haughty pride, do to her as had been done to him.

And why shouldn't he? Didn't the females deserve it?

Perhaps they did. But in order to take revenge, he had to become as vicious as Marlieth, as cruel as Bruefen and Smarro.

But he had enjoyed it. It was such a relief, after having been a victim all his life.

But did that make it right?

Then a further thought occurred to Daveeka. He and Annilee had been here for several nights now. This was probably not the first time she had been raped. It must have been happening repeatedly.

The image of Annilee's exposed genitals flashed across his mind, but this time all he could think of was how it must have felt, raw hurting flesh torn a bit further with each callous thrust. Suddenly, it was no more sexually exciting to him than the memory of having his feet slashed with hurat thorns.

He couldn't stop his mind from dwelling on such gruesome images. His head swam and his stomach lurched. He propped himself against the side of the hut with one hand and vomited.

"You have little stomach for contact with females, Daveeka?" Clarlaw's voice was soft, barely audible above the churring of insects in the woods. "Or is it only this particular female who upsets you?"

"It's not right," Daveeka said, wiping his mouth on his sleeve.

"Right?" The outlaw's voice was bitter. He laid a hand on Daveeka's arm. "Come to my hut, and I'll show you what the females consider right where males are concerned. Then you can tell me how much consideration they deserve."

Daveeka let himself be led inside. Standing in the harsh glow of the illovex on the wall, the renegade leader abruptly pulled up the front of his tunic, exposing his pouch to Daveeka's view.

Only Clarlaw didn't have a pouch. A ragged dark scar outlined the place where the outer wall should have joined his body. At the bottom, just above the base of his penile sheath, where the skin and muscle of the pouch would have been thickest, the scarred area was almost the width of Daveeka's hand, puckered and raised as if it hadn't healed well.

His teat was exposed, the skin around it hanging slack and covered with fine fur. The teat itself looked unhealthy. It was stretched and elongated, as if it hadn't shrunk back to normal size after lactation had ceased.

The enormity of what had been done to the other male slowly sank into Daveeka's mind. This had been no accidental injury. The outer wall of his pouch had been deliberately excised.

Daveeka imagined the knife slicing through living flesh, the awful pain and terror. He felt his stomach lurch and his ears begin to ring. He sat down heavily on his mattress, lowering his head. As had happened previously with Annilee, his mind wouldn't stop showing him the bloody flesh being cut away, the raw wound gaping open.

"So, you seem to have a pretty clear idea of what they did to me, don't you?" Clarlaw remarked calmly. "You needn't get sick again. I was drugged pretty well unconscious at the time. Only came to a little as they were stitching me up. It didn't really hurt a lot until later."

He lowered his robe and sat down next to Daveeka, leaning back against the wall and watching the other male through half-closed eyes. "Didn't you ever wonder what the females use to feed their newly-taken daughters? Do you imagine they'd give kullup milk to such a young infant?" He gave a short laugh. "And didn't you wonder what happened to potential Fathers whose sons died in their pouches, if they never returned from the obligatory examination in the females' Palace?"

"But why excise the pouch wall that way?" he asked sickly.

"Makes it much easier to milk us, that's all," Clarlaw said. "Of course, a certain number of males don't survive the excision, and some who do stop lactating as a result of the shock, but what do the females care? There are always others to be found. It doesn't have to be a failed Father. There are other ways to induce lactation in childless males. It's just more convenient to use someone who's already producing an abundant supply."

Daveeka remembered Teo, and squeezed his eyes tightly closed. Mother of All, had that almost happened to his own partner?

"When you stop producing milk," Clarlaw went on, "you're simply sent to the Farms, where you don't usually last too long. I spent five years in the Thennevar Palace. In all that time, I saw nothing but the four walls of my cell. I was well fed and cared for, just as a valuable kullup might be. Four times each night and twice each day, specially-trained servants came and milked me. Sometimes young females were brought by their teachers for a lesson in male anatomy. We were good subjects, because it was easy to see what the inside of a pouch looked like, without the outer wall to get in the way."

"How many of you were there?" Daveeka asked, unable to quite absorb this further horror.

"I'm not sure. I'd hear doors being opened, sometimes voices screaming or pleading. It seemed like maybe three or four others at any one time. I think I lasted longer than most."

What have we males ever done to deserve all this? Daveeka thought wretchedly. *Elenath, Mother of All: Why?* He hugged his knees to his chest. Resting his forehead on his crossed arms, he began to cry.

Clarlaw sat in silence until the other rillenu had recovered his composure. "Do you still say the female deserves our care and consideration, my friend?" he asked at last.

"Annilee didn't do anything. It isn't her fault." But Daveeka wasn't entirely sure he believed it himself.

"She is a female. Females mistreat males. It's the way they are."

Daveeka shook his head, unable to accept this. Females were wise and beneficent, made in the image of Elenath. Females were ...

"Whose hand held the hurat stick that cut your feet, Daveeka?" Clarlaw challenged, seeing his vacillation.

"She didn't want to. Her Mother ..."

Clarlaw heaved an exasperated sigh.

Daveeka laid a hand on the other male's arm. "Let me talk to Mistress Annilee. Alone. Maybe I can convince her to be more cooperative. She likes me. She'll listen to reason."

Clarlaw snorted and made a dismissive gesture. "Somehow I doubt that she'll listen to anything you have to say, after what you just did to her. Besides, it's not necessary. She'll learn soon enough."

"What harm could it do?"

"All right, all right, talk to her, if that's what you want! But not just now. I have a feeling she's still ... engaged."

"You could stop them, call them off."

"I could, but I won't." Clarlaw leaned closer. "Nextnight you can see her, if you insist. Honestly, Daveeka, I had much higher hopes for you than this. I hadn't expected one of the Kiari to be so squeamish."

"I've seen males die in the Dance, Clarlaw. But that's different. We don't torture people."

"Neither do we." Tilting his ears ironically, the outlaw leader added, "It's just that females aren't people. In time, you'll come to realize that."

Placing a hand on Daveeka's knee, the outlaw leader moved over until his thigh was against Daveeka's. "As the father of a daughter, you'll be in a position of respect and honor amongst us. If you can convince our new female to become more cooperative, that in itself would be a much appreciated service."

"Her name is Mistress Annilee," Daveeka pointed out, not really sure where Clarlaw was going with all this.

"Annilee, then, if you prefer. If she's still a Mistress,—" he moved his hand up to rest lightly over the bulge in Daveeka's pouch "—this would be her first daughter. Am I right?"

"Yes." He tensed at the touch, but Clarlaw was careful, using the barest amount of pressure.

"I won't hurt her, Dav. I know only too well what it's like." His hand moved down and under the hem of the tunic, slowly pushing it up. Daveeka froze as he felt Clarlaw's fingertips barely grazing the fur just below his pouch, making small circular motions in a gradually expanding circle. "You weren't quite finished with the female, were you? You're still upset over that unfortunate interruption in what you were doing. You'll feel better if you can get past all that." His fingers brushed the base of Daveeka's sheath, which had never entirely lost its fullness. "You didn't release your fluid, did you? I could help you with that, you know."

Daveeka shuddered as the fingers traced their way slowly up to the end of his sheath, where the tip of his penis was just now beginning to extend. Clarlaw's other hand stroked the inside of his thigh. Daveeka spread his legs, and Clarlaw moved to kneel between them.

"I'll show you how we do it here, Dav. Don't worry, you'll like it."

Much to Daveeka's surprise, Clarlaw put his mouth over the end of his sheath, licking and sucking gently. He started to protest. "This isn't —"

"Normal?" Clarlaw replied, removing his mouth for a moment to grin at the other male. "Who says? Your precious females? I'll bet all you've ever done with another male is use your hands, right?"

His eyes tightly closed and his body tense with desire, Daveeka gave a stiff nod. His penis had extended even further. All he could think of was how good that warm mouth had felt, tight around him.

"Oh, yeah," Clarlaw said in triumph, leaning down and enclosing the entire length of the throbbing brown shaft in his mouth. It didn't take very much effort to encourage Daveeka to release his fluid.

Nextnight, as promised, Daveeka was admitted to Annilee's hut alone. She sat slumped dejectedly on a very worn mattress, wearing nothing but a tattered blanket wrapped around her shoulders. Her torn ear was caked with blood and one side of her face was swollen badly. She didn't bother to get to her feet as he came into the room.

"Well, look who's here," she remarked with bitter sarcasm. "Are you going to rape me again? If so, you'd better go get a few others to hold me down. Or did you imagine I'd be so glad to see you that I'd fall to my knees in ecstasy?"

"Mistress Annilee, that isn't my intention at all."

She turned her battered face away. "Oh? It's been the intention of every other male who's come through that door."

"Not me. I just want to talk to you."

"So talk."

He squatted alongside her. He could see no evidence of food or a meal tray, although there was a pitcher of water over in one corner. "Have you had anything to eat?"

She shook her head. "Nothing but a bit of gruel each evening. They won't feed me anything else until I 'cooperate' with them."

Daveeka took a large chunk of bread out of his pocket. Her eyes devoured it, but she was too proud to ask. "Go ahead, take it. Just don't let anyone know."

As she ate the bread, he went on, "Maybe you should do as they want, Mistress. I'm sure they'd take much better care of you if you'd be a bit more cooperative."

"I'll starve to death first."

"No. They won't allow that, I'm certain. They want you alive so you can produce children for them."

She seemed a bit taken aback by that news. "Children? I'll never …" Her voice trailed off as she realized the futility of what she was saying. She would have little choice in the matter.

"You could stop fighting them, Mistress," Daveeka said gently. "You can't prevent them from mating you, but you don't have to be beaten each time."

"Relax and enjoy it, eh?"

He winced, knowing full well how callous and stupid that advice was. "No, Mistress. I never said you had to enjoy it. But if you keep resisting, they'll just keep forcing you."

"Why should you care what they do to me?"

"I'm beginning to think that's a very good question," he snapped with growing irritation. "And you're not making my answer any easier by being so hostile. Merciful Mother of All, Annilee, I'm only trying to help you!"

"Then do something useful for me, instead of just offering stupid advice."

"What would you have me do?"

She lowered her voice. "Get me out of this hut. Help me get back to civilization."

"We're in the middle of the forest. Where could we go?"

"Down the river, of course. We could take a canoe. This river must be the Mirr. It comes out of the forest near the holdings of Family Mirn, next to Scheld. It can't be all that far."

"We'd never make it."

"We might. Or is it that you're just afraid to try?"

Daveeka glared at her. "If I stay, no one would take my daughter from me."

"Oh?"

"That's right. Here, Fathers keep their daughters," he announced smugly.

She was surprised, but not impressed. "And how are girlchildren treated, Daveecha? Judging by the way they treat adult females, it can't be very well."

"If you'd be more agreeable—"

"Then I'd be raped less often, perhaps. Shall I learn to like it, since it's to be my lot in life?"

He was beginning to lose patience. They'd been over this ground before. "Why not? Did you ever ask a male permission when you took him to the mating room?"

Now it was Annilee's turn to be taken aback. "I … never hurt them."

"No? How would you know? If you had hurt them, do you think they'd have dared to complain?"

"This isn't getting us anywhere. Are you going to help me escape, or not?"

"Just now, I think not."

Annilee leaned back against the wall. As her torn ear tried to slant down in annoyance, she winced and forced it up once again to a less painful angle. Her long fur was tangled and matted with dirt and dried blood. She was a mess. Daveeka tried not to notice that she didn't smell very good either.

"Listen, Dav, if you'll help me get back to Thennevar, I could do something for you in return."

"Oh? Like what?"

"Like help you defeat Fahlin's proposal at the Conclave, for one thing. And maybe try to alleviate conditions on the Farms."

"Why should you do that?"

Annilee averted her eyes, picking nervously at the frayed edge of the blanket she wore. "I've had time to think about things during the last few nights. Pain hurts. It isn't fun, it isn't exciting, and it isn't a game. It just hurts. Maybe I'd like to make things better for the males. Maybe I'm a little bit sorry for the way they've been treated."

"Sure. And I'm an Exalted Mother." He turned away in disgust. Did she actually think she could fool him so easily?

She clutched at the edge of his tunic, trying to make him look at her. "I mean it, Dav! I swear … I swear by the Holy Name of Elenath, if we can get out of here and return to Thennevar, I'll do everything I can to change things. I'm not a Mother yet, but I will be, when your daughter is taken."

That was the wrong thing to say. Daveeka snatched his tunic away and stood up, intending to leave.

She caught his hand. "Please. I'm only trying to point out the realities. As a Mother, I'll have power. And so will you, as an Honored Father. Just think what we could do! Together, we could make a difference."

It sounded good. But did he dare believe she meant it?

"Look, Annilee, I've got to think about this."

"You'll consider it though? Get me out of here, and I'll be eternally grateful."

"Yeah, I'll consider it. If you'll consider being more cooperative."

She let go of him. Pulling her blanket tighter around her shoulders, she tried to strike a regal pose and glare at him arrogantly. He laughed, took a few steps in the direction of the door, then turned around.

"Listen, if you want to make it difficult for me to get you out of here, just keep on as you've been doing. Let them starve you until you're too weak to escape. Provoke them into beating you until you can't move. Make them so suspicious that they never relax their guard around you. Go ahead, make it impossible. It isn't me who wants to leave, it's you."

Annilee thought about his words in silence for several long moments. Then she rose to her feet and walked unsteadily over to him, biting her lip as if it hurt her just to move. It probably did, considering her ravaged genitals. "All right, I'll play the game your way. But you've got to promise to help me escape."

A year ago, he'd have done anything a female deigned to ask of him. But a lot had happened since then. "I'll consider it. That's all."

She shook her head in resignation, then retreated back to her place against the far wall and crouched down on the floor once again. "Fine. Consider it. I'll be right here when you make up your mind." She gave a short bitter laugh, and rested her head face down on her knees.

Daveeka left, not entirely sure whether he had won or lost the argument.

"Well, I don't know what you said to her, but the female is behaving herself much better," Clarlaw remarked. "Tonight she asked almost politely for more to eat."

"I told you she'd be reasonable, if things were presented to her properly." Daveeka decided to press his advantage. "As long as she's being more cooperative, how about keeping everybody away from her for a while? At least until she heals a bit."

Clarlaw's left ear twisted slightly in amusement. "Bruefen will be disappointed."

"Who's in charge here, you or Bruefen?" He was careful to keep his tone light, so it wouldn't sound too much like a challenge. "Annilee was torn up pretty badly. An infection could be serious. She might die, or not be able to have children for us."

"That's true. Besides, it's possible that she's pregnant already anyway. If not, there's always next nanth." He nodded. "Yes, I'll see that she gets some time to recover. And I suppose she really should be cleaned up. I could send her some water for a bath. And some better food, if she stops throwing it back at us."

Daveeka nodded. It was exactly what he wanted, but he preferred Clarlaw to believe he'd thought of it himself. "I'm sure Annilee would appreciate that bath. You know how vain females can be."

Clarlaw's ears flickered with amusement. "I surely do."

"Oh, by the way," Daveeka began, as if he'd just now thought of it, "how about getting someone to teach me more about living in the forest? If I'm going to stay here, I've got to learn how to get around safely."

"You can learn all that after your daughter leaves your pouch. Until then, just stay in our clearing. No sense in risking your daughter's life."

"Of course not," Daveeka hastened to agree. "But I've got to start sometime, even if I don't venture away from here until later on. I'm bored just hanging around. I need to do something useful, and learning about the forest would be useful, in the long run. It must be very complicated, with all those dangerous things out there."

He hoped he hadn't laid it on too thick. Clarlaw didn't respond right away. Judging by the angle of his ears, he was thinking things over.

"That does sound reasonable, Dav. I'll arrange for Harizi to start your training. He's one of our best scouts. He's also Bruefen's oldest son."

"I think I've seen him. Wasn't he with the party that kidnapped Annilee?"

"He was, indeed. A very promising youngster."

Daveeka had a sudden idea. "Tell me, Clarlaw, do many of your people know how to read and write?"

The outlaw shook his head, his eartips drooping regretfully. "They were all slaves from the Farms. Only a few of us can do that, and mostly not very well."

"Then how about if I offer to teach it to anyone who's interested? Surely, that's the least I can do to help out."

"Deal," Clarlaw replied. "We teach you about the forest; you teach us reading and writing."

"I could also teach them about the Kiari and the dances," he offered quickly.

"Yes, that would be fine also. We could all profit from learning more about the outside world."

And so it went for the next quarn. Only a few of the outlaws wanted to learn to read, but Daveeka taught them what he could. His demonstrations of the Kiari dances drew a larger audience. Meanwhile, Harizi began training him in the ways of the forest. He was never actually taken out into potential danger, of course, but at least Daveeka was getting some idea of what he was up against.

As First Nanth drew to a close, Daveeka deliberately kept away from Annilee. Although he knew she was doing all right, he didn't relish the idea of facing her in person and having her ask again about escape. Maybe she'd come to accept her situation, now that it had been somewhat ameliorated.

Three nights prior to the full moon which would begin Second Nanth, Daveeka awoke late and stretched luxuriously. Reaching into his pouch, he tenderly stroked his daughter. She wriggled with pleasure, now quite at home with his touch.

If he had still been in the Thennevar Palace, this would be the nanth when she would have been taken. His ears slanted at the loathsome thought. That wouldn't happen now.

But he also wouldn't become an Honored Father. Nothing would change, back at Thennevar. The Kiari would continue to be persecuted and childless males would virtually never get Invitations. In fact, when Fahlin's proposal came up in Conclave, it would doubtless be accepted, leaving childless males even worse off than before.

And Teo, if he still lived and had returned from the Farms, would be sleeping alone in their old room. Zillah would still be a slave on the Farms, if he hadn't fallen victim to the forest by now. And goodness only knows what may have happened to Sinda, once Daveeka's disappearance was discovered.

If he went back, perhaps he could change some of that.

But if he did, his daughter would be taken.

But if he didn't …

Daveeka got up, distressed with the direction his thoughts were taking. He left the hut and went over to join Clarlaw, who sat talking with a group of males around a small fire. A pot of thick porridge bubbled over the flame, so Daveeka lowered himself clumsily to the ground and ladled some into a bowl.

"Ah, just the one I wanted to see," Clarlaw remarked. "I've got some good news. Bruefen and I just came from examining your female, and she appears to be pregnant. In two more nanths, we'll have a fresh crop of children. Maybe even a female, although I suppose that's not too likely, since she had one at her last Birthing."

Daveeka wasn't sure whether to be pleased over this development or not, but the outlaws apparently were, so he pricked up his ears to show satisfaction as he scooped a spoonful of porridge into his mouth.

Annilee's pregnancy would assure her of decent treatment, if for no other reason than that they wanted the babies. And perhaps it would make her more docile, less anxious to escape.

He swallowed the porridge. "That's great! Next nanth she can send out Invitations …

The others stared at him. Realizing the ridiculousness of what he had just said, Daveeka laughed at himself. "No, I guess not, huh? So how do you decide who receives a baby, if it isn't up to the female?"

"Wait a few nights, and you can see for yourself," Bruefen replied. And no one else would tell him any more than that.

On the first night of Second Nanth, the entire renegade community gathered in a circle in the center of the clearing. Clarlaw insisted that Daveeka take a place of honor alongside Bruefen, so he made himself comfortable sitting on a folded blanket on the ground, curious as to how they planned to choose the males to receive Annilee's babies.

After seating Daveeka, Clarlaw went into Annilee's hut.

As the light of the rising full moon filtered slantwise through the dense trees, he reappeared at the door of the hut. The babble of excited chatter died quickly away. Everyone seemed to be waiting with bated breath to see what would happen next.

Clarlaw stepped forward, leading Annilee by the hand. The assembled males clapped and cheered. This was evidently what they had been waiting for, a good look at their female.

Annilee was clean and neatly brushed, wearing a plain shift of coarse timmen cloth. The garment hung barely to the middle of her thighs, leaving the fine long fur of her arms and legs immodestly exposed to view, but at least she was dressed in something more than a blanket. She followed Clarlaw docilely enough, but her eyes roved constantly around the outlaw camp, stopping only for a moment on Daveeka as she passed in front of him.

Clarlaw led her over to the circle, seating her on a cushion next to him. Then he placed a woven basket in her lap and turned to address the crowd.

"Our female is believed to be pregnant," he announced loudly. "All those who would receive her children must now indicate their intention to prove themselves worthy." He stood next to Annilee, looking out over the crowd.

Daveeka leaned over to Bruefen and whispered, "This doesn't make sense. Who wouldn't want a child? Everyone in the camp will volunteer."

The scarred male shook his head. His own daughter sat on his lap, fretting restlessly and whimpering now and then. "No, it doesn't work that way. Any male who wants to be considered has to place his name in the basket. We've been without a breeding female for so long that there should be a good number of candidates, but certainly not everyone."

"I don't understand. Who wouldn't … ?"

"Wait and see."

Bruefen was right. Only seventeen adult males dropped their names into the basket. A few of them were comparatively young, but most were older. Many of them showed nasty scars on various parts of their bodies.

"Hold Varri for me, will you, Dav?" Without waiting for an answer, Bruefen handed the child over to Daveeka, then rose. The ears of the other candidates drooped with dismay as he placed his name into the basket.

Varri squirmed uncomfortably in Daveeka's arms. For a moment, he thought she was going to start crying. He tentatively caressed her head and the base of her small ears, enjoying the feeling of the soft fur touching his fingers. Soothed, she closed her eyes and curled up in his lap against the curve of his distended pouch.

Bruefen returned to his seat. He glanced at his daughter, now sleeping contentedly. For a moment, Daveeka got the distinct impression the other male was annoyed that Varri had taken to Daveeka so quickly. But it was hard to read Bruefen's feelings, what with the scar that distorted his face and drew one eye partly closed.

"Well, since she likes you so well," he remarked sourly, "you might as well keep her in your lap. I'm going to be busy very soon, anyway."

"Bruefen, why do you want another child so soon? You'd have to wean Varri immediately, in order for your pouch to be ready for a new infant in two nanths."

Bruefen shrugged. "She's old enough to be weaned anyway. Then I won't have to bother so much with her anymore."

Here I am, overjoyed at the opportunity to keep my daughter, and he thinks of it as a bother!

Aloud, Daveeka said only, "But why do you want another infant?"

"Are you really so naive, or are you just pretending? I have six children, more than any other male in our band. Do you imagine I got them because I loved babies?" Bruefen snorted contemptuously. "It's an honor, Dav. Or had you forgotten? I'm second in command under Clarlaw. How much would anyone respect me if I didn't prove myself worthy of receiving infants, especially from the female I captured myself?" He pointed to Clarlaw, who was mixing the slips of paper around in the basket on Annilee's lap. "Now stop jabbering and watch."

Clarlaw nodded to Annilee. Obediently, she closed her eyes and began picking out names, handing them to Clarlaw one at a time. He laid them on the ground in a straight line in the order in which they had been given to him.

So that was it. A drawing. But that still didn't explain why so few males had entered, nor why Annilee continued until all the names had been drawn. Nine would have been sufficient.

Daveeka watched in puzzlement as Clarlaw unfolded each paper. He read them off aloud by twos, placing the paired names one atop the other before going on to the next. When he had finished, nine piles lay spread on the ground before Annilee.

"Now what?" Daveeka asked Bruefen.

"That's the first round. It doesn't always work out so evenly, of course. Sometimes we have more or less than nine pairs of candidates for the first round."

It still didn't make a lot of sense. Daveeka shrugged and went back to watching. Perhaps they'd draw one name from each two to fill the traditional nine Positions at a Receiving?

Everyone was moving back now, clearing a wide space in front of Annilee and Clarlaw. A good-sized roll of heavy fabric was brought out and spread in the open place. It looked about the size of eight dancing rugs, laid side by side in two rows.

When a boy brought over two heavy hurat branches and laid one at either side of the mat, Daveeka had the uneasy feeling that he knew what was going to happen. Each branch was about the length of a rillenu's arm and twice as wide, with a padded section at one end for use as a grip. In the right hands, these weapons could be used to kill.

Clarlaw read off the first pair of names. Smarro and another male Daveeka didn't know stepped forward and began stripping off their clothing. When they were both down to their naked fur, they went to opposite sides of the rug and picked up a club, hefting it experimentally and taking a few practice swings.

It was all too clear that they intended to fight for the privilege of receiving an infant. Daveeka felt Annilee's eyes on him and deliberately avoided her gaze. Civilized males had stopped fighting over pregnant females, ages ago.

Bruefen nudged Daveeka with his elbow. "Not a lot of competition," he remarked scornfully. "I should be able to get First Position, same as I did last time. All it takes to win a match is to be the first to draw blood from your opponent's head or torso. Other wounds don't count, since they probably wouldn't have been fatal in a true fight. Step off the rug and you're disqualified. There are no other rules," he explained as Clarlaw held one hand up in the air.

Smarro and the other male squared off against each other. "Keep an eye on Smarro. He's good," Bruefen added, apparently enjoying the spectacle.

Clarlaw dropped his arm. Smarro came out swinging his club, driving his opponent into the corner of the fabric. Forced onto the defensive, the other male tried to block without success. Smarro's club sliced a bleeding gash across his chest. Clarlaw shouted the command to stop and the match was over.

Ears at a jaunty angle, Smarro sat down in front of Annilee, while his injured opponent skulked off to have his wound tended. Clarlaw called the next two names.

Before Elnanth had risen much higher in the sky, nine victorious males sat before Annilee, waiting for the second round. Bruefen had beaten his opponent and sat amongst them.

Daveeka eyed the seated males. Several of them sported bandages on arms or legs from injuries received in the previous matches. With one exception, they were bigger, stronger, and older than the average male in the outlaw camp. The exception was Harizi. Although he was still quite young, he already outweighed Daveeka by a considerable amount.

It was easy to see that the babies would go only to the strongest and best fighters in the group. No one else would have much chance.

He shifted uneasily in his place, trying not to disturb Varri. This wasn't necessarily an improvement over having the females choose. All it did was create a different hierarchy than the females had created, but it was a hierarchy nevertheless. Although any male theoretically had the opportunity to compete, it still resulted in an elite corps of Fathers.

Daveeka reflected bitterly about the differences between theory and practice, as the winners' names were again placed in the basket and picked out by Annilee. She sat stiffly, her face a frozen mask, her ears immobile. During the fighting matches, she had fixed her eyes on the treetops and steadfastly refused to show any interest in who won or lost.

The second round lasted longer, since the remaining males were more evenly matched and more experienced. Bruefen dispatched his opponent with a sweeping blow to the head, relying on his superior strength. The other male crumpled to the ground, his skull crushed. There was an excited murmur of conversation in the crowd, but no real consternation. Death must be a fairly common occurrence in these babyfights.

Annilee's eyes swept down from the treetops to catch Daveeka's. Nothing changed in her face or the set of her ears, but he felt her challenge loud and clear. Is this the world you would live in, Dav? If so, you're welcome to it.

He almost looked away. Then he recalled Clarlaw's excised pouch, Myerta's hideous execution. There were wrongs enough on both sides. He stared back at her until it was she who looked away.

With one of the nine finalists already gone, it was decided that Ninth Position would be made available to the least badly injured of the losers in the previous round. Accordingly, those in good enough shape to walk were summoned to come before Clarlaw to be examined.

Only three appeared. Clarlaw made his decision and seated them in order at the end of the line of finalists. Depending on how the rest of the second round went, several of them might have another chance to prove their worth.

The competition was halted for a time to allow food and drink to be served. Daveeka was given a platter heaped with roast bird, crisp chared stalks, nuts, and even a fresh cranel. He noticed that none of the other males had been served anything like his sumptuous repast, with the exception of Clarlaw and the finalists in the competition. Annilee, herself, received the same food as the other males. Well, at least she was eating, he thought.

Varri stirred restlessly in Daveeka's lap. She whimpered, eyes watching the food in his hand. Figuring she must be hungry, Daveeka tried to catch Bruefen's attention.

The scarred male shook his head in annoyance. "Not now, Dav. We'll be starting the competition again soon. Give her a piece of bread." Then he turned back to the other candidates, most of whom were eating only lightly from the plate in front of them.

Daveeka took a small chunk of meat from his platter, and gave it to the child on his lap. She sucked on it greedily, nibbling bits off the edges with her tiny teeth.

The competition resumed, with the four losers of the second round matched against each other. One of them was too badly injured to fight, so he was tentatively assigned to Eighth Position, depending on how the rest of the competition went. The others fought elimination matches until Fifth, Sixth, and Seventh had been awarded. There were no more casualties, but the male in Seventh Position had a deep gash across his abdomen, cutting into his pouch. If that became infected, he wouldn't live long enough to worry about a baby.

That left the winners. Bruefen, Smarro, Harizi, and another male unknown to Daveeka would compete for the top four Positions.

The unknown male put up a good fight, but Smarro eventually defeated him with a vicious blow across the face.

A strange look passed between Smarro and Bruefen as Smarro stepped off the rug. Daveeka was suddenly very sure that he knew how Bruefen's face had been scarred, and who had done it. All along, he had been assuming it was the work of the females, in the time prior to Bruefen's becoming a renegade.

Bruefen and Harizi approached the mat.

Since Harizi was Bruefen's oldest son, Daveeka expected that his father might show mercy to the youngster. He was quickly proven wrong. They moved back and forth across the mat, each striking and blocking with ferocious skill.

Then Bruefen stumbled and fell. Harizi wasn't quick enough to follow up on his advantage, his club coming down where Bruefen's head had been as the scarred male rolled and regained his feet. Bruefen caught his son a hard blow to the shoulder as he rose, winning the match.

Harizi and the other losing male squared off. The other's face was badly cut, his bandage already soaked with blood. He seemed weak and off balance as he took his place.

"This shouldn't be allowed," Daveeka said half-aloud in consternation. "Why don't you call it off?"

"If Lavel doesn't wish to fight, all he has to do is step off the cloth," Clarlaw informed him in an undertone. "Unlike what happens to your Kiari dancers, stepping off doesn't mean being poisoned."

Confident of victory, Harizi closed in rapidly, favoring his wounded shoulder and using his other hand to wield the club. Lavel fell back, blocking clumsily. He staggered sideways, as if he were going off the fighting area. Harizi stopped, certain he had won.

Lavel fell into a half-crouch, twirled, caught the younger male's foot with an outflung leg, and tumbled him to the ground, lashing out with his club to gash his back as he fell.

Much to everyone's surprise, Lavel had Third Position, while Harizi had Fourth.

Bruefen and Smarro were called for the final match. It went on for a surprisingly long time, with a number of near misses on each side. Both males received nasty slashes on arms and legs, but neither could get through the other's defense to score a telling blow to head or body.

At last, Smarro feinted a low swing, jerking his club up at the last minute to aim at Bruefen's scarred face. Bruefen avoided the blow by a finger's breadth, but inadvertently stepped off the mat in order to do so. The crowd went wild, cheering and screaming.

For a brief instant, it seemed Bruefen would charge back into the fight out of sheer fury. Then his eyes locked with Clarlaw's and he dropped his club in acknowledgement of defeat. Smarro would receive the first baby, with Bruefen second.

All Positions for Annilee's Birthing were now decided.

As Daveeka looked them over, this system suddenly became personal. He would never have been among the winners, had he been one of the outlaw band. Size, strength, fighting skill: that was all that made them worthy of receiving children. At Thennevar, such males would have been Palace guards, never Fathers.

As everyone crowded over to congratulate the winners, Daveeka remained seated. He tried to tell himself the outlaws' system was no worse than the females', which was true. But if it was no worse, it was also no better. Somehow, he had hoped for more.

Clarlaw called for everyone's attention, standing up alongside Annilee. "Once again," he shouted, "Bruefen and Smarro have demonstrated their strength and superiority." The crowd quieted down as people resumed their seats. "It seems only fitting that they, who brought us this female, should also receive the choicest of her infants."

The assembled renegades cheered loudly for the winners. Some appeared to be exchanging various articles. It looked to Daveeka as if they had been gambling on the contest, but he wasn't sure.

"Our valiant champions," Clarlaw continued, "shall all have the honor of participating in the final mating of our female, before she is set aside as taboo until after her Birthing. As is our custom, they will do this in the order of the Positions they have so courageously obtained." He turned to the winner. "Smarro, she is now yours until you have finished with her. Take her to the hut."

Daveeka watched in dismay as Smarro went to Annilee, taking her hand and leading her away. She must have known about this already, since she showed no surprise. Other than a quick scornful glance in Daveeka's direction, she went with the big male, her eyes cast down in humiliation, as the assembled crowd shouted obscene suggestions about what Smarro should be sure to do to her.

Appalled, Daveeka tried to pretend he didn't care. But in his heart, he saw only the image of his daughter, twelve years hence, being led away to be brutally and repeatedly mated, as Annilee had just been.

Varri whimpered. Daveeka lifted her against his shoulder, patting her back. Her hands clung tightly to the cloth of his tunic.

Clarlaw sat down next to Daveeka, as more food was brought out and served to everyone.

"Was that really necessary?" Daveeka hissed, his voice covered by the renewed hubbub from the crowd.

Clarlaw picked up a juicy cranel. "It's our custom. I explained it to her beforehand. So long as she shows herself willing to accept them, the males will not treat her as roughly as they did last time. After all, they too are concerned with the well being of the infants she'll bear for them. It's up to her to choose."

"And if she chooses to resist?"

Clarlaw shrugged. "Then that's her problem, not ours."

Seeing Daveeka's ears flatten in anger, the renegade leader went on, "And what exactly do you think the Thennevar females would do if they took you to the mating room and you refused to just lie there like a good male should? Do you suppose you'd get away with that? Hmm?"

Daveeka had no answer. Clarlaw was right. Such behavior would not be tolerated. Just refusing to lie there would be bad enough. Actually attempting to fight off a female would get him a death sentence.

Pressing his advantage, the older male said smugly, "Besides, this final mating serves a good purpose, reinforcing the status of those males who are most worthy of respect and privilege."

"'Serves a good purpose'?" Daveeka repeated acidly. "What would you know about good purposes? All I've seen since I've been here is a struggle for power. What are you doing about the rest of the world? It's still out there, you know."

"Let it stay out there, then. If most males want to spend their lives kowtowing to the females … Well, just like your precious Annilee's choice to fight or not, that's not my problem. We have all we can do just to keep ourselves alive."

In all justice, Daveeka had to admit that was probably true. The more he learned about it, the more he came to realize that surviving in the middle of the forest was a serious challenge in and of itself. And yet, he simply wasn't satisfied.

He looked around at the other rillenus, now talking and feasting happily. Reminded by the voices of the crowd, Daveeka imagined he could hear the Kiari melody to which he had danced, so many nanths ago, when he and Teo had become priests. The music summoned him, called him back. He had a duty, a responsibility …

No! If he went back, his daughter would be taken.

Come back. Or your daughter will grow up to be treated no better than a slave, and your destiny will be unfulfilled.

The voice that whispered those words in his head was the same one he'd heard during that Spring Dance whose melody echoed, even now, in his ears.

Daveeka shook himself. He glanced up at the moon called Elnanth, whose huge disc flickered suddenly out from behind a cloud. The two small moons lay superimposed upon her red-orange bulk, forming circles against her face as they passed in front of her. It had been years since that particular arrangement had occurred, and doubtless would be years before it would occur again.

Come back. You are summoned.

Daveeka bowed his head.

CHAPTER 9

"Clarlaw, what would you say if I asked permission to mate Annilee once more?"

Daveeka picked up his cup of cold river water and glanced across the table and the remains of their meal, leaning back against the wall in an attitude of casual comfort.

"Well, normally we don't allow any more of that, once the female is pregnant. Wouldn't want to risk harming the babies."

"One last time wouldn't hurt. Back at Thennevar, females often took males into the mating rooms during their second nanth of pregnancy. They aren't even officially declared pregnant until the end of the second nanth."

"We like to get things settled well in advance." Clarlaw moved away from the table, still nibbling on a piece of melon.

"So I've seen. Probably a good idea. Having a pregnant female in the camp with Positions still open might incite dangerous feelings."

"Right. We tried having the competition closer to birth, but the fighting seemed to be too fierce. Better early, and if the pregnancy turns out to be a false alarm, there's always next time."

Daveeka considered how he might bring the conversation back around to Annilee, rather than females in general. "How come you don't mate her yourself? Or did you, and I just never heard about it?"

"I wouldn't touch a female if I were the last male in the world. I never want to lay a finger on one of them again, much less any other part of my body. I wouldn't soil myself."

Judging by the contempt in the other male's voice and the angle of his ears, that had been the wrong question to ask. Daveeka backtracked quickly. "About my request—"

"Why are you so anxious to do this all of a sudden?"

"Well, I feel sort of like … I mean, I've kind of been disgraced in everyone's eyes. The way I ran away last time I mated her, you know?" He pushed his ears into the awkward half drooping twist that indicated deep embarrassment, hoping to convince the other rillenu of his sincerity. "That's no way to impress people. If I'm to make a life here, I ought to—"

Clarlaw came around the table to put an understanding arm around his shoulder. "Enough, Dav. I know what you mean. And I'm glad to see you thinking in these terms. Shows you're starting to fit in with us, and I want that."

Despite everything, Daveeka felt guilty about deceiving the older male. He couldn't quite bring himself to dislike Clarlaw. In fact, he had to admit that he even found Clarlaw attractive, and having him sitting so close didn't make this any easier. "Then you'll let me have one last chance at her? I'll bet I can convince her to accept me without any trouble. I won't even need anyone to hold her," he boasted, hoping to provoke Clarlaw into giving permission.

"I doubt that," the other male scoffed.

Daveeka flattened his ears, feigning insult at Clarlaw's remark.

Clarlaw laughed. "All right, Dav. If you think you can mate the esteemed Mistress Annilee without anyone's help, you're welcome to try. But I warn you, having cooperated last time as requested doesn't mean she'll be at all happy to see you standing there with your hand on your sheath and your penis sticking out, after I promised her that the other night's mating would be the last until after she gives birth. She claws like a wild scha'adi, you know."

Meanwhile, the hand resting on Daveeka's shoulder had crept upward to rest lightly against the fur at the back of his neck. "But if you're only looking for a little pleasure, you know you can easily find that somewhere else. And you wouldn't even have to fight an enraged female to get it."

Daveeka looked sideways at Clarlaw's profile, his small ears silhouetted against the glare of the illovex on the wall. *Ah, don't! Please don't. Your offer is too tempting. But accepting it would only make all this more painful.*

Aloud, he said only, "After I've settled matters with Annilee, okay?" He squirmed out from under Clarlaw's arm, getting up and taking a few steps away.

"If it's that important to you, I guess I can wait," Clarlaw replied good-naturedly. "Just don't make me wait too long, eh?"

Dawn was just beginning to brighten the eastern sky as Daveeka approached Annilee's hut. Smarro sat lounging against the wall, peeling a pale white starfruit and munching on the sections. He looked up as the other male drew closer.

"Ah, Daveeka. Don't tell me you're ready to try your luck with the female again, after what happened last time?" Smarro remarked, his ears tilted to show amusement mixed with contempt.

Daveeka nodded. "You guessed it. Clarlaw said it was okay, even though it's against the usual custom."

"I know. He told me. He also said you wanted to do it by yourself. Sure you don't want to change your mind about that?" Smarro asked hopefully as he got to his feet. "I'd be glad to give you a hand."

Daveeka favored him with a confident leer. "I'm sure I can manage alone. She likes me."

The angle of Smarro's ears clearly showed his skepticism. He grinned and said, "Well, make it quick. The sun will be up soon."

"I'll be done before it's full light, don't worry."

Smarro was still grinning as he lifted the bar from the door, but he said nothing, waving the other male inside with an ironically elaborate bow.

Daveeka strode confidently into the hut, hearing the bar drop into place behind him. Quickly, he crossed to the far side of the room as Annilee rose to her feet.

"How dare you come in here?" she demanded. Her voice dropped down to a fierce whisper as she switched into femalespeech. "Arranging esscape ve you ssuppossed, and insstead ve only watching thiss trassh fight for babiess of mine." Her voice rose to normal volume once again. "Get out! I don't want to see you!"

"Be silent, female," he said, loudly enough to be overheard since Smarro would surely be listening. "I have Clarlaw's permission to mate you."

Predictably, her ears flattened with rage. He held a finger to his lips, and turned his ears toward the door. "Be still," he said loudly. "Or I'll call someone in to help me, and he'll have you also.

Take off your clothes. I want a look at you." As he spoke, he shook his head in negation, glancing pointedly at the door. "Yes, that's right. Oh, Mistress, your fur is so beautiful and lush! I've got to feel it under my hands! I want to caress you!"

He kept up the show, appraising Annilee's condition as he spoke. She seemed well and strong, even if she looked truly puzzled over what he wanted. Had she been weak and hurting, he would have postponed his plans. Clarlaw had been telling the truth then: she hadn't been raped and injured after the babyfight. She had been smart enough to do as she was told.

He almost wished she wasn't healthy enough for the escape he had tentatively planned. Now he had no excuse not to do it.

He moved closer to Annilee, bringing his hand out of his pocket and showing her the finger-length hurat thorn he carried, its point embedded in a large jaram seed.

"The guard," he whispered, flicking one ear towards the door. "Insside we lure him, and with thiss drug him."

Her ears pricked up with excitement and the glitter of her dark eyes showed her understanding better than any words possibly could.

"Fighting me hyou pretend," he went on softly. "By door I stand, him ambussh."

Annilee nodded. Grabbing up her sleeping pallet, she hit it a few times and then swung it against the floor to make a resounding whap, simultaneously loosing a stream of invective that amazed even Daveeka.

He pulled the hurat thorn free of the jaram seed, letting a drop of thick fluid run out and coat the tip. Pounding his free hand against the door, he cried out in mock anguish, "Smarro! Hey, Smarro! Help!"

The other male must have been standing with his ear to the door, judging by how fast he came running in. Before he even knew what was happening, Daveeka had driven the thorn into the side of his neck. He pulled the door closed as Smarro reached up to the embedded thorn and realized he had been tricked.

"Why, you miserable traitor!" Smarro went for the knife at his belt.

Daveeka hadn't counted on that. He had expected the concentrated jaram seed juice to take effect immediately. He backed away just in time to avoid the slashing dagger.

Annilee jumped on Smarro's back, clutching his arms and knocking him to the ground. They rolled over several times as he tried to shake her off, but Annilee held fast, hatred for her erstwhile tormentor strengthening her arms as Smarro succumbed to the drug.

Daveeka stayed clear of the struggle, since Annilee was clearly winning. He had no wish to expose his daughter to injury.

When Smarro slumped into unconsciousness, Annilee took the dagger from his limp hand and knelt next to him, panting. Her ears lay flat against her head as she rolled him over on his back and pulled up his tunic. Her fingers closed around his penile sheath and she hefted the knife.

"No!" Daveeka exclaimed, realizing her intent. "Annilee, no! That's not necessary." He knelt clumsily beside her, taking hold of her wrist.

She turned to look at him, fierce hatred glowing in the depths of her eyes. "Many timess hass thiss one forced me. Ish ve owed vengeance, Daveecha."

"Na. Hyou musst na thiss do, Misstress."

She jerked her hand free of his grip. The harsh blue-white light of the illovex gleamed on the blade of the knife. Her mouth twisted into a snarl.

"Na, Misstress. Na will I go with hyou, if thiss hyou do," he insisted.

Annilee took a deep breath and exhaled, fighting for control of her hatred. Her ears lifted slightly from her head and she nodded shortly. "Ve as you wissh, Daveecha."

"Goodh. Now, thiss one'ss clothing hyou put on, him tie up. Then we go."

She reached for the sheath at Smarro's belt. Holding up the knife, she looked a challenge at Daveeka.

"Ish thisss weapon take. In casse Ish need."

Somewhat unwillingly, Daveeka nodded his acquiescence. He had hoped to get the dagger for himself.

As soon as she was ready, he cracked open the door of the hut and peeked around the edge. No one in sight. Not surprising, since the sunlight was already bright enough to force him to squint his eyes. Even then, they stung and watered. He stepped outside, gesturing for Annilee to follow him. In Smarro's bulky tunic and leggings, she was not immediately recognizable as a female, especially in the searing light. Annilee wore Smarro's dagger at her waist.

Daveeka pulled the door silently closed, slipping the bar into place. No one would be likely to investigate until sunset, when the new guard came to relieve him. With luck, Smarro would be out until then.

Together, they slipped away from the village, taking the path that led to the river. Daveeka retrieved the small cache of provisions he had hidden near the beginning of the trail, digging out goggles and sunvisors for both of them and slinging the bag of food over his shoulder.

Birds chirped and warbled in the trees and sunlight fell in dappled patches on the underbrush. He kept a sharp eye on the path, sincerely wishing he had been able to get more practice in actually avoiding the dangers to be found in the forest, instead of just a cursory knowledge of what they were.

They soon reached the river, where three canoes lay drawn up on the bank behind their camouflage of bushes. Taking the largest one for themselves, they knocked holes into the bottoms of the others, towing them out into the water behind them until they sank. The current flowed swiftly, and the two rillenus barely needed to paddle, having only to guide the canoe as it drifted downstream.

Sunlight glinted bright off the water. Even with the protection of the dark goggles and visors, Daveeka's eyes smarted. But he and Annilee were safely away. The outlaws wouldn't be able to catch up with them easily, not without a canoe.

From her place in the front of the boat, Annilee chuckled softly. "That was easy, Daveecha. You planned well."

"Thank you."

"Males are not hard to fool, eh? They're awfully stupid."

"They weren't too stupid to capture us in the first place, Annilee,” he remarked sourly. If she noticed the lack of an honorific before her name, she didn't respond. The current slacked off and for a time they paddled in silence.

"How long until this river reaches civilization?" Daveeka finally asked.

"I don't know. Maybe several nights' journey."

"Several nights! We have to spend that long in the forest?" Maybe he should have asked her that sooner.

"We are not in the forest. We're on the river," she explained patiently. "You needn't be afraid. Eventually we'll come out near the holdings of Family Mirn."

Eventually. Perhaps this hadn't been such a good idea after all. But he reminded himself of Annilee's promise to make changes, and that he had to find out whether Teo was alive. It was easier to think in those terms, than to try to believe that Elenath Herself had called him back.

Glancing across the sun-sparkled water, Daveeka watched the shadowed forest glide by. Annilee was right. If they stayed on the river, they would be okay. There was nothing to worry about.

The cry of a harno lizard cut through the early morning air, sounding like shrill laughter. Although he'd never seen one, Harizi had told him harnos were large and often found near water. They could be dangerous, but only if they were hungry enough to attack a canoe. He shivered and turned his attention back to paddling.

All went well for a while, but he knew there would be rapids ahead somewhere. He remembered how the outlaws had had to struggle to paddle against them. This time they'd be going downstream, so it should be much easier.

Meanwhile, the river twisted and turned, the current sometimes fast, sometimes slow and sluggish. They ate sparingly of the food Daveeka had brought, unsure of how long they would have to make it last. As they ate, they compared notes on what little they could recall about the location of the rapids. All they could decide on was that it couldn't be too far ahead.

As the morning wore on, the river began to narrow, the trees leaning far out from the banks, almost as if they were trying to clutch the canoe. Here and there, glowweed draped through the branches in huge clumps. Uncultivated and wild, it glimmered a pale pinkish-white amongst the shadows.

The river flowed faster, then faster still. The turbulence of the water increased. Rocks began appearing in midstream. It was all the two of them could do to keep their fragile canoe from being overturned. Surely, it wouldn't get much worse than this.

It didn't. Before long, they had gotten through the narrowest part and were once again paddling easily along on the wide and placid river, congratulating themselves on getting through the dreaded rapids and confident that the going would be easier for the rest of the way. As the sun crawled slowly toward the west, Annilee even predicted they would reach the end of the forest sometime before the next sunrise, if they kept going.

Shortly before dark, they stopped for a brief rest, tying the canoe to the branch of a tree that had fallen into the river but was only partly submerged. Despite the sunvisors and goggles, their eyes were bleary and stinging painfully. It was still too bright for them to keep their eyes open, but they removed the goggles and blindly scooped up handfuls of water to bathe their closed eyes. It helped a little.

Waiting for the light of the sun to die out, they ate a sparse meal together.

"I wonder what's going on back at the village by now," Daveeka said tentatively. "With luck, they've only just realized that we're gone."

"We can't be sure Smarro didn't come around earlier on and rouse the others. If so, they've probably tracked us to the river and realized their canoes are gone. They can either follow the riverbank or take the time to make new canoes."

"Or both," Daveeka added.

"Or both," she agreed grimly. "I wish we could stop and sleep. I'm exhausted. But that wouldn't be a very good idea."

"How about if we took turns paddling, while the other person slept a bit? The current is fairly strong here, so we would still make pretty good time."

"That sounds good." Annilee squinted one eye open. "It's almost full dark. At least we'll soon be able to see comfortably."

"How are you feeling? Any problems, like pain or …"

"No more than could be expected," she said shortly.

"That final mating after the fighting?" he suggested. "Did they hurt you much?"

She laughed. "No, hardly at all. The stupid fools! I had them eating out of my hand. I acted as if I wanted it as much as they did, telling each one how brave and strong he was during the competition, and how handsome he looked. I snuggled against them, running my fingers through their mangy fur and allowing them to stroke me in return. You should have seen how easily I manipulated them into being gentle as they used me. I squirmed and moaned and told them how excited I was to be mated by such skillful males. I took the entire length of their penises into me and made them feel so good that they released their fluid quickly, without my having to force them. They never even had time to force their sheathes in also. I had them fooled completely!"

"I imagine you did." *Just hearing you describe it has gotten me all excited. But I'll have to ignore that.* "There's no reason you couldn't do that for every mating," he suggested.

It was dark by now, so she opened her eyes and stared at him in consternation. "I could, if it were worth the time and trouble. Usually it isn't."

"You didn't enjoy it, even a little?"

"Well, maybe just a little. At least it was …different from the usual way."

Daveeka decided this wasn't the time to pursue the subject any further, although he had an overwhelming urge to lie with her in the bottom of their canoe and see if he could convince her to mate him like that. "We'd better get moving again."

"You take the first turn at paddling. I want to sleep," she said imperiously.

As the night wore on, Daveeka drove the canoe steadily onwards, helped by the current.

The moonlight flickered down through the trees, glinting off the water and making Annilee shine with glimmers of light when it fell on any of her exposed fur. He found it hard to keep from stealing quick glances down at her sleeping form, and even harder to resist thinking of how wonderful it would be if she'd treat him as she had treated the outlaw males. *Maybe –- No, you idiot! Stop dreaming. Just keep your mind on what you're doing.*

After finding himself drifting off to sleep too many times, he woke Annilee and they traded places. The river was running a bit faster than before, but that would just make it easier for her to cover more distance. It shouldn't be too long before they reached the edge of the forest, and safety. He wouldn't let himself think beyond that. Not yet.

"Daveecha, wake up! Wake up! Help!"

He was sitting up even as he awoke, expecting to see the outlaws surrounding them. Instead, it was the river he saw, now rushing wildly along and taking the canoe with it. He grabbed his paddle, trying to get things under control.

"What happened? Why didn't you wake me sooner?"

"The current was running faster, but I could handle it. Then we went around a long curve and into this! What do we do now?"

"We have no choice but to go with it and try not to capsize!"

The riverbanks on either side were much higher than they had been, and climbed further as they went, until they were almost like steep cliffs. And the river narrowed steadily. White water foamed around half-submerged rocks and dead tree trunks. Desperately trying to find the safest passages, the two rillenus were soon being tossed around in the roaring, swirling rapids, while the canoe was taking on water and becoming less and less maneuverable. Neither of them dared let go of their paddles long enough to bail.

The river frothed and foamed, sweeping them relentlessly onward. Over the rushing of the rapids, another sound grew in Daveeka's ears. At first he thought he was imagining it, but as it became louder he dismissed that possibility.

"Annilee!" he shouted. "There's something up ahead!

She was crouched over, grimly paddling. He might as well have saved his breath. They were swept into a long bend.

Straining to look ahead, Daveeka saw the river abruptly disappear, water flowing over a clear-cut lip into nothingness.

"Waterfall!" he shouted, but before the word was entirely out of his mouth, they had plunged over the edge.

Daveeka tumbled forward, barely aware of the canoe flipping end over end, spilling both himself and Annilee into space. He had only enough time to realize that he was falling before he hit. He felt a stinging slap along his back, but he had missed the rocks.

As the water closed over his head, he fought his way towards the surface. When he came up, spluttering, he realized he had landed off to one side of the foot of the falls, where an eddy had carved out a relatively quiet pool. He had to get out immediately or his infant would drown. He clutched at the opening of his pouch, holding it tightly closed with one hand while he grabbed at the branches of a fallen tree sticking out from the riverbank, its trunk partly submerged. Laboriously, he hauled himself up onto the slippery trunk. Lifting his sodden tunic, he forced his pouch open as far as he could, leaning sideways to make the water run out. His daughter seemed none the worse for the dunking. Her chest rose and fell evenly. Perhaps there was some kind of a reflex that made babies temporarily stop breathing if they were suddenly submerged.

It was only then that he had time to notice that he had lost his goggles and sunvisor in the fall. He looked around desperately for Annilee.

There she was, lying in the mud on the far shore, face down, half in and half out of the water. She was either unconscious or just exhausted from fighting her way free of the current. Further downstream, a piece of their canoe bobbed briefly in the rapids before beginning to sink. It had obviously not been as fortunate about missing the rocks as its occupants had been.

Between his perch and the nearer shore, the water was relatively still, swirling in a slow eddy. A snake slithered into the water, taking a moment to lift its head and gaze at him. Daveeka wondered with a shudder if it were poisonous. The murky pool between him and the riverbank suddenly did not look very inviting.

He squinted across the river again. Annilee still hadn't moved.

He yelled her name, hoping his voice would carry over the noise of the falls. Maybe she hadn't landed safely after all. Perhaps she had come down onto the mud and was even now unconscious and smothering.

Much to Daveeka's relief, she roused quickly, sitting up and shaking some of the muck from her clothing. Her goggles hung around her neck and her sunvisor lay nearby. Grabbing up the visor, she looked around, taking in the situation at a glance. She yelled to Daveeka, "Stay there! I'll cross!"

He waved to show he understood, although he wasn't too sure how she was going to be able to get to him.

She walked back toward the falls, watching the river carefully. The current was too swift to swim across, and too treacherous. Annilee crept on hands and knees out onto a rocky ledge next to the falling water, partly obscured by the mist at the base of the falls. When she abruptly disappeared, Daveeka gave a startled cry, thinking she had been swept under.

He searched the churning water, expecting her to surface in the midst of the deadly current. He had almost given up hope when she crawled out from under the falls on his side of the river. The rock ledge must have gone the entire way across, behind the veil of rushing water. He didn't dwell on how slippery the rocks must have been, or how easily she could have fallen in. She had made it. That was enough.

Daveeka still sat perched in the crown of the dead tree. He could easily have swum to shore, if not for the infant in his pouch. The trunk of the tree lay in the direction of the riverbank, although he couldn't see it once it went under the surface.

Annilee stood on the bank, staring at him in consternation.

"I can walk along the tree trunk," he yelled to her over the roar of the falls. "It looks as if it reaches most of the way to the shore."

She nodded, then waded out waist-deep into the water, rinsing some of the mud from her fur and clothing. Daveeka pulled off his sodden shoes, tied the laces together, and hung them around his neck. The Kiari beads reflected bright colors in the pale light of early dawn as he threaded his way through the broken branches and into the water, at first sliding along in a sitting position, then squatting, then half standing, and finally standing entirely upright as the tree trunk disappeared deeper beneath the surface. His toes curled around the edges of the slick wood. The scar tissue on the soles of his feet deadened sensation in places, but the uninjured spots still allowed him to feel his way along the trunk.

The water was almost at the level of his pouch when he stopped, perhaps eight body lengths from Annilee. He grabbed the loose skin of his pouch in one hand and held it tightly against his abdomen as he plunged into the water, pushing off as hard as he could and paddling frantically with his free hand.

Annilee waded in deeper, grabbing him and pulling him into the shallows. As soon as Daveeka could stand up clear of the water, he released the pressure on his pouch and breathed a sigh of relief.

They both collapsed into the weeds on the damp riverbank, dripping and out of breath. The sound of the waterfall filled their ears, a constant reminder of their predicament.

Daveeka kept his eyes closed against the glare of the rising sun. Even through his eyelids, it was becoming distinctly uncomfortable. He felt for his Shape, hoping it still hung at his breast, and breathed a sigh of relief at finding the smooth facets of the crystal under his fingertips. At least he hadn't lost it in the fall.

"Well, what do we do now?" he said, keeping his tone as light as possible.

"We could keep following the river. You stay here and I'll take a look beyond the next bend and see if I can locate where the forest ends. Good thing one of us still has goggles."

He thought he heard a gloating edge to Annilee's words, but he ignored it. After she left, he began wringing some of the water out of his clothing, then did the same with his shoes. Running his fingers over the beads brought back fond memories. With a sigh, he slipped his feet into the shoes and tied the laces.

Sitting alone with his eyes closed, he had visions of carnivorous vines and hungry harno lizards slinking towards him through the underbrush. He opened his eyes briefly, squinting and surveying his surroundings as quickly as he could. What had Clarlaw told him about the forest? Do as little damage as possible and create no disturbance.

He sat very still as the shadows of the trees flickered fitfully around him, playing games with his closed eyes. It seemed a long time before Annilee returned, her ears drooping.

"I couldn't see anything that was definitely the end of the woods, but the river seems to run down onto a flat plain not far from here. The banks spread out further on each side, but the forest seems to have approached closer to the water in places."

"Not good, but what else can we do?" he said.

"The river is meandering around, not flowing directly the way we want to go. It might be faster to just travel straight through the forest. We know the woods are north and west of the Farms, so we could go south and east."

"Directly through the woods? Are you serious?"

"Well, if we stay here, Bruefen and his friends will catch up with us."

"Without canoes?" he objected automatically. "On foot alongside the river, they could probably be here in a night or two. We'll be long gone by then."

"But they know the river and know about the waterfall. What if they've already sent another party directly down here through the woods as a back up, hoping to head us off, while the rest of them make new canoes? After all, they have no problem going through the forest. If they don't find our bodies along the shore, they'll surely follow the river looking for us."

Daveeka considered that. "Such a thing would be risky, but they might well do it. They don't dare just let us escape and tell our story. They know they'd be hunted down remorselessly if the females learned where they were and what they were doing." He sighed. "I guess our clever idea of following the river wasn't so clever after all."

They had lost their food, plus one pair of goggles and a visor, and the sun was rising fast.

Demoralized, dispirited and getting hungry, they argued for a while about which course of action to follow, finally deciding to follow the river on foot.

"The river it is, then." Annilee stood up decisively. "Let's get going. But first, let me rinse more of this disgusting muck out of my clothes."

Shortly afterwards, they set off along the riverbank. Annilee had their only pair of goggles, but she did give Daveeka the visor to wear. Although it helped a lot, as the sun climbed higher overhead, he found it impossible to keep his eyes open without risking damage. He ended up just closing them tightly, keeping one hand on Annilee's shoulder so she could lead him along.

At first, the terrain sloped rather steeply down and the river tumbled along with it. The two rillenus were forced to slip and slide for much of the way. Other than small cuts and bruises, they suffered no real injuries, but they were once again covered with mud, much to Annilee's disgust. At least they were able to avoid the forest by staying mostly on a strip of bare land right next to the roiling water. Apparently, the foliage didn't like to grow too close to the river. Now and then, they did have to go through patches of sparse vegetation. Daveeka warned Annilee to create as little disturbance as possible. She tried her best, but every time he felt a twig snap beneath his feet he feared the sting of a poison vine.

By the time they reached the flat plain Annilee had seen below them, the river had grown calm, spreading out on the level ground and giving up its headlong rush. Much to their relief, the clear strip of sand widened also.

Annilee immediately dashed into the river, splashing about and trying to get rid of the mud and dirt on her clothes and matted into her long fur. Daveeka groped his way over to her, breathing a prayer of thanks to Elenath for allowing them to get this far and begging Her protection for the rest of their journey.

The blazing sun beat down on them as they stumbled wearily out of the water.

"I can't go on any longer without a rest, Dav. Not in this horrible daylight."

Shading his eyes as much as possible with the visor, he took a quick glance upriver toward the waterfall, reflecting unhappily that they would now be more visible to anyone looking down from the heights.

Despite his misgivings, he knew Annilee was right. They were both too exhausted to continue.

Closing his eyes again, he began stripping off his wet clothing and wringing it out.

Taken aback at his actions, Annilee asked what he was doing.

"If we're going to stop here for the day, we may as well let the sun dry out our clothes. The night will be chilly enough without our being soaking wet. With any luck, we'll be able to stay out of the river from now on."

Annilee watched him in silence for a while, then began disrobing also. She still wore her goggles, so she was the one to spread out their various articles of clothing on the warm sand. With Smarro's dagger, she cut two strips of cloth from the oversize leg covers she had been wearing.

"Come on, Dav. Let's go under the trees and try to get some sleep. I've made us blindfolds to block out the sun."

"We can't. It's too dangerous in the forest, even in the daytime. We'll have to risk lying out here on the sand and hope no one is close enough to see us."

"But I'll get sand in my fur," she objected.

"Better than having a jinko vine around your neck."

Resigned, she scraped a slight depression in the sand and lay down next to him, facing away and trying to get comfortable.

Daveeka couldn't resist peeking out under the edge of his blindfold, so he could get a glimpse of the beautiful long fur on her back. Even now, damp and matted though it was, her dark pelt shone with glistening highlights, the deep rich color still very apparent even in the harsh light of day.

She reached one hand around, trying vainly to untangle a mat not far below her shoulder. Without thinking, Daveeka rolled onto his side and stretched out his own hand, combing through the tangles gently while working the loose fur away from her skin. In a very short time, most of the mats had been removed and her back was fluffy and dry. Although Daveeka desperately longed to get closer and put an arm around her waist, he thought better of it. That might be taking it too far.

Mistress Annilee had fallen fast asleep. He rolled away from her and did the same.

When they awoke, the sun had set and comfortable darkness blessed the land. Annilee was already up and dressed when Daveeka opened his eyes.

"Before you put your clothes on, let me check on my daughter," Annilee ordered, sitting down on the ground next to him.

He bristled, sitting up and pulling away from her. "It isn't necessary. She's fine."

"Maybe so, but your pouch probably needs cleaning by now."

"I'll take care of it myself."

"You know perfectly well that's not permitted."

"Oh? And just who do you think has been doing it while we were at the renegade camp?"

Her ears twisted sideways in consternation. "It may have been necessary then, but it isn't now. I'm here and it's my right. You probably haven't done a very good job anyway. Now lie down."

A lifetime of veneration for females made it hard for him to defy her, despite recent happenings. It wasn't natural for a male to disobey any female, much less the Mother of his child. He shifted nervously, but didn't move.

"Annilee, it's more important that we keep moving. The baby is all right, believe me. I've been taking care of her just fine."

"Nonsense! A daughter must be tended by her Mother. She has to become accustomed to her Mother's touch, especially when it gets this close to being taken from her Father's pouch. You don't want her to reject me when that happens, do you?"

She had him there. Assuming they both got out of the forest, he would have no other choice than to give up the infant, and soon. Defeated, he lay back down in the sand.

Daveeka hadn't expected to feel such pleasure when she placed her hand on his belly and slid it gently into his pouch. He drew in a sharp breath; his eyes opened wide and his ears jerked up with surprise. When her fingers went in deeper, something else also stirred in surprise.

As Annilee reached for her daughter again after their being separated for an abnormally long time, Daveeka could feel the baby tense and try to pull away. The seeking fingers retreated slightly and became still. After waiting a short while, they again sought out the infant, but more slowly than before.

Daveeka closed his eyes, luxuriating in the light pressure and gentle motion he could feel on the inner wall of his pouch, where soft downy fur now covered his once bare skin. It had never felt so good before. But then, until now, Annilee had always been in a hurry to get this chore over and done with.

Patiently, she worked her way close enough to place the tip of one finger against the baby's head. This time, it was accepted.

"Her first fur is starting to grow," Annilee whispered softly, stroking the small body.

"Umm," was all Daveeka could say in reply. *This is just too good,* he thought to himself. Then another thought drifted through his mind. *No, this is just how it should be.*

To his great astonishment, he realized that Annilee's free hand rested on the side of his hip, tracing small calming circles in his fur.

He relaxed into the delicious sensations flooding his body, all thoughts of anything else driven out of his consciousness.

After Annilee had caressed the infant for a while, she slid her hand down to the bottom of the pouch, expecting to have to collect and remove all of the pellets that had accumulated since her last cleaning. Although she searched thoroughly, there were very few to be found.

Meanwhile, Daveeka simply lay enjoying the probing done by the delicate slender fingers of the Mother of his daughter. Yes, this was indeed exactly how it should be. No pain, no fear. Just floating in the lovely sensations that enveloped him. It was sensual, but it was also sexual. As Annilee withdrew her hands, he was acutely aware of the fact that his penis was halfway extended from its sheath, stiff and dark brown.

Annilee noticed it at the same time he did. For a long moment, they stared into each other's eyes.

Although he would have liked nothing better than for her to take hold of his swelling organ and help him to release his fluid, what he said was only, "Go away for a bit. I'll take care of this. Then we'll be on our way."

With a short nod, she got to her feet and walked over to the river, squatting there with her back to him and drinking the water.

In a very short while, they were ready to move on.

Hungry, but at least not thirsty due to the river, they walked in silence, each seeming unwilling to bring up what had just happened. Finally, Daveeka could stand it no longer.

"Guess I didn't do so badly at caring for our daughter as you thought, did I?"

Huffily, Annilee replied, "As males go, you are somewhat unusual. Most of them are not very fastidious or reliable at such important tasks."

"If we're all so incompetent, why do female infants survive so well in the outlaw camp, while a lot of them die in your Palace? Clarlaw's people keep their daughters in their pouches, just as if they were sons, and they thrive on it. Clarlaw says—"

Annilee's ears flattened. "I don't care what those unnatural perverts do! Why, they're so uncivilized that they still fight over babies! And your precious Clarlaw is responsible. He's nothing but a vicious, cruel—"

Daveeka stood his ground, interrupting her. "If Clarlaw is cruel, it's the females who made him so. His pouch was excised."

Annilee fell abruptly silent, her tirade cut short.

"You know about that sort of thing, don't you, Mistress?" he persisted. "Our daughter would have been fed that way."

Annilee nodded reluctantly. "Female infants are fragile. They can't drink kullup milk, even watered down."

"Then leave them longer in their Fathers' pouches, and you won't have a problem."

"And let their eyes open so they can see their Fathers and remember them? That's a disgusting idea!"

"Well then, if you must have real milk, don't excise the outer wall of the male's pouch. That certainly isn't necessary."

They locked eyes, both pairs of ears flattened. Daveeka could hardly believe he was holding such a stance against a female, but he knew he was right and refused to back down.

Annilee looked away first, staring off into the thick bushes along the bank. Insects whined and rasped, beyond the zone of quiet caused by their voices.

She turned back to him. "Daveecha—"

"Save your breath. There's nothing you can say to justify yourself."

She laid a tentative hand on his wrist. "No, listen to me. When I was a young girl, and I was taken to see one of the excised males for the first time, I couldn't stand it. I ran out of the room and refused to come back. When Marlieth found out, she whipped me so hard I could barely walk. Then she took me back to the room, forced me to touch the male and examine him thoroughly. She even made me milk him. After that, I never went into that part of the Palace again. I couldn't bear to. I tried to tell the others that excision wasn't necessary, but nobody listens to a young girl. What could I do?"

It made a nice story, but Daveeka wouldn't put it past her to lie to him. "Well then, if you're so sympathetic towards us poor males, perhaps you can prove it to me by trusting me to care for our daughter."

Annilee drew back her hand angrily. Then she reconsidered, getting her temper under control once again. "All right. But when we get back to civilization, this has to stop. The other Mothers would never allow such a thing."

"We'll worry about that when we get there."

"If we ever get there," she retorted. "Right now all I want is a nice hot bath and a meal. If we don't find anything we can eat soon, I'm going to eat my fur."

It was only a rillenu expression denoting serious hunger, but Daveeka couldn't resist the impulse to taunt her a bit. "Oh, don't do that, dear Annilee! It would be such a shame to ruin your glorious fur. If you began nibbling on it, it might look almost as awful as it did when it was all dirty and matted."

And that was the closest either of them came to bringing up the subject of grooming for the rest of the night.

By the time Elnanth had passed the zenith, the land had leveled out completely. The river widened further and lost some of its depth, flowing only sluggishly now. The two rillenus had to wade across numerous small rills that ran off from the river, and the going got harder. The forest appeared to thin out some, but the vegetation now grew closer to the river.

When they could avoid the encroaching bushes and scattered trees no longer, Daveeka took the lead, claiming he knew more about how to deal with the forest then Annilee did.

At first, they managed pretty well, encountering nothing but a few small lizards that did nothing worse than startle them while fleeing from their path. Then, shortly before dawn, it started to rain. As the heavy drops pelted down through the trees, they slogged along, heads bent and ears flattened to keep the water out.

The rain made it harder to see, but with luck, it would also drive most of the forest creatures into shelter and deter the carnivorous plants from becoming too active.

Suddenly, Annilee shrieked with pain, rubbing frantically at her face. Before he could react, a raindrop hit Daveeka's ear, soaking immediately through the thin wet fur and stinging as it touched the flesh beneath.

Realizing they stood under a tanchanol tree, Daveeka grabbed Annilee's hand and pulled her out from beneath its large glossy leaves. Harizi had told him that tanchanol leaves exuded a caustic poison meant to deter grazers. That poison must now be washing down upon them with the rain!

Annilee continued wiping at her burning face, even after they were out from under the tree. He had her stick her head into the river in order to wash it off, since the rain only spread the poison further. Even so, both her face and head already bore angry red blisters beneath the fine layer of fur. They were especially bad along the ragged edges of her torn ear, where no fur had yet grown back to cover the healing skin. As he examined her ear more closely, he was pretty sure that it would be puckered and somewhat twisted once it had finished healing. And the fresh blisters would only make the damage worse. Annilee would not be pleased.

Luckier, Daveeka had only one small burn on his ear.

The rain continued falling as they knelt by the side of the river, where Annilee splashed the cold water repeatedly over her face, hoping to keep it from swelling too badly.

"I thought you knew all about the forest," she finally remarked, as the pain eased off a bit.

"I only said I know more than you do, that's all."

Her reply was nothing more than a scornful grunt as she leaned forward to scoop up more water. Then her eyes widened abruptly and her ears stood up straighter, despite the raw places. She pointed down at something in the water. "Dav, what's that?"

At first, he thought she had noticed her ear in a reflection, but he was wrong.

Squinting to see through the rain, he leaned forward and tried to make out what she was looking at. Something floated just beneath the rippled surface, something sleek and white.

Daveeka scooped it out of the water with both hands. It was covered with sharp spines, but it didn't make a move. A big chunk of flesh had been sliced out of its back. It seemed to be dead.

Annilee drew back in revulsion, but Daveeka picked up a short stick and poked it a few times, making sure it was as dead as it looked. He examined it closer, then picked it up.

"This is an onagar," he announced. "Annilee, we can eat it!"

"Are you sure? It looks pretty nasty, with all those pointy things on its skin."

"I've seen this kind of fish at the outlaw camp. They catch them in the river and eat them all the time. I watched one being skinned and cooked."

She gave him a sideways look, her ears twisting into a skeptical angle, forgetting about the burns, then wincing as the pain hit her. But she didn't complain. Drawing the knife from the sheath at her waist, she handed it to Daveeka, glancing pointedly at the dead onagar.

He took the knife and started working on the fish. The skin was tough and more than one of the spines poked into his fingers, but the dark meat underneath was finally uncovered. He sliced off a small strip and held it up.

They stared at the fresh meat, then looked up at each other, each licking their lips and swallowing saliva.

"You're sure this is all right? We don't know how long it was dead, and we certainly can't cook it."

Daveeka took a deep breath. "We don't have much choice, do we?"

He nibbled gingerly at the meat. "If anything happens – " Daveeka began.

"I'll take our daughter and do the best I can. Don't worry."

Nothing happened. No burning tongue or other immediate reaction. With Annilee's hungry eyes watching him, he swallowed. So far, so good. He tried another small bite and they waited once more.

He ate another piece.

Annilee could stand it no longer. She grabbed the rest of the meat and stuffed it into her mouth.

Daveeka went back to slicing up their first meal since they had lost their food at the waterfall. It was the most delicious thing they had ever eaten in their lives.

As soon as they had devoured every bit of the fish, they started walking again, invigorated by their unexpected meal and hoping to make more distance before the day became too bright.

So heavy was the rain and so dark were the clouds overhead that they were able to keep going into the early morning before they finally had to rest. By then, the storm had begun to slacken off and the light was becoming uncomfortable. At the same time, the ground on either side of the now wide river was becoming soft and marshy, covered in tall grass and bushes. While dense stands of trees could still be seen here and there, they were no longer hiking alongside the thick forest. For its part, the river had spread out into several channels, which meandered through the swampy plain.

The rillenus could see further ahead now, but there was still no visible sign of civilization.

They stopped, staring with squinted eyes at the horizon. With the growing sunlight, they would have to decide whether to rest here until dark, or don goggles and sunvisor and keep on going for as long as they could manage.

"Annilee, you've seen the Mirr River in Family Mirn's territory, right?"

"Yes. Why?"

"Is it like what we see now, or does it come directly out of a thick forest?"

"Not quite like this, but not a real forest either. The Scheld land slopes downwards as you go toward Mirn, if I remember correctly. That's why they can't grow jaram as well as Scheld can. Instead, Family Mirn plants things that need a lot of water, like cranels."

"That's encouraging, anyway. At least it means we could still be going in the right direction." He looked at the blisters on her swollen face and ears. "Do you think you can go on for a while longer?"

"Of course. Do you think I'm a weakling?"

"No, not at all. But the stronger the sunlight becomes, the more it will irritate your burns."

"You think I don't know that?" she snapped.

"I have a suggestion that may help. This time, give me the goggles and I'll lead you." He held up a hand to stop the objections that he was sure were on her lips. "We could cut more extra fabric from your leg covers and drape it over your head and ears, holding it in place with the sunvisor, which would help shade your face. You could also use both of the blindfolds we have, with one over your eyes and the other wrapped around the lower part of your face, to better protect you from the sunlight. If all the fabric pieces were frequently soaked with water, it would also relieve the swelling and pain that you must certainly feel, but have been bravely keeping to yourself."

Annilee thought about his suggestion.

"After all, Mistress, it's only common sense to do it that way. Male or not, I know as much as you do about the dangers around us." This time, he refrained from pointing out that, in fact, he knew more about them than she did.

Convinced at last, Annilee nodded, handing him the goggles and taking out her knife to trim more off the overlarge leg covers she had taken from Smarro.

When everything was set up as he had suggested, they resumed their weary trek along the increasingly soggy riverbank, Annilee's hand clutched tightly over his shoulder.

Never in his life had Daveeka expected to be leading a female in any way, shape, or form. But here he was, responsible for the safety not only of his daughter but now also of her Mother. A small patch of pride and confidence glowed in his heart. He kept a sharp lookout for anything in their path, determined not to fail the two lives that depended on him.

The rain stopped. All too soon, the clouds blew away and the sky began to clear. Eventually, the light became too bright for Daveeka to bear, even with the goggles. Finding a relatively higher and drier patch of grass-covered land, he led Annilee over to it.

"This is the best place I can see for us to rest," he announced wearily.

They made themselves as comfortable as possible, shielding their faces and eyes as well as they could before they fell into an exhausted sleep.

It was full dark by the time they awoke. Almost grudgingly, Annilee admitted that her face did feel somewhat better for avoiding the sun.

Lack of food and the unaccustomed exertion was beginning to take its toll on both of them. They had little to say to each other as they plodded doggedly along through the grass, doing their best to avoid the muckiest places. By now, Daveeka's Kiari shoes, already well worn and never meant for hiking on rough surfaces, weren't holding up too well. The soft bottoms were torn almost through in places. The boots Annilee had taken from Smarro were in much better condition. Of course, they were far too big for her, but earlier on she had found enough moss to fill up the extra space and make them reasonably comfortable.

It didn't take very long before their hunger reasserted itself. Daveeka suffered most, with a nursing infant in his pouch. But they dared not risk eating any of the leaves or berries on the unknown bushes that appeared more often now. Death could come too quickly that way. Better to be hungry.

Annilee stopped suddenly, pointing toward a slight depression in the land a short distance from the river.

"Look, Dav. Food!"

The thought of food penetrated his exhausted brain and he stared in the direction she indicated. There was a shallow pond, literally carpeted with odd blue-violet plants, their broad leaves lying flat on the surface in a sunburst pattern with a red center in the middle of each one. The flat leaves were about the length of an arm, while the leaves of each plant seemed to lie just against those next to it, lightly touching.

Daveeka stared at the strange vegetation, but Annilee was already halfway there. He hurried after her, coming to a halt by the edge of the pond.

"We can eat these things?" he asked dubiously.

"Yes, of course. They're cranel plants. The red fruits are in the center. See?"

Daveeka looked closer. There were indeed a number of deep red objects embedded in the spongy-looking mass, just the tops of their curved surfaces showing. Each one looked about the size of a fist. He'd never have recognized them as cranels though. Not surprising, since he'd never seen them growing before. Several rows of tendrils ringed the outside edge of the spongy center, standing stiffly upright.

Cranels. A delicious luxury he had never expected to find in the middle of this desolate wilderness. His mouth watered at the memory of their juice on his tongue, the crunchy seeds with their sweet centers. He leaned over, reaching out a hand. Annilee grabbed him and pulled him back.

"Careful! Brush one of those tendrils and the outer leaves close in. Cranel plants eat small animals." She grinned smugly at knowing something he didn't know. "That's why cranels are rare delicacies. They're nasty things to grow. Just ask anyone from Family Mirn."

With fresh caution, Daveeka inspected the carnivorous plant. Something this size could hardly eat him, but now he could see the multitude of tiny spikes embedded in each leaf.

"Poison?" he asked.

"No. At least, none dangerous to us, but they're sharp and barbed. If a small animal or lizard touches those tendrils in an attempt to get at the fruits, the leaves snap shut and the spikes bury themselves in the creature, slowly liquefying and then ingesting the insides of their prey."

"So how do we get at them?"

"Here. I'll show you." She pulled up her sleeve and arched her arm above the center of the nearest plant. "The tendrils are designed to sense an animal approaching from the side."

Lowering her hand directly downwards, her fingers slowly reached for the fruit.

One of the nearby tendrils quivered. She froze, but nothing happened.

When her fingertips touched the glistening red surface of one of the fruits, she spread them around to the sides, sinking her fingertips into the spongy flesh in the attempt at getting a firm grip. That done, she eased the fruit upwards.

It came free with an audible squooshing sound. Daveeka almost expected that the disturbance would set off the trap, but it didn't. The spiked leaves remained peacefully outspread, not designed to deal with an intrusion from above.

Annilee brought her hand back slowly, then pulled the fruit apart until it split into two pieces, handing one to Daveeka and keeping the other for herself.

Eagerly, he lifted it to his lips and took a bite. *Delicious! Absolutely delicious*! Juice ran unheeded down his chin and into his fur as he quickly devoured the cranel.

They ate in silence, slowly, savoring each bite. Then Annilee went to the next plant near the side of the pond and fished out another red globe.

After that they took turns, until there was nothing left in the nearby plants. Before long, they each had full stomachs and as many cranels stuffed into their pockets as they could fit.

"I guess that's all we can get," he remarked

"Just one more, for good measure," Annilee said, reaching beyond an empty plant and out further toward a full one. But she was careless this time. Her sleeve slid forward and brushed a tendril. The plant snapped closed, tearing through cloth and into flesh as she jerked her arm away barely in time to avoid being caught.

For a brief moment, she stared at the ripped fabric. All across the cranel patch, leaves snapped shut in a spreading wave that centered on Annilee's plant. In the blink of an eye, nothing could be seen but clumps of purple leaves, each one clenched tightly together.

A shudder seemed to pass through the swamp. The ever-present cacophony of insect noises fell silent. A bird twittered tentatively once, then stopped. Leaves rustled, but Daveeka could feel no wind.

"Let's get away from here," he whispered. "Quickly."

Annilee gave a subdued nod. The two rillenus made their way back to the riverbank. Annilee didn't dare stop even to examine her arm, simply holding it cradled against her chest. Not much blood had soaked through the ripped sleeve, so the injury was obviously minor.

When she did look at it, she simply shrugged. "It's worth it. Now we have something to eat."

Daveeka fully agreed with her assessment of the situation, especially since she was the one who had been hurt. But he didn't say that out loud.

They plodded on, invigorated by their luxurious meal of cranels. The landscape continued to change, with tall trees appearing here and there, some fairly close to the river.

Daveeka started to look more closely at the trees, trying to identify them based on the descriptions Harizi had given him. Most remained entirely unknown, but he felt sure of some of the others.

He stopped, staring hard at one of the taller ones fairly nearby. Then he pointed at it. "Annilee, that tree over there is a tamaquino."

"So?" she queried impatiently.

"So it's not poisonous or dangerous. If I were to climb up as far as I could, I should be able to look back over the river for a long distance, and see if anyone is following us."

She measured the height of the tree with a calculating glance. "Yes, that might be so. But I'm the one who'll do the climbing, not you."

He started to object, but she held up a hand to stop him. "Daveecha, look at yourself. You're carrying a good-sized infant. That would make you clumsy and you might fall. We can't risk our daughter's life."

"But if you're pregnant, we shouldn't risk having you fall, either."

"Despite what your outlaw friends think they know, it's really too soon to definitely confirm that. Besides, a daughter in the pouch is worth any number of infants not yet born." She touched his shoulder lightly and smiled. "You had the idea. I'll carry it out."

There was nothing he could say to that. She was right.

"At least let me lead the way over to the tree. The undergrowth is getting pretty thick near the base, and I know better what to look out for than you do."

She nodded and they started off towards the tamaquino.

"The most important thing is to do the least possible damage to the forest. Even breaking twigs or stepping on exposed roots can attract jinko vines, not to mention other kinds of predators," he instructed her, while picking his way gingerly across the riverbank. He avoided any vegetation as best he could, with Annilee following directly in his footsteps. Eventually, the bushes and grasses became too thick, so they had no choice but to step slowly and carefully onto the grass, and gently push the branches of the bushes aside. They spotted and evaded several questing jinko vines, saw a few lizards scuttle out of their path, and encountered a large snake that regarded them with cold unblinking eyes, but did nothing more threatening than watch.

At last they arrived at the base of the tree. The branches mostly grew straight out from the trunk, and they were closely spaced.

Annilee emptied her pockets of the cranels, not wishing to crush them while climbing. Daveeka gave Annilee a leg up to one of the lower branches. She had no trouble climbing the rest of the way.

He shuddered as the smaller branches crunched and creaked under her weight. So far, so good, but there might well be other things out in the surrounding vegetation, less well known and less easily seen.

"Come on, Annilee. Make it quick," he whispered under his breath. "The sooner we can get out of here, the better."

Suddenly, the creaking and crunching increased as Annilee came swiftly down the tree. He was about to rebuke her, but as she swung down to the ground he saw fear in the angle of her ears.

"I could see the Farms ahead and I could see upriver too," she gasped. "There were three canoes on the river, just beyond the waterfall! If they start tracking us from there—"

"Easy, Annilee, easy. It will still take them time to follow our trail. They'll have to keep checking if we've left the river. How far are the Farms?"

She frowned. "Hard to be sure."

"Compared to the waterfall, did it seem to be more or less?"

"Definitely less. But the river disappears into what looks like a thicker section of forest before it reaches the Mirn Farms. I know it's Mirn, since I could make out the numerous ponds and small lakes where they grow their cranels, and other water-loving crops."

"So if we kept going throughout much of the day each time, we might make it in two nights?"

"Maybe one, if we'd stop pussyfooting around and being so careful of the foliage."

"Clarlaw and Harizi both warned me about—"

"Forget them! I'm more afraid of the outlaws than I am of the forest. Merciful Mother, are all males such cowards?"

So saying, she strode back toward the river, shoving the bushes roughly out of her way. With a curse, Daveeka followed her.

When nothing happened, Annilee became even more confident that she was right about ignoring the forest.

Daveeka just breathed a weary sigh of relief as they started along the riverbank once again. He dared to feel hopeful. After all, they were almost there and they now had their pockets full of cranels. They just might make it to safety after all.

He refused to think about what would happen then.

By sunrise, they were struggling through some very swampy territory. There was standing water all the way up to the river in some of the worst places, and that water was crowded with various kinds of plants and strangely contorted trees, with an ever-thickening forest growing closer around them.

To avoid the worst spots, the two rillenus had to wade across shallow inlets along the narrowing riverbank, and sometimes even out a ways into the river, when the vegetation grew too thickly even in the inlets themselves.

The sandy bank turned muddy, making it harder to walk.

As they approached yet another overgrown inlet up ahead, this one even wider than the other and leading into a vast expanse of thick swamp, Daveeka shook his head.

"We're not going to be able to go on much longer. The sun's getting brighter and it'll soon be too hard and exhausting for you to try to follow me blindfolded."

"Don't tell me you're willing to give up that easily, now that we're almost there," she replied scornfully. "Surely, we could make it a little further."

"No. There's too much possibly dangerous stuff growing in that inlet, and we have no idea what may be living in the swamp.

Even with goggles, we won't be able to see well enough to get across safely."

"You're too cautious."

"You're too careless," he retorted.

They stood there at an impasse, glaring at each other.

Neither of them noticed the thick brown vine poke up out of the swamp and slither through the grass until it had whipped its thorny end around Daveeka's ankle.

CHAPTER 10

Daveeka was jerked sharply off his feet, landing flat on his back. He tried to get up, only to find that a mottled brown vine no thicker than one of his fingers had wrapped itself around his ankle, between the top of his shoe and the bottom of his leg covers. He saw the red stain on his clothing even before he felt the circle of burning pain surrounding his ankle. Even worse, it was dragging him slowly but inexorably towards the nearby swamp.

He sat up, grabbing for the vine. Its surface was covered with tiny barbed thorns. He drew his hand away with a sharp cry. The insistent tug on his foot slid him closer to the edge of the dank pool.

Just below the water's surface floated a ropy network of branched and closely intertwined stalks. Pale brown, like the muddy water, it was hard to make them out, but the vines seemed to form a tangled mass of vegetation that stretched back into the deeper part of the swamp as far as Daveeka could see. Wrapped in the mass of squirming leaves was the dead body of what looked like a wild scha'adi, bloated and decomposed and covered with a fine net of tendrils.

Judging by the steady tug of the vine around his ankle, Daveeka was intended to join the unfortunate scha'adi. And the mass of whatever sort of plant that was down there would easily be heavy enough to drag him under and drown him.

Shorter vines crept out of the water now, slithering in his direction. Panic-stricken, Daveeka struggled to get loose, heedless of the way the thorns on the vine were being worked deeper into his flesh.

Annilee appeared alongside him, Smarro's knife drawn from its sheath. She slashed at the vine, but it was tough and rubbery and refused to part easily.

As she sawed at the vine, Daveeka slid closer to the swamp, despite his wild scrabbling at the mud. She was forced to move with him.

A crowd of small tentacles slithered out of the swamp, gathering at the water's edge and clearly anticipating the arrival of their hapless prey. There were more than enough of them to haul Annilee in also, if she got within their range. With the strength born of terror, she hacked even harder at the vine.

At last, it snapped. She hauled Daveeka to his feet, pulling his arm over her shoulder and half-dragging him as fast as she could down along the river, not even pausing as they struggled through the vegetation-clogged inlet that rose almost to their waists. Once they were well clear of the swamp, Daveeka collapsed. The pain from his ankle began to override the panicked terror that had carried him along on their wild flight.

"Annilee—I can't—" he gasped.

"Quiet. Let me get this thing off your leg."

Using the tip of her dagger, she carefully pried the thorny vine away from his ankle, having no choice but to rip the barbs from his flesh. Daveeka bit his lip and tried not to cry out.

She removed his shoe and pulled up his leg cover so she could better inspect the wound. All Daveeka could see was blood-caked fur.

"We'd better wash this off. Can you make it over to the river, if I help you?"

Daveeka regarded the sluggish water with new respect. If that thing wasn't restricted to the swamp …

"You think that's safe?"

"I'll go over and check." She walked back the way they had come, scanning the surface warily. Then she returned and offered him a hand. "Nothing. The river water is clear, so maybe that creature is limited to swamps. But let's make it quick, just in case."

He hobbled over with her.

"Sit down here and I'll scoop out water with my hands. We might attract something else just as nasty if we get blood in the river."

He did as she said, his ankle hurting worse the more he thought about it. He closed his eyes as Annilee sloshed water over his foot. His head swam dizzily. The last thing Daveeka remembered clearly was falling backwards into the sand.

He came to with the feel of someone's hand exploring his pouch and the bright light of day soaking through the rag tied over his eyes. Panic flared in his groggy brain. He grabbed at the intruder, catching wrists, pulling them away with frantic strength.

"Daveecha, stop. It's only me."

Annilee's voice was not reassuring and her hands refused to budge. His torn ankle throbbed with agony. There was no way he could walk. A horrible thought flashed across his mind.

"You're trying to take my daughter," he accused. "You'd leave me here to die."

"No, Dav, no. I was only cleaning your pouch."

He wasn't sure whether to believe her or not. She had good reason for wanting him out of the way. After all, he had been a witness to her humiliation at the hands of the renegades. She might not want him back at Thennevar, telling that story. It could be much more convenient for her to take her daughter and just leave him here to die.

However, judging by the bright daylight beyond his blindfold, he'd been out for some time. If she'd wanted to take the infant, she'd have been able to do so while he lay unconscious. Perhaps Annilee was telling the truth. Or perhaps the idea had only then occurred to her.

Belatedly, he remembered she had called him Dav, rather than his full name. That was never done, unless one was a friend, and even then, not by a female to a male.

He lifted the edge of the blindfold and looked at her.

"You called me 'Dav'," he said bluntly.

"Did I? Yes, I guess I did." Her ears twisted with embarrassment.

"Did you mean it?"

Her ears twisted further, yet she nodded.

Refraining from saying more, he squinted down at his foot. It was puffy and inflamed. He wriggled his toes experimentally, then tried flexing the ankle. Sharp spears of pain lanced up his leg and he winced. He wouldn't be able to walk for a couple of nights at least.

Then an even worse thought occurred to him. He said softly, "Maybe you should take our daughter. I'll never make it. I've already delayed us for too long. Bruefen and his friends must surely be close behind us. If you stay here with me, you could be captured again."

"I know. I thought of that too. I almost …" She stopped. "Anyway, I'm prepared for the outlaws. They won't take me or my daughter alive. Not as long as I've still got my dagger."

Daveeka had no doubt that she meant it. "No! Take the child and leave me. At least then you'll both have a chance to survive. We can't be far from the edge of the forest by now."

Her hand touched his head, caressing the base of his ears with reassuring strokes. "I won't desert you. We've been through too much together."

This wasn't entirely the reaction he had expected. "Annilee, I'm a male. Why should you care what happens to me?"

"I don't know, but I do. You got into this mess because I convinced you to help me escape. I won't leave you here. It wouldn't be honorable."

"Honorable? Is that all?"

Her hand stopped moving, simply resting on his head. "Not quite. I honestly … like you. I don't understand it. I've never felt this way about a male before. I mean, they're all rather stupid and uninteresting and petty and I never thought …"

Her voice trailed off, almost as if she were suddenly ashamed of what she was saying, but perplexed by that shame.

"For a female, you're not so bad yourself," Daveeka remarked wryly.

Then he said something he had wanted to say for a long time, but had been afraid to tell her.

"I'm truly sorry about what I did to you back there."

For a moment, she looked puzzled. Then her expression changed and her ears drew down and back. "You mean mating me against my will?"

He turned his head away in shame. "Yes. And for being so cruel while I was doing it."

"Such an action would condemn you to death," she said levelly.

"I know."

"Yet you were willing to risk that by not merely freeing me, but also helping me get back to Thennevar."

"I was thinking of my daughter more than of you," he admitted, determined to be honest no matter what. He owed Annilee

197

the truth, since she had just risked her own life to save him from the swamp creature. "I didn't want her to be treated like that when she grew up."

Annilee was silent for a very long moment before she spoke. When she did, she placed both hands on his head and recited in formal femalespeech, "Ssswear Ish by Mosst Sssacred Name of Elenath that sspoken never ve, no one ve of thisss told forever."

"Sspoken never ve?" he queried. "She has another name?"

"Yes. It is known only to females, and even we may not use it." She hesitated, as if she had told him too much already. Then, very softly, she said, "This is our most sacred oath. It is sworn only by one female to another."

Realizing the honor she had just bestowed upon him, Daveeka bowed his head. Tears slid unbidden from his eyes and soaked into the short fur of his face.

The rest of that day and most of nextnight passed with Daveeka sick, miserable, and half-delirious from fever as his foot grew infected and swollen. Annilee remained by his side, keeping watch and tending him.

The night sky was lit only by the cold white light of one of the two smaller moons when Daveeka was jerked roughly awake by someone shaking his shoulder and whispering his name.

"What?" he replied muzzily.

Annilee was a dark silhouette against the pale gray of the eastern sky. "Get up. We're moving out."

"Huh? Why?"

"I saw canoes on the river. They're still quite a distance away, but if they notice that cranel patch we raided, they'll know we're not far ahead of them. We have to go. Now!"

She pulled him to his feet. Fresh pain washed up his leg as he tried to step on it.

"Annilee, I don't think I can walk."

"You'll lean on me. If I have to, I'll carry you," she promised.

And it almost came to that, by the time the sun was fully up. With visor and blindfold, Daveeka stumbled along with an arm clamped around Annilee's shoulder, much of his weight resting on the young female, who wore the goggles and led the way.

She gasped and panted for breath, stopping to rest frequently. They didn't move fast, but they covered ground at a steady pace.

By nightfall, the river had widened out into a deep lake. With no other choice, they continued along the shore.

The forest encroached steadily further upon the lake itself, until they found themselves beneath towering trees. Daveeka was, by now, so weak and exhausted by the pain and exertion that he often drifted off into a sort of daze, sometimes not even aware of where he was or what he was doing.

During one of his lucid periods, he realized they were essentially in the forest.

"Must do no damage," he said dreamily. "Harizi. Said not to break anything. Take care."

"Hush, Dav. You've already told me that. Several times. Just keep walking."

"Yes," he agreed. "Must keep walking. Must …"

Eventually, his voice drifted off.

They kept walking.

When they finally staggered out of the forest shortly before daybreak, Daveeka was delirious with fever and the pain in his foot, barely aware of his surroundings. Excited voices buzzed around him and hands reached to support him, but all he cared about doing was collapsing to the ground and passing out.

The trip back to Thennevar was mostly a blur. By the time the infection in his ankle had subsided and the fever had gone down, he was in his old room in the Palace, with nothing but disconnected snatches of memory of being jounced along in a closed litter for what seemed like an eternity of throbbing pain but must in reality have been far less.

In every one of those memories, Annilee had been there beside him, stroking him tenderly and reassuring him that his daughter was well and had not been taken. He couldn't remember much else, but he could recall the feel of her fingers in his fur, relaxing and soothing him.

She was still at his side when he was laid at last on his familiar mattress at the Palace. He was jarred rudely into full consciousness when a Thennevar servant came to treat his ankle, unwrapping the bandages.

"It's all right now, Dav. You're safe. I've told everyone what happened," Annilee said, taking his hand and smoothing the short fur on the backs of his fingers. "In fact, you're a hero."

He blinked, but saw nothing. For a moment he thought he had gone blind from overexposure to the sunlight. Then he realized there was a damp rag covering his eyes. It felt good, so he left it there. It might be awhile yet before he could see clearly, but at least he wasn't blind.

"Hero?" he croaked.

"Sure. You helped me escape. There's an expedition being sent out to capture them already. Clarlaw and his followers may even be prisoners by now, and we just haven't heard."

"Prisoners?" Daveeka asked blankly. Then it penetrated. *Of course.* The females couldn't afford to have renegade males loose in the forest, especially now that their existence would have become general knowledge due to Annilee's capture. Revenge would have to be taken. With the information Annilee must have given about the location, the renegade village would be easy to find, although there would surely be a lot of casualties along the way. But what did the females care about male casualties?

He groaned.

Mistaking his groan for pain, Annilee sharply reprimanded the servant working on his ankle.

"Mistress, can't you do something? If they're captured, they'll surely be executed. Some of them were kind—"

"Like Bruefen?" she interrupted tartly.

"I know. But the others. And some are only children."

"Hush, Dav. Don't worry about them now. Rest and get well. The healers say your ankle is showing improvement. The inflammation is subsiding and you'll soon be able to walk."

He tried to sit up, pushing the rag off of his eyes and wincing in the light from the glowweed. "Annilee ..."

Her ears slanted back, one much further than the other. The torn ear was now badly distorted by the scar that had formed. "We are no longer amongst outlaws, Daveecha. You must not call me so."

"Mistress Annilee, couldn't you do something?"

She dismissed the servant with a wave of her hand. Leaning close to his ear, she whispered, "Shh, we mustn't be overheard. I didn't give good directions, so they may have time to escape. I had to say the camp was along the river, since the kidnappers had been tracked that far. But I claimed I didn't know the exact distance, so that will delay the search."

Astonished, he started to say something, but Annilee put a finger over his lips, saying scornfully, "Why are you so worried about those worthless outlaws? Aren't you even going to ask about that friend of yours? What was his name … Teo?"

Teo! Mother of All, I forgot about Teo!

Seeing his alarm, Annilee laid a hand on his shoulder. "It's all right. He's alive. In fact, once he told his story, he was granted release from the Farms, since he had tried to foil the kidnap attempt and save me."

He was trying to save me, not you, Daveeka thought. But he kept silent. Better for Teo if they assumed otherwise.

"He's back at Marloosh. At last report, his wounds were almost healed. He was most happy to hear that you were safe." She stroked his neck. "Does this not please you?"

"Oh, yes! Very much." Teo was safe, then. Soon they might be reunited. "Mistress, if I'm a hero, perhaps the Exalted Mother might be moved to grant me a small favor?"

"What is it you wish? I'll see to it."

"The servant boy, Zillah. He was exiled by a complaint from Fahlin, but he was my friend. If not for his help, I might not have witnessed the kidnap attempt. If he could be pardoned and brought back from the Farms …"

"It shall be done," she promised. "I'm sure I can convince my Mother. It's only wise to honor those whose actions led to my return, even if only in a small way."

"And the outlaws, Mistress. When they're captured, perhaps they could be granted clemency?"

"Never! How dare you ask mercy for those who dishonored me?!"

Daveeka slowly blinked his eyes, signaling that there was more meaning to be found behind his words than was apparent.

"Not the ones who—" he groped for a neutral word "—assaulted you. But the others. Most of them were not involved. The children surely not."

Annilee thought for a moment. Her flattened ears lifted slightly. Yes, she understood. If anyone were listening, he could not just ignore the fate of the renegades now, having spoken up for them once. And he must appear to assume they would be captured.

"True enough. I will see what may be done, Dav. But remember, I am not the Exalted Mother. I'm not even a Mother yet. I have no power of my own and can only ask."

Her eyes shifted down to Daveeka's pouch, and he saw the hunger in them. It was past time for his daughter to have been taken.

As if reading his thoughts, Annilee explained, "I've convinced the Exalted Mother not to have our child taken as yet, since you're still in bad shape and the additional trauma might prove harmful. In consideration for your heroism in helping me escape, she has agreed. But we can't delay for much longer. It must be soon."

His ears drooped.

"So long as you're still weak and in a lot of pain," she said carefully, "I might be able to put it off a bit longer. I would also be willing to clean your pouch and examine my daughter here in your room, since the strain of the usual sessions might be too much for you just now."

Daveeka nodded his understanding. He must act as if he's worse off than he really is.

"I would appreciate that, Mistress. The longer I can keep our daughter, the better chance she'll have to survive."

Annilee looked away. "That may be so, or not. I sought only to spare you."

"Thank you," he said softly. "I think I really need to rest now, Mistress."

Taking the cue, she rose to her feet. With his more sensitive male hearing, he could make out the quick rustle of footsteps outside the door. Someone had indeed been listening. He inclined his head slightly, and very slowly and deliberately blinked his eyes.

As Annilee turned to leave the room, she returned the signal.

From then on, Daveeka pretended to be much worse off than he was, leaving the cloth over his eyes even after his vision began to clear and feigning exhaustion and pain far beyond what he actually felt. He saw no one but Annilee and, much to his relief, his young servant, Sinda, who had now been reunited with him.

Fahlin's voice could often be heard from the common room beyond the curtain at Daveeka's door. Now and then, stealthy footsteps approached the doorway and the curtain would move almost imperceptibly. He suspected the Honored Father was spying on him.

It was the third quarn of Second Nanth when Annilee brought him news of the outlaws. Her good ear was set at a strange angle and she plucked nervously at a loose thread on the blanket as she sat next to Daveeka.

"The few surviving members of the second expedition sent out by Family Scheld returned two nights ago."

"Second? What happened to the first?"

She shrugged. "No one knows. They may still be out there."

"More likely they're all dead."

"Considering what it's like in the forest, I wouldn't be surprised. Unlike the first, the second expedition was made up of volunteers, who had been promised to be released from the Farms if they were successful. In any case, some of them lasted long enough to reach the outlaw camp. Except for a few of the leaders, the camp was deserted."

"Who—"

"Bruefen and Smarro. They said the rest of their people had already gone deeper into the forest to establish a new settlement. They stayed behind to confront their pursuers and offer them a deal. They would turn Varri over to them and escort the entire party safely back to the edge of the forest."

A faint rustle of fabric came from the direction of the doorway. His ears swiveled, aiming for the soft sounds. The rustling noise was repeated. It could have been caused by someone shifting his weight impatiently or inadvertently brushing against the curtain. Such a sound was beyond the normal hearing range of a female, but Annilee noticed the angle of his ears. She glanced questioningly to the curtained arch and then back to Daveeka. He gave her a slow blink of warning.

"Why would they want to do that?" he asked quickly, not wanting a suspicious silence to alert the possible eavesdropper.

"They figured the females would never call off the search if they knew there was a girlchild out there. It was Clarlaw's idea to give her up. But just turning her over to the search party wouldn't do any good, if the search party never got back to the Farms. Since the renegades had been watching the expedition most of the way, they knew full well how many of them had died just to get there. They also offered anyone who wanted to join them a place with the rest of the renegades, instead of going back to the Farms and hoping the females would actually keep their promise to set them free. A few took them up on that, but the rest decided they wanted nothing to do with the forest, no matter what.

"Smarro led their new followers off to catch up with the rest of the band, while Bruefen took Varri and the rest of them down the river, turning his daughter over to the others as soon as they reached the edge of the forest near Family Mirn. They said he didn't turn a hair at giving away his girlchild."

Daveeka snorted disdainfully. "Knowing Bruefen, I can believe that."

He didn't dare show how pleased he was over the renegades' escape, since he might be overheard. "At least Varri is all right and she'll be treated much better now. I'm surprised they'd give up their only female though."

"What good is a female, if you're hunted to your death as a result?"

"You're right, Mistress. As usual." Although his tone was sincere, the angle of his ears made his sarcasm perfectly clear to Annilee.

"A good attitude to take, Daveecha," she stated haughtily, with a significant glance at the doorway. "You might be interested in knowing that the slaves who brought Varri back were, indeed, treated as heroes and returned to their male Families, as Scheld had promised. They were sworn to silence, on pain of death."

"Hmph. I'm surprised they didn't just execute the survivors instead, in order to maintain secrecy," he said disdainfully. "That would have been more in character for females."

Annilee glanced uncomfortably towards the curtained doorway. "Watch your voice, Daveecha," she warned sternly. "You may not use such a tone to a female."

"You weren't so high and mighty when you were crouched in the corner of that hut, begging me to help you escape, Mistress," he replied with bitter sarcasm, his anger flaring at the memory.

The words were out of his mouth before he realized it.

Annilee frowned and flattened her ears, while her eyes flickered to the doorway again.

His heart skipped a beat. It could be Fahlin. Or it could be the only female in Thennevar who would have reason for eavesdropping on them. Either way, it was time to end this charade.

"Mistress Annilee, someone is perhaps approaching my room," he said. "I thought I heard footsteps, but I'm not sure."

"I'll look," she replied, playing along with him.

Daveeka heard several hasty footfalls retreating backwards. By the time Annilee drew the curtain aside, Marlieth was innocently walking towards the room.

"Resspectss, Mother," Annilee said. "Why ve hyou here?"

Marlieth swept grandly through the doorway. "To ssee Daveecha have Ish come. Daughter, hyou have told him of cowardly outlawss, na?"

"Thiss have we sspoken of, yesh."

Marlieth turned her dark eyes on Daveeka. "Thossse who ressscued girlchild have earlier thisssnight been brought to Thennevar for honor. Finisshed now being quesstioned. Known it iss that my daughter wass mated often by captorsss. Outlawss bragged of it to rescuerss, sssaying you alsso have thisss done."

Her eyes narrowed and her ears folded down flat against her head in her wrath. "What sssay you, Daveecha?" she hissed.

He struggled to overcome his terror, not knowing what he should say. *If I were to deny it, would Annilee call me a liar?* A quick glance at her ears showed only confusion and shame. Surely, Marleith must have known what had happened before now, since Annilee would have been examined and her injuries treated. Maybe even her pregnancy had been noticed. But she must not have implicated him, or he would be dead by now.

He had almost decided to admit what he had done and beg for mercy, when the young female spoke up.

"Lie did they. Daveecha na do. Only othersss."

Marleith regarded her daughter as if she were not sure whether she believed her or not. Then she turned back to Daveeka, demanding, "Ve true, faithlesss male?"

He was barely able to get the words out. "Sssuch thing ve abomination, Exalted Mother. Misstress Annilee ssay true."

Marleith thought about that for a long moment, her eyes flickering back and forth between the two of them.

Annilee forced her good ear forward and upright, meeting her Mother's gaze squarely. "Thiss sswear Ish by Elenath," she proclaimed. "Innocent ve Daveecha."

"According to daughter'sss wordsss, truth mussst ve," the Exalted Mother stated, her ears still held back and sounding as if she wished it to be otherwise. She continued to glare at Daveeka. "Na so caring ve ssshe now, if sssuch abomination had you done. Sssurely sshe ve demanding execution on High Wall, if truth ve ass outlawsss claim. Na ssso?"

Annilee's fingers traced a small pattern on his arm, cautiously smoothing his fur, but he could feel the slight tremor in her hand. She would doubtless be in trouble also, if it could be proven she had sworn falsely.

That was the way it was to be, then. It had never happened. If he wished to live, he would have to keep up the deception.

Daveeka forced his ear tips up as he gave Marlieth her answer. "Ssuch thing na do I. Ve … ve …" He shook his head, as if at a loss for words to describe such hideous actions.

"Othersss did," Marlieth hissed. "Ssstopped them did you na."

"Na ressponssible ve Daveecha for what otherss do," Annilee interrupted angrily. "Na could he sstop it. He ve captive, as wass Ish. Sso have Ish ssaid."

"True. Sso have hyou sssaid." It didn't sound as if Marlieth believed her daughter's story, but she couldn't disprove it either, as long as Annilee stuck by her version of the facts.

His life hung on Annilee's word. This was not a particularly comfortable feeling.

Marlieth went on to inquire about Daveeka's health, but it was clear she wasn't truly interested. "And hyour dhaughter, Annilee? Sshe ve well?"

"Yesh, Mother. Jusst examined her, have Ish," she lied. "Well sshe ve. And sstrong."

"Goodh. Ssoon now, ve taken. Hyou ve Mother, and na longer only Misstress." She laid a hand on Daveeka's head with feigned affection. "Then ve you Honored Father. Ve pleassed, na?"

"Yesh, Exalted Mother," he said firmly, fighting to squelch the fear rising in his mind at the thought of losing his infant.

With a few more falsely solicitous remarks, Marlieth took her leave. Both Annilee and Daveeka breathed a sigh of relief as she swept aside the curtain and strode out the door.

Annilee was clearly upset now, her ears twitching and her eyes darting toward the door, as if not quite certain Marlieth were truly gone. She looked to Daveeka, waiting for confirmation from him that Marlieth had truly left and was beyond earshot.

He nodded.

"I told my Mother I'd just examined our daughter. Maybe I should, just to see how she's doing."

"She's fine, Mistress. I would know if anything were wrong."

"That is for me to say."

He decided it was not worth an argument, considering how she had just saved him from a horrible death. Folding back the coverlet, he pulled up his tunic. As Annilee's hand slid carefully into his pouch, he couldn't help turning Marlieth's words over in his mind. Soon now, he'd lose the child. After that, he would never know what happened to her.

An Honored Father had no assurance that his own daughter still lived, since female children were kept strictly secluded in the Palace and no news of them was sent to the males, not even the names they had been given. Only after a girlchild came of age and gained the official status of Mistress would she begin her dealings with the Fathers of the male Families, and by then an Honored Father couldn't be certain that a particular new Mistress was indeed his daughter. Sometimes one could make a good guess, but there were too many complicating factors to be sure.

Daveeka felt his daughter wriggle with pleasure, as Annilee caressed her gently.

His own fingers yearned to touch her, but that wouldn't be good. She must come to know and trust Annilee now, not him.

It felt so right and comfortable, to have Annilee caring for their child. Now that he'd gotten to know her better, her hand in his pouch was reassuring, not threatening. If only the females would let him keep the infant longer, until she was truly ready to leave his pouch. The baby should have both Mother and Father, not just a Mother.

Then he became aware of the enormity of what he had just thought. *Mother and Father?* The females would never agree to such a thing. It was preposterous.

Daveeka glanced at Annilee. She sat with her back to him, staring blankly at the far wall, her concentration on the hand inside his pouch and the feel of her daughter's silky fur beneath her fingers.

He forced himself to ask a question he'd long been avoiding. "Annilee, how many female infants actually survive being taken?"

He felt her hand quiver slightly. Still not facing him, she answered, "You do not want to know, Dav."

He touched her shoulder tentatively. Not long ago, he would never have dared such a gesture. "Please. This is my child too. I have a right to know the truth. You owe me that, at least."

Annilee continued to caress her daughter. Then, still staring at the wall, she said dully, "Nearly one-third of the babies die within three nights of being taken, with an additional sixth of the survivors failing to make it beyond the end of the first nanth."

Daveeka had had no idea the mortality rate was that high. He lay there in shocked silence, staring at the back of Annilee's head.

When he didn't reply, she went on. "We don't know what goes wrong. Some babies are found dead in their cradles. Others lapse into unconsciousness and eventually die while their Mothers hold them in their arms."

She twisted around to face Daveeka, trying to keep the dry certainty in her voice but not entirely succeeding. "Any infant not strong enough to survive the shock of leaving its Father's pouch probably wouldn't live to adulthood anyway, so it's for the best that the babies die so young. It is obvious that this is the Will of Elenath."

A black wave of sorrow crested and threatened to fall upon Daveeka's heart. What if his own daughter didn't make it? His child, his very own infant, might all too soon be just another number in a scroll recording yearly deaths. He could do nothing to help her survive, once she was taken.

His eartips drooped and he closed his eyes, concentrating on the reassuring pressure of his daughter's fragile body in his pouch, the long-familiar feel of her mouth holding his teat. She must grow strong and large. Then she would survive.

Suddenly, Annilee inserted her other hand into his pouch, stretching him open with a callous disregard that was unlike her. Alarmed, he arched his head and tried to see what she was doing.

The light shone only dimly into his pouch, but even so he could see the uncharacteristic glitter of dark eyes against the fur of his daughter's face.

Annilee drew in a shocked breath. "Infant'ss eyess ve open, Daveecha," she whispered. "Na good. Marlieth ve angry."

"You don't have to tell her yet, Mistress," he pleaded desperately. "We could fool her for a little longer."

Annilee's ears half-flattened.

"Please! Even just a few more nights could help improve our daughter's chances of survival."

Reluctantly, she agreed.

She had almost gotten to the doorway when she turned back. "Oh, I almost forgot. Your servant, Zillah, was brought back from the Farms at the same time Marlieth's 'heroes' returned. He had a few minor injuries on the Farm, but with rest and decent food, he's going to be fine."

"Could I see him? Do you think he could be my servant again?"

Annilee glanced over her shoulder at the doorway. "I don't think that would be a good idea right now, do you?"

"No, you're right," Daveeka replied, taking the hint. After all, Zillah must need to recover from his ordeal for a while before returning to his duties. "Thank you for getting him back, Mistress. I am truly grateful."

"I'll tell him you asked after him," she offered before she left his room.

Two nights slipped by without incident. Daveeka's ankle had healed to the point where he could walk short distances without undue pain, but still he kept to his room, not wanting anyone to know he was feeling better than he pretended to be.

He stared at the carpet moss on the floor. A discolored section showed where the chalk marks he and Zillah had used for rug-dancing had been scrubbed away. At least Zillah was safe, for now. After he became an Honored Father, he would be able to request Zillah's services again. Maybe he could even get the youngster out of the Thennevar Palace and take him back to

Marloosh as his secretary. Maybe he could also request Sinda to remain with him.

By then, Teo should be recovered. It would be so good to be with him again!

Cheered by the thought, he looked again at the fading marks, remembering that last time he had been in a Dance.

And that led to another thought. At the beginning of Fifth Nanth it would be time for the Kiari Winter Dance. With a lot of practice, even with the scars on his feet, he might be able to perform one of the simpler dances. It would be the first time that a Father, much less an Honored Father, took part in such a thing!

Then reality crashed into his hopes: as an Honored Father, would he dare to participate? That was the real question, and to that question, Daveeka did not know the answer.

On the night of the full moon beginning Third Nanth, Annilee came to tell him she had officially been declared pregnant. Her ears stood straight with joy as she sat down beside him and described the ceremony.

"Fahlin was there too, way in the back," she concluded, with a short laugh. "He didn't look at all pleased."

Fahlin. Daveeka hadn't so much as seen the other male since he'd returned to Thennevar, nor did he wish to.

"Oh, by the way, Mistress Chezoar was also declared pregnant, but given her past history, no one was very impressed by that. She'll be lucky to have even a few sons that survive, at her age."

Chezoar. How long ago had she last mated him? Was it possible that some of the infants –no, he couldn't remember for sure.

"Dav?" she questioned.

He blinked and brought his mind back to her words.

Her ears drooped. "You're not going to like this, Dav, but I had to do it. I told my Mother the baby's eyes are open."

He sat upright in sudden shock. "Annilee—"

She put a hand over his mouth. "Shh. We can't keep fooling her much longer. It had to be soon, you knew that." Annilee glanced to the door. "Would you rather she came in and examined you herself? That's what she planned to do tonight. Mistress Chezoar warned me." She touched his head gently, rubbing his ears. "The taking will be at next moonrise. She wanted it to be immediately, but I reminded her it is customary that the male have a full night to prepare himself, so she had to agree to it."

Daveeka found his voice. "Couldn't you get her to wait a little longer?"

Her hand stopped caressing his ears and her voice reflected impatience. "Dav, you must stop this. It's already way past time for the baby to be taken. If I were to say anything more, everyone would think I was crazy."

"But you know how it was among the outlaws. You know what they said about—."

She shrugged. "A bunch of ignorant, crude males. What could they know? A few of their female infants survived. So what? They might have just been stronger than usual. It may have no connection with their staying in their Fathers' pouches too long."

"It isn't too long! Clarlaw's group was right. I know it!"

Annilee blinked her eyes slowly, warning him of the danger of his raised voice. "Were they also right to treat their females as they did?" she asked sternly.

Daveeka had to duck his head and let his ears droop at her remark.

"So they may just as well be wrong about other things also, na?"

"But Mistress, if there's even a possibility this would give our daughter a better chance to live, what harm would it do?" He stopped, warned by the angle of her ears.

"What harm? You have already carried this child an entire nanth longer than is customary. Her eyes are open. She will have some memory of you. Perhaps that alone will make her less willing to accept my care and she'll be more likely to die. It's as possible as your theory."

"But—"

She rose to her feet. "Na, Daveecha. There's no use discussing this further. You will not impress the Mothers with your behavior. You have a chance to gain favor in many females' eyes because of the part you played in destroying the renegades. Now you could lose all that by acting like a hysterical male afraid to give up his daughter." She held up a hand to silence his protest. "Na. Hear me out. There are a few of us who are willing to consider the merit of your suggestion about giving more of our Invitations to childless males."

Daveeka's ears stood upright with surprise. He tried to say something, but again she gestured him to silence.

"Oh, we're not in favor of that nonsense you've been claiming you're going to propose at the Conclave. Restricting Greater and Honored Fathers to Fifth and Sixth Position is ridiculous. They've got to be in the higher Positions, since female infants carried by experienced Fathers have a much better survival rate. That's clearly documented in our records. Thennevar will never approve of excluding them from higher Positions, even if all of the male Families approved it.

"However, it might be possible to work out some less extreme proposal, something that the females would go along with if you could bring it up at the Conclave."

Daveeka stared at her in blank astonishment. He hadn't realized any of the females might be on his side, even if only partially. Before, he was certain he had been fighting a losing battle. Now it was beginning to look as if that might not be the case. "Mistress, I had no idea you agreed with me."

"I don't exactly agree with you, Dav. I just said some of us are willing to entertain the possibility of making some changes in the way Invitations are given. But if you expect a female to take you seriously, you've got to stop acting like a typical cowardly male. Whether you like it or not, your credibility is going to depend not only on what you have to say, but also on how you act. I can't argue in your favor unless you give me something to work with. Once you're an Honored Father—"

"I can't, Annilee!" The words poured from his mouth, as visions of his helpless infant being taken from his pouch overwhelmed his mind. "I won't let them take her! I'll run away, I'll hide—"

"Hush," she said gently. "Most first time Fathers do try to escape before their daughters are taken. But if you get beyond the confines of the Palace and we have to bring you back, this draws the attention of other males. In that case, Marlieth is justified in refusing to confirm you as an Honored Father. Wouldn't it be better if you didn't do anything foolish like that?"

Refuse to confirm him as an Honored Father? After all he'd been through?

Annilee studied him intently. Reaching into a pocket, she pulled out a small roll of parchment. "Look at this."

Daveeka took the parchment and opened it up. For the second time in his life, he found himself holding an Invitation to Annilee's next birthing. But this time he was being offered First Position.

His hand shook. *First Position.* That virtually assured him of a child, most likely a son, but possibly even a second daughter.

"Two Invitations in a row from the same female is a great honor, Daveecha. Everyone would know you had found favor with the prospective heir to Thennevar. But if you wish to be able to accept, you must stop this talk about keeping our daughter any longer. Unless she's taken immediately, your pouch will not be ready to Receive a new infant in time. Indeed, one nanth is barely long enough as it is."

That was all too true. His body would need time to adjust to the loss of his present infant, not to mention getting into condition to accept a new baby. His teat, now enlarged by the demands of his daughter, would have to shrink back to a size that would fit the mouth of a newborn. His stretched pouch would have to contract, at least enough to hold a tiny infant snugly. In a nanth, with proper care, he might be ready.

She had him, and Daveeka knew it. He stared at the Invitation in his hand. Did he dare to negotiate further? Swallowing the lump in his throat, he said hesitantly, "Mistress, perhaps for the other Positions you would consider some childless males? It would set an example for other females to follow."

"I … I'm not sure I could get away with that just yet, Dav. There will be protests when I make your Invitation public. Marlieth—"

"Annilee, please! You said you'd be on my side. We'd change things."

"We will, Dav. But not right away. It will take time."

He sank back against his pillow, forbearing to mention that the time Annilee pleaded for was exactly what she was unwilling to grant to her daughter.

But she was right. Further protest would serve no purpose. He was going to lose his daughter nextnight. He'd just have to accept that fact.

He nodded shortly, feeling the tears well up in his eyes.

Maybe he'd been a fool. Maybe he should have stayed with the outlaws.

CHAPTER 11

As the sand slid inexorably down in the yellow timeglass, building to a pile that meant sunset was not far away, Daveeka tossed and turned on his mattress. He was tempted to take a draught of jareesh in order to sleep, but something inside him resisted being drugged. This was the last little bit of time when he would still have his daughter. He couldn't bear to waste it in a drunken stupor.

He curled around his pouch, bitter tears sliding down the fur of his cheeks. He tried to tell himself he was being irrational. His daughter was an entire nanth older than most female infants were when they were taken. She would survive.

The more he reassured himself, the worse he felt. Annilee would reach inside him, force the child to release its hold on his teat, and take her away. He couldn't bear the thought.

The horrible image grew and grew in his mind, Annilee's face turning into a demonic caricature.

No! I can't let them do it! I won't!

But in the end, he had no choice. There were guards outside his room. Escape would be impossible, and if by some chance he did escape and get outside the Palace, he would surely be captured. After that, Marlieth would never confirm him as an Honored Father.

There was no way out.

When Annilee came for him, accompanied by a cadre of Mothers, he donned the black, open-fronted tunic they gave him without protest. He even insisted he could walk, rather than being carried. Leaning heavily on Annilee's arm, he limped to the Temple, sitting on the cushion they indicated for him directly before the statue of Elenath.

Behind him, the females' voices droned through prayers for the survival of the daughter he carried, imploring the Deity's favor, asking strength and courage for Annilee in what she must now do.

No one prayed for him, he noted bitterly. His usefulness was almost at an end.

He stared up at the face of the statue, wondering if there even was a prayer for him to say. Firelight flickered, casting shadows across Elenath's graven countenance, constantly altering the apparent angle of Her ears. It was impossible to tell if She was pleased, or angry.

He narrowed his eyes, trying to see beyond the deceiving shadows. Suddenly a cold thought entered his mind, colder than the fear in his heart. In reality, Elenath is neither angry nor pleased. Rillenu imagination attributes those feelings to Her. She only watches and listens. And does nothing.

He shivered at that chill realization.

And then he grew angry. What good was this thing they worshipped, if it did not care? If Elenath could not, or would not, help, then why implore Her favor or sing Her praises?

No, he wouldn't stand for this any longer. She would answer him, if She could. Here. Now. Or he would worship Her no more.

He rose to his feet. Limping over to the steps that led to the raised platform, Daveeka struck the crystal chimes in the melody indicating he sought to go before the Deity for a Shape.

The evening ritual halted abruptly. Outraged voices broke the sudden silence. Marlieth turned from her place on the platform and stared at him in disbelief.

He sank to his knees and covered his face with his hands, waiting to be questioned.

Skirts swished and a female voice sang hastily, "You wisssh before Elenath to go?" It was not Marlieth. The voice sounded like Mother Magdael, who had been leading the prayers.

"I wisssh ssso to do," he replied.

"What ssseek you?" she sang.

He drew a deep breath and continued in a quavering and difficult melody that he was far from certain was correct. "I Challenge. An ansswer do I demand from Sshe Who Ruless."

Stunned silence fell over the vast expanse of the Temple.

A female might Challenge Elenath during times of stress, but no one had ever expected a male to have the courage to try it. To humbly seek a particular Shape was one thing, but he risked provoking the Deity's wrath by a Challenge. Now he was bound to plunge his hand deep into the pot and take whatever Shape presented itself to him. Such a thing was chancy, since he would be obliged to live according to the concept signified by the crystal he received, whether he liked it or not.

Daveeka felt the light touch on the top of his head that signified his quest had been accepted.

"Go you," Mother Magdael sang in the final tune, gesturing toward the statue that towered over them both. "To your Challenge, ve Ish witnesss."

Opening his eyes, Daveeka rose and climbed the stairs to the platform. Once again, he stood before the curtain and the flickering firepot. Gathering his courage, he reached through the heavy folds of the veil.

A strange calm enveloped his mind as he plunged his hand into the hot crystals. He must not attempt to identify the Shapes, but simply take whatever one he was inspired to grasp. Heat scorched through his fur as he forced his hand further down. His entire forearm was immersed now. He was determined to take one of the complex, many-facetted crystals from the very bottom of the pot, to do what few females ever accomplished. The cold rage in his heart quenched the burning pain in his fingers.

Dark Mother of the Kiari, speak to me now! You WILL reply. Do You hear me? Do You care? Are You even there at all? What is the meaning of my life?

His knuckles brushed the hard surface of the bottom of the firepot. He opened his hand, then closed it around the first Shape to slide into his palm. Quickly, he wrenched his arm out of the heat. The fur on the back of his hand and lower forearm was completely burned away, while the bare brown skin was scorched a reddish color.

He dropped the Shape into the cooling dish, then clutched his throbbing hand against his chest. The Shape bounced and rolled to the center of the shallow ceramic cup.

A plain round crystal. A Sphere? What did that mean?

He thought frantically back to the Scroll of Meanings he'd studied nanths ago. Smooth, unfacetted crystals were extremely rare. He hadn't paid much attention to the meanings of those Shapes, since he'd never expected to get one.

Magdael sucked in a startled breath as she looked into the bowl. "Ve Ssphere of Unity and Wholenesss," she said, voice quivering with disbelief.

Excited whispers broke out amongst the watching females.

"Na can it ve," Marlieth announced, striding up and across the platform. "In thirty-ssix lifetimess, na hass ssuch a Sshape been given. Ve misstake."

"Na misstake, Exalted Mother," Magdael said firmly. "Ve Ssphere."

Marlieth gestured her impatiently away, then stared into the cooling dish. Her ears flattened, and her fingers curled into fists. She shook her head. Daveeka thought he heard her mutter a short curse, but he couldn't be sure. The pain in his hand grew worse, demanding his attention.

The Exalted Mother sank to her knees, covering her face with her hands and chanting softly to herself. Some of the other females followed suit, but others merely stared at the male who had received such a Shape from the Hand of the Mother of All.

Daveeka was somehow not impressed. Unity and Wholeness? What kind of an answer was that?

He glared up at the statue, the face and body strangely foreshortened when seen from so close and below. He laid his ears back and whispered barely audible words through teeth clenched in pain and anguish. "Is this all? Just this enigmatic reply? Dark Mother, it is not enough! Why do You not act? You watch, while males die in agony on the Farms. You watched, while a female who should have been sacred to You was brutalized by renegade males. You will watch, while my daughter is torn from my pouch. You listen to our prayers and shrieks of pain, and You do nothing!"

What would you have Me do, foolish child? Do you wish to live within My pouch like an infant for all your life? Or will you grow up, and take responsibility for your own world and what you do with it? Shall I take that away from you, then? Or will you keep your freedom, knowing its cost?

Daveeka was at first too amazed to know if the strange answer had truly come from Elenath or from his own imagination. But it made a sort of sense. You cannot have both freedom to make your own choices and a Deity Who constantly interferes with Her world, nullifying the consequences of that freedom.

Yet something about that answer disturbed him. Why would Elenath refer to Her pouch?

Puzzled, he continued to stare up at the statue. It was, of course, not the reality. It was merely a reminder, a focus for eyes and mind. All but the most coarse and ill-educated males knew that.

Then something slipped in Daveeka's mind. As a brilliant image reverses itself inside your eyelids when you close your eyes, the statue flickered and turned inside out. And was not Mother, but Father of All.

He stared incredulously at the statue, and for the first time, really saw it. The rounded ears: almost female, but too large; almost male, but too rounded. Her fur too long for a male, but too short for a female. Even the color of that ambiguous fur was wrong; too light for a female, too dark for a male.

The ancient statue, always there, always seen until no one thought to wonder at it anymore.

Elenath was no female, nor yet again was She (She?) male. Females were not the only ones made in Her image.

No, it could not be. Such a truth shook the very nature of Daveeka's being. And the very nature of rillenu society.

If She Who Rules is not She at all, then what … who …? The Mother of All surely could not be male. That made no sense.

Or it did make sense. And the differences became meaningless, and the meanings meant nothing at all. Elenath, Who was the essence of all things, was something not-male, not-female. And possibly not even rillenu.

Impossible! Everything was one or the other. He could not even speak of such a thing. Which pronoun, which verb inflection, could be used?

There must be two Deities, one male, one female. Yes, he could think of that. He had the grammar and the words.

Elenath was one, female singular. Elenath was one, male singular.

He shook his head. No, it wouldn't do. For two to be one made even less sense.

Daveeka looked down at the Sphere in the ceramic dish. That had been the answer to his Challenge. Unity and Wholeness. His mind bent suddenly around a corner he hadn't realized was there. If Elenath was one, alone and only, might not all other rillenus, male and female, be truly only one kind, one nature? It was the language that was wrong, for it distorted reality.

Have we persisted in seeing Elenath in our image, bound by the forms of our bodies, although in truth S/He could have no body at all?

The statue brooded in the shadowed light, mute testimony to the vision of its original sculptor. Daveeka tried out this unaccustomed perception, attempting to force Her into an image that surpassed both male and female. Almost, when he silenced the words in his mind and simply looked through his eyes, he got a brief glimpse of such a Being.

But he couldn't hold the image. It was as if a thick curtain had been pulled back, exposing sensitive eyes to raw daylight, and the light was too bright. He looked away, unable to continue staring.

Elenath was Mother. That category was comfortable and familiar, not mind-bending. Forget the rest.

But if it were not so, if the Ultimate Essence of Being was not exclusively female, then a male was not something else and other, auxiliary, extraneous to the real thing. His existence was as valid as any female's, and as valuable.

Could it be? Dare he believe that? Even the renegades hadn't claimed such a thing. They had simply torn the Mother from Her place and cast Her to the ground, to be raped and terrorized. Somehow their solution seemed only the same conditions in reverse, as if they had carved an exclusively male statue of Elenath and declared it to be the new reality.

Understandable, yes. Ultimately useful?

He shrugged uncomfortably. Did it matter? The renegades had been dispersed, their only female lost, as a consequence of his decision to help Annilee escape.

But all this might be the result of his own overwrought imagination. How could he find out if that strange flash of insight about Elenath's true nature might indeed be true? The statue was deliberately ambiguous. That had to mean something. Someone else had to have thought of the same thing, or such a statue would not exist.

The females might know. But would they tell him, or simply lie?

He noticed Mistress Chezoar in the back row, seated humbly behind the Mothers. The Shape she wore was Truth in All

Circumstances. She would have no choice but to answer truthfully, if she knew.

Daveeka took up the Sphere from the cooling dish with his uninjured hand. "Elenath ve na female only," he said clearly, looking down at the females. "Na sso?"

Marlieth's ears flattened. "Ssuch thingss ve na fit to hear. Na sshall you sspeak more."

Opening his hand, Daveeka held out the crystal on his palm at arms length. It caught the light from the glowweeds overhead, seeming to burn with its own brightness. He locked his gaze deliberately on Chezoar as he demanded, "Ve na truth? Misstress Chezoar, ve na truth?"

All eyes turned to the aging Mistress. She hesitated, but she had to speak, or dishonor the Shape she wore. "Ve truth, Daveecha," she replied, eyes downcast and ears laid flat. "Elenath ve na flessh and blood. Ve sspirit, and sspirit ve na male,—" she lifted her gaze to the enigmatic Statue, a hint of triumph in her voice "—na female."

Ask the Name, my child. Ask the Name.

"Misstress Chezoar, what ve the Mosst Sssacred Name of Elenath that sspoken may never ve?" he demanded.

"Elnatha," came the reply. The "A" at the end and the change of letters made it definitely male.

"Ssilence!" Marlieth roared. But it was too late. Daveeka had heard enough. The gathered females stared at him, dumbfounded, outraged, shocked and confused.

Satisfied, he strung his new Shape on his beadstring. Clipping it back onto his collar, he turned briefly for one last glance at the statue, then strode down the altar steps and over to Annilee.

The answer he had received had gone much further than the question he had asked. Something had crystallized in his mind, something as hard and glistening as the Sphere he now wore at his breast. He was not an afterthought, not a secondary and extraneous being. He was rillenu. Male and female ceased to count.

For the first time in his life, Daveeka felt a stirring of pride in what he was. He held his head high and his ears staunchly upright as he addressed Mistress Annilee.

"Ve now ready to go to Taking," he declared firmly.

Marlieth glared at him as she led the way out of the Temple and into a nearby chamber. Daveeka clasped his hands behind his back and kept his head up proudly. No matter that part of him still felt like screaming and pleading for mercy. He wasn't going to give them the satisfaction.

And so it was that Daveeka looked more angry than afraid as the females filed into the room behind him. When he was led to the couch, he sat down with his ears still cocked insolently forward.

Annilee offered him a cup of jareesh, seeming confident that he'd take it. Judging by the oily sheen on the surface of the liquid, it was strong. Drain this cup, and he would know nothing, feel nothing, until long after the Taking was over.

He shook his head.

"Dav, please," she whispered. "Don't make me do this to you without the jareesh."

"I'm not the one making you do it, Annilee. Whether or not I'm conscious makes no real difference."

She fumbled with the cup, some of the jareesh running over the side and slipping to the floor in a lazy, elongated droplet. Marlieth came over to her daughter, a question in her eyes.

"Na wisshess he jareesssh," Annilee said in a shaky undertone.

Marlieth's fingers curled under his chin, but he met her eyes of his own accord. For a moment, he wondered if she would try to force him to drink.

"Let ve," she hissed to Annilee. "Sssoon enough for it he beg."

Daveeka glared at her and turned his head away. Unfastening his crystalstring and clutching both Shapes firmly in his unburned hand, he opened the front of his black tunic and laid back on the couch without having to be told to do so. He held his hands up behind his head so one of the attendants could grasp his wrists. A murmur ran through the group of assembled Mothers.

Annilee went to the left side of the couch; Marlieth to the right. Since the young Mistress had never done this before, she might need her Mother's assistance. Daveeka sincerely hoped not.

He cocked his head forward. He intended to watch, to get one really good look at his daughter before they took her away from him forever.

As Annilee hesitated, Marlieth said, "Proceed, dhaughter. If dho thiss can hyou na, na ve hyou worthy to ve Mother."

The young female swallowed and nodded, her hands shaking visibly as she reached out to touch Daveeka. She opened his pouch carefully, keeping her wrists against the outer wall to stretch it fully open. Somewhere behind Daveeka's head, someone held a bright glowweed, its deep red light directed into his pouch so Annilee could see as well as feel what she was doing.

She stroked the child, reassuring it with her familiar pattern of caresses. Then, with her fingers gently around its body, she slid it slowly from its normal position lying across the bottom of the pouch, bringing it around to one side, feet first, and drawing it out as far as she could as long as it still held his teat in its mouth.

Daveeka swallowed the scream that rose to his throat. Part of his mind clamored that his child was being attacked, endangered. He ignored that. It was an instinctive reaction, and it was true. And it had to be ignored.

Females were holding his legs and shoulders, but he didn't try to get away. He knew what was going to happen, and he refused to be afraid.

But the infant was frightened, despite Annilee's reassuring caresses. Her eyes were open, staring. She kicked futilely, tiny fists drawn up tight against her chest. Her mouth clamped hard on his teat, sucking frantically.

Daveeka clenched his teeth, trying to engrave every last detail of his daughter's appearance on his memory, the silky fur and her small rounded ears, now flattened against her head in fear.

He longed to touch her, to stroke her small body and ease her fear. But strong hands held his wrists. His fingers clenched in helpless longing as tears came to his eyes. The hard crystals bruised his palm.

"Na watch, Daveecha. Pleasse." Annilee's voice, a cracked whisper barely audible despite the hushed silence in the room. Her eyes pleaded with him.

Daveeka ignored her. His daughter's eyes were on his face now, pupils constricted against the unfamiliar light. Perhaps she could even see him. *Remember me,* he thought. *Oh, my child, remember me!*

It was a foolish wish, and he knew it. Still, she was more than a nanth older than most female infants would be when taken, and her eyes were already open. And she had felt his forbidden touch, although none of the Mothers knew it. She might keep some of that in her memory.

"Annilee," Marlieth prompted her daughter as she made no further move. Her voice held a warning.

"Na can Ish dho."

"Hyou musst."

Marlieth held the drugged cup to Daveeka's lips, triumph in her face, sure that he wouldn't refuse it now.

He turned his head away.

"Proceed, Misstresss," Marlieth hissed meaningfully at Annilee, dashing the cup to the floor.

"Go ahead, Annilee," Daveeka said. "I trust you."

She looked at him wide-eyed, as some of the other females gasped in surprise.

Annilee nodded numbly. She forced her little finger into the infant's mouth and down the small throat, despite its resistance.

Her finger pressed painfully against Daveeka's teat as she tried to break the baby's grip and release the suction that held it deep in the infant's throat. Agony blossomed through his abdomen as she grasped the base of his teat with her other hand and tried to pull it out of the baby's mouth.

The old fear of having his insides torn out swamped Daveeka's efforts at remaining calm. If a child were actually to be pulled from its Father's pouch, still holding his teat, it was, indeed, likely that the teat and much of the structure of the underlying mammary glands would be pulled out with it.

To Daveeka's terrified mind, that seemed to be about to happen to him now. The females would lose patience, would simply jerk the infant away.

He forced himself to see Annilee's fingers, to watch what she did. She was not tearing him open, even though she pulled painfully hard. Her finger was working his teat out of the baby's throat as she pushed brutally at the sensitive skin, but she was not really trying to injure him.

Still, it hurt. A trickle of blood showed around his daughter's mouth, mixed with the milk that still flowed into her throat. The baby gagged and struggled, trying to clamp her mouth tighter.

But Annilee had loosened her daughter's grip. She slid a second finger into the baby's mouth, preventing it from closing. Pulling steadily with her other hand, she began to draw his teat out.

The pain let up when the teat was free of the baby's mouth, but it didn't stop completely. The infant, shocked by the unfamiliar sensation of being disconnected from her Father, stopped struggling. She opened and closed her mouth several times in confusion. Her hands flailed for security, and closed on the tender skin just inside Daveeka's pouch. He winced, but kept his body relaxed. Let her not pick up fear from his tension, poor little terrified thing.

The baby gave a thin wail of despair as Annilee took hold of her, loosening her fingers and lifting her the rest of the way out of the pouch. Daveeka kept his gaze glued to his daughter, drinking in the sight of her with greedy eyes as Annilee wrapped her in a soft blanket and cuddled her against her chest.

Quickly, before Marlieth could stop her, Annilee leaned forward with the baby, holding it close to Daveeka. He kissed the top of its soft head, knowing this was the last time he'd ever see her.

Marlieth slapped Annilee viciously across the face. "Na ssshow sssuch weaknesss," she hissed. "Ve na fitting."

Annilee ignored her. The baby began to wail as the young female stood up and walked out of the room, followed by the entire crowd of Mothers. They would go into the Temple now, for the ceremony of Naming and to confer the title of Mother on Annilee.

Daveeka was left alone on the couch, tears running down his cheeks.

No, not quite alone. The female who had been holding his wrists released him and moved into his line of sight. He recognized her as Mistress Chezoar. He turned his back to her, curling into a miserable ball around the aching emptiness of his pouch.

Chezoar sat down next to him, lightly caressing his back and his neck. "Daveecha, jareesh?" she inquired. He could almost imagine a hint of tenderness in her voice.

He shook his head. His courage faltered and he began to sob. Chezoar sat behind him in silence, stroking him and waiting until he stopped crying.

Then she coaxed him onto his back again, opening his pouch and cleaning it carefully and with great gentleness. He just stared up at a strand of glowweed on the far wall, not really caring what she was doing. His daughter was gone, so what did it matter?

She covered his teat with soothing ointment and placed a soft pad of clean cloth inside his pouch before she let it close. She urged him to sit up, pulling a fresh robe over his head.

A long robe, some part of his mind noticed. The robe of a male not carrying a child. He almost began crying again.

The elderly Mistress took his Shapes from his clenched fist and fastened the clip to the neck of his robe. She bound crushed jaram leaves loosely around his burned hand, then held a cup of jareesh, once again, to his lips.

"Brave were you, Daveecha, but now ssshould ressst. Drink."

He almost pushed her hand away, then relented and took several sips of the concentrated liquid. The ordeal was over. He would need something to counteract the depression and insanity that was likely to follow. Not too much though. He didn't want to spend the entire night unconscious.

Chezoar smiled, stroking his head. "Ressst. Ssstrong enough mussst you ve, to ve confirmed Honored Father at next moonrissse."

He tried to follow her advice, forcing his thoughts away from his empty pouch and on to the ceremony that would confirm him as an Honored Father. And not long after that would be Annilee's Birthing, with he himself in First Position. He would have a child again, in just a nanth's time. Everything would be all right.

Daveeka awoke to quiet and dim red light. Chezoar had gone, but she had covered most of the glowweeds in the small chamber. His burned hand throbbed and his pouch ached, the teat raw and tender and the mammary glands swollen with milk. The sense of hopelessness and despair that weighed upon his mind seemed almost palpable. He felt as if he might at any moment leap to his feet and run wildly around the corridors of the Palace, screaming for his baby.

No, he told himself firmly, this is nothing. Just the normal psychological reaction of a male who has lost a child. He remembered that Teo was half out of his mind for three quarns after it happened to him, but Teo's infant son had died. His own daughter was alive and well, in the care of her Mother. The craziness will pass. He must not give in to it.

Memory of the Taking seared across his mind, but he pushed it aside, thinking instead of the Challenge and the strange insight he had had in the Temple. He fingered the Sphere at his breast to reassure himself that it truly had happened.

What other Honored Father would wear such a Shape? There were few even among the females who wore the many-facetted, complex Shapes.

He tried to find satisfaction in that thought, but it wouldn't hold. Suddenly he felt stifled, as if the very walls of the Palace would collapse upon him. The High Wall, the heavy stones, all cut him off from the open air and broad sky. They held him prisoner, far from Teo and the rest of his friends. He had to get out of this buried chamber, and sit in the soft red-orange light of Elnanth for a time. Perhaps then he'd be able to think, to banish some of the confusion fogging his brain.

Still somewhat groggy from the jareesh he'd drunk, he got to his feet. Limping unnoticed through the passageways, he climbed the winding stairs that led to one of the roof gardens. His ankle began to throb, but it was just one more pain on top of his burning hand and aching pouch.

At last he reached the roof. Elnanth hung halfway down the western sky. Dawn would be coming soon.

He walked across the garden. The moonflower bushes were in full bloom, their large blossoms spreading cloyingly sweet perfume on the cool night air. An elderly servant worked among the tall flowers, plucking off the dead blossoms in order that new ones might take their place. He bowed respectfully to Daveeka, who returned the bow with a slight nod of his head before continuing on to the opposite side of the wide garden.

He sank down on the broad, waist-high parapet that overlooked the Marloosh lodging house. He leaned forward, peering over the edge. The buildings sprawled below him, the guards' barracks where he had spent so many unhappy nights off to one side and the luxurious main building running along the Palace wall in the other direction. Was Teo waiting anxiously for his return, somewhere in that vast warren of rooms?

Nextnight they'd be together again. Nextnight he'd be an Honored Father. He would make decisions, give orders.

A wave of dizziness overtook him. He sat back, away from the steep drop. The new Shape bumped softly against his chest as he moved, reminding him of the concept he was now obligated to live by. Unity and Wholeness. If Elenath is One, then male and female are also one. He must begin making changes, tear down the walls that separated the sexes. He could do it, as an Honored Father. The Kiari would support him. He would counter Fahlin's proposal, for a start. Introduce sweeping changes at the Conclave. Once he told everyone what he had learned, everything would change. It would all be different. He could do it! He could …

His thoughts crashed in upon themselves. This was frantic delirium, nothing more. It was all hopeless. What could he realistically do to change the world? He was only one male.

But he would soon be an Honored Father. He turned the idea over slowly in his mind. A year ago, he'd never have imagined such an outcome, yet now the title was ashes in his mouth.

He looked away from the Marloosh holdings, his eyes sweeping the ramparts of the Palace at the other side of the roof garden. Here, inside these walls, was where the real power lay. Without some support from the females, he might as well be knocking his head on the cold stones of the High Wall, for all the good it would do.

He glanced at the sky, where a thin white crescent moon struggled up from the eastern horizon. That's all he was, he thought sadly, a small male moon, hanging unregarded in the sky compared to the vast bulk of red-orange Elnanth. What did it matter how brightly he shone? The larger moon would always eclipse him.

No, he mustn't think like that anymore. It was foolish. A moon was a moon. It was no more male or female than Elenath was. Or should he say, Elnatha, the forbidden Name? No wonder it was never to be spoken. Some female, somewhere, very long ago, had forbidden it, lest the ancient truth be known, or at least hinted at. But that would mean that sometime far before that happened, the truth was known to everyone.

He shook his head, overwhelmed by the sheer weight of his thoughts. Could he be losing his mind?

Fresh awareness of his misery assailed him. The inside of his pouch ached. The mammary glands, engorged with milk, were swollen and inflamed. He was tempted to reach in and squeeze some of the milk out to relieve the pressure, but that would only encourage lactation to continue and he needed to make it stop as soon as possible, if he were to be prepared to Receive again at Annilee's Birthing.

Daveeka shook his head, trying to banish the sodden hopelessness that weighed upon his mind by telling himself this was only the normal depression from losing the baby. Things would be better in a while. There was the Conclave coming up. He could make a difference there. If nothing else, at least try to stop Fahlin's proposal from being passed.

The seesaw of his moodiness sank deeper down on the side of depression and he shook his head. No, even that wasn't possible. Not for him. He was no politician. He wouldn't be able to influence other Fathers or gain the support he'd need. Couldn't he just go back to being what he had been: a simple childless male and a Kiari priest? Let someone else be responsible. Let someone else make the decisions.

And let someone else face the inevitable conflicts that would erupt if anyone tried to change things. He needed peace and quiet, a chance to pull his shattered wits together and assimilate all that had happened to him. He just wanted to curl up into a ball and never move again for a year or so.

In an attempt to break the deepening cycle of misery, he leaned once more over the edge of the parapet, looking straight down on the courtyard below. Two males strolled across the flagstone, oblivious to his presence high above. He felt dizzy at the sheer drop before him, but he kept on looking. A light wind ruffled his fur, tickling his ears.

A sense of deja-vu played around the edges of his thoughts. He had stood at the top of a cliff like this before, and heard the waves crashing below him.

Waves? No, never. He'd heard of the sea, but never seen it in person. Then he had it. Jeremael, the old Kiari priest, had been teaching him to dance. Daveeka had been tired, careless, bored by the endless repetition necessary to engrave the steps upon his memory.

"No, no, no!" Jeremael had exclaimed. "Not like that!"

"But what's wrong? I did it correctly. I didn't step off the rug."

The old priest gave him a strange look. "And that's all there is to dancing, Daveeka? Just do it correctly?"

Puzzled, he nodded. "What else?"

Jeremael rose to his feet, coming over to stand alongside Daveeka on the practice rug. He took the younger rillenu's arm, positioning him so that he stood with his toes just touching the long edge of the rug. "Now," he said, "close your eyes."

Daveeka complied. What sort of senile nonsense was this?

"Imagine you're standing at the edge of a cliff. In front of you is a sheer drop. Far below, the ocean breaks against sharp rocks. Feel the breeze ruffle your fur. Listen to the frantic crash of the waves."

The image floated clear in Daveeka's mind, conjured up by the old priest's words. He could almost feel the giddiness of standing a mere step from empty space, the temptation to let himself plunge over and down. His ears twitched with imagined terror.

"Got it?"

Oh yes, he had the image, all right. Daveeka nodded.

"Now," Jeremael said softly, "dance."

Daveeka's thoughts jerked abruptly back to the reality of his present position, the old priest's words still ringing in his ears. At the time, he hadn't entirely grasped the lesson, but he had felt a chill of awe as he realized he played a game with far more serious consequences than he had ever imagined. A misstep would cost more than he had thought. The poisoned thorns had been an abstraction to him back then; it was before he had taken part in a real Dance.

A vast abyss stretched before him now, in the form of his life as an Honored Father. A misstep could cast him into the depths. Not only that, but he would take others down with him, their lives and hopes dashed on the rocks below.

The world was far more complicated than he had ever imagined. Wielding power would be a much more difficult thing than simply talking about what he'd like the world to be and complaining about how it was.

Staring out over the countryside beyond the roofs of Marloosh, Daveeka wondered if he had the courage to participate in that Dance.

Footsteps sounded behind him, and a rustle of fabric. His ears swiveled, catching the pattern of the steps.

Oh, no! It would have to be Fahlin, the last rillenu in the world that he wanted to see just now!

He got quickly to his feet, turning his back towards the Honored Father as if he had not heard him. If he hurried, he might avoid meeting him.

"Daveeka, wait!"

Cursing his ill luck, Daveeka halted.

Fahlin came up alongside him and leaned on the stone rampart with one arm. "When I heard you had left the Taking chamber, I thought I might find you up here."

"Oh? Why?" Daveeka kept a tight rein on his temper. He didn't want to get into an argument with Fahlin just now. He felt too close to the edge of insanity as it was.

"Because this particular garden overlooks the Marloosh House. You'll be going back there nextnight as an Honored Father, so I figured you might be gloating over your new domain, so to speak."

"Right now I'm gloating over nothing but an empty pouch, Fahlin. I just want to be alone," he said pointedly.

Fahlin ignored that. "Maybe now you're willing to start thinking like an Honored Father? Once they fasten the collar around your neck, life will be different."

Daveeka turned away. He wasn't in the mood for political wrangling. All he wanted was Teo's arms around him and a warm furry shoulder to cry on.

"I suppose you plan to go back to that useless partner of yours, eh?"

Daveeka nodded, deliberately not responding to the insult.

Fahlin gave a snort of disgust. "What a waste! All those handsome Fathers in Marloosh, and all you can think of to share your mattress is a worthless childless male."

Daveeka's ears began to slant, but Fahlin ignored that. "Or maybe your taste runs more towards boys, as mine does? Oh, I know you'll deny it, but you seemed pretty fond of that servant you had. What was his name? Zillah? I understand he's back from the Farms now and has been taken in by our Family."

"I liked him. That's all," Daveeka replied cautiously.

"Uh-huh. Do you seriously expect me to believe you and he were doing nothing more than dancing together? Why, I'll bet it wouldn't have been long before you'd have had his pouch open."

"What?"

"Now you're going to play the outraged innocent? I suppose you've never opened a boy's pouch?" Fahlin laughed. "Oh, it's a lot of fun. You don't know what you've missed if you've never forced a terrified youngster to endure your hand in his pouch for the first time. They scream and plead and cry. Really adds to the fun."

Daveeka's ears flattened completely, but Fahlin appeared not to notice.

"Try it sometime, Dav, before you condemn it. Maybe with your new boy, Sinda? I'd be glad to show you how it's done."

"I have no reason to torture my servants," Daveeka replied icily.

Fahlin shrugged. "Oh, it's not all that bad. After a few times, they learn to enjoy it. It's very exciting if it's done right. Or didn't you know that?" He shook his head. "You have so much to learn about the powers and privileges of an Honored Father. But you can't afford to be tender-hearted and soft-headed. I mean, look at that whole mess with the outlaws. Sure, you came out of it a hero of sorts. But if you'd asked my help, I could have managed things so that you'd have some real influence with the most powerful Mothers. You had a chance to become someone important, but you missed it. Such a shame!"

Fahlin shook his head in disgust. "Oh yes, I heard about your new Shape. Of course, like the fool you are, you tried to get something really impressive, didn't you?" Without waiting for an answer, he went on, "That's absolutely the worst thing you could have done. Males should never try to out-perform females. All you get is their anger, not the sort of admiration you were seeking."

Astonishment washed over Daveeka. He wanted to protest that sort of thing wasn't what he sought, but no words came.

Fahlin continued obliviously, "In fact, the females are a bit on edge just now about those outlaws, so I figured this might be a good time to warn the Exalted Mother about the danger of letting the Kiari continue to spread unrest amongst the childless males. She agreed with me and we've worked out a plan to get rid of them once and for all." The Honored Father leaned back against the parapet again, enjoying the horrified expression on the other rillenu's face.

"How?" Daveeka forced the word past his lips, managing to disguise his anger in the effort to get more information.

"Most of them are here right now, waiting to see you confirmed as an Honored Father. It would be simple to haul them all in, while they're gathered to hear the announcement. The leaders and priests could be quietly executed, and the others sent to the Farms."

"Fahlin, you—" Daveeka began.

The old male waved one hand, dismissing whatever it was Daveeka was about to say. "This wasn't just my idea, you understand. I have quite a few allies amongst the Honored Fathers of the other male Families. Very soon now, I'll be Father of another daughter. Then I'll have even more power. The leaders of the other male Families will all want to be allied with me. We worked out this plan some time ago, but your escapade with the renegades gave us the opportunity to carry it out sooner." He glanced sideways at Daveeka. "Of course, if you wanted to reconsider supporting my proposal at the Conclave, I might be willing to see that a few of your friends are left unharmed. I'm not unreasonable. We could come to an agreement."

But Daveeka wasn't listening anymore. His outrage and anger at Fahlin's machinations had reached the flashpoint and exploded into rage. Hardly aware of what he was doing, his hands reached out and closed around Fahlin's throat.

The Honored Father's mouth opened in a silent scream. He clawed at Daveeka's fingers, trying vainly to pry them away. As the air in his lungs ran out, he began to thrash around in panic. They stumbled against the parapet, with Fahlin's weight forcing Daveeka down on his back across the top of the low wall, his head and shoulders suspended over thin air.

But Daveeka refused to let go. Fahlin's eyes bulged and his tongue protruded from his mouth. His struggles seemed to be weakening.

Then the old male jerked himself upright, pulling Daveeka with him. Fahlin raised an arm above his head and spun to one side, simultaneously bringing his upraised arm down hard across Daveeka's wrists, breaking his grip. He twisted away and Daveeka's hands were left clutching empty air. The Honored Father sucked a precious breath into his lungs.

But the violence of his spin sent him off balance. As Daveeka lunged towards him again, Fahlin threw himself sideways in a desperate effort to evade the younger male.

And sprawled across the parapet, his momentum carrying him almost over the edge. Fahlin's fingers scrabbled for a grip on the smooth stones.

Time seemed to slow down for Daveeka. He saw the other male fighting to save himself, but Fahlin's feet were off the ground and his body was still sliding over the edge. Daveeka could have grabbed his legs and pulled him back. Having lunged at the Honored Father, Daveeka was already in motion, could reach him in time. But why should he do that? This was the male who had schemed to destroy his friends. He wanted to kill Fahlin, not save him.

As he fell forward against the parapet himself, Daveeka shoved Fahlin with all his strength, breaking the other male's tenuous hold on the stones and rolling him over the edge.

Daveeka almost followed him over. He ended up sprawled on his stomach on the wall, watching Fahlin tumble to the courtyard below. Fahlin's short scream was cut off by the paving stones on which he landed, face down and spread-eagled.

In the time it took for Daveeka to grasp what had happened, several Marloosh males had come running from their rooms to gather around the Honored Father's body. One glanced up to the Thennevar wall, pointing at Daveeka. Someone else gingerly turned Fahlin over.

Even from far above, Daveeka could easily see the red-soaked front of the Honored Father's robe. Fahlin had to be dead. He could not have survived the fall.

And neither could his infant daughter. Daveeka pulled back from the wall, retching at the thought of such a thing happening to a female infant. And he was responsible for it!

As the first angry shouts drifted up from below, he realized the full enormity of what he had done. Bad enough he had caused Fahlin's death. He might have been able to get out of that, since they had been fighting and it might have seemed like an accident, but there was no extenuating circumstance for someone who caused the death of a female infant, regardless of intention. The death penalty was automatic. And particularly gruesome.

In sudden panic, Daveeka struggled to his feet and looked around. The servant who had been working at the far corner of the garden stood staring at him, mouth and eyes gaping open in horror. He must have witnessed the conflict, even if he hadn't heard the words.

Daveeka ran for the exit from the roof garden. He had to escape from the Palace or he was doomed.

CHAPTER 12

When Daveeka realized that his feet were taking him towards the main entrance to the Thennevar Palace, he stopped. There would be guards at the entrance. He couldn't get out that way. In fact, he wouldn't be able to simply walk out through any of the entryways. They were all guarded and he was well known. He wasn't thinking clearly at all.

He leaned against a wall, knees trembling. He had to figure out what to do, but his mind shied away from anything useful, picturing only Fahlin's broken and bloody body. Had he really done that? He must have been crazy, still in shock over losing his daughter.

Think, you idiot! The females won't care if you were crazy or not. All that matters is that you killed Marlieth's daughter.

Perhaps if he went to one of the lower roof gardens around the back of the Palace, he could slip over the wall and get away without being seen.

Now, which stairway led to those gardens? Wasn't it the one near the laundry?

He slipped cautiously through the corridors, listening for any pursuit. He avoided the servants, stepping behind curtains or into alcoves whenever he heard footsteps coming his way. If they weren't looking for him now, they soon would be.

He started up the stairway he thought led to the roof garden. The promise of open air and freedom beckoned him on. Somehow, he'd get over the wall and then sneak into the Marloosh lodging house. If he could find Teo, his partner would surely hide him.

But he had taken a wrong turn. The stairway led only to a number of unused storage rooms. Daveeka tried to think calmly, but panic rose up and engulfed his mind. He fled blindly down the staircase and around a corner, imagining he heard footsteps pursuing him.

A pair of guards stood at the next intersection. He drew back before he could be seen, darting down another corridor and down a curving flight of stairs. He had already lost track of where he was in the huge Palace.

He heard voices up ahead.

"Find him?"

"Nah, not yet."

Across a doorway to his right hung a heavy curtain decorated with the Thennevar symbol, ornate warning that a male might not enter. The sign above the door read "Meditation Chambers" in femalespeech.

Daveeka ducked inside, hearing footsteps coming down the hall. None of the guards would dare to go through that doorway.

A small octagonal room. In the center of each wall, a heavy curtain. Had he reached a dead end?

He ran to the doorway directly across from the entrance, hoping it wasn't already occupied by a female.

Black darkness surrounded him, with here and there a brief sparkle of light. His eyes adjusted rapidly and he found himself looking into a labyrinth, its walls made of panels of clear glass. From apertures in the walls on either side, beams of focused light played redly upon the transparent maze, picking out sudden sparks and flashes in the dark chamber. He could see no exit nearby, but the labyrinth blocked his view of the far recesses of the room.

Daveeka stared at the improbable construction, his eyes seeming to play tricks on him even as he tried to make sense of the whole thing. The shifting sparkles gave the impression that the maze was moving.

In his wildest imaginings, he had not expected to find such a thing in a meditation chamber. Darkness perhaps. Silence.

And it was silent. Totally, numbingly silent. His ears strained for any sound, swiveling to their fullest extent. Nothing. He could not have heard less had he become stone deaf.

There had to be a reason behind this uncanny glass maze. What purpose could be served by such a thing? How could it promote meditation?

He fought down his growing panic. One thing was certain: a maze was meant to be entered, to be explored and solved. Perhaps it led to a secret way out.   The Palace was rumored to be honeycombed with hidden passages, although he had never seen one himself.

Daveeka took several uncertain steps forward, his hands held before him, groping for the unseen surfaces. There had to be an entrance to the maze. If he felt around carefully, he should be able to find it.

Crimson sparkles flared and died at random intervals in the room. It was difficult to see an invisible wall of glass. In the dead silence, even the size of the room was hard to judge.

Maybe he should go back to the door and try a different room? No, someone might be there by now. He dared not risk it.

He stopped, reached out to touch the glass wall that appeared to be directly in front of him.

His hand went through open air. There was nothing there.

But his eyes still interpreted the shifting shapes and sparkles as indicating something solid.

This must be the entrance to the labyrinth. It was an optical illusion, his eyes misled by the shimmering surfaces around him. He should move forward, ignoring the illusion. That's what a female would do—refuse to be deceived by appearances, seeking instead for the solid reality underneath.

Commending himself on this insight, Daveeka stepped confidently forward into the maze. Hands outstretched, fingers spread apart, he felt for the opposite wall of the glass corridor. If he could touch it, perhaps he could follow it to the end, ignoring the treachery of his eyes.

Once again, his hand went through what should have been a solid surface.

Confused, he stood stock-still for a moment, ears drooping as he searched for a clue to the mystery. Was it all an elaborate hoax, insubstantial shapes projected somehow into the room for the sole purpose of deceiving anyone who entered? Was Marlieth even now watching him from some secret passage, laughing heartily at his lack of understanding before his pursuers closed in on him? Had the females deliberately had him chased here, just to enjoy his frustration?

No, that made no sense. He was being crazy again. They wouldn't go to such lengths simply to make a fool of him.

And yet, he couldn't quite banish the feeling that he was being watched.

He surveyed the dark chamber again. The glass panels wavered, as if swinging freely and responding to the air currents stirred up by his movements. The intermittent reflections came primarily from what he had assumed to be the edges of the sections of glass. Strange.

Daveeka moved to the nearest zone of scintillating flashes, ignoring the uneasy feeling that he would smash his nose into a solid wall with each step.

He stopped, squinting. The random glistenings around the room distracted his eyes, making it hard to focus on any one thing.

He reached out, wary of being fooled again.

His four fingers closed around a narrow strip of mirror, which hung suspended from the ceiling. He turned it around, catching and reflecting light as he did so. Very softly, Daveeka laughed.

It had been illusion after all. The narrow strips of mirror gave the impression of being edges of large plates of glass, and imagination filled in the rest. Although his eyes still insisted there was a maze, his mind knew the apparent emptiness was solid, just as what appeared solid was in reality emptiness.

Seek for the reality to be found behind the outward appearance. That must be the lesson to be learned in this strange chamber. He had solved it. He, Daveeka, a mere male, had grasped the hidden meaning.

But it brought him no closer to escape. If the maze was illusion only, it led nowhere. He crossed back to the door by which he had entered. Then he stopped, ears pricked forward. Voices came from behind the heavy curtain, from the octagonal room beyond.

He backed away silently and began feeling his way along the wall on the slim chance there might be another entrance somewhere that he hadn't noticed. He glanced around the room, trying to gauge its depth. His eyes were caught once more by the scattered sparkles.

He came full circle, back to where he'd started. There was no way out, only solid rock. If his pursuers came through the door, they had him.

Retreating to the far end of the chamber, Daveeka sank to the floor in defeat. They were sure to search this room sooner or later. His only chance was that they might not notice him, if he stayed very still and they were distracted by the glass strips hanging between him and the entry.

He looked across the darkness of the room, expecting at any moment to hear footsteps at the door. If he concentrated, he could see the mirrors now. No puzzling labyrinth. Only mirrored strips in the darkness. Half-hypnotized by the sparkles, his bemused mind ran to strange considerations.

Was the reality truly any less marvelous than the illusion it had replaced? Was it simpler to understand, or more complex? He knew the seeming-random flashes were actually governed by angles of reflection. When a mirror made a certain angle with his eyes, he saw the light. When it didn't, he was aware only of darkness. But if he moved, the pattern would change. And in the infinity of other positions in which he might have been but wasn't, there would be a corresponding infinity of patterns.

Daveeka shook his head. Such thoughts helped him not at all. He would soon be captured. He blinked back tears of bitter despair, setting the twinkling glimmers to swimming before his eyes.

The beams of light impinging on the room were invisible, until they struck something that would reflect them. If there were nothing there, there would be no glimmer, however brief, in the surrounding darkness.

He shook his head. Useless thoughts. *Where were they coming from?* But he couldn't keep his eyes from the mirrors. Time seemed to stop, or drag on forever.

Daveeka. The time draws near for you to separate truth from illusion.

The voice whispered in his mind, as he had heard it before at the Spring Dance and in the outlaw camp, then again in the Temple.

But what did it mean? "Separate truth from illusion?" It couldn't mean just the maze. He had solved that already.

Then a horrible sick thought flashed across his mind. In his rage, he had killed Fahlin, the one he'd thought was his enemy. But Fahlin, for all his status among the males, was not his true opponent. Marlieth and all those females like her; they were the ones who held the real power. Fahlin was just another victim, although a privileged one. The anger he should have felt against the females had exploded against another male. Killing Fahlin had been useless, for it solved nothing and changed nothing.

The curtain at the door swung briefly aside. Someone entered the room.

"Meditation chamberss ve interessting, Daveecha. Na sso?"

Marlieth's voice cut harshly through the heavy silence of the room. Daveeka rose to his feet, his back pressed against the wall.

Her footsteps sounded lightly on the carpeted floor. Mirrored strips tinkled as she thrust them aside, setting red sparkles dancing crazily in the darkness. He could see her silhouette where the sparkles were blotted out.

"Sso, danser, you ve good at esscaping, na? Why ve you na esscaping now?" She stood directly before him, her voice soft.

Angered beyond caution by her taunting, Daveeka struck his hand against the rock surface behind him. "SShall I run through wallss, female?"

He heard her indrawn breath at his contemptuous manner of addressing her. Then a wicked laugh teased his ears, barely audible.

"Wallss na alwayss wallss ve, ignorant male. Ve sometimess empty spacess."

Daveeka heard the swish of her garments as she moved closer to him. There was a rapid rustle, then a slight grinding noise, as of rock moving against rock. An opening appeared in the wall. It was barely waist-high, dimly lit from the inside by old and fading glowweeds.

Escape! He bent over and stared into the tunnel, unable to believe his good fortune.

"Follow left branch, go up, left again. Right twice, then sstraight on. Come out in closset of Fahlin'ss quarters in Marloosh. Go," Marlieth urged.

Yes! If he could get into the Marloosh lodging house, he could get to Teo. Surely the Kiari would hide him, smuggle him out into the country. He wasn't dead yet.

Daveeka bent lower and took a step towards the tunnel.

"Hurry! In here come ssoon otherss."

A faint scent of food drifted out of the tunnel. One of its branches must go past a kitchen. The smooth walls curved down and to the left, blocking his view of what lay beyond. It looked cozy and safe. Inviting.

"Na wait!" she hissed impatiently. "Go you!"

He turned, staring at Marlieth's face in the dim illumination from the tunnel. Behind her, flashes of light continued to reflect off the phony maze. Her ears stood rigid, pricked forward and quivering in her eagerness.

The tunnel beckoned, offering safety. But why did she want him to escape?

Daveeka turned. As with the maze, there was more to this than met the eye. He took a step back into the room. Marlieth's ears flattened.

"Go!" she hissed. "There ve way out. If na go, die." She gestured imperiously toward the tunnel.

"Why are you letting me escape?" he demanded. "Why haven't you called the guards?"

"Ve na time for quesstionss! Run!"

She was pushing him, not giving him time to think. What was it she didn't want him to realize?

"If I go, I won't be confirmed as an Honored Father," he said. "That's what you want to prevent, isn't it?"

"Fool! Why care if Honored Father ve, when you ve dead?"

But there was a hint of uncertainty in her voice, just enough to make him suspect that he had hit on the truth.

If he stayed here, the females would have no choice but to confirm him as an Honored Father, and an Honored Father could not be put to death without a public accusation and execution. He would be permitted a formal statement of fifty-one words, before his death on the High Wall. Marlieth would be bound to let him speak. He could warn the Kiari to go into hiding, exposing Fahlin's scheme before it could be carried out.

Marlieth had no way of knowing Fahlin had told him of their plans, so it must be that she feared the impact his public execution might have on the other childless males. He would be an example, a martyr whose death might stir up trouble, especially combined with some of his radical ideas, which had already gained circulation outside the Palace.

An Exalted Mother feared the influence he might have? Could it be possible?

But what if he ran?

The answer came to him with a cold assurance. Marlieth could easily have him killed, with little publicity and fanfare. She might well have guards waiting to ambush him already, over in the Marloosh lodging house. They would set it up so that he would be seen outside the Palace, a craven male fleeing for his life and being unfortunately slain by the Thennevar guards as they attempted to capture him. His death would ultimately be unnoticed, despite his having killed Fahlin and Fahlin's daughter.

You have no real chance at escape, he told himself grimly, *regardless of what Marlieth says.*

Seeing his hesitation, the Exalted Mother went on, "Know you penalty for killing of female infant, Daveecha? Ve na pleassant. Male ve chained on High Wall, just before ssunrisse. Outer wall of pouch ve cut off, alternating from one sside to the other, each cut going further, while wall of pouch is pulled away a bit more each time, finally being torn off completely. Teat ve grassped with pincerss and ssslowly pulled from body. Then ve left to die in ssunlight. If ve sstill alive by ssunsset, ve mercifully evisscerated. Body left hanging asss example to othersss for two nanthsss, or next execution."

Daveeka knew the penalty was death, but hearing the exact details sickened him anew. That was worse even than Myerta's execution had been, since that had at least been done quickly.

He couldn't face such a gruesome death. The tunnel beckoned invitingly.

But what if Marlieth had already arranged for him to be ambushed by the guards once he was outside the Palace?

His death would be quick, but it would serve no purpose. He would die with his warnings and insights unvoiced. The Kiari would never know of their peril.

What had Marlieth told him before? Something about walls and spaces?

Light flickered around the chamber behind her shadowed form. The mirrors twirled in the disturbed air from the tunnel, sending glowing red worms of reflections dancing against the rock walls.

"Ssometimess empty spaces, even tunnels, ve in reality wallss. Na sso, Exalted Mother?" he said, switching to femalespeech as he re-phrased her earlier statement and threw it back at her.

He heard her draw in a startled breath. Her robes rustled faintly as she made a slight movement with one hand. Drawn by the noise, Daveeka looked down to see the glint of light on the dagger she held.

"Go, worthless trassh. Or die right here," she hissed.

He made as if to flee into the tunnel, then dodged aside, evading her strike. Racing through the center of the room, he lashed out at the mirrored strips, making them swing and sending flashes of light careening wildly around the room.

The momentary distraction was enough to delay Marlieth. He dashed through the door, through the central room, and out into the corridor, where he surrendered to a group of astonished guards.

Daveeka sat staring at the yellow timeglass, watching the sand slide from the top to the bottom. When it had all run out, the day would have ended and his life would have run out also. It had been almost sunrise when he'd surrendered, and the ceremony to confirm an Honored Father traditionally took place shortly after sunset. Once it was over, they'd be free to have him executed.

Just now, the day was almost half finished, and the sand was falling all too fast.

He closed his eyes and sank back against the cushions on his mattress, his eyes roving restlessly around the familiar room. He had tried to pray, but his words echoed hollowly in his head. Besides, what was there to say? If there was any sort of life after death, he'd know about it soon enough. Other than that, all he could ask of Elenath was courage, and the more he thought about that, the more afraid he became.

You fool! You should have run when Marlieth gave you the chance. You might have made it. If not, at least you'd have been dead by now, and it would all be over.

No, he mustn't think that way. He must be brave. Think of the moment he had stood before the ancient statue and gotten a Shape few females had ever received. Think of how it had felt to hear Marlieth's displeasure when he had said he wouldn't run.

Think of how the knife will feel, slicing through your flesh.

He pummeled the mattress in frustration. This wasn't going to work. He was terrified.

If only he could see Teo one last time, just to say good-bye.

He heard footsteps approaching, the guards in the common room shifting quickly to alert attention.

Go *away*, he thought bitterly. *Whoever you are, I don't want to see you.*

Mistress Chezoar pushed aside the curtain. Daveeka turned his back on her, facing the wall. He had nothing further to lose by being discourteous to a female.

Unperturbed by his attitude, Chezoar settled herself cross-legged onto a cushion. "Daveecha, listen," she said softly in reasonably good malespeech. "The Exalted Mother wishes to make you an offer."

Reluctantly, he sat up, turning to face the elderly Mistress. "What sort of offer?"

"If you will use your permitted words to recant your Kiari priesthood and renounce your position on the rights of childless males, Marlieth will arrange an easy death for you."

"An easy death? How?"

"The executioner's blade will be dipped in poison. It wouldn't kill you right away, because that would be too obvious. But you would pass out shortly after the excision begins. You need never feel the rest of the procedure. You would lapse quickly into death."

He laughed rudely. "This is what Marlieth calls easy?"

She ignored his laughter, responding in all seriousness to the question. "Compared to what you now face, yes. A male may take a long time to die this way, Daveecha. Many survive the entire day, to be eviscerated at sunset. Even then, death may not come quickly. I have seen such executions, and I have read accounts of others. The Exalted Mother offers you great mercy, believe me."

Daveeka's small store of bravado dissolved. "Exactly what does she want me to say?"

"That you regret causing the death of her daughter. That you throw yourself on the mercy of Elenath and realize the error of your ways, repudiating the Kiari and their heretical ideas. That your mistaken beliefs have brought you to this sorry pass." She shrugged. "The exact wording doesn't matter, as long as you confine yourself to that sort of thing."

"And if I do that, the executioner will use the poisoned blade?"

The female nodded. Her ears twitched once, but she forced them back to an upright position.

"What guarantee do I have that Marlieth will keep her word?"

"Only that she has sworn it before Elenath in my presence, charging me to make it known to the other females if she breaks her vow. My Shape constrains me to Truth, Daveecha. Everyone knows I may not lie. That's why Marlieth sent me to make the offer, and not one of the Mothers."

"Does Annilee know about this?"

"No. Mother Annilee has not been told."

Mother Annilee. The title sounded strange. Yet she would be a Mother by now, whether or not their daughter still lived. Not long ago, Annilee had promised to try to make things better for childless males, once she herself became a Mother. But she could easily forget those promises now. She would be too interested in consolidating her power and making alliances, looking forward to the time when she would take over as Exalted Mother of Thennevar.

He could not count on help from Annilee. She would turn against him, if for no other reason than to protect herself.

"Mistress, why are my words of such importance to the Exalted Mother?"

Chezoar glanced over her shoulder at the doorway. Lowering her voice to a faint whisper, she replied, "There has been trouble. Several Thennevar guards have been found dead, with a note pinned to the bodies that read, 'Free Daveeka!'" She leaned closer, her voice now barely audible. "The bodies were found in the Honored Father Syron's office. He's terrified."

Daveeka had to smother a pleased laugh. Whether or not this was the doing of the Kiari, at least someone was protesting what had happened. A few disgruntled males couldn't do much good in the long run, but it was still nice to know.

Yet Chezoar's ears quivered with barely controlled anxiety. The females must be quite upset over this small show of resistance. Perhaps they were right and his death could cause widespread unrest and dissatisfaction with the present system.

Or was Chezoar worried about something else?

"Mistress, do you believe I should do as the Exalted Mother asks?"

She turned away, saying only, "What I believe makes no difference. It is not I who will die on the High Wall this night." But the bitterness in her voice betrayed her feelings.

Daveeka realized something he should have noticed sooner. "You agree with me, don't you? About the way childless males are treated. And about the true nature of Elenath."

Chezoar's fingers played thoughtfully with the topmost Shape hanging at her breast before she answered. That Shape was the crescent of Obedience to the Will of Elenath. From its position, it would have been the first one she had ever obtained.

"I have borne many children in my life, but none of them were daughters," she replied at last. "I know there is nothing I have done to deserve this, and lately I have wondered if it truly does reflect Elenath's judgement against me." Her dark eyes met his, her voice shaking with suppressed passion. "I have wondered if the ability to bear daughters has any connection at all with a female's ability to rule, or the ability to Receive an infant with a male's true worth. These are heretical ideas, but I have not been able to banish them. So, yes. In some things, I do agree with you," she finished defiantly. Then her ears wilted. "But I can do nothing. I am only a Mistress."

"Are there others among the females who also feel this way?" he asked, somehow not entirely sure he wanted to hear the answer.

She bowed her head. "A few, scattered amongst the Families. Mostly Mistresses and those without power. There are several Thennevar Mothers who would be receptive to the idea of alleviating conditions on the Farms, if a practical approach were to be suggested. But few would go farther than that."

He was surprised at even that small amount of opposition. If there were only some way of forcing them to act, some way to convince the Kiari to stop dancing on rugs and start putting pressure on the female Families, so that something would have to be done.

No, it wouldn't work. He was dreaming. And he'd soon be rudely awakened from that dream to die in agony.

Suddenly it seemed absurd to believe his death would serve any purpose at all. Nothing would change. Slaves would continue to die on the Farms. Childless males would still be unvalued and worthless. The Kiari would dance across poisoned thorns, choosing the risk of ecstatic self-destruction over meaningful action. The Fathers would rule the Families, as always. And the females would oversee it all, in the Name of Elenath.

So had it always been. So would it always be. He was but one hapless male, caught between the twin grindstones of tradition and history. His life would make no difference, nor would his death.

So why not make it as easy as possible?

"Tell the Exalted Mother I accept her offer. I will do as she asks."

Chezoar's ears drooped in what might have been disappointment, but she acknowledged his answer with a brief nod, then rose and left the room.

The sand continued to dribble down into the bottom of the timeglass.

Sunset, and Daveeka was brought to the Temple for the confirmation ceremony. Annilee walked beside him as they went in procession down the length of the huge chamber. One of her hands held his elbow, as if she might have to help him along. Most potential Honored Fathers would have been so drugged from the taking of their daughters that they would still be groggy for this ritual, so that hand might well have served a useful purpose.

He forced himself to keep moving, keep his ears from drooping forward. Only a little longer.

He could hold together just a little longer. He fixed his eyes on his feet, willing his knees not to tremble. He could get through the confirmation ceremony. After that, it would soon be over. The poison would kill him quickly, he was sure. Chezoar wouldn't lie, and Marlieth wouldn't take a chance on his living long enough to change his mind. He had his speech all thought out, the words carefully counted to fit within the fifty-one word limit. It was appropriately humble and repentant. Marlieth would be satisfied.

He glanced sideways at Annilee. Her profile was stern and hard in the deep rose light from the glowweeds, her good ear pricked stiffly forward. What was she feeling about all this? Did she hate him for causing the death of a female infant? Momentarily, he left off worrying over his predicament to wonder about his own daughter. Was the baby still alive, or had she died already? Now he'd certainly never know.

Off to one side of the Temple, separated from the females by a strip of glowweed strung between a row of low posts, stood the Fathers of Marloosh, along with a number of visiting Fathers from other Families. The Honored Father Syron was in front, leaning on the arm of a younger colleague.

They must know about Fahlin. Do they know what's going to happen?

Daveeka drew himself up stiffly as they reached the platform before the statue and Annilee released his arm. He climbed the steps without her assistance, although she followed close behind him. There was no spoken part in the ceremony for him, but he wanted it to be clear to everyone that he was alert and attentive, not still drugged.

He strode over to Marlieth and knelt at her feet, his back to the assembled crowd below.

The Exalted Mother spoke the ritual blessing. Daveeka stared past her, up at the statue. Then his eyes fell. He was planning to betray all he knew and believed. He dared not raise his eyes to Elenath. He was not worthy.

Annilee approached him, holding the wide embroidered collar of an Honored Father in her hands. Marlieth moved aside and he rose, to stand facing the Mother of his daughter with downcast eyes.

She placed the collar around his neck with a dramatic flourish, fastening the hooks at his throat. Taking the clasp of his crystalstring from the neck of his robe, she clipped it over the stiff collar, one finger grazing the Sphere. He glanced at her, but her face showed no expression, her ears held steady.

He thought of their time together in the forest, when they had been just two rillenus, struggling to survive. Male and female had not mattered then. Now it made all the difference in the world. The wall between them was back in place, just as solid as ever.

She placed a hand on each of Daveeka's shoulders, looking beyond him to where the Marloosh Fathers stood watching. "Daveecha sardhan Marloossh-Ssharemmi," she said loudly, "now and forever, Honored Father ve."

Behind him, the gathered females began a loud chant that should have been joyful but somehow managed to sound somber instead. Annilee whispered under cover of the noise, "Daughter lives."

Daveeka had barely recovered from his surprise at this unexpected, but welcome, disclosure when her hand went to her crystalstring, pulling it away from the folds of her robe so he could see it clearly. At the bottom, she wore the teardrop Shape of Respectful Disagreement with Authority. "Invitationss for my Birthing ve to childlesss malesss, and always sso ve," she promised softly, meeting his eyes with a determined gaze.

He had not expected that either. If he were to recant now, Annilee would be left publicly supporting the theories of a dishonored murderer. She had been given that Shape by Elenath and risked her Mother's anger, just in order to show her support for him.

But Annilee did not face death, as he did. It would not be her body being torn apart to witness to the truth she had belatedly chosen to affirm.

The chant ceased, to be replaced by an expectant silence. Annilee turned him around to face the crowd. This was the time when he should have been free to leave the platform and join the other Marloosh males, but he knew that wouldn't happen.

And, of course, it didn't.

Marlieth moved to block his way, standing between him and the stairs leading down from the platform. She took a rolled parchment from her pocket, pointing it at him as if it were a knife. The paper was tied with a black band, symbol of an official decree of the Exalted Mother and her Council. With her other hand, Marlieth pointed to the floor.

Daveeka knew that command. He dropped to his knees in front of her, bowing forward until his ears brushed the ground.

A faint rustle as Marlieth unrolled the parchment. Then her voice, loud and gloating. "Honored Father Daveecha ssardhan Marloossh-Ssharemmi ve here condemned to death on High Wall, for causing death of female infant. Execution ve performed."

Daveeka rose to his feet. If he did not follow her now of his own free will, he knew guards would be summoned to drag him, so he stood regarding Marlieth calmly, as if he were not terrified.

She led the way down from the platform and out of the Temple by a side entrance. Daveeka walked behind her, head held high. He turned only for a moment, to look up at the huge statue one last time. *Mother of All, Father of All, forgive me,* he thought sadly. *I have not enough courage to be Your witness.*

The statue only sat there, eyes staring down at the platform and at the heated pot of Shapes behind the veil.

Daveeka walked out onto the execution platform on the High Wall, naked except for his embroidered collar and the Shapes hanging from it. The square below was packed with males, but the noise from the crowd ceased abruptly when he appeared. The platform itself wasn't large and there wasn't even a railing along the outside edge. Nothing must be permitted to block the view of the execution from the square below. Two guards flanked him now, each holding an end of the rope that encircled his waist, in case he should attempt to throw himself off the edge and escape.

It all seemed unreal somehow. He could not be about to die. This was a farce, a game. But the executioner stood to one side of the platform, a short knife held in one hand. Iron shackles fixed against the back surface of the Wall were open and waiting for Daveeka's wrists and ankles.

No. They wouldn't do such a thing. Not to him.

He shied away from the thought. Revulsion rose in his throat and he wanted to throw up. It wasn't quite like being afraid. It was more as if his mind simply rejected what was going to be done to him, too appalled to accept the truth.

Marlieth came out onto the platform followed by Chezoar and Annilee. He had expected Chezoar, but not Annilee. Mistress Chezoar was, doubtless, here as a witness. She would report all that happened, truthfully, to the other females. But Annilee wasn't involved anymore. She didn't have to be here. He wished she weren't here at all.

The guards took Daveeka's arms, leading him forward so that he stood at the very edge of the platform. Marlieth took her place next to him, reading the formal accusation again to the crowd.

He looked down at the gathered males, almost hoping Teo wouldn't be among them. He wasn't sure he wanted his partner to see what was going to happen. But selfishly he knew he wanted to see Teo's face one last time, wanted to know he cared enough to be here.

The Kiari were grouped together over to one side of the base of the High Wall. Teo was in the middle, with Jeremael next to him. Daveeka saw Zillah there also, and Sinda standing just behind Teo.

Marlieth fell silent, the accusation done. Everyone looked to Daveeka, to see what he was going to say. He could almost feel Annilee's eyes boring into him, probably hoping he would back up her choice to support his cause. The crowd was utterly still.

He had his speech all planned, the words carefully memorized. It was just a matter of saying them. Teo would be shocked, the Kiari shamed by his repudiation.

He shrugged slightly. That was too bad. Had they done anything to save him? They were prepared to stand there and watch him die.

As you watched Myerta die. And did nothing. What would you like them to do? Speak now, my child. Or come to Me with your truth left unsaid.

The same whispered voice, which might have been his imagination, or something more.

What good was his life, if he was willing to die with a lie on his lips? Although he was shaking with fear, Daveeka took a step forward to answer that silent challenge.

"Kiari: Dance no more on thorns! Dance now in world! Elenath does not demand our lives in ritual sacrifice, but in making the world as it should be!"

Marlieth hissed a sharp curse at this unexpected declaration. Glancing back over his shoulder, Daveeka saw the executioner lay down the knife he had been holding and pick up another one, looking to Marlieth for confirmation. In her turn, the Exalted Mother looked to Daveeka. His heart leaped into his throat. There was still time. He calculated quickly. He had twenty-two words left.

He couldn't betray his friends. He just couldn't.

"Females plan to capture all Kiari here! Run! Hide! Never give up!" he shouted loudly.

Daveeka fastened his gaze on his partner. Their eyes met across the distance separating them. "Teo, I love you."

He had intended to finish by saying more to Teo, but suddenly there were other words on his lips, another phrase burning in his brain. On a sudden impulse, he wrenched the crystalstring from his neck, holding the Shapes above his head.

"Hear!" he proclaimed, switching now to femalespeech. "Elenath ve All, na female only!"

Stunned silence met this declaration. Few of the listening males knew femalespeech well enough to understand what he had said, but he saw Zillah speaking urgently to Teo and Jeremael, translating. Then Teo looked up.

Daveeka tossed his Shapes far out over the crowd in Teo's direction. The crystals fell short of his partner, but someone caught them, and others handed them along.

As soon as Teo held the crystals in his hand, he was lifted onto the shoulders of several nearby Kiari. He raised the Shapes above his head, repeating Daveeka's last words in malespeech. His voice set off a rising murmur in the crowd.

At a sharp gesture from Marlieth, the guards jerked Daveeka back from the edge of the parapet. The harsh light of early dawn picked out gleams of color from the beads and bright threads of his collar. His body might be left to rot on the High Wall, but it was forbidden to remove that collar. It would remain, to bear mute testimony to the identity of the one who had died here. And perhaps to inspire the Kiari, whose ragged shouts had crystallized into a loud chant that repeated Daveeka's last sentence.

Here and there, fighting had broken out in the crowd, Kiari scuffling with the Thennevar guards. Under cover of the disturbance, most of the priests were getting away, leaving the square. Only Teo, Jeremael, Zillah, and Sinda remained where they were, surrounded and protected by several ranks of dancers.

The chant still continued. Chezoar's voice joined in, hesitant at first but gaining power. Then Annilee took it up also.

Iron bands clamped around Daveeka's wrists as his arms were pulled out to either side. Shackles closed around his ankles. But he would not be gagged. The females would want him to scream, to impress his suffering on the ones who watched. He felt sure he'd never he able to die silently and bravely, but how much did that matter? He had delivered his warning and proclaimed his truth. It would be up to the others to act on it.

The executioner approached, his knife bared. Daveeka shrank away against the cold rock wall at his back, the wall that had separated male from female for as long as rillenus could remember.

As the executioner's hand reached for his pouch and wrenched it open, Daveeka clamped his eyes and his lips shut, knowing full well he would start to scream and beg for mercy, but determined to keep silent as long as he could.

The knife cut slowly into one side of his pouch, just a little way. Then the other side. He bit his lip to keep from crying out at the pain.

As the executioner pulled and cut and ripped, Daveeka had time for one last rational thought before his mind could feel nothing but agony and he could do nothing but scream:

There was much of good and much of evil on either side of these walls. But, though he would never live to see it, the walls would fall—someday.